SINGAPORE 52

Also by Murray Bailey

Singapore Girl
Singapore Boxer
Singapore Ghost

Map of the Dead
Secrets of the Dead

Black Creek White Lies

I Dare You
Dare You Twice

SINGAPORE 52

Murray Bailey

Heritage Books

First published in Great Britain in 2017 by Heritage Books
Second imprint published 2018

1125

copyright © Murray Bailey 2017

ISBN 978-0-9955108-5-2
e-book ISBN 978-0-9955108-6-9

Printed and bound in Great Britain by Clays Ltd, Elcograf S.p.A

Heritage Books, Truro, Cornwall

It's been a long time coming but
this one's for you, Dad.

ONE

Friday the first of February 1952, the sixth day of the Chinese New Year and my first in Singapore. I was here for two reasons: partly, because a friend had asked for help but also because I needed to get away from Palestine. Quickly.

On the flight from India a young army lieutenant told me everything he knew about Singapore. Which wasn't much. He said it was run by the British and strategically important both militarily and for trade. He said it was the best place to get posted and get laid. Nestled in the tropical jungle, the place was as exotic as the women were beautiful. He told me it was the size and shape of the Isle of Wight but upside down and with ten times the number of people. I'd never been to the small island on the south coast of England but I guessed it wouldn't have been as packed as the streets where I was now. I was in the Chinese quarter of the city and heading for the docks where my friend worked.

I sidestepped a street vendor who tried to block my passage with his tray of steaming noodles. He touched my arm. "English. I have something you like."

Even before he'd spoken I knew it was more than noodles he wanted to sell me. He had a large bag over his shoulder. A protective hand hovered over the opening.

He'd have stolen goods in there. Watches maybe. I stood out, a white man in shorts and a short-sleeved shirt. Not an army uniform but not a labourer. If I didn't buy his watch maybe the plan was someone else would pick my pocket. I moved on.

Observation and deduction. We do it every day, often without realizing it. It's instinctive and vital for my line of work. My previous line of work. The crooked street vendor selected me because he spotted me and deduced I was a prime target. It works the other way too. Recognizing something that's out of the ordinary, out of place.

The first rule of covert surveillance is to blend in and act natural. Tailing someone is easier when there's two or more of you, but a good operator on their own should be fine when in a crowd. And this was a crowd. The man I'd spotted could have been a dock worker, dressed in brown overalls and a cap. After all, the docks were about a mile away and there were other labourers dotted around. Most of them were in clusters and walking with purpose. This guy acted more like a tourist. He slowed down and sped up and never overtook me. The real give-away was his shoes. Not dockers' boots, not army boots. Smart brown shoes. Probably Brogues.

I had two choices: evade or confront. It was an easy choice. We were in public and the guy didn't look a threat. I continued to walk along the street as though acting like a tourist without a concern. Rain drops, the size of small marbles, smacked the exposed skin of my arms and I glanced up. People around me started to scurry. A tropical downpour was coming. The timing was perfect. I saw an opening to what looked like an undercover market and stepped inside. It smelled of roasted chicken, incense and dust.

2

Doubling back, I stood by the entrance, hidden from the approaching tail. He'd come inside and I'd grab him.

Ten seconds passed. Twenty seconds. The guy didn't enter and he didn't walk by. A whole minute must have passed before I was tempted to step back into what was now a torrential downpour. The sound of trade was masked by the rain as it crackled like an intense wood fire on the canvas roof above. And then I heard another noise above the racket. Shouting.

I looked around. Smoke wafted, green in the thick air. The undercover market extended for at least a hundred yards and probably had offshoots I couldn't see. Stalls and customers were everywhere with hardly any space to move. At six-two I could see over the heads of most of the crowd. And then I saw a definite movement like a wave of heads. In an area about a third of the way down people were moving away, hustling, pushing one another. There was no panic, just an urgency to get away. Some of the people at least. It seemed to be the source of the commotion too.

I headed in that direction and as I drew closer I could see the problem. A stall had been overturned, the wares scattered on the cobbled floor. Three British soldiers were remonstrating, shouting and throwing things around.

I moved closer still. There were just two rows of people in front of me now.

I heard one of the soldiers say something about dirty Japs and I moved through the last remnants of the crowd. I could see him now: a fourth person, on his hands and knees. With a white band tied around his forehead and a red dot in the centre, he was clearly supposed to look like a Japanese suicide pilot.

3

One soldier kicked the prone man in the rear while another forced his boot into his face and indicated that it should be kissed or licked.

"Enough!" I shouted. Either they didn't hear me or they were distracted by a young white woman who threw herself at the nearest soldier. She flailed her arms and screamed and was batted away like an annoying fly.

I helped her to her feet. She was just a teenager.

"You all right?"

There was dust all over her pretty white dress and tears streaked down her cheeks but I could see she wasn't hurt. She sobbed something about protecting the vendor and I nodded.

In the voice I'd used many times in similar situations, I bellowed, "Military Police!"

For a moment even the crowd fell silent. All three soldiers stopped, frozen to the spot. Then the guy who was clearly the leader stared at me, eyes cold and hard. I could read doubt on his face.

"Military Police," I shouted again. "Get out! Get out now!"

Two moved. The leader didn't. Then he laughed.

"Bugger off. You ain't an MP. Where's your red cap?" The other two closed ranks, pushed out their chests.

No point in getting into a discussion. I skipped forward. One step. Two steps. Punch. It was a straight right to the guy's nose. Just a tap, but it spun him around. Before the blood appeared I was already sidestepping to hit the next guy with a left hook.

The third man was a problem. He was the one behind the Japanese vendor who was starting to rise. Still only half upright, the vendor was pushed and fell towards me. I instinctively caught him which was a mistake. It slowed me down. The bloody-nosed leader was up and also

4

lunging. I tripped on something on the floor and we fell together, knocking over a trestle table.

I felt a blow to my head, scrabbled to my feet and blindly tangled with another of the soldiers. I hit him hard but again found myself tumbling to the ground.

And then suddenly there was an eruption of noise: whistles and shouts. Strong hands pressed down on me, pinning me to the ground. I expected more blows but there were none. I breathed in the hot dust. *What the hell?*

"Stand up!" a voice barked in my ear. He spoke with the same authority I'd tried just a few minutes earlier.

With my arms locked behind my back I was pulled to my feet and held by two men in uniform. They had red caps. Royal Military Police.

A major glared at me. Behind him I could see the three soldiers I'd been fighting, each of them also held in an arm-lock.

I saw the girl in the white dress. She was kneeling by the vendor, offering him a drink. She looked over and seemed to smile, perhaps apologetically. The items that covered the floor looked like Japanese war memorabilia which made sense for a Japanese vendor. I spotted a sheathed Samurai sword under one of the over turned trestles. Thank goodness the soldiers hadn't noticed that. I looked at the trouble makers. Not one of them could have been twenty. Just kids probably high on booze and adrenaline. They hung their heads now, no fight left in them. Which was a good thing because you don't mess with the military police.

The three men were dragged away and the crowd immediately parted to let them through.

My captors didn't move and the major continued to glare at me, unblinking.

I nodded. One officer to another. "Thank you."

5

The major said nothing.

He seemed to wait until the last of the three was almost out of the covered market. Again I nodded. "Right. You can let me go now."

Only now did he change his expression. The glare became a kind of smirk.

"Let you go?"

"Yes. I was just—"

The major barked, "You are going nowhere, matey boy." He spun on his heels and I was nudged forward, my arms locked behind my back. "You are under arrest."

TWO

I blinked in the bright sunlight. Water sloshed from pipes and ran over the cobbles down the street. A truck with military police markings was pulling away and I figured the other three guys were in it.

A second vehicle waited, its rear doors open.

"I'm a civilian," I said to the major but he ignored me. He walked to the front of the vehicle where a beetle-browed sergeant opened the door for him.

A second later I was bundled into the back of the truck. At the last moment, I caught a glimpse of the guy who'd been following me earlier. He was leaning against a wall, cigarette in mouth, watching. He inclined his head, perhaps as a courteous nod. It was the first indication that maybe something was going on.

The MPs snapped cuffs on me behind my back then attached the cuffs to a metal bar in the rear of the truck. Once secured, they sat either side and slammed the door shut.

"Where to, lads?" I asked trying to lighten the atmosphere. They didn't respond but then again I didn't expect them to.

I couldn't see outside but the bumpy ride took no more than ten minutes. We were still in the city. When we stopped, I heard the front passenger leave. Then the two in the back got out and shut the door again. It was hot inside, maybe eighty degrees Fahrenheit, maybe more. I tried to stay relaxed with shallow breaths. *Don't think about the heat.* I knew what was going on. I'd done or instructed the same thing many times. This was about weakening a prisoner's spirit. Exhaust him, break him and gain control.

Thirty minutes later, the doors opened.

The sergeant with the eyebrows looked at me. I'm sure I was dishevelled, my short hair plastered on my head, my clothes soaked with sweat. Not an impressive sight. But that was the point.

"Welcome to Hotel Bras Basah," the sergeant said in a Welsh accent.

He climbed in and detached the cuffs from the bar. My arms ached from the uncomfortable position.

"Could you uncuff me, Sergeant?"

"When we've got you inside, sir."

I could see from his eyes that he'd made a mistake, shouldn't have called me sir. But there was no point in confronting the situation, not yet anyway. I may have been hot and bothered and thirsty and quite pissed off, but I was also intrigued.

We were parked on a street behind a Land Rover. The other truck was there too, the one from outside the market I guessed. Since I hadn't heard anyone get out of it, the squaddies were either still inside or hadn't been kept waiting.

We were outside a single storey brownstone, just wider than the parking space for the Land Rovers. It had large windows and glass doors which were wide open to the street. Five stone steps took us into a foyer. There was a long desk in front of me and three MPs behind it, one an admissions clerk. They all looked hot and I figured that was why the doors were open, trying to get some air into this hothouse.

The corporal behind the desk watched us approach. He would log the prisoners in and ask for the usual details: name, number, rank and regiment. He'd also note the reason for arrest. I knew that the majority of soldiers that I'd seen were on shore leave. The three I'd fought were from the Staffordshire regiment and had come ashore a couple of hours earlier.

"Causing affray," Eyebrows said. The admissions clerk wrote it down and then reeled off the usual questions aimed at me.

"Ash Carter," I said. "No number. No regiment. Civilian."

Even though I put emphasis on the last word, the clerk didn't bat an eyelid. He just grunted, "Cell one."

Eyebrows led me around the desk to a corridor. On the left was a door that I suspected led to a couple of offices. On the right was the main cell. It could probably take over twenty men comfortably. Double that uncomfortably. But there were just three today. The squaddies. They sat on the bench, looking sorry for themselves—especially the one I'd jabbed on the nose. It was stuffed with cotton wool and his face was swollen.

To a man they looked up and tracked me through the metal bars as I was led past the pen and through a door at the back. There were four individual cells here. Each about eight by six feet, each with a stubby wooden bench.

Eyebrows opened the gate and I stepped inside. He removed the handcuffs, stepped outside and locked me in. He left me for a minute before returning with a metal mug of water.

I drank it and sat on the bench to wait. Through the door I could see the corridor that led to the foyer. I

9

couldn't see the large pen or the squaddies but sometime during the next two hours, I heard the three Staffordshires close-quarters marched out. I heard one of the guards say the name of a troopship and surmised they were being taken to brig aboard the ship. Soldiers would never be retained on land if their ship was about to leave. But they wouldn't be free. All troopships had their own equivalent of these cells.

Later, I heard two drunken soldiers dragged in and dumped in the pen. Unlike the Staffordshires, the two new prisoners argued and, when the clerk shouted at them to shut up, their abuse turned to him briefly before they resumed their argument.

I had been dozing when I heard my door unlock.

Two guards stood in the corridor.

"You're to see Major Vernon," one said.

The other one said, "It's a long walk."

I stepped outside the cell and they stood one in front and one behind as though we were about to march close-quarters. The one in the front stepped forwards smartly and I waited for the inevitable prod in the back. It didn't happen.

The guy in front opened the door to the corridor and I took a casual step forward. The guards walked awkwardly for five paces and then stopped. I stopped.

The man in front opened a door on the right and we filed through. As suspected there were two offices here, one on either side. He knocked on a door and we waited.

After a count of twenty, a voice called, "Come."

The guard opened the door and we stepped in. I was wrong. It was more like an interview room than an office.

The major stood with his back to us, looking out of an open window. There was a large oak desk between us and one large chair on his side, one small chair on my side.

The guards left.

"Sit, Mr Carter," Vernon said.

I remained standing.

He turned and glared at me. He had small, cold eyes and a half-bald head. As a civilian he may have been tempted to shave it all off or have a comb-over to hide the lack of hair. Instead, he had shaved his scalp halfway like two heads had been stuck together, one bald and one not. It was some kind of signature look. Whatever, he was clearly proud of the unusual hairstyle because he smiled after I looked at it.

On the desk was an open book. He glanced down. "Causing affray, it says here."

I said, "The three Staffordshires were bothering a local market trader. A girl was knocked off her feet. I stepped in to help."

"They were on shore leave. A little merry from drink and having a bit of fun."

"I judged the situation—"

"Judged?" Vernon shouted. He slammed both hands on the desk and leaned forwards. "Who the hell are you to judge?"

I didn't respond.

Vernon made an exaggerated show of turning a page.

"Witness statements," he said, spitting the words.

"Good."

"Not good." He stood ramrod straight, maybe trying to look big though he was a couple of inches shorter than me. "Have you wondered why you are here rather than in a police cell?"

I didn't respond.

"I have witness reports that say you shouted, 'Military bloody Police'."

11

"Without the bloody."

Vernon said, "Military Police. Impersonation of a military police officer."

"Who were the witnesses? Did you get a statement from the Japanese market trader?"

"Impersonating a member of His Majesty's armed forces—a military policeman not least—is a criminal offence." He trotted off some regulations and then waited for me to say something.

I met his glare and said nothing.

"The witnesses all claimed you started the fight."

They hadn't interviewed anyone from the market. It wasn't standard procedure, not unless there had been criminal damage or grievous bodily harm. All Vernon had were three statements from the Staffordshires.

I shook my head and waited.

Eventually he flicked over another page and pointed to a line of type that I couldn't read upside down.

"Palestine," he said in a tone that was almost reasonable.

"That's right."

"Just off the boat yourself?"

"No, I caught a flight into Changi."

He waited. When I didn't elaborate he said, "Captain Ash Carter. Assigned to Royal Military Police seventy-fifth Provost. Special Investigations Branch. Palestine."

It seemed to be the only information he had about me. I nodded and said, "Retired as of two weeks ago."

The cold, hard stare returned and I wondered if he ever blinked.

I added, "Honourable discharge."

Vernon puffed himself up again. His teeth were clenched as if he wanted to say something but was unsure what it was.

Finally he bellowed, "Guard!"

The door opened and the two MPs stepped smartly inside.

"Take Mr Carter back to his cell."

THREE

Night approached and slinked slowly across the corridor leaving just a dim light from the room beyond. I leaned on the wall and dozed. Something you learn in the army is to sleep when you can. You also eat when you can but all I was given was a chunk of bread and another mug of water. It was lukewarm and tasted of tin.

During the night there was a lot of noise and activity. Many drunken soldiers came and went from the pen next door. At one point the sergeant with the eyebrows came through and asked if I wanted a blanket. The heat was unrelenting so I used it as a pillow and curled up on the floor.

It was still dark when I woke up just before six in the morning. I rubbed the stiffness from my joints and returned to the bench. A guard brought me a mug of tea and a billycan with watery porridge.

"What's next?" I asked him.

"No idea," he said. "Except…" He looked uncertain.

"Go on."

"Well, sir, you've caused a bit of a kerfuffle." That was all he would say before he left me.

Thirty minutes later, Eyebrows came back. "Sleep all right?"

"I've had better nights. But I've also had worse."

He nodded. "You're staying at The Queens?"

They'd obviously checked up on me whilst I'd been in the clink. "In theory," I said. "I checked in but haven't actually stayed there yet. Yesterday was my first day."

Eyebrows cracked a smile. "Well then, welcome to Singapore." He led me into the corridor. I counted eight men in the pen, looking tired with hangovers and bruises from fighting no doubt.

Eyebrows checked me out at the desk and showed me a map.

"This is the Military Police Head Quarters on Bras Basah road. Your hotel is here—" He pointed to a crossroads not far away. "A maximum of ten minutes' walk. Get yourself cleaned up and I'll pick you up outside the hotel at oh-eight-twenty."

"Pick me up?"

"Yes," he said and became more serious. "I'm to take you to Government House."

I expected a vehicle, but I was wrong. *Pick you up*, just meant that Eyebrows would meet me at The Queens Hotel and we would walk. Showered, shaved and with clean clothes I felt like a new man. On the steps of the hotel I formally introduced myself.

Eyebrows replied with a nod. "Sergeant Dave Hegarty."

We set off at a brisk pace.

"What's at Government House, Dave?"

"Sorry, sir, that's all I've been told." After that, he said nothing.

We walked in a straight line with the rising sun at our backs. There were occasional blocks of shop-houses— two storey buildings each with a retail shop downstairs and living quarters upstairs—but within minutes we were in the area I learned to call the Government sector. White Georgian properties gleamed in the sunlight.

Hegarty stopped at a shiny black door with a silver knocker and door pull. He knocked and the door was opened by a Malay butler who bowed curtly.

Hegarty indicated that I should enter and said he'd wait outside.

The butler led me down a corridor and parquet flooring clicked under my shoes. I glanced at large oil paintings and expensive looking ornaments. He stopped at an open door and waved me inside.

The room looked like a cosy private library. There was a plush rug and leather armchairs. It smelled of cigars and polish and was cool compared to the street with a giant fan turning lazily in the centre of the room.

A man wearing a black suit and white wing-collared shirt sat in one of the chairs. His legs were crossed and he had an unlit cigar in one hand.

"Captain Carter," he said rising. "Very pleased to meet you." The way he stood made me think he either had a false leg or a knee problem.

I shook his hand. It was soft.

"And you are?"

"Secretary Coates."

He was a small, relaxed man but with a natural air of authority. Public school and army, I figured, but a long time ago. He was over fifty and gone to seed though his pale eyes were still bright.

We both sat and I decided his movement suggested the leg was indeed false. Between us was a round mahogany table. I placed a hand on it and said, "Secretary?"

He smiled. "I work for the Governor. As I'm sure you know Singapore is a Crown Colony. We have a

Legislature, a government if you will, and I'm the Secretary responsible for internal security."

I nodded and took in the room. The books crammed on shelves were leather bound and looked more like journals or record books than for entertainment. There was a globe to Coates's right—the sort that was really a drinks cabinet. I could see Asia, but Singapore was too small to make out.

He saw me looking. "Strategically important," he said. "Raffles realized it as soon as he spotted the island and pictured it as the gateway to the Orient. Pretty much everything going east or west by sea goes through Singapore." Then he pierced me with his bright eyes and asked abruptly, "What are you doing here?"

"I believe you wanted to see me."

"I mean in Singapore."

"I'm visiting a friend." Which was true. I'd received a telegram from an old school chum, Tom Silverman.

SINGAPORE GREAT BUT SOMETHING AMISS -(STOP)-
INVESTIGATING -(STOP)- NEED YOUR HELP -(STOP)- PLEASE CALL

I could do better than call. I needed to get away from Palestine and had nowhere better to go, so a few days later I jumped on a ship to Egypt. Then I caught a ride on a DC 6 to India and then another flight to Singapore.

Coates was appraising me with his bright eyes. Maybe he doubted my story, but I saw no reason to elaborate or prove its veracity.

I smiled. "Perhaps now, you could tell me what I am doing here. In your office I mean."

The politician lit his cigar with a motion that was both languid and considered. After it was lit he took a long draw and the space between us filled with blue smoke.

17

I said, "You had me followed. Before I was arrested I spotted someone tailing me."

"We knew you were coming." He took another long draw and set the cigar down. "Captain Ashley Carter."

Only my father called me Ashley.

I said, "I prefer to be called Ash."

"You resigned your commission from the Royal Military Police two weeks ago after seven years of distinguished service. Why would you do that?"

I looked over his shoulder at an oil painting of elephants in the jungle. The detail was almost good enough to be a photograph.

Coates said, "You were awarded the Distinguished Service Medal. Which is ironic really. I understand you were instrumental in stopping a bomb plot against the United Nations building."

"It was more the occupants—the international delegates—than the building but apart from that you are correct."

"And then you resigned."

"Yes. It was time to move on."

"Really?" He picked up his cigar and blew another cloud between us. I wondered if he was using it as symbolism—a smoke screen. I wasn't going to tell him anything he didn't know. And then I discovered he knew more than I expected.

He said, "You resigned because you were unhappy. You were unhappy because your snitch—if that's the right term—was murdered and you could do nothing about it."

It was much more than that. I tried to stay relaxed and not let my face betray my feelings.

Coates said, "The suspected perpetrators—four of them—were found dead three days ago. The same day you left the country."

I said nothing. It had been the day I'd left. Coates knew a great deal but not everything. I suspected he was filling in the gaps in his intelligence with educated guesses.

He continued: "As an MP you were powerless to take any action against the murderers. So I think you resigned and took independent action. You found the perpetrators and you killed them. You revenged your snitch's death."

"That's pure speculation," I said.

"For now."

I stood. "Thank you, Mr Coates. It has been an interesting meeting."

"Sit down, Ashley."

I remained standing and looked at the fine detail of the oil painting.

He said, "I have a proposition for you," and pointed to the chair. "Please sit."

After I had taken the seat, he rang a silver hand bell and the butler appeared. "*Stengahs*," he requested. When the butler returned with two tumblers, Coates explained that they contained weak whisky and soda. He took a sip in the same languid fashion that he smoked.

I waited.

"I want you to work for me," he said with a beatific smile.

"I'm in Singapore to visit a friend. I'm not staying."

"Let's be frank. You aren't leaving without my approval. Since I suspect you of murder, I could incarcerate you here on the island."

"Under what charge?"

Coates waved a hand. "I don't think you understand the situation here, my boy. I am responsible for the security of the island. I am responsible for the police and

19

the law as it concerns the wellbeing of the population. My God, man, do you not know we are at war?"

"I'm aware of The Emergency," I said. Since 1948 we had been fighting the communists in the north. It wasn't the scale of the war in Korea, but it could develop. I was well aware of the tensions.

"Bandits are everywhere."

I nodded. Bandits were what they called insurgents back then.

Coates continued: "And it's just a matter of time before the Reds attack us at home. In Singapore."

"And this affects me, how?"

"I want you to make sure it doesn't happen."

"You have the police and the army for that. You said yourself that you're in charge."

"I want you between them."

"That's Liaison's job."

Coates took another slow sip of his watered-down whisky. "I don't want a liaison officer. I want action. I want someone who can work with the army and the police. I want someone who can also be independent."

"And I'm your ideal candidate?"

"Although you're a civilian, you'll be accepted by the army." He gave me the smile again. "I also know who your father is. And because of your father I know the new Commander-in-Chief for the Far East won't have a problem either. General Gaskill is based here on the island."

This was crazy. Coates was well informed about my recent past and, despite the angelic smile, could make it seriously difficult for me.

"All right," I said, "I get why you've chosen me but why now?"

"Because of two things. There's a rumour that someone is buying arms on the island. Someone—most likely a group—is arming themselves."

"And the second thing?"

I was intrigued when he pulled a piece of paper from his pocket. He leaned forward and handed it to me.

It was about six inches by four with red symbols on one side. It looked like an advertising flyer. There was a circle with a paw print in the middle. Underneath were four characters that I assumed were Chinese.

"What is it?"

"Precisely? I don't know."

"How did you get it?"

"From a reliable source."

"And what do they think it is?"

"Best guess is it's a secret code."

I handed it back but he wanted me to keep it. "A code for what?" I said.

He finished his drink and for the first time I thought I detected a chink in his façade. He was worried.

"What do they think it is?" I asked again.

"An attack," he said quietly. "There's suspicion of a plan to attack us—an imminent security threat."

FOUR

Dubious of the Secretary's motives, I walked back to The Queens Hotel, thinking. At the reception desk, I asked if I could use the telephone. There was only one for the whole building. At first the receptionist dismissed me so I told him I was working for the government. I couldn't get in any more trouble, could I? I flashed my old warrant card, like the police show and moments later I was alone in the manager's office and speaking to the operator. She put me through to the colonel of my old regiment, Dexter. He was pleased to hear from me and gave no indication that he knew why I'd left so abruptly although he must have guessed.

I cut to the chase. "Colonel, I need to know—what's the situation there?"

Dexter didn't immediately answer. I knew him well enough to know he was choosing words carefully. When he spoke he said, "Everything is tickettyboo. There is no problem."

So I wasn't wanted in Palestine for murder. "Thank you," I said. "It's just that someone here seems to think there is."

"Army?"

"No."

"Government?"

"Yes."

"My advice would be to play the tourist somewhere else. Or go home to Blighty."

I didn't say anything.

"Ash?"

"I'm thinking of staying. For a while at least."

"Take care and if there's ever..."

I thanked him and ended the call. While I was speaking I twirled the warrant card between my fingers and imagined it was the government ID card Secretary Coates had promised me.

When I'd said I'd think about his offer, he'd responded, "You have twenty-four hours," and I reckoned that would be plenty of time to check out how serious the threat was and see my friend. If I then needed to get away, I was certain Tom could help. He was an engineer at the docks and could get me on a boat and off the island.

Outside the hotel, a porter hailed a trishaw for me. These, I was told, were everywhere in the city and better than a taxi for short distances.

As skinny as a whippet and speaking no English, I guessed the driver was Bangladeshi. However, he understood when I asked for the docks and we set off at a brisk pace.

After the Esplanade, which everyone called the *Padang*, we passed an obelisk and crossed the Anderson Bridge. Its white, arched girders resembled a rail bridge. On the far side we went through a square crammed with cars. As we approached the docks, the road became dense with traffic and the air filled with choking fumes.

We made slow progress through a gaggle of people and animals before stopping by a pier. I located the harbour masters office and was told that the maritime engineers were based at the end of the main docks. The office was a stone's throw away but we needed to circle around to Keppel Harbour.

Using sign-language, I directed my driver back to the long congested road that took us to the docks supervised by the navy. The navy's shipyard was to the north of the island but they had an HQ here and oversaw both the troop and commercial shipping.

At the entrance, a manned barrier ran between high fences and we were stopped by a Masters-at-Arms, the naval equivalent of an MP. He let me enter and I signalled the trishaw driver to wait for me.

There were no troopships in and, apart from a commercial ship being unloaded, the docks were quiet. The ship was to my right and I could see half a mile of storage areas and warehouses. Just inside on my left was an MT yard, a compound inside which included a motor pool. There were various size trucks and three identical pale blue cars. I'm not a car expert but I could see they were all Ford saloons.

I continued on past the yard and the dock swept around. Here was a long warehouse, workshops and offices. The Master-at-Arms had pointed to the far end of the wharf and I could see a couple of guys working on something that looked like a giant pulley system.

As I approached, I called out, "I'm looking for Tom Silverman. Is he about?"

When they looked up, I read something in their faces: uncertainty or concern maybe. They exchanged glances and one pointed to a door.

Ducking inside, I saw men working at benches and others sitting around a table drinking tea. The air was filled with a hum of machinery and screech of metal. There was no sign of Tom. I asked the group drinking tea and again received the look.

A voice behind me said, "Who wants to know?"

I turned and introduced myself to the guy who explained he was the gaffer.

"He's my friend," I said. "Something's wrong isn't it?"

"I have bad news, I'm afraid."

I waited and could tell he was unsure how to explain.

"Just say it," I said.

He shrugged, released from the need to be sensitive and just said, "He's dead."

FIVE

Instantly, my guts constricted. "Dead? What the hell…?"

One of the men at the table spoke up. "A car crash at night out on the road to Nee Soon."

"When? How'd it happen?"

"Ten days ago."

"We don't know the detail," the gaffer said. "Really bad downpour. An accident. Just lost control they think."

"Who thinks?"

"The police."

I nodded. That made sense. But an accident? He'd sent me a telegram asking for help ten days ago, so he'd died that night.

"Did he tell anyone of any concerns?" I swept my gaze across the group. To a man they all looked baffled. I switched back to the gaffer. "And the police definitely think it was an accident?"

"That's right." Now he looked uncertain. "Are you suggesting otherwise?"

"I don't know but you can be sure of one thing. I'm going to find out." Again I turned to the group. "If you find out anything, hear anything that might be remotely significant, please let me know."

"How will we…"

At that moment I decided I was staying. I also knew I was moving out of The Queens Hotel. "Get a message to me. My name's Carter. Ash Carter. I'll be at Gillman Barracks."

Gillman Barracks was the home to Singapore's Military Police 200 Provost Company. I figured I needed to be either close to the police or MPs and my background made the army the obvious choice. Of course there was also the consideration that they had quarters whereas I didn't know the situation with the police.

Back at the hotel I spoke to the operator again and was put through to Secretary Coates.

"I have two conditions," I said. "Firstly, we draw up a proper contract. I will work for you until the incident you are concerned about occurs or three months. No more. After that, I am free to leave the country."

"What's the second condition?"

"You get me into Gillman."

Coates actually laughed. "Of course, dear boy. I'll agree to both of those. I'll have our agreement drawn up by the end of the day. In fact I'm one step ahead of you. Major Vernon is already expecting you at the barracks. I'll also send you the government warrant card in case you need it."

I checked a map and decided to get a proper taxi. However, before that, I walked to the police HQ. It was an imposing building on the corner of Hill Street and River Valley Road. There was an open door on the corner and I went through. I expected it to be a staff entrance, however it led to a piazza and what looked like a parade ground. There was no one around. I continued round the side and found a door marked *Public Entrance*. Oversized, aged teak doors were closed but opened as I pushed one. Warm stale air and the smell of a day's worth of body odour immediately assaulted me. Giant fans slowly turned in the vaulted ceiling causing air to circulate, but do little else. It was warmer inside than on the street.

The room was crowded, people standing in the centre or sitting on benches around the side. For the large number of people, I was taken by how quiet and calm they were. Or weary. I eased my way to the desk where a sergeant was dealing with a small Chinese lady surrounded by a gaggle of children.

The sergeant, himself Chinese, glanced at me as I approached and called something over his shoulder that I didn't understand. A moment later another sergeant appeared. This one was maybe Malay but spoke excellent English.

"Can I help you, sir?"

I looked around at the many faces watching me. I had jumped the queue but saw no malice.

"I'd like details of an accident—I have discovered my friend was killed in a car crash ten days ago." I showed the sergeant my new warrant card and he almost leapt out of his skin and then stood to attention. He took a couple of beats to compose himself and then ushered me around the desk. Moments later I was sitting in an office. The window was open and I moved the chair to get as much air as available.

"My name is Inspector Anand Rahman." The man in the doorway had a generous smile on his Indian face. He held out a bony hand and pumped mine warmly.

I introduced myself.

"Yes," he said, "I've been expecting you. Secretary Coates himself spoke to me this morning. Welcome Captain."

"Please, just Ash. But that's not why I'm here." I went on to explain about my friend's unfortunate death and asked if I could view the file.

He nodded and then shook his head. "I am afraid I do not know about this accident. As I am sure you appreciate, there are many, many incidents that occur each day. Most of those involve the soldiers off the boats and my role is to work with the military—the military police in particular. But if you would excuse me for a minute, I will request the report... Mr Silverman you say." He checked a calendar. "On the twenty-third."

He spoke to someone in the corridor and I glanced around the office. It had certificates on the wall and a photograph of a large family gathering. There was a clock the size of a dinner plate that ticked slow and loud. His desk was small and functional: just an in-tray and out-tray with papers and nothing personal.

When he returned he gave me the generous smile again. "It won't be long, Captain... Ash."

While we waited he asked about my background and experience in Palestine. Half an hour went by and he talked about the need to work more closely with the MPs. An operation had recently gone wrong because of failed communication. The MPs had ruined an investigation into drug smugglers by chasing a soldier who had tried to deal in the stuff. Rahman grinned. "I think with your help, we will find we work so much better together."

"How do you find the Special Investigation Branch officers here?"

He cocked an eyebrow and waggled his head. "I have never met them."

I was surprised, being SIB myself—at least I had been until two weeks ago.

"I believe they are mostly in Malaya because that is where the trouble is."

And yet the inspector had just described a classic SIB issue: a soldier involved with drug smugglers. I took a mental note to ask about it at Gillman. For now I moved on and handed him the flyer of the circle with a paw print and said, "Secretary Coates gave this to me."

Rahman studied it, turned it over, studied it some more and handed it back. "What is it?"

"Coates's evidence of a security issue. Have you seen it before?"

"No. But then…"

"What are you thinking?"

"Well, I wondered whether the source was us, the police. And we have a large force—almost a thousand men. So it could have come from us. I'll try and find out. I was also thinking about the numbers."

"Numbers?"

"The writing appears to be a series of numbers: four, ten, two, ten. I'll ask around about those. I'll also ask whether anyone has come across a lion's paw in a circle before."

"Lion's paw?"

"That's what it looks like to me. Of course lions feature a lot in Chinese imagery."

He passed the flyer back to me as a young policeman came into the room. He gave the inspector a file and I noticed how deferential the junior man was towards his superior. The chap practically bowed as he backed out of the room.

Rahman opened the file in front of me. It was typed and in English but consisted of two pages of foolscap paper and five photographs about eight inches by six. I read it. The report was by an officer called Sergeant Kee and was reasonable for someone whose first language wasn't English.

Tom had been driving south on the road from Nee Soon to Singapore City. The road was made of small stones called laterite and was rutted in places. There was thick jungle on either side of the road. It was judged to be about one in the morning. The sky was overcast and it had rained heavily in the hours before. It was totally dark except for the headlights of his small car. It was referred to as a Toyota SA Compact. I didn't know it.

There were no other vehicles on that stretch of the road. The report said the car was old, the tyres were bald and the windscreen wipers broken.

During a sudden torrential downpour, the car hit a rut and the driver lost control. He couldn't see where he was going and drove at speed into a tree. He travelled through the windscreen and died immediately from the impact.

I put the report down and studied the black and white photographs. There were two from the front, one focused on the impact and the other on my friend's body trapped between the car and tree. The windscreen was in two main parts but looked like it had come out whole and broken when it hit the ground.

The third photograph showed a tyre with no tread. The next was a shot from the rear showing the ground and what looked like a skid mark. The back of the car was clearly visible on this photograph. However the next picture showed a dip in the road. It was filled with water and the stones again appeared to show something heavy had skidded over it.

I sat back.

"Satisfied?" Rahman asked with a smile.

"No," I said with concern. "There are many things wrong with this report."

"Really?"

I handed the inspector the photograph of the skid. "I'm not convinced this was an accident."

SIX

Now Inspector Rahman's face creased with unease. "Please explain."

"Is your sergeant available—the one who wrote the report?"

Rahman ducked out and a few minutes later returned with a sweaty Chinese police sergeant. They were a similar height—about five foot eight but where Rahman was wiry, Kee was about three times the width. His demeanour was also less friendly than the inspector's.

I handed Kee the report.

"This is yours I understand."

"Yes."

"Have you been trained in investigative work?"

Kee frowned and looked at Rahman and then back at me. "Of course I have."

"Then why haven't you followed procedure? This is not a thorough accident report. It's a bloody story."

"I—"

"Where's the coroner's report?"

"The death wasn't suspicious so I—"

"Where are the witness statements?"

"There were no witnesses. It was late at night. There was no one else around."

I nodded. "And yet you know the time of the crash. You know the weather conditions. And stating that there were no witnesses is pure supposition. You wrote the report at 11am the following day and it's clearly daylight when the photographs were taken."

Kee bristled but said nothing.

I continued: "You have written a story that explains what you saw. It sounds convincing but does not mean that is what actually happened." I pulled out the photographs and spread them on the table before continuing. "I agree that it looks like the car skidded into the tree. I can see evidence that the tyres are bad. However you cannot possibly know that this occurred during a downpour. And the windscreen wipers broken? I can see that the wipers were down so they don't appear to have been on. If indeed you checked whether they worked then it could have been a result of the accident. Did you check?"

"No."

"There is no connection between the hole in the road and the skid. That mark on the road could have been caused by any vehicle. And even if we accept that the wipers didn't work and that he hit a rut, why would he be travelling at speed in those conditions? Let's assume you are right and it was pitch black, then it would have been hard to see the edge of the road even if it weren't raining."

Rahman nodded thoughtfully.

But I hadn't finished. "Your statement that there were no other vehicles on the road achieved two things: it reinforced your view that there was utter darkness. It also removed the problem of witnesses. This accident required a proper investigation. Not a story." I handed Rahman the photograph of the skid in which the rear of the Toyota could be seen clearly.

"The bumper appears to be damaged," I said.

Kee looked at the photo and Rahman nodded. The left hand side was flattened and buckled.

"That didn't happen as a result of the impact with the tree. In this one—" I handed Rahman the photo from the front "—we can partially see the left hand side of the car. That looks dented to me."

"An old car," Kee said.

"The car was heading south to the city and was on the correct side of the road?"

"Yes." He used his sleeve to wipe sweat from his forehead.

"If the car skidded and went straight off the road, the left would be the most likely direction."

Kee shrugged then reluctantly agreed.

I looked at Rahman. "The car will be in a compound somewhere?"

"Yes. Eventually it will be junked, but it's too recent so it will still be there."

"Good," I said switching back to Kee. "Then I want you to go and take another look at the car. I want you to examine the car thoroughly."

Again the sergeant wiped away the sweat. "What am I looking for?"

"Confirmation that the dents and scrapes weren't old. There will be rust in them if they were. And—" I pointed to the side of the car where there may have been a light coloured line against the black paint of the Toyota. "If this is paint, I want to know what colour it is. This doesn't look like an accident to me. I think my friend was forced off that road."

Outside the police station a Land Rover jeep was parked half on the kerb. Sergeant Hegarty waved at me from the driver's seat.

35

I was still in a foul mood from the confrontation with Kee and his useless report. Rahman had been apologetic and wanted to give me a tour of the station but I had declined.

"Everything all right, sir?" Hegarty said with his Welsh lilt.

"No it isn't, Sergeant. I hope I don't find the 200 Provost Company is as ineffective as the Singapore police appear to be."

Hegarty grinned. "Well let's cut and run and you can find out." He then used his thumb to point to my suitcases on the back seat. "Already picked up your stuff, sir."

I jumped in beside him and tried to shake off the bad temper. I tapped the dashboard. "OK let's go, and there's no need to call me sir. Ash will do just fine."

Hegarty gave me a natural grin. "I'll call you Boss then if that's all right... Boss?"

We bumped down the kerb and followed the same route I'd taken earlier in the trishaw. At Empire Docks he pointed out the naval HQ, a house more than an office, on the opposite side of the road to the main Keppel Harbour entrance.

"Cut and run," Hegarty said.

"Yes?"

"It's an old naval term for getting away quickly when under attack."

"Makes sense."

"They would cut the anchor and run on the wind." He grinned. "Just saying that's all. It's an interest of mine... understanding where expressions come from."

We headed north through a tangle of roads. Ten minutes later we were on the outskirts of the city. Around a sweeping bend we came to a drive and a gate manned by a redcap. Hegarty didn't slow and the guard jerked the barrier up for us. Just in time.

Gillman Barracks, home to the British Royal Military Police 200 Provost Company, was set on a small hill and surrounded by a high wire fence. A third of the way up, we passed a single storey building. White and plain except for square pillars. A Union Flag hung limply on a pole outside.

"Offices," Hegarty said.

Over to the left I could see the MT yard. To the right I could see what looked like a diving board.

"Swimming pool," Hegarty confirmed.

Ahead I could see a three storey block that was clearly the main barracks. As we got closer I saw a bathhouse and a block that Hegarty told me housed the rec-room where we could play billiards.

He stopped outside a smart building that could have been a grand two storey home.

"We've put you in the Officers' Quarters," he said as he took hold of my two cases and showed me to my digs.

It was a simple room, not unlike the one I'd had in Palestine but larger. Stone floor, unadorned white walls, a single bed with sheets and a grey blanket—which I doubted had ever been used—a freestanding wardrobe and a chest of drawers. At least I had a room to myself.

A shower room and toilet was shared by four officers in the house. Hegarty also told me where the mess hall was. I was suddenly famished. It was almost the middle of the afternoon and I'd had nothing since my watery porridge.

Hegarty said, "You've got a few hours."

"Until?"

"Major Vernon." Hegarty pulled a face and I realized then that the sergeant didn't think much of the major.

"You have an appointment with the major at nineteen-hundred hours."

I cleaned myself up for the second time that day. The humidity clawed at my skin and my clothes were damp just from walking around. At the rate I was going I would need to buy new clothes every day.

Due to the size of the company, there was no separate Officers' Mess but they were happy to serve me in the canteen providing I had sausages and mash. Due to the hour I was the only one eating and got talking to the Indian chap who served me. I mentioned the humidity and my clothing and he promised to send someone straight over to collect my laundry. It would be returned by the evening. He also fetched me a map of the city.

After eating my fill, I strolled around the grounds. I chatted to a few men and gained a little information. Finally I stood alone at the top of the rise and got my bearings.

Gillman Barracks was in an area called Pasir Panjang. The centre of the city was a little over three miles to the east. To the south I could see the straits with its islands and shipping. The islands appeared to be uninhabited jungle from this vantage point. In fact I could see jungle in every direction, except the city. I knew there was thick jungle to the north that ended at the Straits of Johor and that there was a causeway between Singapore and Malaya up there somewhere called Woodlands Crossing.

Tom Silverman had died somewhere to the north and I decided I'd need to visit the scene of the crash myself.

The main army barracks at Tanglin was also north—about two miles as the crow flies—although the obvious route was circuitous—along the coast road, past the docks and then up through the city.

The docks were just a couple of miles south east of me but hidden by the coastal hills.

I stared out to sea and thought about what Coates had said: munitions coming into the country. Someone was arming themselves. I reckoned there were three options. The first I dismissed for the time being as highly unlikely. By land the munitions would need to come over Woodlands Crossing. A corporal I'd spoken to confirmed my expectation. The crossing was secure and well manned by the army. No way was anything coming over the causeway that we didn't want. In 1942, the Japanese had cycled across to take the island by surprise. With the present threat from the Reds in the north, the British Army would not be caught out like that again.

Keppel Harbour, with its ocean going ships could be dismissed for the same reason. I had seen the naval presence there and was confident there was a similar level of security as for Woodlands. However, I had been over the river a number of times now and I'd seen the frenetic trade coming in by sea. I set off towards the city to find out how easy it would be to smuggle arms via that route.

SEVEN

Getting a sense of the balance between incoming and outgoing trade, I stood on Coleman Bridge, the fourth of many that spanned Singapore River. There was a steady stream of traffic crossing between New Bridge Road and Hill Street, cars, bicycles, trishaws and electric buses which ran on cables like dodgems. I chose this bridge because it was less busy than the industrial, dual-carriage Elgin Bridge, and had a good view of the wharves that lined this part of the river inland from here.

The air was filled with an intoxicating concoction of rubber and spices from cargo on the myriad of boats running below me. My spirits might have been raised if it weren't for the fact that my old friend was dead. I didn't really know if the crash was an accident or not but I knew I'd get answers by suggesting it wasn't.

Of course, it could have been a coincidence but my gut said not. Tom Silverman had sent me a telegram asking for help and now he was dead.

I let my back-brain process everything I was learning and just stood watching the activity. There were two types of boat: barges and a smaller squatter equivalent that I later learned were called *tongkangs* and *bumboats* respectively. A line spaced no more than five seconds apart, headed for open water and an equally regular stream of boats returned. A high number of the ones leaving had giant black bales that I realized was unprocessed rubber. Of the overladen boats coming in, I couldn't tell what the cargo was. Many of the boats were stacked with sacks and others had wooden crates; impossible to know what was inside.

On the east side of the river was a wharf and I could see more around the next bend. Each wharf had giant wooden warehouses—called *godowns*—with names written in both English and Chinese.

Most of the workers appeared to be Chinese and they worked like regimented ants ferrying goods from boat to warehouse, loading flatbed waggons which they pulled by hand. I realized there was no room for horses to work here so human power did everything.

Occasionally I saw a man stopped and asked to provide something. The customs officials were easy to spot in their white shirts and shorts in contrast to the dock workers' dark greasy garb. The customs men checked bills of lading but also picked on junior labourers. I was intrigued at what these dock workers were being asked.

I walked along on the opposite side of the river following a customs man, hoping to see him do it again. He stopped someone who was carrying a sack on his back that was as big as himself. The docker dumped it down, straightened and then pulled something out of his shirt. A necklace maybe.

The customs officer examined it and then moved on. I shadowed him on the opposite side.

When I came to another bridge I crossed over and began to follow through the wharf. Then I saw it. The dockers were being asked to show a small medallion they had tied with string around their necks. I got closer. It was like a bronze coin with a hole in the centre.

I made a mental note to ask about it back at the barracks when something caught my eye. Movement between the *godowns*. Someone in a suit ducked through a side door.

Maybe it wouldn't have attracted my attention if the warehouse concerned had been busy but it was the only one with its main doors closed. The buildings on either side were a hive of activity. This one was different.

I crossed the busy quay and entered a dark alleyway about eight feet wide. The warehouses loomed overhead. At the far end, about forty yards away, I could see the road that ran behind the wharf. There were no windows in the side wall, just a small wooden door a third of the way along.

There was no one about. I tried the door handle. It opened and I entered.

Inside was even darker than the alleyway. High up I could see skylights and dust motes spiralling down.

I could see the warehouse was stacked with boxes and I could hear voices. I walked towards them and then pulled up short.

A Chinese guy stepped out from behind a tower of crates. He was burly and maybe an inch taller than me. Initially he looked surprised and then alarmed. He shouted something. Not at me. To someone else. Someone who understood Chinese I guessed.

A moment later a guy who could have been the first man's twin scooted around the crates and glared at me.

"Sorry, took a wrong turn," I said with an innocent smile.

Another guy, smaller but with an air of authority, appeared. He stood behind the first two and looked between their shoulders.

"Who are you?" the third guy asked in broken English.

I looked around.

"What's going on here?" I asked in my best polite but commanding voice.

The third guy wasn't biting. "You leave," he snapped at me.

Again I said, "What's going on here? Why are the doors closed?"

The guy said something and the other two flexed their hands as though ready to fight. Their size didn't bother me. As my trainer had said early on, "The bigger they are the harder they fall," and most times it was true. I changed my stance, relaxed my shoulders and rehearsed the moves in my head. I'm a south paw and normally a counter-puncher. I expected the one on my left, the guy who had arrived second, to move first. As soon as he twitched I would step forwards, jab him with my right and follow through with my left. *Bam bam*. With the momentum I would then crouch and swivel to the right and catch the other big guy in the gut. He would double over and catch my uppercut on his chin. That went through my mind in a millisecond, followed by the memory of the market, how I'd not planned on the third guy and stumbled over the Japanese vendor.

I looked at the smaller guy in the middle trying to assess him. And then it was too late. He yelled and the two big guys virtually jumped to my left. I tracked their sudden movement and in that same instance felt something strike my right leg, just above the knee. It felt like I'd been sliced. The smaller guy stepped back. In his hand was a stick about one and a half arms' lengths that he held at his side.

The twins looked like they were waiting for me to buckle but I fought the urge and gritted my teeth.

I took a short step back to cover all of them, wondering what their next move would be. The smart

43

move would be to go for the guy with the stick. But then they'd expect that.

The guy raised it as though about to whip my legs again. "Go!" he snarled at me.

I began to work out my moves.

Third guy stepped back but I could see in his eyes it was a feint.

"Wang! Stop!" A woman's voice cut through the tension.

The man stopped his move and waited. At first I couldn't see her clearly and then she stepped between Wang and me, and Singapore suddenly became interesting for a very different reason.

EIGHT

Happy to talk, I gave her my name and she introduced herself as Su Ling, just a translator. In the warehouse she had shown control over the guys. When she snapped at them they'd just melted away into the dim interior. She was more than just a translator.

She walked me outside and we stood on the footbridge. I knew I was staring, but couldn't help it. She was Eurasian, half English and half Chinese she later told me. For now I just saw a golden brown skin and dark almond-shaped eyes. When the light caught them I registered how green they were. Her hair was tied up in a swirl held on with a needle-like stick. She wore a shimmering blue cheongsam and glittery, dark blue shoes. She was elegant, moved with poise, and knew she was perfection.

I noticed she wore a matching silk strap on her right wrist like a watch.

"How is your leg?" she asked and looked at the red welt rapidly growing on my flesh.

"I'll survive."

"I am sorry," she said for the tenth time. "Wang and his men were just protecting the property. You know you were trespassing."

"I made a wrong turn."

She smiled at me. "Yes you did." I knew she wanted to know why I had entered the warehouse and who I was, but I wasn't offering information. Not yet anyway.

As a way of diffusing the situation and getting me outside, she'd invited me to eat with her. On the far side of the bridge she hailed a trishaw and took me up Orchard Road to a small restaurant. We didn't speak on the short ride but she kept glancing at me making an assessment I think.

Even though I'd eaten at the barracks, I ordered the same as her: Singapore noodles and a beer.

"So Mr Carter, you are an enigma." She paused and smiled. "You are not military although from a distance you could be mistaken for one in those clothes. You are not Customs because I would have seen you before. You are obviously not from the police because you are white."

I took a sip of my beer when it arrived. "I'm just a civilian," I said.

"With an interest in warehouses no doubt?" She laughed. "Shall we say you are a student... no, a professor of commerce?"

I chinked my glass with hers. "I like the sound of professor, but to be honest I'm more of a scientist."

She studied me with her dark eyes and then nodded. "So please do tell me. What was your interest in Mr Yipp's warehouse?"

"Mr Yipp?"

"You don't know who he is?"

"No."

"Mr Yipp is the head of the largest Chinese business empire in Singapore from rubber plantations, manufacturing, sawmills, canneries, real estate, import and export brokerage, ocean transport and rice trading. He is also well known as a philanthropist."

46

"And you work for him?"

"As I said, I am a translator but I also act as his personal assistant." She smiled again and I was becoming accustomed to enjoying it.

"You still haven't told me the truth," she said, after a few heart beats of silence. "You have an easy style of answering a question with a question. Were you a policeman from somewhere else?"

At that point I realized she was playing with me. She knew or at least suspected what I was.

"How do you know?" I asked.

"You're doing it again, Ash. Question with question."

I waited.

She took a slow sip of beer and flashed her smile. "Mr Yipp knows everything."

"Does he know about arms coming into the country?" As I said the words, I knew instantly that she didn't know. Surprise flickered in her eyes before she hid it.

"Is that what Secretary Coates believes?"

"Now you are answering with a question." When she didn't immediately respond, I asked, "How long have you known who I'm working for."

"Pretty much from the moment that Secretary Coates decided to employ you. And, yes, I know about your background: British Military Police Captain from Palestine—until you retired two weeks ago. You are acting as liaison between the police and military. Why you came though, I must confess, is less clear."

"I'm here because a friend asked me to come—asked for my help."

"Help with what?"

"I don't know and I'm unlikely to find out. Because he died in a car crash before I arrived."

She said she was sorry to hear that and asked his name. We finished our meals and she ordered some kind of aromatic tea which I didn't like.

"The warehouse—" I said. "Will you tell me what was in it and why were the doors closed?"

"Mr Yipp has many warehouses. About a third of those on the quay were his. The one you entered is small and simply wasn't moving goods today."

"Really? It's as simple as that?"

She inclined her head with a smile.

I asked, "Why then were those men there? The big ones are clearly heavy security... or protection."

"I can't answer that."

And then the big question: "And you, as a translator, why were you there?"

Her green eyes studied me for a while. Perhaps she was assessing, deciding how to respond. When she did, I believed she was telling me the truth. She said, "I was following you. I saw you enter through the side door. I came in from the main road."

As I've said before, I'm good at spotting a tail and yet I hadn't spotted her—a beautiful, elegant woman.

"How long—"

"Have I been following you? Just through the quays."

So someone else must have been following before. They had handed over to her. "And what about yesterday, were you following me then?"

"No."

"But you know where I was and what happened."

"At the market? Yes. And then the police station."

"So Mr Yipp has eyes everywhere?"

She inclined her head with the smile. Yes. "I understand you were defending a Japanese market trader."

"Not because he was Japanese, if you're asking that."

48

"You will find out about the Japanese," she said. When I looked inquisitive she smiled. "It's what you do, Ash. You are an investigator so I am just saying you will want to understand." With that, she stood up.

I waved to the staff for the bill but Su Ling told me it was paid for.

"I need to go," she said and held out her hand. I was surprised at how cool and smooth it felt, whereas mine felt bloated by the heat.

I checked my watch and realized I had to get a move on.

"A quick question," I said, fishing out the piece of paper that Coates had given me. I showed her the red symbol. "What does this mean?"

"Can I take it?" A question in response to a question.

"It's all I have and would like to keep it for now. Do you know what it means?"

"Maybe," she said. "Let me think about it and I will let you know."

"I'm at Gillman Barracks," I said unnecessarily.

She left me then and I hailed a trishaw.

I had an appointment with Major Vernon.

NINE

Eyeing me with suspicion, the desk clerk told me to knock and wait at the door. Vernon kept me waiting a few minutes before he called for me to enter.

I sat opposite him at a grand desk with a burgundy leather inlay. I guessed it had once had a gold trim but it had worn away. He had a long credenza and an array of filing cabinets, the tallest of which was metal with multiple drawers.

"So how does this work, Mr Carter?" Before I could respond, he continued: "You are here as my guest. As you probably know, I am the acting CO of 200 Provost Company. It is my camp and the rules are my rules. Whilst you are here you will respect those rules. Yesterday you tried to pass yourself off as an MP. The deal is that you will act as an MP. I am an officer short, so while you are here you will wear the uniform." He looked me up and down slowly, deliberately. "Which is basically how you are already dressed, but you will put on your insignia and wear the brassard." He then gave me a smile laced with irony. "But you will not have a service revolver. Don't try signing one out from Armoury because they will be under specific instructions—"

"That's fine," I said, because at that point I had no intention of shooting anyone or even threatening to use a gun.

"And there will be no trouble. If there is, I will have no hesitation but to put you in the clink again. Is that clear?"

"Of course. I get the deal. But don't expect me to call you sir."

I could see his chest constrict with annoyance but he managed to control his anger. Instead of shouting at me he said, "All I require is respect."

"In public."

His head nodded although his eyes were saying something different. But he didn't dwell on it. Instead, he switched subjects and said, "We have our own liaison officer, Lieutenant Robshaw. The police have theirs—Inspector Rahman—who I understand you have already met. The reason we need you is because the police are utterly useless. They are fine at traffic problems, they are fine with minor public order offences, but when it comes to crime... they are either headless chickens or incompetent fools. Quite frankly they are a bunch of monkeys. If we have an investigation or exercise then I want them kept out of the damned way."

"Secretary Coates is concerned about security."

Vernon scoffed. "That's his job."

"He mentioned specific intelligence about arms coming into the country."

"Your point is?"

"That's my job. To find out if it's true and identify any threats."

"You're my guest and I say your job is to stop the bloody police blundering into our affairs."

I said nothing for a while. A fan turned slowly on the ceiling.

51

He watched me with his small eyes. Finally he said, "Dismissed."

I stood.

"Another rule," he said. "You will keep me informed of everything you do. Give me a report at the end of each day. Verbal if I'm here, otherwise in writing." He smiled without moving his eyes. "Is that clear?"

"Anything you say."

He desperately wanted a *yes, sir* but he wasn't getting one. The meeting was over.

The desk clerk showed me a small common room and an office where I would work. He said I'd share an office with the liaison officer and a sergeant.

There was a phone in the room but it was only connected to the desk clerk. If I needed to make a call he'd call the operator and my phone would be rung when the connection was made.

I checked the time. It was half past eight in the evening. That meant it would be one-thirty in London.

I asked the clerk to place a call to Whitehall, the Department of Energy. I gave him my father's name.

A few minutes later the phone in my shared office clicked and then rang.

"Connecting you now," a voice said.

"Ash?" a woman asked. "It's Sam Duffield, here."

My father's secretary.

"Is he there please Sam?"

"He's at lunch I'm afraid. So you made it to Singapore all right?"

"Yes," I said and then asked when he'd be back. She informed me his diary was blocked out for the whole afternoon. He was a man in demand it seemed.

"I'll pass on a message, if you'd like."

"Sam?" I said realizing something. "How did you know I was in Singapore?"

"You needed to leave the Middle East fairly quickly."

"Yes."

"You asked your father for help…"

And then I understood.

"He had you sort out the travel for me."

I could almost sense her smiling down the phone.

"He may have the connections, but… you know how it is… behind every good man…" And then she stopped herself finishing the sentence. My father and mother hadn't spent much time together during the war. In fact she'd virtually brought me up alone. After she died I had taken her surname. I'd never met Sam, but wondered at that moment whether she was more than just his secretary.

I shook the thought from my mind.

"It's OK," I said. "Thanks for sorting the transport then."

"Your father cares about you Ash."

"That's the reason I rang."

"Oh?"

"Who did he tell I was coming?"

Again I sensed a hint of pride in her voice. "He sorted out a job for you. I put him through to someone in the embassy there and also a general called Gaskin or something."

Not the embassy. He'd spoken to someone in the government. "Was the embassy man called Coates, by any chance?"

"Yes that's the name."

I thanked her and ended the call. That explained everything. That explained why Secretary Coates knew so much. My father probably thought he was getting me a little civil service role. A job to make sure I wasn't

53

footloose in Singapore. I don't know what my father had said, but it wouldn't have surprised me if he'd even told the man I was in trouble. Maybe they'd cooked up the whole plan between them. To make sure I took the job. He was a military strategist. Maybe brilliant and with good intentions, but he was naïve when it came to politics.

I was also no politician and I went to bed resolved to play along. I would find out what had happened to Tom and then get the hell out.

In the morning, I dressed in my shorts and shirt. I wore the standard belt but, since I would have no side arm, I didn't bother with the cross-strap. I attached the captain's epaulets that I never imagined I'd wear again. And that was as far as I would go. It may have been childish but as an act of rebellion I wasn't going to wear the hat. After all I was officially SIB and had been plain-clothed for more than half of my time in Palestine.

I discovered my office was shared by all the officers although that just meant me and Lieutenant Robshaw at present. He was with Hegarty in the common room when I arrived.

They insisted I call them Hedge and Robbo and I instantly liked them both. They were open and friendly. The lieutenant was tall with blue eyes and straw-blond hair that wasn't as short as most of the lads'. Hedge later confirmed my suspicion that he was a bit of a lady killer.

The sergeant himself was more relaxed with me than he had been the day before. He used his Welsh accent and bushy eyebrows to comedic effect and seemed to relish working with a captain without the need for formality.

"How did it go with Vernon?" Robbo wanted to know after introductions and tea brought in by a cha-boy.

"All right."

"He's a royal pain in the arse that chap," Hedge said. "Acting CO—you'd think he had been promoted to God the way he acts. Off the record—" he dropped his voice "—Vernon is a stickler for punishment."

"Don't you mean rules?"

Hegarty waggled his eyebrows to tell me he meant what he'd said. "There have been more men on *jankers* this past month than Lieutenant Colonel Ambrose had in the last two years."

"So where is Ambrose?"

"On compassionate... Back in England to look after his wife. He was only expected to be gone a couple of months but it's been four with no news of his return."

The officers' quarters had four rooms and only Robshaw and I were there. "What about the other two OQ rooms?" I asked.

"Vernon has taken a house off base," Robshaw said, "And Lieutenant Cole is on R and R. He's taken two weeks in Penang."

"And your Special Investigations Branch? Are they based here?"

Robshaw nodded. "We have two officers: Green and Jenkins. Do you know them?"

I didn't. I had been in SIB Three Company and these guys would be in Two Company.

Robshaw ran a hand through his straw-coloured hair. "They're based out of the Bras Basah HQ but they're up in Malaya. No one knows what they're working on. As far as I know, they've not been back for a while—maybe five or six weeks."

"But they report to Vernon?"

"Yes."

So Vernon knew what the SIBs were doing but didn't share it with his other officers. I wondered if they knew anything about arms coming into Singapore but then I would have expected them to have a presence here. I made a mental note to try and find out what they were working on.

"Why is Vernon so upset with the police?" I asked.

"A couple of weeks ago there was a bit of a balls up," Hegarty said. "We had a tipoff that a corporal from Tanglin Barracks—Webster—was trying to deal in drugs. He was spotted making contact with a Chinaman."

"Chinese," the lieutenant corrected.

Hegarty shrugged. "The Chinese man was believed to be an opium and heroin dealer."

"The day before, Webster spent time in the dock's backstreets before withdrawing a large sum of money from his General Post Office account. We think he was checking out a rendezvous before getting the money. Anyway we had a unit there who followed him back to the docks and saw him enter a building. Before we could move in, there were gunshots."

"Coppers were already there," Hegarty said. "Messed up the whole thing."

"No one was hurt but when our boys got inside, there was no sign of the drug dealer or the money. And Webster's not talking."

I asked, "What did Inspector Rahman have to say about it?"

"He agreed we should have coordinated efforts. But they were investigating the Chinese dealer and didn't know about Webster."

Robshaw handed me a piece of paper. "Almost forgot. You had a call yesterday. The telephonist didn't know what to do with the message so just left it with the general messages and post."

It was a typed note, the record of a phone call. Pope for Ash Carter it said. There was a telephone number for me to return the call.

"Pope?"

Hedge raised his eyebrows. "Only one of the wealthiest people in Singapore. You must have noticed the Kelly and Pope Building in Commercial Square…"

"Why would he want to speak to me?"

"The disturbance you interrupted at the market. He's connected in some way I think, being the big trader in Japanese goods that he is."

Robshaw winked at me. "You also had a phone call from someone else."

I held out my hand expecting a note.

"No message, I'm afraid. All I know is the desk clerk said it was a woman and she sounded Chinese. She wouldn't leave a name."

TEN

Likely-lad, Hegarty turned out to be my designated driver although I knew this was more for Vernon's benefit than my own. He wanted someone close, keeping an eye on me. I wasn't going to keep Vernon fully informed and I guessed Hegarty was his contingency plan. The sergeant had a comfortable chatty way about him and Vernon probably thought I would tell him everything.

I asked Hegarty to take me to Tanglin Barracks and he didn't disappoint. Like a tour guide, he pointed out and explained the most mundane things.

When we turned off Orchard Road, I noticed large houses festooned with pink bougainvillaea and Hegarty told me that Pope lived in one of these although he didn't know which one.

On the approach to the barracks, we heard church bells peeling for Sunday worship and soon passed St Georges. Hegarty pointed and said, "It doesn't look much now but apparently it used to have the most beautiful stained glass windows you can imagine."

"What happened?"

"In the war. The story goes that they were buried to protect them." He laughed. "Trouble is, no one knows where, although one theory is that they are under Changi. Anyway it's remained windowless since."

We reached a long dirty-white wall that ran parallel to the road for almost half a mile ending in a sentry gate with pill boxes either side of the barrier. As the guard moved in, Hegarty said, "Remind me to tell you about the holes in the wall when we leave."

With a quick scan of our credentials, the guard retreated and raised the barrier.

"Which is the quartermaster's office?" I asked as we trundled past him.

The soldier pointed to the right hand side. "Beyond the parade ground. You'll pass the Officers' Mess. Then it's the second building. Block K, sir." The MP also indicated where we should park.

The main British camp on the island, Tanglin Barracks was the furthest from the centre and, unlike Gillman, had few redeeming features. I noted the small patches of grass were sun-scorched and a handful of trees appeared stunted and struggling to survive. Compared to the lush greenery of the jungle close by, this was a stark contrast, like the exact opposite of a desert oasis.

Hegarty continued into the complex and parked where instructed. Like many pre-war bases, most of the quarters were ship-built wooden slatted huts. They were arranged in clusters of five known as *spiders*. Every now and again there was a modern concrete hut. Same design, just newer: grey with flat, yellow roofs. The Officers' Quarters was a superior block, still single storey but with some consideration to design and aesthetics— but only a little.

We walked across the parade ground towards the Officers' Mess. A few squads were marching up and down, square bashing. That would be over shortly.

Before midday it would be too hot for marching in the sun and the parade ground would be deserted until late afternoon.

Block K had a large wooden sign in front with equally large white lettering: "Stores". The door was open and I could see a soldier standing behind a long wooden counter, his head down and his eyes half closed. The noise of two men entering made the man start, look up, see the MP uniform and register panic on his face. He snapped to attention and saluted.

"At ease, soldier," I said. "Where can I find the QM?"

He looked from me to Sergeant Hegarty and back, clearly trying to assess who I was since I didn't have a red cap.

"The quartermaster?" Hegarty prompted.

"Round the side, second door, sir,"

We left him wondering who I was and whether we'd noticed him sleeping on the job and followed the directions. Again the door was open and I realized it was necessary for these rooms without fans.

Inside there were two men sitting at desks. They looked up as we stepped over the threshold.

"Captain Carter," Hegarty announced as we walked into the room.

"Regimental Sergeant Major Sinclair," said the senior of the two with a salute. He walked around his desk and shook my hand. "This is my assistant, Staff Sergeant Cooke," he nodded towards the other man who was now also standing. "How can we help you, Captain?"

I explained that I was working for the government and with the 200 Provost. I handed him my papers as a formality. He glanced at them and handed them back.

"The question remains. How can I help?"

"I'd like to look over the inventory."

"Of course. Billy here will give you what you need."

Cooke pulled a four inch-thick ledger from his desk drawer, placed it on his desk and spun it around. There was a tab that he used to open the ledger at specific page.

"Anything missing?" I asked after flicking through twenty or so pages of current inventory.

Sinclair smiled. "Not on my watch," he said with pride.

"No knives and forks? No kettles?"

"Not a one."

"No blankets, buckets or billycans?"

"I know it's unusual," he said, "but I run a tight ship here. Everything is logged in and everything is logged out."

I nodded.

"Most of the problems occur due to not checking the goods when they arrive," he said. "Doesn't happen here. Everything is opened and counted and noted in the ledger."

Cooke pointed to an entry. "See this for example." He went to a filing cabinet and pulled out a sheet. An army delivery note for eight-hundred buckets. He pointed out the reference number in the ledger was the same. The number of buckets however said seven-hundred and eighty-nine. "Eleven short," Cooke said unnecessarily. Behind the delivery note was attached a pink slip. This noted the discrepancy and had three signatures including Sinclair's. The goods came in, Sinclair's men counted them and any discrepancy was double checked and signed off. Then Sinclair signed it before the actual number was entered into the ledger.

"Guns," I said, "Stens, Brens, rifles, handguns, anything... I'd like to see any pink slips you have on those."

Sinclair and Cooke exchanged glances.

Cooke said, "We've never had any issue there."

"Never?"

Sinclair said, "Not on my watch."

"Would you mind if we went through the ledger and cross checked?"

"Be my guest. Can you tell me why... why guns in particular?"

"Just a concern."

"Based on?"

"Based on a concern."

Sinclair nodded. "Rightho, I'll leave you in Billy's capable hands. If you need me I'll be in the Mess."

We spent almost an hour in that stuffy office, finding an entry, pulling the delivery note and checking the number of items. When we'd finished with the current log, I had Cooke work backwards so that we covered all the stock of guns that had moved within the past year. At the end I had a summary note of the movement in and out and balancing stock.

"Let's go and kick the tyres," I said to Hegarty who blinked sweat from his eyebrows.

"Boss?"

"Let's count the actual stock of guns."

The three of us trooped back to the Stores. The private behind the bench lifted it to let us through. The room was shallow with multiple shelving like you see in some libraries. There wasn't much on the shelves, just everyday stuff that a Tommy might need. We slipped past these to a door behind. Cooke produced a key and opened it. The heat immediately blasted out at us. There were no windows and the air was hot and stale, like old blankets.

"Only RSM Sinclair and myself have keys," Cooke said in answer to my unasked question. He switched on the lights.

The room beyond was a long storage unit again with shelves although these were deeper and taller. We walked past these to another locked door.

"Same security?" I asked.

Cooke nodded and opened it with a key. Inside were lockers and crates containing arms and munitions. He gestured for us to begin and stepped back. He leaned against the door, arms folded watching us.

Everything we counted, matched the figures in the ledger. Not a thing missing.

"OK," I said.

Cooke waited and I just looked at him. Eventually he said, "Is there anything else?"

"Maybe, but let's get some air."

Cooke looked uncertain. He hurriedly locked the door and caught up with us as we walked out.

"All the stock is accounted for," he said trying to prompt me.

"Yes." I smiled. "But what's not accounted for?"

"I don't know..." he began, but by then I was heading for the jeep with Hegarty scurrying after me.

As we pulled out I glanced back. Cooke was standing at the office door watching us. I nodded at him but the man didn't respond.

"What?" Hegarty asked as we drove under the security barrier.

"Later," I said. "Tell me about the holes in the wall." I was referring to damage to the barracks perimeter wall that Hegarty had mentioned as we had driven in.

"It's where a soldier was executed for mutiny. At least that's the story."

"The story?"

"I heard it was on the second day of the invasion. A man showed cowardice and was shot as an example to the others. The irony is that the war was over a few days later. To be honest, I don't know the detail. If you're interested, one of the lads back at Gillman is an expert on the war."

We drove in silence for a while before Hegarty said, "Run a tight ship. It's another old navy expression."

I thought it was obvious but he continued to explain anyway. "A tight ship referred to the rigging. If it was slack the sails wouldn't be in their optimum position."

"Like sailing close to the wind?" I said.

He looked over at me. "Not at all."

"I know."

I could see the cogs turning in his mind. "You don't think Sinclair was being straight with us?" he asked.

I said nothing.

He said, "Cooke was uncomfortable."

"Yes he was. He was trying too hard to be relaxed but he wasn't."

"So what are they up to?"

"I have no idea but I can tell you one thing: if they have a perfect record of stock with no losses then it'll be the first time in the history of the British Army. Any army for that matter."

ELEVEN

Part way up the winding road to Fort Canning, Hegarty stopped briefly and pointed out the tropical trees and flowering bushes. He joked that it looked more like a botanical garden than a military post. This was where the general was based.

Moving once more, Hegarty rounded a bend and as we approached a barrier, he slowed and flashed his ID at the MP on duty. The check was more thorough than at Tanglin but moments later we were driving beneath a white portico entrance with high walls on either side. Beyond was a courtyard the size of a football pitch with a grand colonial residence surrounded by more trees and gardens.

I got out and absorbed the strange sense of tranquillity. There were no people. I started to walk towards the house and could hear the sweet sound of birdsong quickly replaced by the sharp crunch of gravel under my feet.

Hegarty waited in the car as I entered the building and walked across a marble floor into a grand foyer. It was empty except for book cases, paintings, a bust and a clerk behind a reception desk. He looked up at me.

"I'd like to see General Gaskill," I said.

The clerk looked down at what I guessed was an appointment's diary, frowned and looked back at me. "Sorry, sir. You are...?"

I introduced myself and said I was there on important security business.

The clerk jumped up as though he'd just sat on a drawing pin and scurried away. A couple of minutes later he walked smartly back to his desk and avoided eye contact.

Another minute passed and I heard shoes clacking on the marble floor. A door opened and an officer appeared. He had a broad smile and an even broader moustache.

He held out a hand. "Colonel Simon Atkinson," he said, "adjutant to the general."

I placed him at mid-forties although his hair was already steel-grey. The hard lines on his face and strong handshake told me this man was no pen-pusher and had likely seen action.

I introduced myself and Atkinson nodded.

"We were told to expect you though not quite so soon."

Of course they had been told. My father had spoken to Gaskill and Coates. Maybe Gaskill was also in on the arrangement.

"My father rang a few days ago?"

"Last Monday," Atkinson said after a second's thought. "I'm afraid the general hasn't got much time but would like to meet you. Please follow me."

Despite the hard features, Atkinson's tone was relaxed and welcoming. He led me to an antechamber from which more rooms fed off. Here, he went straight to a door, knocked and entered.

The room was like a comfortable British study or small library with dark oak tables and chairs with burgundy upholstery, brass lamps with tasselled shades and a large rug that muffled their footsteps.

General Gaskill sat at an oak desk big enough to be a family dining table. There were two reading lamps, both on but adding no additional illumination. There was a huge blotter pad with a pile of documents on it plus a copy of the London *Times* newspaper folded in front of him. There was also an array of photo frames that I guessed were of his family but couldn't see. At the general's back, was a bay window overlooking the gardens.

My first impression of the general was of an eagle. He was heavy framed, balding with a slightly hooked, beak-like nose. I felt inclined to salute and did.

The general reached across the table and shook my hand. Then he waved at the chairs in front of the desk. "Sit down man. Simon, you too."

As soon as we were settled, he said, "I know your father." His bright blue eyes sparked as if recalling something. "A British hero through and through."

I said nothing. My opinion of what my father had done in the war differed from many.

The general's head cocked slightly to one side, complementing his bird-like appearance. I wondered if he could read me but didn't comment on that. Instead he said, "You changed your surname."

"It's my mother's maiden name. I didn't want my father's reputation to go before me."

"Ah," he said as though that explained it and I wondered whether he knew there was more to it. But he didn't comment. Instead he continued: "I'm sure Simon has explained that I haven't got much time today but he is more than capable of handling any questions you may have. I understand that the secretary has appointed you to liaise between the army and police regarding security matters." He gave me an avuncular smile. "Don't worry, we will be most cooperative, but do bear in mind there will be no need to baby sit me. I may be the new commander here, but it is like coming home. We were last here just before the Japs invaded. At the end of forty-one, I was transferred to Hong Kong. Sometimes the hand of fate can be on your side. Who knows? A few months later and I would have been with the other unlucky bastards who died in Changi."

"Can we talk about security, sir?"

"Simon's your man for that," he said and leaned across the desk to shake my hand. And I knew the interview was over.

Atkinson took me through another door and into another office similar to Gaskill's only the desk was a few inches shorter.

He sat in a leather chair and indicated that I should sit next to him. For the first time, I noticed his moustache twitch. I later realized it was a nervous tick.

"You used to be a boxer," Atkinson prompted.

"At college."

"And in the army. You won the Golden Gloves competition in Palestine three years back. Then two years ago you dropped out after winning your bout."

Atkinson had done his research. I didn't like talking about it so gave my stock answer, "Injury." What I didn't say was that the injury was to my opponent who lost an eye. A freak accident and I thought it honourable to retire at that point.

"And what of Palestine?"

"It's a damn mess. It's hard to tell who the good guys are over there and the League of Nations doesn't seem to know how to resolve it. It's like being in a pit of smiling vipers. You have to treat everyone as a friend and yet anyone could be a potential terrorist."

68

"Must have been tense." His moustache did its twitch thing.

"All the time. Every day we went into the streets, we were on edge. In the last few months before I left, there was no downtime. Men were exhausted and exhausted men make mistakes."

"Did you make a mistake?"

"I felt so."

"Tell me," Atkinson said kindly.

At this point I started to realize the colonel was adept at getting people to talk. I needed to get onto the main reason for the visit. But I could see this man was a politician and an abrupt switch of subjects wouldn't work in my favour so I humoured him a little longer.

"There were always meetings and negotiations. The multiple factions were kept apart except for critical points of mediation. On the whole the security was well controlled. Of course there were threats and even murders, but nothing directly related to the negotiated settlement. And then the League announced a big conference in Palestine with the unofficial aim of achieving a resolution at the same time."

"A political leader's publicity stunt? It happens all the time."

"I had information that there was an assassination plot by an extreme Israeli faction aiming to break up the talks. For them compromise was unacceptable. Ironically the League called the conference off anyway."

"Doesn't sound like a mistake."

"My mistake was not protecting my informant and his family."

"Ah."

Like Secretary Coates, I was pretty sure Atkinson didn't know the truth. I hadn't protected my Palestinian informant but he hadn't been murdered. It had been his wife and five children. I knew them. I considered them my friends. Abdul was made to watch them die and then had his eyes gouged out. He was still alive with his pain and torment. And I was told it was not my concern. So I had resigned, found the perpetrators and killed them. I wasn't proud about it. It just needed to be done.

Atkinson stood. "Let's take a walk around the grounds."

"I need to talk about security."

He nodded and led me outside to an orchard at the side of the building. I could see the sea through the trees.

When he stopped, he said, "Politics."

"Sorry?"

"Who is in control here—on Singapore I mean?"

"The government?"

"That's what the Governor and Secretary Coates would like to believe. But take a look around the city. Who do you see more of? The police or the army? We are everywhere and guard the causeway from Malaya and manage the docks. We also manage the security of the Straits. So who is really in control? The government are also in a state of transition and the Second Legislative Council has only been established for a matter of months."

I remained silent. This was something I knew nothing about.

He continued with a smile: "Democracy is coming, Ash. Only nine members were elected out of thirty-two but the government of this country is changing. Maybe slowly, maybe more quickly."

"So you're telling me that my role is just political?"

"Palestine all over again, I'm afraid," Atkinson said with a smile that creased his face even more. "Now, come. Let's take a look at the spice garden."

As we walked, I said, "The Secretary is concerned that there will be an attack on the island. He has intelligence—"

"Really?"

We passed through a gothic gate and followed a narrow path. "Look at this—a spice garden designed by Raffles himself." He waved his hands as if directing the scent towards his face. "Just breathe that in, Ash. Now the whole island smells of spices, but in the early nineteen hundreds this was a revelation; a hill amidst the jungles with a manicured spice garden at the top of it!"

"Real or not, how could bandits get weapons into the country."

Atkinson looked at me as if wondering about dismissing my question. His moustache twitched before he eventually spoke. "Via the private wharves."

"I've had a look around. Customs seem to have a tight control over it."

Atkinson was walking again. He led me down the gentle slope to the island-facing side of the fort. He pointed to an iron gate in a grass embankment and said, "A sally port. There are three of them. Tunnels that led down the hill for emergency escapes."

"It comes from Latin, I believe. From *sallir*, to jump."

"Excellent. What's the Latin for making or being safe?"

"I don't know."

"Exsisto tutus. We've seen the *sally* now let me show you the *totty*!" The colonel laughed at his own pun. He had clearly used the line many times before. He stroked his moustache. "I know, I know it's a bit of a stretch, but funny anyway." He pointed to a short grey concrete wall with a metal door. It was a bunker. *The* bunker, more formally known as the Battle Box.

71

Although my First World War history was patchy at best, I'd heard of this. "So this is where we surrendered Singapore to the Japanese?"

"Of course everyone knows the official surrender was signed at the Ford factory, but this is where Lieutenant General Percival surrendered." Atkinson took out a key and opened the door. Inside, the lighting was dim with a grey-orange tint. In the centre of the room was a large table—the size of two end-to-end table tennis tables—with a relief map of South East Asia. The rest of the room was sparsely furnished with the exception of four metal filing cabinets and shelves with books and papers on. It was a stark contrast to the sumptuous feel and opulence of the main building.

"The official reason for the Battle Box is for campaign planning and troop movements. It is my responsibility to maintain the records—to keep the map up to date with where the regiments are. I must also track the Chinese Red Army and our friends the Americans. Officially the general and I spend time in here every day. Truth is there's little need for him to be here."

Although I hadn't mentioned it, Atkinson was telling me he had the general's own security in hand.

We stepped outside into the bright sunshine and the colonel locked the heavy door. Then he surprised me by handing me the key.

"The general wants you to have a key. Traditionally the adjutant has one and the officer in charge of security has the other."

"So you're giving it to me as such an officer?" After all he had said it seemed to be a contradiction.

Atkinson patted me on the arm. "He wants you to have it because of who you are, not what you do."

"I'm flattered," I said but wondered if there was more to it, whether this was also a political play. In any case, I put the key in my pocket.

Atkinson held out his hand as if in farewell.

"One more question," I said.

"Yes?"

"Let's just for argument's sake say that munitions could be stolen from the army here. How would you do it?"

For a brief moment Atkinson's face became serious. Then he gave me the broad smile again. "You've been over to Tanglin Barracks I hear."

"I have."

"Sinclair is a good man."

"I have no doubt—"

"Goodbye, Captain Carter," he said using my old title. "Good luck with handling the role but I assure you there are no guns missing under Sinclair's watch."

TWELVE

Hegarty wanted to know how my meeting had gone and I gave him a high-level summary. I had no doubt the information would go straight back to Major Vernon.

"What's the general like?" Hegarty asked.

"Friendly enough," I said. "Atkinson is a difficult one to read though."

"He has a reputation."

I waited for an explanation that was delayed as Hegarty manoeuvred around a trishaw that suddenly stopped in front of us, blocking the way as a passenger climbed in.

"He was here during the war, at Tanglin. When the Japs invaded, I mean."

Gaskill had said they had both been here and said he'd been posted to Hong Kong. He didn't explain what had happened to Atkinson. I wondered if the colonel had been one of the unlucky ones imprisoned at Changi.

"Must have been difficult," I said.

"Anyway, he's supposed to be very religious. Whatever he went through changed the man."

Back at Gillman Barracks there was a shiny black Bentley waiting by the barrier. The driver wore a chauffeur's uniform and stepped out as we drew alongside.

"Ash Carter?" he asked.

"Yes."

"Sir, Mr Pope should be honoured if you would accompany him at The Singapore Club. If you have the time, sir."

The guy sounded intriguing, so I climbed into the back of the luxury car and was driven back the way we had just come.

When we arrived, Fullerton Square was a chaos of cars. The Bentley parked in front of the Fullerton Building, a grandiose four storey structure with many columns and buttresses. A stone staircase and grand entrance dominated the front and the sign above proclaimed this to be the General Post Office. However, the Fullerton Building was much more than an elaborate post office, I had been told. It also contained the Chamber of Commerce, Marine Offices and The Singapore Club.

The chauffeur pointed out a discreet side door and informed me it was the club's entrance. I walked over and took a flight of steps to the first floor where a Punjabi doorman—typically dressed in a white uniform, gold trimmed sash and matching turban—asked for my identity and the purpose of my visit.

Once past him I was met by a broad reception desk and more questions. A young man in a green and gold uniform was waved over and sent off to find my host while I was directed to sit and wait.

Within a couple of minutes a portly gentleman in a morning suit appeared. Apart from his girth the most noticeable attribute was the man's skin, white like tissue paper.

"Captain Carter, Captain Carter, my dear chap, how good of you to come and visit me," Pope said effusively. He offered a plump and impossibly soft hand.

I explained my recently acquired civilian status but it didn't seem to register. He just led me into a glorious lounge which must have been almost two hundred feet long with sumptuous leather armchairs around tables. Everywhere, gentlemen sat smoking, reading newspapers and having meetings.

There was a view of the sea and open windows allowed the delightful sea breeze to cool the room. The fittings were all brass and the floor was a rich brown marble.

"Tampines marblette," Pope said after he noticed me looking down. "All made in Singapore, you know." Then he pointed beyond the bar. "Over there we have the reading room and a library next to it. Upstairs there is a billiard room—with six tables no less! There is also a dining room for two hundred and on the upper floor there are the bedrooms. Everything a gentleman could wish for! Now, Captain, please take a seat."

We sat by a window, the chairs making a comfortable sigh as we sank into them. Immediately, a waiter came alongside and Pope ordered two *stengahs*.

As the drinks were served along with iced water, I studied my host. Pope looked to be in his mid to late fifties, and I wondered if he'd ever been in the sun or done a day's work.

"So. Good of you to come," Pope said and raised his whisky as a toast. "And thank you."

"I understand you are the owner of the market stall."

Pope laughed. "No, my dear chap, no. Much too small for me, but I do supply all the traders of Japanese merchandise. No, the reason for my gratitude is really

76

for my daughter, Amelia. I understand from her that you protected her and tried to stop the affray."

Now it made sense. The girl in the white dress who had been pushed over. So she was Pope's daughter.

The other man took a gulp of his drink. "I do love my whisky and won't give it up even though Mrs Pope does nag and my doctor disapproves." He dabbed at beads of sweat which had appeared on his forehead.

"Now are you hungry?" he asked and before I could respond had called a waiter.

"Yes, *Tuan*?" the waiter said respectfully.

"Sandwiches for both of us."

As the waiter scurried away, Pope turned back to me and said, "I also need to apologize to you."

"You do?"

"Ah, you see, before I understood the full situation I complained to the Governor. He is, of course, a member here. I rather misunderstood what happened." He held up a pudgy hand to make sure I didn't interrupt. "You see my property is not far from Tanglin Barracks and there has been trouble with the army before. Amelia is a pretty girl and of a dangerous age," he said and winked.

The waiter returned with a tray of small, single slices of bread topped with smoked salmon.

Pope resumed: "As a father I must be careful, you know. Anyway in the excitement I blamed the army for risking my daughter's life. However after I had spoken to my wife I realized you were in fact her saviour. I understand that my complaint was passed to the Commanding Officer at Tanglin Barracks and then to your CO at Gillman."

I didn't bother explaining that I didn't really report to Vernon and frankly didn't care what he thought. However I said, "I still don't understand."

77

"I didn't fully grasp the situation. I thought you were involved rather than intervening." He laughed, uncomfortably this time. "I seem to have become overexcited with half the facts. Anyway, I would like to make it up to you, Captain. Again, I am truly sorry if I have caused you any problems."

"There really is no harm done."

Pope seemed to ignore me for a while as he devoured a few sandwiches. I suspected it would be unseemly to make my excuses and leave already so I decided to try small talk after taking a sandwich myself.

"And how is business in Japanese goods? Is there much demand?'

"The Japanese are now our allies." Pope took another gulp and finished his drink. He signalled for a fresh glass then said, "Ironic isn't it, how our darkest enemy can become our friend when faced by a new foe. Have you ever been to Shanghai, Captain? What a terrible place. Singapore may be overrun by Chinese, overcrowding and slums and child labour, but at least it is not Shanghai. You know, they collect thousands of dead bodies off the streets each year. Starvation and murder. Where a life is not worth a penny. That is Communism for you, my dear chap."

He paused but I could see he was about to continue so waited.

"Of course we are building businesses to create wealth and wealth means jobs and food. Don't give me any of this tosh about equality and welfare and Chinese nationalism. It's all very, very dangerous, Captain, don't you agree? Did you know that during the war General Yamashita and other senior officers of the Japanese Imperial Army used The Singapore Club as a headquarters?"

I shook my head and ate another sandwich.

"Oh yes, well I do have a tendency to ramble," he chuckled and dabbed at the sweat. "Let's see if I can explain. The British used to totally control international trade. All the big merchant houses were British and then of course the war put things on hold for a few years. However, although the British rule Singapore and control the harbour, there has been a gradual erosion of the control of the businesses. The Chinese are not only more numerous, they are also becoming business heads and I worry about where all this will lead. My own business used to be twice the size. Fortunately there is also the brokerage business that is doing extremely well, but again I fear the Chinese will soon move into this market."

"And the Japanese connection?" I prompted.

"There are Japanese businesses in Singapore, but I am the largest employer of Japanese. Not all of them are Japanese you understand, but a goodly proportion."

"And has there been any trouble?"

"Like tarring of buildings, you mean? Yes, but not of my warehouse or offices. The Japanese were hated after the war, but within five or six years things improved dramatically. Sometimes soldiers hurl abuse at the Japanese. You know how it is. I think high spirits and alcohol can make some of your chaps forget the war is over. The incident in the market was the exception. Recently however, we have seen an increase in the intimidation."

"By soldiers?"

"By the Chinese."

"Have any of your staff been intimidated?"

Pope dabbed at his forehead. "Indeed they have. We've had a couple of cases of assault. But, I don't think you will find such things reported to the police."

I tried to connect the dots to his previous rant about the Chinese. I asked, "And do you blame the Chinese for these attacks?"

"Chinese gangs, yes indeed!" Pope observed me glance at a large junk that swept majestically across the mouth of the Singapore River. It had a billowing white rectangular mainsail and a smaller one at the rear.

He said, "Magnificent isn't it? It's a Japanese junk called a *sengoku-bune*. Modern cargo ships may have huge capacity, but they have no style. I finance a handful of *sengoku-bunes* for my business. It's very expensive and inefficient but I never tire of watching them."

As I watched the beautiful boat a thought struck me. Could there be a connection?

"I'm sorry to be so bold," I said, "but could I ask whether there's a chance munitions could be brought ashore via your junks?"

He smiled. "No. I know exactly what comes and goes. And even if they were, why on earth would anyone be smuggling? I assume that's what you are alluding to. Why on earth would anyone smuggle in munitions? This is not Malay, Captain!" He studied me for a second then said, "Why do you ask?"

"Secretary General Coates has intelligence that there will be an attack of some sort on the island, specifically involving guns." I showed him the piece of paper with the strange symbols.

He turned the paper upside down and around. "I don't know what this means. It is not Japanese, if that's what you're asking. The writing is traditional Chinese, I can tell you that. And the paw print is probably that of a lion. Perhaps that is your Chinese gang symbol?"

I reached across and shook his hand. "It was a pleasure to meet you, sir. If you hear anything..."

"Of course. And Captain?"

"Yes?"

"If you think of a way I can show my gratitude for helping Amelia then please do let me know."

On the drive back to Gillman I thought about my meetings with Atkinson and Pope; two very different men with different backgrounds and outlooks. However both men were concerned about the Chinese. Could this be an uprising against the local Japanese population? I thought it unlikely and yet ten minutes later something made me think again.

THIRTEEN

A young Chinese woman was waiting for me in an office at Gillman Barracks. When the desk clerk told me a woman had asked for me I had expected Su Ling. After all she was the only woman I'd properly met so far. However it was not the alluring Su Ling who stared at me with red-rimmed eyes as I opened the door. This young woman was petite and fragile looking, like a frightened sparrow. She had a glass of water in one hand that trembled slightly.

"Hello," I prompted.

She pushed up from the hard backed chair and said something.

"I'm sorry," I said, "I don't understand Chinese."

"You are... Captain Carter?" she said in faltering English.

"Please call me Ash." I smiled encouragingly and sat on a similar chair opposite her. "How can I help you, miss?"

She introduced herself as Mei Fen and, in sentences punctuated with pauses as she thought of the words, she said, "I come here last... evening and... asked for you."

I was confused. How could this girl have known who I was and that I would be here?

"You came here looking for me?"

"Tom say you will come. He say... you will be here."

Now she had me even more intrigued. "You're talking about Tom Silverman?"

She nodded vigorously and a flicker of a smile appeared before she started to sob.

She held up her left hand and I saw a delicate ring on her finger. Tom hadn't mentioned a girlfriend, but then he hadn't said very much at all in his telegram. I guessed it made sense and she was clearly distraught.

"I'm so sorry. I found out about Tom... about the crash only yesterday."

She took a shuddering breath and looked at me, her eyes streaming uncontrollably. She tried to speak but for a moment the words didn't come.

"I saw pictures of the car crash," I said. "The police believe it was a simple accident, that he lost control in the dark in bad weather."

She shook her head.

"I suspect he was forced off the road."

Mei Fen pressed both palms against her eyes to wipe them and breathed in again. She took another sip of water as she composed herself.

"He say he was... shadow..."

"Shadowed? Followed?"

She nodded. "Followed. He say someone was following him. He worry... was worried."

"Mei Fen, do you know why Tom asked me to come?"

"I not know. He not say. He say he thought... something—" She struggled for a word and made a few attempts before she got it. "—dodgy, yes that what he say. Dodgy. He not say more. He say too dangerous to say."

So Tom hadn't told her what was concerning him, only that he was being followed and it was dangerous.

83

Perhaps Tom had told someone else, maybe reported it to the police. I asked her.

She shook her head vigorously. "Only you with the detail. He say he trust only you."

I was disappointed. It appeared that Mei Fen knew little more than me but I said, "Thanks for coming to see me. I'll do my best..."

She nodded and I saw belief in her eyes, like she knew I would find out what happened, investigate and perhaps resolve whatever my friend had been concerned about.

We both stood and I shook her hand. It was about half the size of mine. She seemed so small and thin I wondered if she hadn't eaten since learning the news of Tom's death.

"Do you live far, Mei Fen? Do you have someone to take you home?"

She looked at me and her eyes seemed to glaze over as if she was about to faint.

I helped her back into the chair and helped her take a drink from the glass of water.

As I waited for her to recover her strength and answer my question about getting home, I wondered if I was missing the obvious.

"Do you know where the accident happened?" I asked.

She blinked and seemed to be gathering strength.

"The car crash. Do you know where it happened?"

"Yes. Road from Nee Soon."

I didn't know the place. "Outside of the city?"

She nodded.

"So he was travelling back towards the city at night?"

"Yes."

"Where had he been?"

"Nee Soon... village."

84

This was the bit I didn't get. How did she know? "But you weren't with him and he wouldn't tell you."

She looked at me blankly and I spoke slowly and rephrased the question.

"Ah yes... He say he go to Nee Soon." She stopped as if suddenly recalling something then said something like, "Dongzing de fangzi."

It sounded like Chinese again. "I'm sorry I don't..."

She put her hands together as if praying, her eyes bright with excitement. "Yes," she said. "I know... I remember. He say he go to Dongzing de fangzi. I not think..."

I shook my head and she must have seen it still meant nothing to me.

"House of Tokyo," she said nodding. "He say he go to House of Tokyo in Nee Soon village."

FOURTEEN

Reappearing in the office, Hegarty agreed to drive me to Nee Soon. Five minutes later we were in the jeep. Mei Fen sat in the middle of the back seat. She had agreed to show us House of Tokyo and then we'd drive her home.

When we'd arrived back at Gillman Barracks, the sun was just about to set. Now it was fully dark and I was reminded of how quickly night fell in Singapore.

Hegarty knew the way and took us to the far side of the city and onto Thompson Road. This took us north and we were soon beyond the lights of the city and the shop-houses. The road twisted and turned through the darkness following what I guessed to be old trails through the forest. Trees closed in and the darkness with it. To me it looked like we were immediately in the jungle but Hegarty laughed at me.

"These are the suburbs," he said. "The lights you can see through the trees are houses and this on the left—" the headlights picked out a sign and a side road "—is the island golf course."

The road became bumpy and occasionally the wheels spun on the loose stone covering.

In the darkness with so little detail it felt like we'd been travelling for ages, but in reality we'd covered about four miles since leaving the city.

"How much further?" I said.

"Not sure. To be honest, Boss, I've never been out this way. Nee Soon is an Out Of Bounds area and I've never had reason—" We hit a bump and Hegarty fought the steering back on line.

He laughed. "Sorry, I'll slow it down. We're in the jungle for real now."

Only three cars had passed coming the other way since we joined this road. Another one headed for us, its lights temporarily blinding me. We cut through two villages with ramshackle huts strung along the road and people standing about. Outside each of them was a small fire and I saw children playing as though it were daylight. The last hut had tyres piled up and a gaggle of kids tried to tell us to stop and buy some pans—at least that's what I guessed they shouted as they ran alongside for a few yards.

The darkness closed in again and I noticed Hegarty was having more difficulty with potholes.

"Here!" Mei Fen shouted. It was so loud and sudden that the sergeant automatically slammed on the brakes. The tiny Chinese girl fell between the two front seats and scrabbled between us. I just managed to stop my head colliding with the windscreen and then helped the poor girl up.

Hegarty was very apologetic but I was more interested in why she had shouted.

"What did you mean by shouting here, Mei Fen?"

"It is here," she said as if I would understand.

I looked around. In the headlights I could see the red, laterite road, short grass verge for a foot or so then long grass and then, after another few feet, trees.

I turned back to her. "Are you telling me this is where the crash happened?"

She pointed behind us. "There!"

I asked Hegarty to turn around and the headlights swept across the forest before settling on the road again. We edged forward and then I saw what Mei Fen was pointing at. The lights picked out a tree with its bark torn away. Beside it the undergrowth looked disturbed and a smaller tree was bent over with a jagged break.

Using a torch, I got out and headed towards the damage. Hegarty was by my side but the girl stayed in the car. As soon as I stepped into the long grass it squelched.

"Lots of surface water around here," Hegarty said.

I shone the torch at the damaged tree and then at the ground. The ground had been disturbed by the people who'd removed the crashed car but I could roughly make out the route Tom's car had taken.

"What are you thinking?" Hegarty asked.

I played the light along the ground.

"That I may have been too quick to assume foul play." I stepped back on the road and swept the torch over it. The track was wide enough for two cars but only just. Tom's car being on the wrong side wasn't as conclusive as I'd imagined. The ground was rutted and in the rain it could have been treacherous.

Hegarty seemed to read my mind.

"If it was raining cats and dogs and your friend was travelling too fast... well, he could easily have lost control."

I walked south and saw where a heavy vehicle, maybe two, had crossed the verge, heading for the crash site. I followed the tracks in and then out again. I now judged it was one vehicle in and then laden with the Toyota on the way back.

I walked back to the Land Rover and studied the line of Tom's tracks. They were angled from the road but they appeared to curve towards the tree rather than away. Surely he would have realized he was heading for the jungle and tried to steer away? I kept walking and then I saw what I suspected: another tyre track. It was three paces on and just a single rut as though a front tyre had slipped off the road and then back again. And in my head I pictured Tom's car struck from behind on the left hand side, being pushed to the right, curving more and more to the right. Tom's car hit the wet ground and slid into the trees. The other car veered away but just too late, clipping the verge and leaving this tell-tail skid.

"OK," I said.

"OK?"

I climbed back into the jeep, nodded at Mei Fen and then to Hegarty, and said, "Let's go and find this House of Tokyo."

FIFTEEN

Doubtless, Nee Soon was an important crossroads town but when it started it was a smattering of shacks. It mainly ran north-south. At the heart, red lanterns hung outside many buildings. Lights blazed and people moved about as though it were daytime. Hegarty slowed the Land Rover to a walking pace as bicycles, trishaws and people got in the way. In the city, it was busy and the roads wide, but everyone observed the British rule of driving on the left. Here in Nee Soon the rule seemed to be little more than a suggestion.

"There!" Mei Fen said with less excitement than at the crash site so that Sergeant Hegarty didn't do another emergency stop. "House of Tokyo."

Hegarty pulled up outside a superior-looking building festooned with lanterns. The front had eight foot glass windows that showed willow patterned screens in black and red. Beyond the screens I could see lights but nothing more.

Through a heavily black-framed door, I could see a tiny entrance and a second door to the left but nothing more. The outside door was locked so I yanked on the bell-pull. There was no sound but a later, a woman in a red kimono and comb in her hair, appeared through the side door. Her forty-something face immediately turned to a stony frown as she saw us: me, an MP and a diminutive Chinese girl.

For a moment I thought she wasn't going to open the door but then she did.

She opened it barely wider than her head and spoke to us rapidly in what I guessed was Japanese.

Mei Fen said, "She wants know who we are."

I produced my new government ID and she squinted at it but didn't move the door any wider. Hegarty produced his warrant card which was pointless since she could see who he was.

"She say, no army here," Mei Fen said.

"We aren't looking for anyone from the army." I looked at our Chinese translator encouragingly and she spoke to the stony-faced lady.

Mei Fen repeated, "No army here," and the lady closed the door. She disappeared behind the second door.

I knocked but no one came.

Mei Fen said, "Sorry, my Japanese not good and lady not speak Chinese."

"It's better than mine."

I took a step back into the street and looked at the building.

"What now, Boss?"

"What kind of a place do you think this is, Hedge?"

Without hesitation, he replied, "A brothel."

That was my impression too. Why would my friend have come to a brothel—except for the obvious reason of course?

I realized Mei Fen had said something quietly.

"Not brothel," she said.

"Tom wouldn't come to a brothel or this is not a brothel?"

91

"Not a brothel. Japanese... happy," she said and I could see she knew it was the wrong word.

"Japanese men?"

"Yes."

It looked and sounded like a brothel to me but I accepted Mei Fen's word for it. I started walking.

"Let's just take a look around," I said.

The property had two floors and an elaborate roof. On each corner was a mini pagoda perhaps emphasizing the Japanese nature of the building. I counted what looked like eight rooms on the second floor at the front. Using our torches we took a narrow alley before the adjacent property. After the building, a high wall continued, preventing us from seeing over. There was a smell of cooking here, perhaps noodles and meat and then, further on, the smell became distasteful. Rubbish and rotting things I guessed.

At the back we came out on an earthen track that serviced the rear of the commercial properties. The wall continued but there was a wooden gate, lower than the wall but still too high to look over.

Hegarty found a couple of crates and piled one on top of the other. I climbed up and peered over the gate.

There was a courtyard with outside storage rooms and bins. I could see a kitchen with at least three men working in it. A metal fire-escape reached the upper floor and I counted sixteen rooms up there.

A Japanese man with a white apron opened a rear door and stood in the courtyard. I ducked down and to one side.

He looked up at the dark sky and lit a cigarette. Then he looked down and straight at me.

His banshee screech almost made me fall off the crates. I kept watching and the guy with the cigarette just shouted in a foreign tongue. And then another man rushed out of the door. This man was bigger. Bigger than me. Square and solid and brandishing a meat cleaver.

"Time to go!" I said as I jumped down.

We were still running down the alley as the big guy appeared at the bottom. But he didn't chase us. When I looked back he was just standing at the end shouting aggressively.

Hegarty gunned the engine. "My God, my hands are shaking!" he said.

Mei Fen also had concern etched on her face.

"It's all right, he just wanted to scare us off," I said. "What was he shouting?"

"I not know," she said. "He speak Japanese."

That made sense and I figured the guy with the cigarette had also spoken Japanese.

"Frustrating, having come all this way for nothing," Hegarty said as he spun us around and headed back south.

I shook my head but said nothing. I was thinking.

We passed the crash site a few minutes later and noticed that we all took a long look.

Hegarty said, "Raining cats and dogs."

"It certainly does pour when it rains here," I agreed.

"It comes from Norse mythology. Odin had a pack of wolves and he controlled the weather. If it was so bad then the wolves would also fall from the skies."

"And the cats?"

"Witches' cats blown off the broomsticks."

I chuckled. The sergeant was trying to lighten my mood. "Thanks, Hedge, but nothing's ever wasted."

"What do you mean?"

"I convinced myself that Tom really could have been driven off the road and we took a good look at the place we believe he came to that night. We also learned that they weren't happy to see us at the House of Tokyo."

He seemed to think for a while and then shrugged. We were back in civilisation with better roads and lighting. I sensed Tom Silverman's girl finally start to relax and wondered whether she'd expected someone to be following us. I regretted not comforting her more.

I leaned back and said she should give Hegarty directions to her home.

When we dropped her a mile or so later, north of the city, she said, "Please... find who did it."

We sat for a moment and watched her disappear inside a block of houses. Hegarty said, "Do you think this has anything to do with the guns?"

I shrugged. "I have no idea."

"And what about security—generally I mean?"

"I have no idea."

Of course he wasn't my driver for personal matters but he didn't say anything for a while.

We crossed the river and cut east towards Gillman Barracks.

"What did you mean?" he said after the long silence. "What were you thinking when you said nothing's wasted?"

"Like I said they didn't want to talk to us."

"Right..."

"A Chinese girl, and two white men; an MP and someone with a dubious role. But there is someone they will talk to. No matter what."

He waited.

"The police," I said. "I'm going back there with the police."

SIXTEEN

Cicadas no longer chirped but it was still dark when I got up. I did the exercise routine that I'd started more than half my life ago for boxing. I finished off with twenty minutes of skipping and hit a cold shower. Refreshed and ready for whatever the day may bring, I put on my uniform and jogged down the hill to the office block.

The night-duty clerk looked disappointed as I entered.

"Thought you were my relief," he said with a shrug. "You're keen, Captain."

"Is there tea?" I asked.

"The cha-boy will be here soon but the canteen will be open. You could get breakfast..."

I thanked him for the suggestion but that wasn't my plan. I asked for the reports from yesterday in case anything relevant had happened. After he'd handed a pile of papers to me in a tan-coloured folder I asked him to place a call to the police station and get hold of Inspector Rahman for me.

"I could put it through to you," he said pointing at the shared office.

"I'll take it here."

A minute later he was handing me the telephone.

"Inspector?" I said into the mouthpiece.

"So sorry, Captain Carter but Inspector Rahman was out during the night and hasn't reported in yet this morning."

I took the clerk's name for reference and asked him to take a message. "Please would you inform the inspector that I need his help. I would be grateful if he would accompany me to House of Tokyo in Nee Soon. Secondly I would like to know what his sergeant discovered about my friend's car."

After handing the receiver back, I went into the office, opened the file and began to read the reports.

I heard someone else enter the building and after the night-duty clerk ordered tea, guessed the cha-boy had arrived. An old Indian, who looked like he had never been a boy, soon looked in at my open door.

"Tea, sir?" he asked without eye contact or waiting for a response. He used an ugly metal tea pot, poured into fine china and placed the cup and saucer on my desk before silently leaving.

More people came in. I heard the desk clerks change shift and Hegarty say that he didn't want a cup of tea.

I called him and he immediately popped his head round the door.

"Morning, Boss!" he said with a grin. "I just heard you hadn't had breakfast. Want to grab a bite?"

Lieutenant Robshaw appeared holding a delicate cup of tea. "Morning. Anything interesting in the overnights?"

I waved them in and asked them to sit down.

"Here's what I would like," I said. "Robbo, I'd like you to find out as much as you can about Sergeant Major Sinclair. In particular I'd like to know if there's a link between him and Colonel Atkinson."

The lieutenant looked surprised but just nodded.

I continued: "Meanwhile Hedge and I are going to Tanglin Barracks for breakfast."

Hegarty waggled his bushy eyebrows. "I get all the bum jobs," he said.

"We'll be there for a while so come and find us as soon as you have anything to tell me. Also, if Inspector Rahman calls while I'm out, please have him put through to me at Tanglin."

Robshaw ruffled his blond hair and frowned. "So what are you thinking?"

I stood, took a quick slurp of tea, and said, "I'll tell you when you get there. And, Robbo... make sure you look formal when you arrive. Imagine you have some serious news for me."

We attracted surreptitious glances in the Officers' Mess at Tanglin. Just a sergeant, Hegarty hadn't eaten here before and I had to ask him to stop grinning. "We're on serious business, remember," I whispered.

I found a corner table and we both sat with our backs to the wall so that we could see who came and went. Not that I cared, I just wanted to be blatant.

A waiter asked what we'd like from the menu and we both chose full English breakfasts and tea.

As the man left us, Hegarty said, "Crikey, so this is how the other half live?"

I opened the top incident report. It wasn't at all interesting, just a log of the arrest of some squaddies enjoying too much R and R. I pointed at some of the timings and Hegarty squinted at the page.

"What am I looking at?"

"Whatever I point to," I said. "And then talk to me. Tell me about the incident."

Hesitantly he began to talk and I pretended to be attentive. We went through the first two reports and stopped as our food was delivered. The third report was one I was genuinely interested in.

I let him take a few mouthfuls before saying, "Tell me about Madam Butterfly."

"Was there another one last night?"

I opened the third report between us so that he could see.

"Jesus," he said. "Vernon isn't going to be happy."

"Why Vernon in particular?"

"Because he's sworn to bring that damn woman to justice. She's a royal pain in the backside and has been for more than six months now."

He went on to tell me that Madam Butterfly was the name given to an attractive woman of Chinese descent who had the tattoo of a butterfly on her thigh. "She lures soldiers with the promise of sex and the next thing they know, they've been knocked out and had all their valuables stolen."

"And always soldiers?"

"Any military it seems—at least they're the ones we hear about and it makes sense."

"Because?"

"Well especially anyone on shore leave. You'd be amazed at how much cash some of the guys carry around. It's partly because they've been on board ship for weeks and suddenly have both cash and something to spend it on. And partly because they've got their pay and don't want to leave it for someone else to half inch whilst they're ashore."

The latest case was a twenty-year-old Royal Engineer from the 27th Regiment. He had been drinking with his mates at the Penny Black pub. They went shopping and then some of them reconvened at Happy World, a dance hall. He carried on drinking and bought too many dances to remember. In his own words, he thought he had pulled one of the taxi dancers and left with her. He had another drink with her in a bar he couldn't remember the name of. After she'd finished he asked if she had somewhere to go, assuming they were going to have sex. She had slapped him and disappeared before he returned to his senses. Then he found himself talking to an even more attractive girl. She seemed to like his attention and he bought her a drink. As they chatted, she put her hand on his leg and she gave him *that look*. Seconds later, they were outside hailing a trishaw. She gave instructions to the driver and they were rapidly cycling through the streets, kissing and fondling as their carriage bounced along. He said he suddenly felt sick and emptied the contents of his stomach just as the tricycle stopped.

He remembered the girl helping him out of the trishaw and leading him down an alley towards a door. He assumed this was where she lived and she was taking him upstairs but he never got that far. He blacked out and woke with a stinging lump on the side of his head. His watch was gone. So was the cash in his pocket and the more serious money in his boot.

"It's typical," Hegarty said. "And I see we don't have a clear description of the girl except she wasn't short, she had a nice dress with a long slit up the side and she was very pretty. The problem with these guys is they are so blind drunk it's lucky they can remember as much as they do."

Hegarty wanted to know if I was leaving my black pudding. I let him have it and waved to the waiter to bring us some toast. I started talking to Hegarty as he polished off my food. When the waiter was within earshot I said, "It'll be interesting about Sinclair because—" I stopped suddenly as though not wanting the waiter to hear our discussion.

After he'd left a rack of toast and poured us more tea, Hegarty looked at me. He said, "You were just saying...?"

"I wanted the waiter to hear Sinclair's name. If you notice he'll shortly go over to the far table with four officers on it and give them an update. He's been trying to hear us for the past ten minutes."

Sure enough, the same waiter made his way over to the table and poured the men tea. They hadn't ordered any. I could see him talking and one of them couldn't resist a glance in our direction. As soon as the waiter moved away, all four got up and left.

We kept going with the tea and toast for almost an hour. The number of diners waxed and waned until we were the only ones remaining.

"What now?" Hegarty asked after long minutes of silence. "Even I can't eat any more toast."

I was about to answer when Robshaw burst through the door. I'd wanted him to be serious but his wild eyes said something very different. They said he had shocking news.

SEVENTEEN

Lieutenant Robshaw sat opposite us and took a long breath. "You won't believe it," he said.

"You found information on Sinclair."

"I certainly did. And you wanted a link between him and Atkinson, Gaskill's adjutant."

I waited and Robshaw enjoyed the tease. He delayed by slicking back his straw-coloured hair.

Finally, Hegarty crumbled, "For Christ's sake, tell us Robbo!"

"Sinclair was in Korea until eight months ago. He was with the 54th Commonwealth. The move to Singapore was a promotion."

"OK," I said. Nothing shocking so far.

"His reassignment and promotion was signed off by one particular officer."

"Atkinson?"

"Right. Atkinson was also in the 54th. He left a month ago to come here to work for the new general."

I looked at the lieutenant. There was more to it.

He said, "Atkinson was at Tanglin during the war."

I already knew this. "But he left with Gaskill before the invasion."

"No, he was badly injured. One of the few who made it off by boat."

"Anything else?"

He looked crestfallen. "Isn't that enough to go on? I assumed you had something on them and just needed the link."

"It's not much."

"How about that my source said Atkinson and Sinclair were as thick as thieves—that's the actual term he used. Thick as thieves."

I said nothing.

Robbo said, "So...?"

I took a sip of cold tea, thinking. "I'd like both of you to go over to the Stores office and get the inventory ledger.

"But we checked it only two days ago," Hegarty said.

I smiled. "Maybe we missed something. Maybe we didn't, but let's take another look at it again anyway."

As they left, I told them to remember to be formal. I smiled as they stood to attention, saluted and marched out of the mess.

They'd been back for forty minutes. I was disappointed that Sinclair hadn't been in the office. Warrant Officer Cooke had handed over the ledger and the three of us were now looking at the entries, line by line, with me turning the pages. The words and numbers were starting to blur because I wasn't expecting to see anything. As Atkinson had told me: *Sinclair runs a tight ship.* We wouldn't find anything in here even if there was something to find.

I was starting to think our little trip and the gallons of tea were wasted when the door opened sharply. Sergeant Major Sinclair stood in the doorway. He surveyed the room and immediately matched towards us. He was in full uniform, his medals worn proudly on his left chest and he had a swagger stick under his arm.

This was the other side of the man. Formal, probably dictatorial like most sergeant majors I'd known. It was a role they had to play and this guy could play it well.

He stamped his feet like he was standing to attention, his body ramrod straight. But he didn't salute and his arms weren't by his side.

He took the stick in his left hand and leaned on the table, glaring at me.

"Who the hell do you think you are?" he barked.

I smiled. "Sergeant Major, how nice to see you again."

"Someone has been poking around asking personal questions about me."

I sensed Robshaw wince but he said nothing.

"Do you have something to hide, Sergeant Major?"

He glared. "I do not. But I do not appreciate disrespect even from a superior. And by the way, I know you have retired—under suspicious circumstances."

I didn't bother rising to the bait. He had clearly been finding out about me but I didn't care.

He leaned closer to me and I could smell coffee on his breath. "You have a brass-necked cheek, Carter. Prove what you think you can or back off!"

I inclined my head. "Are you done, Sinclair?"

He snapped up straight, tucked his stick under his arm again, spun and walked out.

"Bugger me!" Hegarty said as the door slammed. "I thought he was going to hit you with his stick. I need a stiff drink."

"My legs were shaking," Robshaw said.

"He's just a sergeant major with a controlled temper." I waved to the waiter and asked him for three small beers. When the others shook their heads as if to say they were on duty I told them to remove their brassards and relax. For the next ten minutes they were off duty.

"So," Robshaw said, after a slug of his drink, "you were going to tell me what you are thinking."

"I'm thinking this morning was a success."

"But we didn't find anything in the ledger."

"I didn't expect it to. I just wanted to stir things up and see what happened. I'd say we certainly got an interesting result."

EIGHTEEN

Undeterred, Hegarty chuckled as he drove us back. Finally he said, "Brass-necked cheek."

"Are you're going to tell me where it comes from?"

"An English highwayman—don't ask me his name or the year but I'd guess late seventeen hundreds."

"OK."

"They used to hang them. No judge or jury as such. If you were caught holding up a carriage, the army had the automatic right to string you up. Anyway there was also a rule that if you survived three hanging attempts, you were free."

I laughed. "That's a quirky interpretation of justice."

"So there was this highway man who was caught and hanged three times and survived. In those days you died by suffocation, by constriction of the windpipe rather than by breaking the neck. Anyway our guy survived through a trick. He swallowed a brass tube so that his throat couldn't be crushed."

I laughed again. "Seriously? How do you know these things?"

"It's my hobby. You like boxing and I like the origin of expressions... and billiards."

"That's good to know—about the billiards that is. Now I know not to play you for money." We turned off the road and up the hill towards Gillman. I said, "Hedge—see if you can find me a brass tube. I suspect I might need it if I'm wrong about this thing at Tanglin."

Vernon had me in his office. "I hear you've been playing at your old role," he said between clenched teeth. "Seems we've been here before, eh? So, what have you got to say for yourself?"

"I achieved my objective."

"What, on this cock-and-bull hunt for guns? There are no guns. There is no security issue." He paused, looking at me through small black eyes.

"Carter?"

"Yes?"

"I'm tolerating you here, you know that, right?"

I met his stare and said nothing.

"This whole security thing is a political game by the Governor."

"I'm working for Secretary Coates. I'm sure his role responsible for internal security is genuine."

"Whoever. Whatever. Where did this intelligence come from about guns?"

"I don't know."

"Then maybe you should find out."

"Anything else I should do?"

Vernon's jaw muscles worked as he clenched his teeth. "Well, Carter, since you are the great investigator I think you should prove yourself. If you want to stay here—and satisfy the control that Coates has over you—then I want you to do a proper job."

I'd predicted this. When I read the report on Madam Butterfly and Vernon's desire to resolve it, I guessed he'd enlist me.

I said, "Madam Butterfly."

He failed to hide his surprise before saying, "Yes. That damn woman is an embarrassment."

"It's not just a woman."

"What?"

"Well based on last night's incident report I'd say there's at least one other person involved, maybe the trishaw driver, maybe someone waiting in the alley."

Vernon processed this for a moment then said, "Dismissed, Carter. Catch Madam Butterfly or any trouble with Secretary Coates will be the least of your problems."

NINETEEN

Eager to speak to the inspector, I rang the police station again but only got another clerk. As before, I was told they would pass on my message. With nothing more pressing to do, I spent the afternoon reading through Madam Butterfly reports.

The first reported occurrence had been in June last year. It took four incidents over a period of seven weeks to realize they were linked. She wasn't called Madam Butterfly until the tenth incident, when the unfortunate Tommy had groped her and seen the tattoo at the top of her leg. He'd received a cracked skull for his trouble, the worst of the sixteen reported injuries. Most men said they either suspected being slipped a Mickey Finn in their drink or had received a blow to the side of the head.

I looked at the dates and saw no obvious pattern although they were all timed with the arrival of a troopship and shore leave.

Was it one girl or many? The tattoo had been mentioned eight times, three of which were reportedly in about the same place. Two early reports mentioned a butterfly tattoo but no one had thought to ask where it had been seen. Apart from that it was difficult to know from the descriptions whether it was a single woman. They all claimed she was stunning with long blue-black hair and golden skin. She was tall although estimates ranged between five-nine and six foot. All bar four claimed she was Chinese. Three others said Eurasian and one said Filipino although he seemed very unsure due to his previous drunken state. All agreed that she was in her twenties but that still gave a ten year spread. In every case the men reported she wore an attractive dress. Some described it as Chinese with a sexy long slit up the side. Others knew this was called a cheongsam.

"What do you think?" Hegarty asked me.

"There's not much to go on."

"I know. There must be hundreds of girls who could match those descriptions. The problem we have is all the guys were so drunk they can't remember much."

"Including which bar they were picked up from. If we knew that—"

The desk clerk poked his head round the door. "Telephone, sir," he said looking at me. "Hill Street police station."

I hurried to the phone and picked up the receiver. "Inspector?"

"It is Sergeant Kee. You wanted to know what I found," he said in his strong Chinese accent. "I looked at your friend's car and you could be right."

"The mark I saw was new?"

"I cannot say for certain that it occurred during the crash. But yes, it is more recent than the rest of the marks on the Toyota."

"Colour?"

"White."

"White?" I was disappointed. The majority of the vehicles were either white or black—or military green of course.

"Or maybe a very light grey or blue."

I thanked him and asked about the inspector.

"I have not seen him today. Let me find out."

There was silence on the line and then he was back again. "Yes, Inspector Rahman has been out at an incident. I am sure he will be back soon."

I killed another hour chewing the fat with Hegarty. In his opinion, treating Madam Butterfly as a priority was nonsense.

"We should make sure anyone coming ashore is warned," he said angrily, his Welsh accent more pronounced.

"And why aren't they?"

"It's like an admission of failure. Vernon won't have it."

"You don't like the major much do you, Hedge?"

He raised his bushy eyebrow with an ironic smile. "Is it that obvious?"

"Yes."

"When the major's in a bad mood everyone knows it. His shouts can be heard from one end of the base to the other. He also expects men to perform drills in full uniform in the heat of the day."

"He certainly likes his rules, but that's not such a bad thing for a CO."

"Really? However illogical or pointless? If he's in a particularly bad mood he'll insist on FSMO," Hegarty said with a shake of the head. Full Service Marching Order meant men had to carry their heavy kitbags and equipment as though they were off to war.

Robshaw joined us. "What are you talking about?"

"A certain bastard," Hegarty said with feeling. I wondered then whether he had been on the receiving end of FSMO.

Robshaw sighed resignedly. "Have you mentioned the fencing club?"

Hegarty shook his head.

"Everyone has to pay a subscription to a fencing club that's supposed to be established. Vernon gets you as soon as you arrive. It's like part of the initiation. You don't know any better and basically feel pressured to sign up."

Hegarty said, "He claims it's really a savings scheme and we'll get any unused money when we leave here."

I shook my head, not liking the sound of this fencing club-cum-savings scheme.

"He's also very odd," the lieutenant said breaking into my thoughts. "Most of the officers take their breaks in Penang, but Vernon goes to Johore Bahru."

I'd seen that name on a map. "In Malaya?"

"Just the other side of the causeway." He shook his head. "Odd place, odd chap."

I checked my watch. There were no windows in our little room and I realized it was now dark outside.

Where was Rahman? Why hadn't he called back yet?

"Come on Hedge," I said standing and stretching.

He grinned and jokingly said, "You're going back to see Vernon and tell him where to stuff his fencing club?"

"Maybe later. No, we're going to the police station. I've had enough waiting around. I want to get us back to that House of Tokyo."

TWENTY

Cigarette smoke was still thick in the air at the police station but the heat had eased. A couple of people waited on benches in sullen silence.

A tired and hassled desk sergeant straightened up when he saw me.

"Inspector Rahman please," I said.

The man scurried off and returned a minute later.

"Someone is looking for him," he said and asked me to wait.

I sat on a bench and studied the two men opposite me. One looked Indian and the other of Malay descent. Their body language said that they were avoiding one another, sitting at either end of the bench, about eight feet apart and turned away.

A police officer appeared and I looked up expectantly but he asked for the two men to come forward. He said they would get a room to talk and led them away. Before they disappeared I heard them start to argue. Something about stealing trade.

Now I was alone and the station fell quiet. I stood up.

"What's taking so long?"

The desk sergeant jerked up from his register and looked apologetic.

"One minute. Please. One minute." He scurried off again.

Hegarty came in. "Everything all right, Boss?"

"Sick of waiting," I grumbled.

The desk sergeant bustled back. "So sorry," he said and bowed servilely. "Inspector Rahman is not here."

"Good grief! Where the hell is he then?"

The police officer moistened his lips. "So sorry. He is at an investigation."

"Where?"

"Nee Soon. The inspector is at a village called…"

He didn't need to say anymore. Hegarty and I were already running back to the jeep.

Since Nee Soon was a small place I figured the inspector would be at House of Tokyo. But I didn't get it. How did he know? Had I discussed it with someone? Hegarty denied telling anyone, even Vernon. He claimed to have only reported that we'd gone with Mei Fen to the crash site. Perhaps Mei Fen had told the police. Whatever, I was annoyed that Rahman hadn't contacted me first. He was the liaison officer for the police and supposed to be working with me. So far all I had done was work with the MPs and investigate my friend's alleged accident.

Hegarty drove us again; an exact repeat of the night before except that we didn't stop at the crash site.

We arrived in the village to find two police cars parked directly outside the House of Tokyo. Two constables stood by the front door, turning people away and making sure no one lingered too long outside.

Hegarty bumped up onto the kerb and we got out. Together we marched up to the officers, flashed our IDs and kept going. One of the men said something but I ignored him, opened the heavy front door and then the second one.

As soon as I was in the room, I spotted the inspector at the back with the stony-faced Japanese lady in the red kimono. He glanced my way and I couldn't read the expression on his face. Concern or surprise maybe, but then gave me a friendly wave.

He left the woman and met me in the middle of the room.

I said, "I've been trying to get hold of you all day."

My gruffness made him frown. "I'm sorry, Ash. I didn't know. I've been busy all day and then this."

"But you are here without me!" I snapped.

He shook his head. "I am sorry."

I wondered then whether I had got it wrong. I was making an assumption. "So you aren't here because of last night, because I wanted you to come here?"

Now he looked more confused. "What are you saying? That you knew about this last night? But it happened today."

"What happened today?"

"The attack on the girl."

I pointed to a sofa. "Let's both start at the beginning," I said.

Once seated, I told him about our trip the previous evening because Mei Fen mentioned House of Tokyo.

He interrupted, "Who is Mei Fen?"

"My friend's girl. She says they were engaged."

"But you don't know. I mean it sounds like it was news to you—your friend never mentioned her?"

"No, but—"

He raised a hand. "All I'm saying is that may not have been true. You met a girl who wanted you to come here."

Hegarty was listening and I noticed his eyebrows rise.

"Now you," I said. "Please explain what you are doing here if it wasn't to help me gain access?"

"Seriously," Rahman said, "I didn't know about your trip here. We are responding to an incident. A young girl was possibly attacked today. We think this afternoon but I'm struggling to get any details and she can't tell us because she is unconscious."

"And that's it?" I said amazed. "Not connected to me investigating Tom Silverman's death?"

Rahman touched my arm. "I am sorry about your friend, but no, this is not about that. If I had known then I would have come here with you today."

For the first time I took a good look around. The room was a comfortable lounge bar of sorts. There was a pleasant atmosphere with the perfume of flowers, possibly lotuses. Music played quietly and the lighting was subtle. Although there were blues and pinks, the predominant colours were black and white. Large black willow paintings adorned the walls. Initially, I thought they were trees but then I realized that they were cunningly suggestive of the female form.

Overall the room had an obvious Japanese theme and feel which made sense. The only things that didn't seem to fit were two golden Chinese lions guarding the entrance.

"What is this place?" I asked the inspector.

"What I prefer to call a bordello."

That was my assumption yesterday although Mei Fen had disagreed. I'd been in many brothels as an MP and it seemed to fit even though this was by far the most tasteful I'd ever seen.

"So what do you know?" I asked.

"At three minutes past four this afternoon we received a phone call from Tan Tock Seng—a public Chinese hospital—to say that they had a patient that had been brought in and were suspicious of foul play. An officer was despatched and decided we should investigate. Her name was given only as Tai Tai. Her residence was noted as Dongzing de fangzi here in Nee Soon and so here we are."

"And you have been here, waiting how long?"

Rahman waggled his head. "Over an hour, but at first, the big woman wasn't here. One of the staff showed us where Tai Tai had been found near to the foot of a fire-escape at the back. There's a large courtyard out there behind the kitchens. It has rubbish and waste, storage and a toilet."

Rahman stopped.

I said, "There's a track behind the building that leads to a road off the main street. There's also an alleyway between this building and the next."

The inspector looked surprised.

"As I said, I was here last night. We tried to gain entry so I could ask why my friend might have come here but the madam—" I nodded towards the lady in the red kimono "—refused to open the door."

"She's difficult, that's for certain," Rahman said. "She seems to have stopped people talking to us."

"And only speaks Japanese."

"Yes. She started off seeming reasonable but made it clear we are to wait for someone to arrive."

"Do you know who?"

Rahman shook his head.

I said, "The girl—why do you think there is foul play as you put it?"

Rahman didn't answer immediately and then said, "Later. You will see."

I got up. "All right, let's take a look from upstairs?"

As we walked to the stairs, the stony-faced madam seemed to consider barring our way. She looked long and hard at the inspector and he asked her firmly in

English to move aside. She did so but I couldn't help thinking there was something odd about her.

At the top of the stairs stood a cluster of young women seemingly desperate to know what was going on. I counted seven girls. The tallest must have been no more than five-foot-four. They were pressed in the corridor, huddled together, worried and skittish.

The corridor had rooms running off it left and right, white partitions in black frames. Some of these were the rooms I had seen from the street.

The girls parted to let us through and closed ranks again behind us. They all turned and watched as we continued down the corridor to the back of the building. We passed through a more conventional door and down a couple of steps.

Here the décor was different; no longer luxurious, but in a state of squalor and neglect. Paint peeled off walls, the floor boards were bare except for a worn rug-like covering that appeared to be made of reeds.

"The girls' living quarters," Rahman explained.

At the end of the corridor there was an outside door that led to the metal staircase I had seen last night.

I tried the door and it opened outwards. I stepped onto rickety metal and looked down. It was steep and someone could easily lose their footing.

Rahman pointed to where the body had been found, about ten feet directly after the foot of the stairs. Beyond this was the courtyard gate. It was open.

"If she fell," I said, "then she must have rolled afterwards. I expected her to be closer to the bottom. Injuries?"

"A single blow to the head."

Ah, so that was part of why he suspected something. If the girl had tumbled down the fire-escape, she would likely have multiple injuries.

Rahman said, "Shall we go down?"

"Which is the girl's room?" I asked. "Let's take a look at that."

It was the first internal door of eight and adjacent to the fire-escape. Rahman opened it and we stepped into another shabby room although, unlike the hallway, this had personal touches that made it homely. Stark and square room, the room had a single mattress in the centre. There was one window with matting for a blind and the only light bulb was pallid and hanging forlornly from the ceiling above the bed. Cushions provided softness and colour. A bamboo wardrobe and chair were on one side of the room. A hard wood dressing table and chair were on the other. The table was covered in bottles that I assumed to be cosmetics. There was also a photo frame although there was no picture inside.

The chair was at an angle that made me wonder if it had been knocked over and repositioned. The table looked disturbed and items also lay on the floor.

"Was the room like this when you found it?"

Rahman looked embarrassed. "No, we searched it for evidence just in case she didn't just fall. Unfortunately my constable was less than careful."

"Did you find anything of interest?"

"No."

I went to the window and looked out. I couldn't see the base of the fire-escape but I could see where she'd been found.

"That's it," he said leading me back into the corridor. "Shall we take a look in the courtyard, Ash?"

Before I could respond, the constable who had been downstairs called to us from the door to the girls' quarters.

"What did he say?" I asked since the man had spoken Chinese.

Rahman closed Tai Tai's bedroom door and then indicated that we should head back up the steps and corridor beyond. The girls were still clustered together talking loudly.

The other policeman spoke again. I heard a word that sounded like "hip". It may as well have been the sound of a falling guillotine, the way it immediately silenced the chattering.

The girls watched us. Rahman looked agitated.

I said, "Anand, what is it?"

"They are ready to talk," he said giving little away. "The person we have been waiting for has just arrived."

TWENTY-ONE

"How nice to see you again Ash Carter," Su Ling said. She was standing in the lounge next to the madam of the house.

She looked as surprised as I felt but gave me a slight smile and held out her hand. I registered that she barely looked at the inspector and didn't greet him.

She pointed to a curving sofa with an oval table in front and said, "Please. Let's sit."

Rahman and I sat at one end and she perched delicately on the other. Hegarty and the police constable hovered within earshot.

Su Ling spoke to the madam in a harsh tone and then turned her attention back to me.

"Mr Carter—or is it Captain now?—what brings you here?"

I wanted to ask her the same question, but explained that I was investigating a case.

"Ah," she said as though that explained everything.

The madam shuffled to the table, her face a mask of pleasantness. She placed a cocktail in front of each of us: a Singapore Sling. Rahman pushed his away but, out of politeness, I copied Su Ling and took a sip.

She smiled at me. "You are wondering why I am here. Well, I work for the owner of this establishment.

You will recall from our meeting at the warehouse that my employer is Andrew Yipp."

I realized then that upstairs the policeman must have said Yipp rather than hip. His name had abruptly silenced the chattering girls.

She continued: "One of my roles is as translator because I speak many languages including Japanese. I am here to ensure that the police—and of course you, Mr Carter—gain the information that you need to investigate this disturbing situation."

"You told me that Mr Yipp was a philanthropist and one of the largest merchants in Singapore. I didn't realize that it included brothels."

Her eyes widened with horror. I'd previously thought her eyes were green, now in this light I saw they were more brown, possibly warmer than before and even more attractive.

"This is not a brothel," she admonished me. "This is an exclusive house of gentlemen's company and entertainment."

Rahman smiled then nodded towards the big Japanese lady. "Ask the madam what she knows."

Su Ling ignored Rahman's abrupt request and took another sip of her drink. "What do you think of our interpretation of a Gin Sling, Mr Carter?"

"A little sweet for me," I said and then added: "Would you mind if we could talk to the madam of the establishment?"

Su Ling shook her head with a sad smile. "Please, Mr Carter, you aren't getting it. This is not a brothel. Her name is Mai Wan Murasaki. She is not a madam but rather the manageress."

"My apologies," I said. "Please may we speak with Madam Murasaki?"

Rahman bristled with irritation but said nothing.

121

Su Ling waved and the woman came and stood by her. The contrast between the two women was extreme and I was reminded again at just how stunning Su Ling was.

Rahman said, "Please talk us through the events of this afternoon."

Murasaki spoke and Su Ling translated. She had been getting the House ready for the evening's guests when she heard a scream.

"Was it Tai Tai?" I asked.

"No," was the reply. "It was one of the other girls."

"Sorry for the interruption," I said. "Please continue."

Su Ling smiled at my politeness as though it were unusual and appreciated. She continued to translate and told us that the other girl had gone to find Tai Tai and saw a body in the courtyard. The other girls came out to see what the problem was and Madam Murasaki said she was the last of them to see her.

"Did you know it was Tai Tai?" I asked.

Murasaki said she wasn't sure. She ran downstairs and through the kitchen and then realized it was Tai Tai.

I asked, "Where were the kitchen staff at this time?"

"They were not yet on duty."

"Even the big guy?"

Murasaki looked at me strangely, maybe wondering how I knew about the man I'd seen with the meat cleaver but then repeated that the kitchen staff were not there.

"The gate was open," Rahman said.

"Yes. The kitchen staff use it for deliveries. It should have been locked at that time. I went outside and looked down the road."

"Did you see anyone?"

"No."

Rahman asked, "How do you explain the open gate?"

"I cannot."

I said, "Was the door to the fire-escape unlocked?"

"Of course."

"Do you think that Tai Tai fell down the steps?"

Murasaki paused as if considering her response. Then she said, "No, I think somebody hit her."

"Someone who then escaped down the road at the back?"

"It was no one here who did it so I believe that is what happened."

Rahman had been taking notes and looked disappointed. "Is there anything else you can tell us?"

"That is all I know."

I said, "Can we talk to the girl who screamed, please?"

Murasaki agreed and went to get her.

While we waited I asked Su Ling, "Where are the evening's customers, surely this place should have customers at this time?"

Murasaki returned with one girl and Su Ling directed the question to her.

The woman failed to mask her annoyance before she spoke. Su Ling repeated in English: "They disappeared like incense into a fog. As soon as there was sign of trouble, the customers left immediately. The police have been here too long for such a minor matter, Mr Rahman."

I looked at the inspector who was clearly going to ignore the comment. I nodded towards the young girl. "So who do we have here?"

"She is called Keiji."

I introduced us and asked her to tell us what happened.

The girl said something about preparing a schedule and Su Ling explained that the girls were all trained musicians and dancers. They served the gentlemen who often came here for meetings but also relaxation. "Most of the evenings are formally planned," she said.

Keiji said that Tai Tai was her best friend and she went to discuss the plans with her.

"When I got to her room, there was no answer. That's when I saw the man running."

I leaned forward. "Where did you see a man running?"

"Out of the courtyard. And then I saw a body..." she started to sob and we waited for her to calm herself. "I realized it was Tai Tai in the courtyard. I ran down the stairs—"

"The fire-escape?" Rahman asked.

"Yes. I ran to check how she was."

"Was the fire-escape slippery? You were able to run down it?"

"Yes."

I said, "What about the man you saw running away? What can you tell us about him?"

"I saw him run out through the gate."

"Anything else?"

"He was wearing dark clothes."

Rahman said, "Was he Chinese?"

She seemed to think hard, trying to picture him, probably. Eventually she said, "Yes," but I thought she sounded less than certain.

When nothing more was forthcoming I asked about the photo frame in Tai Tai's bedroom.

Keiji smiled. "Tai Tai's man."

I said, "The frame was empty. Do you know why she would have taken the photograph out?"

"No."

"What's her man's name?"

She looked uncertain or unwilling to tell us. I tried another tack: "What does he look like?"

"Like you."

"Me?"

"Yes, white only not as tall." She paused and Su Ling prompted her to speak.

Keiji said, "And a soldier."

"Is the boyfriend a member here?"

"Maybe once but not since I have worked here."

Rahman said, "So it wasn't the boyfriend you saw running away?"

Keiji looked unsure perhaps confused and Su Ling had to repeat the question. When she spoke, the girl said she thought the man running away was Chinese.

I looked at Rahman. He didn't seem to have any more questions so we let the girl go.

"Can we get a list of customers?" Rahman asked Su Ling.

The interpreter got up and spoke with Murasaki. At first it looked like the woman refused to comply as her face turned stony, but Su Ling seemed to insist. They talked for a minute.

While they were away I said, "You're thinking that whoever did this—whoever Keiji saw running away is a member."

"Right. My working assumption is they knew her."

Su Ling returned and said, "Inspector, you will appreciate that discretion is paramount in this establishment. They protect their patrons' identities."

"Get the register," Rahman said abruptly and Su Ling waved to the madam.

Moments later Su Ling had a heavy, leather bound ledger handed to her. She opened it and we saw it was clearly a register of sorts. However, instead of names against the dates there were stamps.

"What's this?" Rahman asked.

"The stamps represent the patrons," Su Ling said.

I looked down the column showing animals and flowers of all sorts.

I pointed to one. "Is this a symbol or a name?" The print looked like Chinese writing rather than a picture.

"That represents the wind," Su Ling explained. "The symbols are all mah-jong tiles. When a member joins he chooses his tile."

The madam said something that sounded like *pin zoo*.

"What did she say?" I prompted Su Ling.

"She said, 'five wheels'. It's a mah-jong tile."

Rahman was clearly irritated. "This is not good enough," he barked. "I just want a list of all the people who have been here recently. I don't want stamps, I want names. You can tell your Madam here that if she doesn't give me the names, I will arrest her for obstructing justice."

Su Ling spoke sternly to Murasaki and sent her away.

Before she left I thought she smiled strangely at Rahman.

Su Ling said, "You shall have your list, Inspector." Her tone said she was offended by his bluntness. However, she stayed impeccably calm, stood and bowed.

Rahman said, "You are going? What about the list?"

She looked at him with hard eyes that appeared to be darker than before.

"As I said, Inspector, you will get your list but it will take a little time. May I suggest we bring it to you at the police station tomorrow?"

He started to complain but Su Ling had already turned her attention to me. "Mr Carter, I wonder what you are doing this evening?"

I was taken aback by the sudden switch. I had no expectations other than returning to the barracks at some point.

She smiled alluringly at me but I was disappointed by her next statement.

She said, "Andrew Yipp would like to meet you."

TWENTY-TWO

Any other situation and I may have asked for an appointment on my terms. But I travelled back to the city in Su Ling's car and asked Hegarty to follow. Like Pope's, her ride was a Bentley but white and much older; from the nineteen-thirties I guessed.

Su Ling and I sat in silence as the jungle moved past in the darkness. I had smelled her scent earlier but in the enclosed area it was now stronger and I enjoyed breathing it in. This girl was quite intoxicating.

Finally, to break the spell, I said, "You don't like him, do you? The inspector I mean."

"Am I so transparent?"

"Not at all. I just—"

She cut me off, ending my discomfort. "I think the feeling was mutual. Normally it is nothing personal but the police can be an irritation. They are ineffective and in the way most of the time."

I understood her point of view. In my limited experience of the island, I had seen poor policing twice. Once with Sergeant Kee's accident investigation and now the way they had handled the potential attack of the Japanese girl. If someone had been in Tai Tai's room, why had he taken the photograph of the boyfriend? Was that his reason for being there or was he looking for something too? Simple crime scene preservation and fingerprinting might have given them some clue. Whilst I liked Inspector Rahman, I had also noted that his questioning was awkward. When the witness had told us about the man, he shouldn't have suggested he was Chinese. It was possible he influenced her answer.

"Do you think it is possible that an attack is planned against Japanese people on the island?" I said.

"By whom?"

"Chinese—a group of Chinese. I don't know. I'm grasping at straws. I'm still struggling to understand whether there's a connection."

"Chinese men are particularly fond of Japanese girls, Ash. The House of Tokyo is extremely popular and I find it hard to believe a member—especially one who is Chinese—would attack one of the girls like that."

I was thinking of the security issue and the role Secretary Coates had given me. "But what about a wider tension, not just the members of the club?"

She shook her head. "I still don't think so. Hopefully when you have spoken with Mr Yipp, you will understand a bit more."

I looked behind and watched Hegarty's lights. Had it been like this for my friend? Had he just been driving along pleasantly and then the other car come up behind and hit him? Or had he known he was being followed? I seemed to be collecting questions rather than answers.

"Everything all right?" she asked.

I wanted to change the subject and not think about Tom's death for a while so I asked about the piece of paper Secretary Coates had given me and said, "Have you had any thoughts about the flyer I showed you?"

"The one with the red circle and paw print?"

"Yes."

"And the numbers: four, ten, two, ten."

Rahman had translated the same thing, but I was hoping for more. "Do they mean anything to you?"

"No."

"What about the lion's paw?"

"Is that what it is?" She looked apologetic. "Again, I don't know. But I think Mr Yipp intends to cover that."

We sat in silence for the rest of the way. A couple of times she caught me admiring her. I looked away but not before I noticed a coquettish gleam in her eye.

The car stopped outside the Cathay Building. I walked around to look at the beautiful vehicle from the front and then looked up at the tower.

When I'd finished my circuit, Su Ling led me towards the steps. "It's Art Deco—very modern," she said.

I knew it was the tallest building on the island and could be seen across the city. "How many floors are there?" I asked squinting up through the lights.

"Sixteen. There's a radio mast at the top. Oh and of course there's a thirteen-hundred seat, air-conditioned cinema." She hesitated by the glass revolving doors and studied my face. "You are easy to read, Ash Carter. You don't like it do you?"

"Yes and no," I said trying to be diplomatic.

"Very English of you." She flashed a provocative smile at me. "You can see the good and the bad. Or does that mean you are indecisive?"

She was teasing me so I laughed. "That's not something I've ever been accused of."

I signalled that I wanted Hegarty to stay in the car and turned back to Su Ling. As I did, she linked her arm through mine.

"Come," she said, pushing the doors. "Let's get inside into the cool."

I'd never experienced air-conditioning before and the cold blast of air hit me like stepping from the Tropics into the Arctic.

"Your first time?" she asked with an impish look and then two heart beats of pause. "I mean your first air-conditioned building?"

"Yes."

"Not yes and no?" She laughed.

She continued to hold my arm, her body brushing against mine, and I found it hard to think.

She said, "Well then, let me tell you that this is the future. One day all buildings will be this cool. Heat saps energy and the right temperature stimulates the mind. This is why Andrew Yipp has both his office and residence in this building."

She led me forwards towards a rank of elevators. A bell boy stood to attention, pressed a button and then held the door open with a gloved hand. Inside another uniformed man nodded a polite acknowledgement of Su Ling and pressed a button.

I noticed that neither man had made eye contact, both studiously looking down as if concentrating on their work.

When we reached the twelfth floor, Su Ling let go of my arm and moved a respectful distance away. The door opened and we walked through a reception area.

We passed numerous people—all of whom appeared to be Chinese. Again no one looked directly at us. All except one man who stood by a door. The man from the warehouse. The man who caused the livid bruise on my thigh. Wang.

He focused on me without any facial expression. Then, at the last moment, he smirked and stepped to one side. I kept my eyes on him as the beautiful translator led me into the room. It was large—about ten yards long—and minimalist. There was no furniture, just a giant rug that covered most of the floor. We kept walking until we stood in front of broad windows.

"The view is spectacular in daylight," Su Ling said.

There were plenty of lights and I could see the dark snake of the Singapore River running past the quays and warehouses.

I said, "Are we meeting your boss here?"

"Mr Yipp is in the room there." She indicated a side door. "He knows we are here. It'll just be a matter of minutes."

I continued to look at the lights of the city and her reflection next to mine.

She said, "You haven't asked me why Mr Yipp wants to meet you. I also expected you to ask me about him."

"I'm sure I'm about to find out."

She nodded at me in the glass. "He admires patience."

"I'm not sure—"

"He also respects integrity."

I wondered if she was hinting at how I should handle the man but, before I could ask her, the side door opened. A young lady stepped through, bowed slightly and exited.

It was time to meet the mysterious Andrew Yipp.

TWENTY-THREE

Pointing to the second room, Su Ling indicated that I should enter. She followed one step behind.

The wall lights were dim and there was a faint smell of incense from a long thin candle burning in a pot. The pot was on a low table covered by a red velvet-looking sheet. The only other thing on the table was a bucket covered with a white cloth.

This room had cushions on the wooden floor and no rug this time. By the window stood a man. He was Chinese, lithe and of indeterminable age. I guessed maybe fifty but he could have been twenty years older.

He was dressed in what looked like red and yellow silk pyjamas. He had a wide stance and moved his arms fluidly through the air, changed his stance and repeated the arm movement. I was transfixed because it was the first time I'd seen anyone do Tai Chi.

Without looking at me, Andrew Yipp said, "You are a boxer, I believe, Mr Carter."

"I used to box as an amateur."

"Do you stay fit?"

"I like to think so," I said. "I have trained every day since I was sixteen, when I started boxing."

Yipp completed another series of moves before he spoke again.

"Are you brave, Mr Carter?"

"I think so," I said again.

"On the table is a bucket. I want you to punch into it—through the cloth."

"I might be brave but I'm not foolish."

"And what if I tell you, you will not be harmed? Please punch into the bucket about halfway."

I stepped over to the table. The cloth was silk and impossible to see through. There could be anything inside but this was clearly a test. I stood side on, raised my weaker, right hand above the bucket and punched through the silk.

I connected with something that felt like sponge. Left my fist there for a second and withdrew it.

Yipp stopped his exercise routine and bowed slightly. I returned the gesture.

"Now sit, Mr Carter," he said and pointed to a cushion.

He sat opposite, about two arms' lengths away. Su Ling took a cushion and sat behind and to the right of him.

He said, "I am concerned about the piece of paper you showed my assistant."

"What does it mean?"

"I do not know but I can tell you what it isn't. It appears to be like the symbol of a secret society but, Mr Carter, the Singapore Government banned such things more than fifty years ago."

"Secret society?"

"They are more crudely known as Triads in some countries."

I waited.

"There is no Triad in Singapore, Mr Carter. I have wondered perhaps whether a gang has tried to form but this is not possible without my knowledge."

"I see. So what do you think the symbol means?"

He looked at me with thoughtful eyes. "I wonder whether you are supposed to think that there is a gang problem, Mr Carter. The paper came from someone in the government, yes?"

I nodded.

"Do you understand politics, Mr Carter?"

All too well, I'm afraid, and it seemed I was about to get another lesson.

"As you know, this is a British Colony. Four years ago they held elections for a Legislative Council although only British subjects could vote and only a handful of seats were electable. You are new to the country so you may not know that shortly afterwards, the war broke out in Malaya." He gave an ironic smile. "Although you call it the Malaya Emergency rather than a war."

I nodded and said, "Communist insurgents."

"*Bandits* is the term you should use, Mr Carter. It sounds so much quainter. However this led to the Governor introducing the Internal Security Act. Anyone suspected of terrorism may be held indefinitely without trial." He shook his head and I detected sadness as he said, "Can you imagine it: a suspect imprisoned without question? How is that fair? How can that be justice?"

I could see his point but said nothing.

He continued: "There is a struggle going on, Mr Carter. Forget the communists, forget the bandits. The struggle is between the ten per cent of people who run the country and the rest of us. We are the commercial heart of this country. We are the future, Mr Carter."

I understood what he was saying. He thought the piece of paper and probably my whole assignment was fake. He was telling me that he was not an insurgent but perhaps the government would like to arrest him as one.

"Please don't misunderstand me," he said, "I am very loyal to the British. I am fourth generation. My great grandfather was one of the first Chinese labourers who arrived in the late nineteenth century. This is a multicultural community, mostly of Chinese descent, but we are happy with our heritage. We are Chinese Singaporeans rather than Chinese. We are not leftists."

He stood then and bowed. I was being dismissed.

"So nice of you to visit me, Mr Carter. I wish you success."

He turned to the window and smoothly began his Tai Chi once more.

Su Ling led me back into the first room. She smiled at me.

"You did well. He likes you."

I had the sense of calm but great power in the man. I certainly wouldn't like to get on the wrong side of him. But if I had to, I would.

I said, "I liked him too."

She shook my hand and flashed her enchanting eyes at me. "Would you see yourself out?"

"Can I see you again?"

"Of course." She smiled and pointed towards the exit.

As I left, I noticed her go back into Yipp's room.

Wang was still by the door.

"I wish I had my stick," he said and his smirk seemed to transform into a leer.

Brave or foolish, I don't know. I put my left hand in my pocket and felt the MP's brassard I'd worn at the start of the day. I pulled it out and he glanced at it. Perhaps he thought I'd say something about being an MP. I didn't.

He lunged as though to strike my leg. It was like a schoolboy prank: make the other person flinch. He started to laugh as he saw my movement but I wasn't flinching.

With a counter-puncher's instinct, I had stepped away and then forward to deliver my blow just as he retreated. The uppercut lifted him off his feet and the way he landed let me know he was out for the count.

There had been a slight buzz of noise before. Suddenly the hallway was silent. Five members of staff stared in disbelief. I unwrapped the brassard from my knuckles and walked down the stairs.

Sleep eluded me and for a long time I watched a lizard on my ceiling. I wasn't getting very far investigating the death of my friend. I didn't understand the connection with Nee Soon, if there was one. I appeared to have an impossible job, preventing an imaginary attack. And I appeared to be in the middle of a political game between the army, the government and now Andrew Yipp. He might not be part of a Triad but I had the distinct sense of power. He was in charge and control of something and maybe the government were afraid of him or what he represented.

By the time the lizard finally disappeared through the slats in my window, I had decided to focus on Tom Silverman. I'd find out whether Mei Fen was genuinely his fiancée and I'd question his co-workers. I'd also work with Inspector Rahman to find out if there was a connection with the girl from Nee Soon.

The rest of it could go to hell.

That was my plan but, as I'd learned in the army, when the action starts, all bets are off. However it would be another day before I learned two things that would change everything.

TWENTY-FOUR

Training in the pre-dawn darkness I felt strangely dissatisfied. Instead of stopping, I decided to run as well. I pounded the streets going south a short distance and then along the coast road towards the city and the quays. I passed Keppel Harbour and then Empire Docks, both of which were lit up, and I could see docked ships and people working. This was the night crew and I knew it would get much busier later. I knew this partly because I was now running against a tide of workers, heading for the start of their shift.

I ran around Fullerton Square and then looped back. I was probably at the sixth mile by the time the exercise-endorphins started to wear off. The combination of little sleep and pushing myself hard for ninety minutes made the final mile a bit of a slog.

I showered and dressed for the day and headed for the mess. Robshaw was just finishing his breakfast but hung around to keep me company. He didn't comment on my red face and did a lot of talking until he could see I had my wind back. He told me about the incident reports and that there had been little trouble overnight, just the usual drunken and disorderly behaviour. He then told me about some news of Malaya, that a train had been attacked by bandits. They had been lying in wait at a cutting through the hills and shot down into the carriages. Seven soldiers had been killed and dozens wounded.

Fighting had seemingly reached a peak in the summer of fifty-one and had been relatively quiet since.

"There's a concern it's picking up again. In fact last night there were even shots reported across the Straits near the crossing." He paused and looked at me then said, "So what do you think?"

"About what?"

"About the imminent threat on the island?"

"I don't know." I told him about meeting with Yipp and his view that the symbol was fake, that there were no secret societies any more.

"So what next then?"

"First on my agenda is Inspector Rahman. I want to know if he found out where the flyer came from."

"You think it's the police—that they're pretending there's a security threat?"

"I don't know," I said again. "But I'd like to know. I also want them looking into the Madam Butterfly case."

Robshaw looked shocked and ran a hand through his blond hair. "Major Vernon won't like it."

"I don't care what he likes."

He thought for a moment then said, "Do you think they'll help catch her then?"

"How else are we going to catch her, Robbo?"

He said nothing.

"If all we do is wait for an attack to be reported then it's already too late. Every single case has been reported in the morning. Long after the woman has gone."

"So how can the police help?"

I studied him for a moment. I hadn't realized how young he was; maybe only twenty-two and with limited experience. No wonder they had a liaison issue.

Robshaw had no real experience of the police and the police it seemed were ineffective. I explained that we were supposed to be working together. I'd been reminded in Nee Soon that the army and police still weren't acting in harmony. It hadn't mattered to me last night, when I thought my role was political. However, I realized I should be going with what I knew and not what people told me.

I smiled and said, "Let's just see. I'll let you know how the meeting goes."

Hegarty also wanted to know why I would tell Rahman about Madam Butterfly. It looked like an early rain so we'd selected a Land Rover hardtop and were heading out of Gillman.

I didn't bother with a full explanation and just repeated the "let's see" line.

"You still haven't told me about your meeting with Mr Yipp," he said.

"And?"

"Did you learn anything?"

"Lots and nothing."

Hegarty waited for more. When it wasn't forthcoming, he said, "What's he like?"

"Imagine Major Vernon only without the shouting. Imagine someone who knows they have power but doesn't need to prove it."

"Did you hit him?"

I looked down at my left hand which ached. I wasn't very used to punching anything without gloves on. And if I did, I hit soft tissue. I knew a man could break his hand hitting a hard target.

He said, "I noticed you nursing it, just didn't like to ask—before."

"No. I hit someone else. One of his goons."

"Did he go down?"

"Like a sack of potatoes."

The sergeant grinned. "So you won hands down?"

I shook my head in dismay. "You're just using that expression so you can tell me its origin. Right?"

"It comes from horse racing. If a jockey is well ahead, he doesn't need to whip his horse. He can hold his reins so his hands are down."

"Just drive," I said.

When we arrived at Hill Street Station I asked him to wait for me. Large raindrops began to fall and I sprinted the short distance into the reception area. A twinge in my right calf reminded me of my early morning run.

The area was already half full and the desk sergeant looked hassled. I marched up, stood beside the desk and said, "Is Inspector Rahman in his office?"

Only half looking at me, I got the response that he'd just returned. Without waiting for more, I moved beyond the desk and into the hall. I found the inspector's office. The door was open but he wasn't at his desk.

I let myself in and waited.

There was a framed photograph on his desk. I turned it around and looked at it. It was of a squad of Indian men in Second World War British Army uniforms.

"Oh hello, Captain," the inspector said, coming into the room.

I shook his hand and wondered if he seemed a little anxious. "I hope you don't mind me being nosey."

"Of course not."

I pointed to the photograph. "Who are they?"

"My father and uncle in the 4th Indian Regiment," he said. "Both died in the war—on the first day. The anniversary is just in…" He paused and looked at the photograph. Maybe something caught in his throat.

141

Then within a second he had composed himself and said, "...three days' time."

"I'm very sorry," I said.

He smiled. "No need to be sorry, Ash. War is war and I've come to terms with it. They died defending their country."

Of course, I realized. He was from Singapore so it made sense his father lived here too.

He sat down and indicated for me to take a chair. "I hope you haven't been trying to get hold of me. I'm afraid I've only just arrived. I don't know if you were told but I haven't been in this liaison job long. In fact I was only recently promoted—well the point is, I'm still half covering my old job."

I nodded, the overwork showed in his agitation at times. Like his annoyance at the House of Tokyo.

Rahman continued: "I went over to Tan Tock Seng Hospital this morning to see how the girl is—in case she could tell us what happened."

"How is she?"

"In a coma, I'm afraid."

"That's a shame. I'm hoping she'll tell us whether there's a connection with my friend's death."

I recalled the strange look on Murasaki after she had been told to give us the list of members. "Why did the Japanese madam at the House of Tokyo give you a funny look," I asked him.

"What funny look?"

"When Su Ling told her to get the ledger and sent her away. And then she said, 'five wheels' for no reason."

He shrugged. "I really didn't notice. Who knows what she was thinking? She seemed a bit odd to me. By the way, I heard Sergeant Kee checked your friend's car. He told me the other vehicle we are looking for is white."

"Or a light colour of blue or grey."

142

"How did your meeting with Andrew Yipp go?"

I started to summarize the encounter but Rahman stopped me at the bucket story.

"You punched blindly into a bucket? Goodness me!" He almost choked and shook his head in disbelief. "There could have been bricks in there or maybe glass... or perhaps snakes."

"It was a test," I said. "He wanted to know if I would trust him. It seems integrity is an important value."

"Even so..."

"He told me the symbol on the piece of paper was fake. He said there are no secret societies in Singapore."

Rahman laughed. "He wanted you to trust him and then he told you a lie. Yipp is the head of the biggest secret society on the island."

"That wouldn't surprise me. But he had no reason to lie about the symbol being faked."

The inspector waggled his head as though thinking.

"Have you found out who gave the flyer to Secretary Coates?"

"It was one of our men. I don't know who but we found a whole batch of flyers. Someone here must be passing him information."

I nodded. It happened all the time.

"Any thoughts about it here—internally?"

"The theory is that it's a date." He scrabbled in a drawer probably looking for a copy of the flyer.

I said, "Four, ten, two and ten."

"Do you know any Chinese, Ash?" When I shook my head he continued: "The four, ten could be forty. The two, ten could be February the tenth."

"And the forty—what would that mean?"

"Ah that's where the theory breaks down. Maybe forty means something to the gang."

143

"Or four, ten," I said. "That could be a time. Ten past four."

He looked surprised and pointed at me. "You could be right. I'll pass that on."

If he was going to say something else, I never got to hear it because a junior clerk came in and put some papers in his in-tray. Rahman picked them up and flicked through them. "Busy day," he said. "Is there anything else I can help with, Ash?"

"Madam Butterfly."

"The opera?"

"A woman who is preying on drunken soldiers."

"Tell me more," he said, putting his papers down again, and I told him everything I knew.

"I can't believe it. This is the first I'm hearing of this. Eight months you say?"

"It's precisely the sort of thing that the army and police should work on together."

He agreed and said he'd make sure all officers were informed.

I thanked him and stood.

"You are getting on well with Su Ling?" he said somewhat awkwardly. When I nodded he continued: "Perhaps you could ask her about the code. Perhaps forty will mean something to her."

Of course I'd already asked her about the code and she hadn't known but it was worth asking about forty. I wondered whether Rahman was implying that forty would somehow connect to Yipp's alleged secret society.

"I'll ask, but first I'm off to Keppel Harbour," I said. "I want to talk to my friend's workmates."

"I'll come with you."

I waved him back to his seat. "It's a personal matter, Anand. Thanks for the offer but you appear to have enough on your plate. Plus I'd rather you focus on where the piece of paper came from and telling your men about Madam Butterfly."

He reluctantly agreed and I was soon back in the Land Rover with Hegarty, heading for the harbour.

the place of ... while your men shout

He continued ... went back to the

bowl-lined ... at rest ...

TWENTY-FIVE

Exactly timed, the downpour stopped as we arrived at Keppel Harbour. The Master-at-Arms was sheltering in his box. Upon seeing us approach he just raised the barrier and waved us through. Steam rose off the concrete and, as we passed the motor pool, I again registered the cars. Three of them, like the first time I'd seen them. All identical. All pale blue.

Hegarty continued to the end of the wharf where an engineer was wiping the rain water off a ship's propeller the size of two people. Another couple of guys started work on something that may have been part of an engine but I was no expert.

The main doors were wide open and we could hear the hum and screech of the machine tools. Hegarty and I went inside and found the gaffer at his desk.

"Ah, Tom's friend," he said when he looked up. "Any luck investigating his death?"

"Did Tom have a girlfriend?" I asked.

"I think so. Chalky should know." He leaned out of his office and bellowed to the men outside. Moments later one of the engineers, in overalls and covered in grease, joined us.

The gaffer shut his door to reduce the noise of lathes.

"He was pretty sweet on her, was Tom," Chalky told us.

"Engaged?"

He smiled. "You know how it is, right?"

I think I did. Away from home it was somehow acceptable to give a girl a ring and say you'd marry them even though you knew it wasn't true.

"What was her name?" I asked.

"Mei Fen. Sweet little Chinese girl."

I nodded. So she was who she claimed to be and I believed what she'd said about the House of Tokyo in Nee Soon.

I asked them both if they had heard Tom mention the gentleman's club or brothel, whatever it was. Neither man knew it and both said they'd never been to Nee Soon. In fact when we walked around the shed and asked the other men, we found out that no one had heard of it.

"Frustrating," Hegarty muttered.

"Not really, sometimes a null result is information in itself."

He didn't get it. "Like what?" he said.

"It's important for scientists. When they test something they are as happy learning what it is not as what it is."

"I still don't—"

"It's the same for detective work. We eliminate what it can't be and whittle down the possible answers until we're left with the answer."

We got back in the Land Rover and I asked the sergeant to drive slowly along the wharf. Then I said, "For example, I've learned that it looks like another vehicle forced my friend's car off the road."

"Right."

147

"And that it was probably white or maybe light blue or grey."

"Right."

"Did you see me walk around Su Ling's car last night?"

Hegarty thought and then nodded. "Yes, I wondered at the time why you'd done that."

"The Bentley was white. I was looking for damage."

"And was there any?"

"No. A null result."

My driver still looked uncertain.

"Stop here, Hedge." We were next to the motor pool.

We got out and stepped into the compound. I started to walk around each of the three Fords.

"Can I help you?" a voice called and a naval warrant officer approached. Behind him was a small office and garage workshop.

"Are you responsible for these?" I asked.

"I am."

"Mind if I take a look? They all appear to be in pristine condition."

He beamed proudly. "I do my best. Can I ask…?"

I showed him my government ID. He raised an eyebrow.

"You know this is navy property right? Neither of you… neither the government nor the army have any jurisdiction here."

"It's not a matter of jurisdiction," I said placating him. "I'm just admiring the condition of your cars." I pointed to the Land Rover, dented and mud splattered. "If only the army was as meticulous as you."

He beamed again.

I said, "I bet you fix these cars up pretty damn quickly if anything gets damaged."

"Too right I do."

I smiled, "And have you had to fix anything recently?"

"All the time."

"Any had damage to the right front wing?"

He patted the car next to us. "Crashed a couple of weeks ago by some fool officer driving too fast in the rain."

I felt my heart pounding in my chest. It could have been when Tom Silverman had died. I tried to stay calm.

"Was it Thursday the twenty-third?"

For a second his brow creased in thought then he responded, "Yes, I believe it was."

"You described it as a crash..."

"Pretty bad and a bit of mess to clean up too."

"Was there more than just the front wing damaged?"

"Yep. The driver came off the road and hit a bank or something. One headlight was smashed. The bumper was crumpled. A bit of denting to the bonnet and the grill."

That was far too much damage for the prang that had forced my friend off the road.

"So which *fool officer* was driving that time?" I said lightly. "Perhaps I know him."

The man grinned. "I'm not an idiot, you know. You two asking questions about a car crash. If you want information like that then you'd better go and see Commander Alldritt." He pointed to a grand colonial-style house about two hundred yards beyond the guard post. "Royal Navy HQ," the man explained.

I thanked the warrant officer for his help and asked Hegarty to take us over to the HQ.

In the Land Rover Hedge said, "But that was a null result wasn't it?"

"Maybe," I said. "Maybe not."

149

We crossed the manicured garden to open double doors and found ourselves in a foyer converted into an office. Royal Navy clerks, heads bent, pored over ledgers. One man looked up. "Can I help you?"

"I'd like to speak to Commander Alldritt please."

"Do you have an appointment?"

I explained who I was and that I'd just like a few minutes of the commander's time. The clerk nodded and sauntered off down a corridor. After a few minutes he returned and instructed us to follow.

Commander Alldritt stood and walked around his desk. He was about an inch taller than my six-two. In his early forties, he had a tired face with neat, salt and pepper hair and gave the impression of a man who had gone to seed sitting behind a desk for too many years.

He held out his hand. "What can I do for you Captain Carter and Sergeant Hegarty?"

He sat on the edge of his desk and we remained standing.

I decided to stretch what the car pool guy had just said. If I were wrong, Alldritt could easily correct me. So I said, "We've just been over to your MT yard. A Royal Navy staff car crashed the week before last on the road near Nee Soon village."

Alldritt raised a casual eyebrow and cleared his throat.

I said, "I would like to know who was driving the car."

"Which vehicle are we talking about?" Alldritt asked.

I reeled off the service number from memory.

"I'll have to check." He smiled.

When he said nothing more, I said, "Will you let us know?"

"You know there's a war going on?"

"Malaya or Korea?"

"Korea, specifically," Alldritt replied and he suddenly seemed more animated, light returning to his weary eyes. "You might not think it is our war, but our boys are also out there with the Americans. A lot of boys are getting killed out there, you know. Could be fifty thousand by the end of the war. Damn fine boys fighting in a God forsaken patch. And do you know who makes sure our boys get the help they need: the munitions, the medical supplies, the food and clothing?"

I waited for Alldritt to continue.

"We do, Captain. We do. We may look like pen-pushers, but fifteen-hundred troops come in and out of this harbour each and every day. Ten thousand tons of supplies go through here each week. We are the supply line. Without us, this war could not be fought. Without us, it would grind to a halt. This is the hubris of activity – the end of a funnel if you like, Captain."

"I'm sure that's true,' I said trying to be diplomatic. I knew the Americans did come through the harbour, but they also had Manila in the Philippines. I looked Alldritt in the eye. "I'd just like to speak to the driver of the vehicle please, Commander."

"You don't have jurisdiction here, Captain Carter. As a government official or—" he turned his attention to Hegarty "—the Military Police."

"I understand that, sir—"

"If a crime has been committed by someone in the Royal Navy then the navy will investigate it. Mark my words that it will."

"But you don't know what the crime is?"

"Tell my clerk on the way out," Alldritt said, standing. "Good day to you gentlemen. Thanks for popping by and saying hello. Now, I have important business to attend to, if you would excuse me?"

151

Before we left, I located the clerk who had originally welcomed us.

"How many naval officers are there on the island?" I asked.

He thought for a second like he was adding them up. "Counting the naval base that would be eighteen."

"And could you let me have a list, please?"

He looked at me through narrowed eyes. "You'll have to ask the commander for that."

I nodded and we strode out of the building.

Hegarty said, "Another null result?" I think he was trying to be humorous.

"Take me to Fort Canning, please Hedge," I said. "I know where we can get that list."

TWENTY-SIX

Realizing Colonel Atkinson was under no obligation to help, I told him I was investigating a car crash on the road from Nee Soon. I explained that I suspected a naval officer was involved but had got nowhere with Commander Alldritt.

Atkinson stroked his moustache and nodded. "If you were with your sergeant, he'll have seen you both as Army. There's always been and always will be tension between the army and navy."

"All I needed was the driver of the car."

"And what would you have done with the officer's name?"

"Asked him some questions."

Atkinson nodded again. "And there you have it. I bet the commander said he'd have it investigated."

"He did but he didn't ask for any detail."

"So you don't think he'll do anything?"

"I'm certain he'll do nothing. So, that's why I'm hoping you'll help me, sir?"

Atkinson looked thoughtful. "Is this connected to the internal security issue that Coates has you running around about?"

I hesitated and then decided to be honest. "No," I said. "This is personal. I think my friend was killed in that crash."

"All right, Ash," Atkinson said patting my arm. "I'll see what I can get for you."

"Success?" Hegarty asked as he spun around in the courtyard and headed for the white portico gate.

"Colonel Atkinson will try and get it for me. Since General Gaskill is CIC for the Far East, he coordinates all services. He and Atkinson are effectively Alldritt's superiors."

We looped down the hill and Hegarty started to turn right.

"Let's go left," I said.

"Left?" He stopped and looked at me. "Do you have somewhere in mind for lunch other than Gillman?"

"Forget lunch. I want to go back to where my friend died."

We got out of the Land Rover after turning it around just south of Nee Soon. I could feel the post-noon sun through my hair and turned up my collar as protection. It hadn't rained for more than three hours. Even though it must have been ninety degrees, the ground was sodden and steam rose from the long grass.

Last time we were here, there was the constant loud buzz of cicadas. Now I heard a cacophony of birdsong and the occasional whoop of a monkey.

Hegarty watched me. "What are we looking for, Boss?"

I took him fifty yards up the road and positioned him on the left, a pace in front of me.

"Let's imagine we're cars," I said. "You're my friend in his little foreign car and I'm close behind." He started to walk and looked at me over his shoulder.

"Like this?"

"Remember, it's night, it's chucking it down and my lights just dazzled you."

I pushed him and he staggered but kept going. Then I leaned on his left shoulder with my right hand and kept the pressure up. Hegarty went with it and started a curving walk towards the other side. I pushed harder and he jolted off the road into the grass.

"No need to keep going," I said and he stood still, probably grateful he didn't have to wade across the damp verge. I imagined I'd given a final shove to get a car to the trees but couldn't stop. Then I followed the line I'd spotted before, assuming one side of my car had come off the road. I'd be afraid of losing control as well. I imagined steering away. There was a three inch ridge and I pictured the car bumping back onto the laterite.

Maybe I wasn't in control. Maybe I'd skidded a bit. Maybe I over compensated.

If I were travelling at thirty miles an hour I would cover about one and a half feet per second. In my head I counted seven seconds on the verge. That seemed too long. Perhaps he was going faster: fifty, maybe sixty miles an hour. In bad conditions the driver was indeed likely to be fighting with the steering.

I walked forwards, imaging my car was moving back to the left hand side. A pot hole caught my attention a few feet ahead. What if the second car had hit that with a front tyre?

I pictured him swerving back to the other side following the same trajectory. Twenty yards later I was at the opposite verge. And then I saw it: another rut driving through the grass. It was ten more yards ahead.

155

Maybe the car had been going even faster or perhaps my assumed trajectory had been wrong, but here was a clue that the other car had swerved from one side to the other.

Hegarty joined me. "You think...?" He pointed ahead about another twenty yards. The verge here undulated, rough terrain even for a Land Rover. We could see two tracks across it. And they aimed straight for a bigger mound.

Up close, I could see that the mound was in fact a scattered pile of bricks probably shed by a lorry at some point. It had been buried by earth and grass but now it was partially flattened. Something had hit it at speed, stopped and manoeuvred back and forth until it had come free. The ground had been carved up by spinning wheels. I could see tracks go beyond the debris and back to the road further down.

"Not a null result after all, eh Hedge?"

"The staff car at Keppel?"

"I'd bet my lunch on it," I grinned.

I spent the afternoon at Gillman Barracks hoping for a phone call from Colonel Atkinson to tell me who the driver had been.

I had just finished swimming when I got a phone message. But it wasn't from Atkinson. A corporal handed me a yellow slip of paper.

"From your interpreter," he said with a smirk.

Intrigued, I opened it up. It said: Pick you up at seven tonight. Dance. Dress code: informal.

I checked my watch. Two hours away.

"You dark horse!" Robshaw said when I turned up at the office. I was dressed in my best casual clothes for my date.

Hegarty said, "She's tall, Eurasian, pretty and has great legs."

"Sounds like a taxi-girl—one I recently picked up at New World," Robshaw laughed and flicked back his straw-blond hair.

I'd only been on the island five days at this point but I had heard a lot about the New World entertainment park. Men off the boat often went straight into its sister, Great World. There was another to the east called Happy World. New World was out-of-bounds for shore-leavers and had a popular dance hall, a huge room, like a featureless church with columns either side and between them, card tables and cane chairs. The central space was for dancing, at the far end was a band. The halls were cheap and basic, full of cigarette smoke and ideal for picking up a girl. Robshaw and many of the lads went there every Saturday night. The girls were mainly Chinese and Malay, but there were others such as Siamese and of mixed race. These were not prostitutes, they were dancers. The men would buy a book of tickets at the door and for a dance they would select a girl and give her a ticket. Of course the men usually selected and went back with a girl who was willing. They would have sex and the girl would expect to be paid.

"Eurasian," Robshaw said pretending to struggle to remember. "Dark hair, golden skin, beautiful eyes and pretty good in bed. Did the Singapore grip as I recall."

I ignored Robshaw's crassness.

Hegarty said, "This one is no taxi-girl. She's way out of your league, Robbo."

"Rubbish! Sounds like my kind of girl! Perhaps I should come with you to the dance tonight. Perhaps she'll prefer a blond."

I sat down, waited a minute and said, "You missed an opportunity there, Hedge. Where does the expression *dark horse* come from?"

"Too obvious," he said. "It's from horse racing where a horse is unknown."

Robbo laughed. "And so was your change of subject!"

Hegarty fetched us tea and I asked the lieutenant whether he'd obtained anything from the newspaper.

"All the old editions are on microfilm, these days," he said. I had to put in a request and they'll let us have it as soon as they have something. It'll be a big job and they let me know what a big favour they were doing us—or more specifically you. It seems you have more clout as a government man than an MP with the press."

"Politics," I grumbled. "It's everywhere."

"Always has been, always will be," Robshaw said. "For me, the main difficulty is with the police. What did Rahman say when you told him about Madam Butterfly?"

"He said he'd inform the other officers."

"And did he?"

"I don't know."

"You see, I wonder if he did."

I shrugged.

As Hegarty returned with a tray of cups, Robshaw said, "Hedge was telling me about your friend's car crash. It looks like a naval officer was involved."

After I had given him my version of what we'd learned, he said, "And the security issue. It sounds like you think there's no progress."

Hedge said, "Because there *is* no security issue, right Boss?"

I was about to answer when the desk sergeant ran into our room.

"Sir," he said, breathless from running only twenty yards. "There's been a sighting... of Madam Butterfly. An incident near Happy Palace... It's on-going."

TWENTY-SEVEN

Shouting our destination to the desk sergeant, we ran from the offices and took a jeep. Hegarty and I were in the front, Robshaw and a corporal in the back—the one who had reported the sighting.

Just as the security barrier was raised for us, a gleaming cherry-red convertible pulled up. The lights of the security gate sparkled off the body and made its white-walled tyres both attractive and stark in the same instance.

Su Ling leaned out of the window. "You are leaving?" She could have been annoyed but her pretty face showed nothing but the pleasure of seeing me.

Hegarty was rolling passed. I leaned across him, "Something's come up. Another time?"

"Yes," she said.

"Sorry…" I started to shout but it was lost in the rush of air as Hegarty hit the accelerator.

Robshaw pressed his face between the front seats. "Oh my God, she's a knockout. Outrageously gorgeous!" he said.

The corporal leaned forwards next. He said, "I'd have stayed with the girl."

"And that was a brand new Pontiac Chieftain," Hegarty said with serious awe. "What a fantastic car. I bet it's the only one on the island."

"All right, enough all of you!" I said. "Let's focus on the job in hand and catch us a butterfly."

The streets were alive with people. In the area of the two main fun parks, the ratio of soldiers and sailors to civilians was more than two to one, I estimated. And then most of the civilians were young women.

The jeep had to slow to a crawl to avoid the revellers in the narrow streets.

"There!" The corporal pointed out a policeman standing on the street close to the entrance to Happy Palace. The officer flagged us down and then stood on the jeep's footboard.

"We've cornered her," he said with breathless excitement. "Up two blocks we're in Little India. She ran into a Hindu temple there."

Hegarty pulled up outside the temple that was garish and yet somehow didn't look out of place. It was as though a slice of India had been blended with the Chinese. Every side of the fascia was covered with images of gods and animals and painted in many colours.

On the ground, a crowd of about thirty people stood around either looking uncertain or excited. Half of them were soldiers, probably from the Windrush troopship that had docked at Keppel Harbour during the day. An Indian-looking policeman stood guard in front of giant doors, large enough for someone three times my height.

He saluted. "We have trapped the Madam Butterfly inside."

"What happened?" Robshaw asked.

"A Staffordshire private picked up a Eurasian girl at a club called Happy Palace. She took him out back for sex. When his trousers were down, she tried to mug him and take his money. Luckily his mates were suspicious and we arrived just in time. We chased her in here and I've been guarding the door since."

"There isn't another way out?" Robshaw asked.

"No, sir."

"Why didn't you go in and get her?"

"Sanctuary, sir. And the chief said we had to wait for you."

I said, "Is she armed?"

"No, sir."

I kicked off my shoes. Robshaw did the same and told the corporal to come with us. He asked Hegarty to stay outside and make sure none of the mob got in.

I'd never been inside a Hindu temple before. It had the echo-quietness of a church but there were mats and a couple of stone benches instead of pews. At the far end was a wooden screen about a yard high. Behind that was a neutral coloured curtain.

The lieutenant and I exchanged looks. The room appeared empty so the only places she could be were behind the screen or curtain.

She wasn't behind the screen.

I pulled back the curtain and revealed a dimly lit, short corridor with rooms off to the left and right. Directly ahead there was a teak door covered with brass bells. The other men looked into the side rooms and I went to the teak door. As I started to turn the handle the door burst open.

Because of the gloom it was too late by the time I realized what was happening. A long pole glanced off my side as I tried to twist away.

Then the pole thrust out again but clattered to the floor and the door swung shut.

Robshaw eased it open with his foot and shone a torch through the opening. We could see it was a small room with items draped with sheets. Robshaw checked the gap by the hinge to make sure she wasn't behind the door. She wasn't.

"Wait here," he said to the corporal and he stepped forwards. Immediately, the torch flew from his hand. In that same instant our assailant flew at us with animal ferocity, arms windmilling, legs kicking out.

She had planned a shock attack to break past us, but Robshaw and I both lunged forwards. He yelped in pain and I grabbed anything I could. Then I let go and stepped back in surprise.

"What?" Robshaw asked me but before I could answer, the girl lashed out again and again like a wild cat.

In the faint light, we forced her back until she walked into a sheet. The statue underneath clattered to the ground and she followed. I pinned down her arms and Robshaw snapped cuffs onto her hands. Then we pulled her to her feet and dragged her kicking and screaming through the door into the light.

"Accompany her to the police station for processing," I said to the corporal.

"Ash?" Robshaw said.

I dusted myself off and walked to the temple entrance.

"Ash?" Robshaw said again at my side. "It's a military matter. We should take her to the Bras Basah cells."

I shook my head.

Outside, Hegarty was also confused. The crowd of soldiers cheered and catcalled as the policemen marched the girl away.

"You don't seem very pleased, Boss," Hedge said, "We've got Madam Butterfly. If nothing else at least Vernon will be happy."

Robshaw was looking at me curiously. Then he said, "That wasn't our girl was it?"

"No," I said. "Tall enough, possibly good looking enough, but not our butterfly."

"How—"

"Two reasons. The modus operandi was all wrong."

"And the second reason?"

"Without question," I said, "we just arrested a man."

TWENTY-EIGHT

On the way back to Gillman I explained, "The first time I tried to grab the girl, I caught hold of something I didn't expect!"

Hegarty gave a booming laugh. "You mean: meat and two veg?"

I put my hand on the steering wheel, as he almost lost control.

Robshaw said, "Don't worry. We won't tell any of the men that you've been handling the forbidden fruit."

Hegarty was still laughing. "Speak for yourself! I'm not promising anything of the sort."

"It's ironic," I said. "I could have been dancing with a beautiful woman right now. Instead I've had my first introduction to a transvestite."

"We call them Ruby-with-the-bollocks here, Boss."

"Charming."

"But you have to admit it—" Hegarty started laughing again— "he was very good looking. Perhaps you could have a dance with him."

It was almost midnight when the night clerk knocked on my bedroom door. He stood apologetically in the dimly lit hallway.

"Yes?"

"Sir, Sergeant Hegarty has asked that you return to the office as a matter of urgency. Something has come up."

I was tempted to ignore the request. Hegarty was up to something and I suspected there would be a welcoming committee and reminder of my evening's experience, grabbing a man's tackle. However I decided to humour him.

When I arrived, Hegarty was grinning.

"Couldn't resist, could you?" I said. "OK let's do this."

Hegarty carried on grinning but shook his head.

"What?"

"There's someone at the main gate to see you. I thought it best that you went now. You know, repair your reputation after the incident with the Ruby."

I went outside, wondering what Hegarty meant. In the sodium lights by the gatehouse I could see a red convertible. Su Ling stood up and waved.

I jogged down to her and ducked under the barrier. "Hello. How was the dance?"

"Wasn't much happening," she said. "No fun. So I thought I'd come back and see if you were available."

She patted the passenger seat and I got in beside her.

"What do you have in mind?"

"Let's go for a drive. I'd like to show you somewhere."

She pulled away smoothly and soon the open top car made her luxurious hair stream behind. For the first time I saw that she wasn't dressed in her usual formal clothes. Her style was American. A short polka dot dress with bobby socks and black shoes, presumably for dancing. Her silk wrist strap was white with black spots.

"You are staring," she scowled with reproach and then smiled to let me know she was joking.

"Guilty as charged. You have beautiful legs."

Like she hadn't heard, she said, "Mr Yipp was impressed by you, Ash."

"I'm pleased."

"But you took a big gamble when you hit Wang."

I nodded. "What did Mr Yipp think of that?"

"He didn't say, but I suspect he respects you."

"And Wang? What does he think?"

She laughed. "He's just a thug. I'm pretty sure he will show you more respect in future as well!"

She drove us west along the coast road and felt the fresh wind in our faces.

"Any luck with the Chinese numbers," I asked.

"Four, ten, two, ten? I'm afraid they don't mean anything to me."

"Could four, ten actually mean forty?"

"Yes."

"The police seem to think two ten could be February the tenth. But don't know what four, ten or forty means."

I watched her face and saw no clue that the numbers meant anything to her. A silence grew between us until she made small talk. I wasn't really paying attention when she told me the names of the small islands and bays. I found myself more interested in her profile and flowing black hair than the dark coastline.

I don't know how far we had travelled before she turned the car around. I thought she was going to take me back but we went past Pasir Panjang with Gillman somewhere to our left. Instead she turned into a car park at the foot of a hill.

"Come. I have something to show you."

In contrast to the lights of the city at night, the hill was lit only by the stars. I could see a path leading from the road. Su Ling looped her arm through mine and we walked up.

It was hard to see the path as it wound through dense trees. Gradually they thinned to nothing and we walked up towards a clear, grassy knoll.

At the very top, she sat and patted the ground. "This is Mount Faber. It used to be called Telok Blagah Hill which means Clay Pot, in Malay. I have no idea why it was called that. It should be called something more fitting, more attractive. This is my most favourite spot on the island."

She pointed below us, to the south. "The harbour is there and you can just see the small islands behind it."

We sat down on the warm grass. Through the trees I could just make out a few rooftops and knew that one of them was Commander Alldritt's HQ. The trees ended and the harbour began with its long wall and fence. In the dock, I could see the two funnel troopship, Windrush lit by the orange sodium glow. I could just make out the odd soldier or dockhand moving on the harbour front. I could make out the depots and the offices. Beyond I could see the mounds of jungle in the sea that made up the islands; the smaller, Pulau Brani, was in the foreground to the left. Cargo ships were anchored in between the harbour and islands.

I spotted a patrol boat as it manoeuvred between the ships, on the lookout for illegal activity.

"Lovely," I said.

She pointed north east towards the city. "You're looking the wrong way," she said. "The city's my favourite view."

It was a beautiful display of light patches in the darkness. The city centre was bright with activity. From this radiated the spokes, roads that stretched away, each with their ribbon developments and night-time activity.

The lights sparkled like diamonds and reminded me of a butterfly brooch my mother had worn on special occasions. I could picture her, in happy times, standing resplendent in a ball gown the colour of dark red wine.

"There," Su Ling said, pointing at the body of the spider. "You can make out the Colonial Centre and there is Boat Quay, Clarke Quay to one side and Robertson Quay to the other. The dark area behind the quays is the hill where Fort Canning is. And the Cathay Building is behind that to the left."

We absorbed the view for a few moments in silence. Then she said, "So what was so important this evening that you had to stand me up?"

"Madam Butterfly."

"The opera?" she asked, just like Rahman had.

I explained what was going on and why she'd been nicknamed Madam Butterfly. I also told her about the transvestite we'd captured.

She laughed lightly.

"I suppose it is funny," I said.

"Why haven't I read about the incidents? They sound like front page news."

"The army is embarrassed about it," I said.

She lay back and looked at the stars.

"Could I ask a favour?" I said.

"To see if anyone has information? Because I'm one of them—because I'm Eurasian?"

For a moment I thought she was annoyed. It wasn't what I meant, so I quickly added: "Because you have a lot of contacts."

"All right, I'll see what I can do." Then she patted the ground and I lay next to her.

A dog barked somewhere in the dark.

When she spoke again her voice had a dreamy quality. "Did you know the stars are very important to

169

the Chinese people? Here, without the trees and lights, the night sky is so clear."

She told me the Chinese names of constellations. She moved her hands across the sky in a delicate, sensual way.

"There are four quadrants to the heavens," she said. She pointed them out: White Tiger, Red Bird, Green Dragon and Black Tortoise. He's in control of the monsters."

"It's a nice idea." I had too much of a science education to believe in astrology."

"What? You don't believe that the stars were placed there by the gods? Surely you can see the deliberate patterns? There, you must be able to see the tortoises' beak." She pointed, outlining the image.

"It's a two dimensional illusion, I'm afraid," I said. "Some of those stars are thousands of light years apart and some points in the figures aren't stars at all, but galaxies even further away."

Su Ling looked horrified. And then her face transformed and she laughed. "You are very easy to wind up."

I put my head in my hands with mock distress. When I looked up she looked more serious again.

"So are you a scientist, Ash?"

"I suppose I was at university. It seems such a long time ago now—a different world."

"There are many things that I don't understand, but one that makes no sense to me is how light comes from the stars. I have heard that light is a wave. A wave moves through the sea, sound moves through the air. Surely light moves through the air as well, or is it something called ether?"

"Goodness! You don't pick easy questions, do you?"

She cocked her head to one side and looked into my eyes. "What is the point of easy questions?"

I told her how tests for the ether had failed. Then I tried to explain photons.

She said, "You get very serious when you explain things."

"I'm struggling."

Su Ling turned her face and our noses were just a hand's width apart. She had a mischievous look in her eyes when she said, "Can you explain Einstein's theory of relativity to me, Mr Scientist?"

I had a go but after a minute she stretched and I guessed my explanation wasn't riveting.

When I paused, wondering what else to add, she said, "I know what the problem is, Ash. You should give your explanations with a romantic twist. Tell them as a story."

She turned her attention back to the stars. "For example you could explain relativity by saying there are two lovers. One of them, the beautiful girl, has a terrible illness. Her lover, a brilliant chemist, is working on a cure. However the cure will take too long to find. So the girl gets on the fastest aeroplane in the world and travels. Time goes slower for her..." She checked and I nodded. "The boy finds the cure so that when the beautiful girl returns she has not aged as much and is saved."

"That's excellent," I said.

A fine streak of light briefly stretched across the heavens. Su Ling pointed. "Now tell me about shooting stars."

"Well, they aren't stars at all, but—"

"Oh, you're going to tell me they are just rocks falling through the atmosphere, aren't you!"

"Yes. I'm afraid I'm not very romantic."

"You see," she said, sitting up with a petulant look on her face, "science is no good. I think I prefer the Chinese approach—myths and legends. They are always romantic. Look!" She pointed out two stars that spanned the Milky Way and told me a story about how the Sun Emperor allowed a herdsman to marry his daughter. Later he banished the herdsman to the other side of the Silver River. All the magpies in China were summoned to link their wings so that once a year a bridge could link the two lovers.

I had to admit it was a good story. Not very scientific, but did that matter? Sitting on a hill, under the stars with a beautiful woman, it didn't seem to matter at all.

She told me more stories, getting softer and quieter with increasing pauses, comfortable silences, until it was just her voice rather than the tale that I listened to.

A cool breeze blew off the sea and Su Ling shivered. I took off my jacket and wrapped it around her shoulders. She snuggled close and I knew it wasn't just for warmth.

As she moved to get comfortable, her shape against mine, I felt an electric tingle of desire. I breathed in her exotic scent and closed my eyes.

I thought about the stars and started to see the Chinese gods and spirits moving through the night skies. I opened my eyes. My head was in her lap.

"You've been asleep," she said softly.

"It's been a long day."

"I need to get back. Thank you for spending this time with me."

I stretched and followed her down the hill to the car. She drove me back to the barracks and stopped at the barrier. I climbed out and walked around to her side of the car. She took off my jacket, all the time looking into my eyes. Even though the camp spots cast a harsh light, I thought her eyes were definitely more brown than green tonight.

I leaned forwards and found her leaning towards me. The kiss was tender. It seemed the most natural thing, her lips soft and welcoming.

"Will I see you tomorrow?" she asked.

"Count on it," I said.

As I watched her drive away I wondered about the effect she was having on me. I heard my father's voice telling me that it was all happening too fast, that I didn't really know the girl.

I forced the thoughts out of my mind. I was looking forward to what tomorrow would bring.

However, I was in for a big surprise.

TWENTY-NINE

"Morning, gents," I called as I arrived late at the office.

The desk clerk handed me a message at the same time as I heard Hegarty shout something from the common room.

"Tell me over breakfast," I said leaning into the room.

"At Tanglin again," he said, "because of Sergeant Cooke?"

"What about Sergeant Cooke?"

"Like I said: AWOL. Staff Sergeant Cooke has been reported AWOL this morning."

I asked the desk clerk to call the police station and ask if Inspector Rahman could meet us at Tanglin Barracks.

Ten minutes later we were in Sinclair's office.

"The day before yesterday, I was pissed off with you," he said. "I took it personally but you were just doing your job."

I said, "You've reported Cooke as AWOL. Tell us what happened. How long has he been gone?"

"Over twenty-four hours. They're the regs."

"So missing since the night before last?" I said, disappointed that he'd not reported it sooner.

"Yes. At fifteen-hundred hours Sergeant Cooke asked if he could have a couple of days' pass. He wasn't due any leave and I refused. He should have reported for

174

duty at nineteen-hundred hours but didn't. The gate logged him out fifteen minutes earlier, wearing civvies and carrying a kitbag."

"Do you think we spooked him by rechecking the ledgers?"

"He was twitchy all day," Sinclair said, with a thoughtful nod. "You were irritating, yes, but it didn't warrant his agitation."

"So, what is he hiding? Have some guns gone missing?"

Sinclair briefly looked annoyed but brought it under control.

"As I said, I run a tight ship. There has been no fiddling the books, by Cooke or anyone else. It just couldn't happen."

I thought for a moment then said, "You arrived eight months ago. What were the books like then?"

"A bloody mess."

"And you cleaned it all up."

"Yes. We did a full inventory and brought everything up to date. Even got rid of obsolete stock. It was why Colonel Atkinson wanted me here—to clean it up."

"How long had Cooke been working in the stores?"

"Twenty months."

"So where do you think he would go?"

"I have no idea. We weren't friends."

We sat in silence for a few heart beats then I said, "Anything else?"

Sinclair told us he would think about it, but there was nothing at the moment.

We went to the communications office and I asked for the time Cooke was reported AWOL. They confirmed that Sinclair had been prompt—exactly twenty-four hours after Cooke was seen at the gate. All checkpoints and bases had been notified.

We headed over to the Officers' Mess for breakfast. I said, "Why wasn't I told last night, Hedge?"

"The report came in but the night clerk didn't realize the importance. There was more focus on Madam Butterfly as you'll recall."

I expected him to laugh but he didn't.

"Why the long face?"

"Vernon is on the warpath. I was up late writing up the incident report. Vernon isn't happy we let the police have her... or him."

"But it wasn't the girl."

The waiter took our order of English breakfasts and lashings of tea.

When he'd left, Hegarty said, "Vernon says it could have been."

"Then let him pick her up from the police."

"They've already let Angel go with a warning."

"Angel?"

"The name he gave."

Our food arrived and we ate. Hegarty asked about my date with Su Ling and I told him we'd just gone for a drive along the coast.

I could see he expected more but didn't push it.

After helping himself to my black pudding he said, "So what's next."

"You interview anyone who bunked with Cooke or he was friendly with. Let's find out where he might have gone."

"And you?"

At that point I remembered the note the clerk at Gillman had given me. I pulled it out of my pocket and read:

Meet me at Goodwood Park for lunch? Kisses SL

I put the note in my pocket. Hegarty was watching me.

"You're smiling," he said.

"Am I?"

"So?"

"I was hoping the inspector would meet us here," I said, switching back to our morning. "I'll take the jeep and go over to the police station. I'd like them to look for our missing sergeant too." I also wanted to know whether there had been an update on the customers' names and Tai Tai's condition.

Inspector Rahman said, "When you were at Tanglin, you were trying to unsettle Sinclair, right? But could it be that Sergeant Cooke is missing for a different reason?"

He was sitting at his desk looking hassled, his in-tray pile was higher than I'd seen it before.

I leaned on his wall so he knew I wasn't going to disturb him for long.

I said, "Hell of a coincidence."

"You said that Cooke asked for a pass just before he left. Perhaps he had a personal matter he needed to attend to. Perhaps he thought it would be all right to take time off." Rahman shrugged. "Perhaps he will just walk back into the barracks today and there's been a misunderstanding. I'm just saying this because sometimes we like to think something is more than it really is."

I had to agree the majority of AWOL soldiers reappeared before they were classed as deserters. However it usually occurred when someone was already on leave and returned late. It was rare for an innocent man to just walk out of the barracks.

Despite this, I asked the inspector to put out an *all points* for Cooke. I provided him with details and Rahman disappeared to issue instructions.

When he came back he said, "I've only just been given your message about meeting at Tanglin Barracks. I've let you down again. I'm sorry."

"It's fine. I'd just like us to work closer together. For example, I'd like to go with you to see Tai Tai."

He shook his head. "I was at the hospital again this morning, I'm afraid she is still in a coma. As soon as she comes round, I will have you notified."

"And what news about the mah-jong tiles?"

For a second I thought he didn't know what I was referring to. Then he said, "Ah, yes the members list from House of Tokyo! It was delivered yesterday and there are sixty names. However we have reduced that to twenty-four. These are members who were there within three days of her attack."

"How are you approaching it?"

"We have four teams of two men. They are visiting each of the addresses and interviewing them. Again as soon as I hear something interesting, I will let you know."

I thanked him and we shook. Again I was reminded of how skinny the inspector was, his bones feeling fragile in my hand.

I had taken Hegarty's Land Rover jeep and so was surprised to see him on the steps of the police station. He looked serious.

"What are you doing here?" I asked.

"Vernon ordered me back to base—and to bring you with me."

THIRTY

Eventually, after a long glare, Vernon said, "Last night was a bloody disgrace."

I smiled. "Which one?" I said.

"This is no laughing matter, Carter."

I said nothing.

He then went on a rant about how foolish it was for me to inform the police about Madam Butterfly.

"But they can help us catch her," I said.

"Did it help last night? No it didn't. All it did was embarrass us. The least you could have done was process the woman at our HQ."

"It was a man," I said.

He reddened. "I know it was a man. That just adds insult to injury."

He was silent for a moment and a knock on the door broke the tension. The desk clerk appeared when Vernon eventually answered.

"Sir," the man said nervously, "I have something for Captain Carter."

Vernon said, "It can wait," and waved the man away.

He immediately turned his attention back to me and seemed to have calmed down. He smiled.

"I'm sure it isn't really urgent. Please give me a quick update on your progress with the security issue that Coates is worried about."

"None," I said.

"None? But you've been doing a lot of running around. And what's this I hear about you upsetting our friends at Keppel Harbour?"

"I just wanted to find out who was driving a car on a certain night."

Vernon shook his head. "I can't have you investigating personal matters, Carter. Understand? I especially can't have you upsetting Commander Alldritt. The Navy at Keppel are the funnel—an important part of our operation—the shipped and stored goods, the men troops to and from warzones."

I shrugged and could see Vernon didn't like it.

He said, "You won't upset them again."

I said nothing.

"Commander Alldritt doesn't want you setting foot in the controlled area. And, quite frankly, I'm forbidding you as well."

He studied me as though trying to read my thoughts. Then he added: "Whilst you are acting like an MP, you are going to behave like an MP. And number one that means you'll not upset the Navy at Keppel. Got it?"

I said, "Yes," but didn't mean it. I'd get what I wanted and didn't care how.

He nodded, satisfied.

"So tell me about the symbol: the lion's paw in the circle."

"It's possibly a Chinese Secret Society or Triad mark. Yipp denies it's anything to do with him or any knowledge of it."

"What about the guns?"

I had no doubt that Vernon knew about my prodding about at Tanglin Barracks. "No sign of any missing from us."

"Have you thought about the merchant quays? Guns could be smuggled in as some other goods. Maybe the Chinese are getting them through there."

"It's possible," I said.

"And what's this I hear about you going over and over the documentation at Tanglin?"

"I wanted to make a hundred per cent sure—and see what would happen. The junior quartermaster has gone AWOL."

"And you think it's linked?"

I could sense he was dubious but trying to hide it.

"It could be a coincidence," I said.

"All right," he said in a friendly tone, "carry on. Keep following leads on Secretary Coates's security issue and solve the bloody Butterfly case. But—" he switched to his usual voice "—no more personal investigations and no more upsetting the navy."

When I left the major's office, the desk clerk was practically hopping from foot to foot outside.

"Captain," he said excitedly, "I have two things for you."

He handed me a piece of paper that I opened up. On it was a list of twelve names.

"From Colonel Atkinson," the clerk explained.

This was the list of naval officers that I'd requested. I thanked the clerk and asked what the other thing was.

"Lieutenant Robshaw and Sergeant Hegarty have gone to Woodlands Crossing."

This was the causeway, the only land route to Malaya.

"And?" I prompted.

"You should meet them there. Apparently your AWOL warrant office has been spotted. Sergeant Cooke may have tried to cross."

THIRTY-ONE

Finding a driver, I headed north on the main road through the island and watched a constant flow of traffic coming the other way.

After we passed through a village called Bukit Timah, my driver, a young lad called Private Evans, said it was how far the Japanese had made it with limited resistance when they invaded.

"Caught us by surprise, they did," he explained. "The Japs just cycled over the causeway while our guns were pointed out to sea."

I had heard the story about the guns.

He continued: "But that wasn't the issue really. The shells were armour-piercing not explosive. When the guns were turned inland they had little impact."

He told me that it only took a week for Singapore to fall and mentioned that the first attack was met by Australian battalions and 44th Indian Infantry. Then he went on to tell me in great detail about the Jurong Line and the battle on the high ground of Bukit Timah. It had been short lived because the line was too thin and collapsed.

Private Evans was undoubtedly the expert that Hegarty had referred to.

When he paused, I said, "I saw the holes at Tanglin where someone was executed for cowardice."

"Just a rumour. Allegedly a group deserted their position at Bukit Timah and their ringleader was executed. It might be confused with a misunderstanding of orders that caused the line to break up because I've never read anything to back up the story."

He went back to telling me details of the invasion and strategic errors, clearly used to the sound of his own voice and pleased to have a captive audience.

When he started talking as though he relished the idea of Malaya turning into a conflict like Korea, I tuned him out and thought about Cooke.

Had the sergeant gone AWOL because of our pressure on the quartermaster's office or was it something totally unconnected? If he had been at the crossing, had he gone straight there and what transportation had he used? There were plenty of trucks on the road and hitching seemed commonplace.

We had been travelling on laterite-covered roads through uninterrupted jungle. Suddenly the surface changed to concrete and the jungle thinned. We rounded a corner and I could see the Woodlands Crossing post. There was a queue of people and vehicles. In front of them, the road was blocked by a checkpoint. A short distance ahead, a second set blocked the causeway. There were three wooden huts: two for accommodation and one an office for processing people crossing into Singapore. There was a separate, more substantial Customs building.

My driver scooted around to the head of the queue. After a brief word with the guard, the first barrier was raised for us and we were directed to a parking spot next to another jeep and a troop carrier.

Robshaw and Hegarty were there talking to a tall soldier. They waved me over and I was introduced to a lieutenant in charge of the post.

"There's been a sighting of Sergeant Cooke?" I asked.

Hegarty said, "Night before last I'm afraid."

The lieutenant said, "We've only just been issued with the bulletin and called it in straight away."

I asked my driver to wait in the jeep and the lieutenant led us into the office and introduced us to Private Allen.

"Allen here is the one who recognized our man."

"At least I think so," Allen said nervously.

We sat down and I said, "Tell us what happened, soldier."

"Two nights ago," the man began, "I'd been on duty since nineteen-hundred hours. It was busy... busier than usual. We'd had a lorry breakdown on the causeway so there was quite a queue of traffic."

He paused, perhaps envisaging the evening.

The lieutenant said, "Go on. What did you see?"

"There was a car in the line that turned around just before it got to the front. I thought it was a bit odd. I mean, why queue for a good half an hour and then give up? So I shone the light at it and saw his face. Only I didn't realize it was his face, of course."

"But you remembered it," I said.

"Yes. I thought he looked familiar. Turns out he's from the Stores at Tanglin, so I'll have seen him there."

"Although you didn't recognize him at the time?"

The lieutenant chipped in, "There's almost a thousand men at Tanglin..."

The private said, "It wasn't until I saw the AWOL bulletin that I realized who it was. He'd been in civvies and we see so many people up here."

I nodded.

"What time was this?"

"Must have been about two. It was definitely before two-thirty-six."

"Two-thirty-six," the lieutenant confirmed, "that was when we heard the gun shots from across the water. Every time there's potential bandit activity over the way, we have to report it. The shots were at two-thirty-six that night."

To the private I said, "What else can you tell us? What about the type of car?"

"Sorry, I've tried to remember..."

The lieutenant said, "Allen, tell them what happened next."

"The car drove off. South. Only I'm not sure it did."

"What do you mean?" I asked.

"Well, after he turned around, he drove slowly away but then the rear lights went out. I was still watching, see, wondering what on earth was going on."

"Show us. Let's go outside and show us where you were standing and where the car was."

We walked out of the office and stood by the first barrier.

"I was on the causeway side," Allen said. He pointed to a truck third in line on the left hand side of the road. "The car was where the truck is now. I didn't pay it any heed until it was side on in a three-point turn. That's when I shone my torch at the window."

"From here?"

"No, I started walking towards it as it pulled out of the line. At first I thought he was going to overtake. You know, every now and then someone tries to queue jump. I was also a bit nervous, though if there was ever going to be any trouble, it would be from the other side, right?"

I looked up the road. The queue went around the bend about one hundred and fifty yards ahead.

"You say the lights went out. Could he have just driven around the corner so you couldn't see the lights anymore?"

For a moment the private looked uncertain.

The lieutenant prompted him: "How far along do you think the car got before the lights went out?"

"Maybe a hundred yards. I can't be sure. It was pretty dark. It could have sped up I suppose."

We left the lieutenant and private and walked back up the road on the left hand side, the queue of traffic on our right.

"It's very odd," Hegarty said.

I had to agree. "What was he up to?"

The other two didn't respond. We got to a hundred yards out and looked back at the post. The private signalled we should go a little further. We walked another twenty.

Robshaw rubbed at his blond hair. "The chap's mistaken. Cooke drove away. The lights didn't go off. Why would they?"

I was looking at the ground, reminded of the location where my friend's car had been driven off the road. Unlike that site, there was no verge here, but the ground beside the concrete was soft.

"Let's keep walking," I said.

We were out of sight of the guard post when I stopped and checked the ground. A car had recently driven over it.

"But we're round the bend," Hegarty said in response to me pointing it out. "Allen told us the lights went out well before."

"But maybe he didn't stop straight away. Maybe he saw where he wanted to stop and turned the lights out early."

Robshaw looked back the way we'd come. "You think he parked here and snuck back on foot?"

"No," I said, pointing to the trees. "I think he went that way."

The other two shook their heads as though I were mad. But it looked like there was a route through the undergrowth and between the trees.

I could sense they were sceptical but they followed me into the jungle.

"It's an animal path," Hegarty said behind me just as I spotted something.

"That's the oddest looking animal track I've ever seen," I said and pointed to a footprint.

Hegarty checked it against his own boot. "About size, nine," he said. "Could be Cooke."

We kept walking and I could see clear signs that something human-sized had been through here. Branches were bent back and broken. We also found a footprint going the opposite way, which puzzled me.

"Perhaps he wasn't sure of the way?" Robshaw suggested.

"Maybe he doubled back or we've missed a turn he made?"

The trail suggested he'd carried on, at least for a while and so did we.

We covered about a mile when I asked, "Where does this eventually come out do you think?"

"The main naval base is on the north coast," Robshaw said. "But that's quite a few miles further."

"At night, walking through this jungle on a difficult trail. Why?" I asked more to myself than the others.

Then Robshaw said, "The water."

We could see the straits through the trees and the path was now heading for it. There was a slight clearing with a churned up muddy area. Again size nine boots.

We looked around and decided he hadn't continued along the coast. There were two options: Cooke had doubled back into the undergrowth or he had gone into the water.

"He swam for it," Hegarty suggested. "He couldn't cross at the causeway for fear of being recognized so he swam across."

We decided to keep on going, just in case Cooke had gone into the water and had come out again further along. We walked for another ten minutes and then Robshaw spotted something in the water. It was snagged on a submerged branch.

After a bit of complaining, Hegarty removed his boots and socks, and waded in. The water was splashing the hem of his shorts by the time he reached the object.

"What is it?" I called.

"Could be..." he started to say as he tugged the item free. "Yes it is. It's a kitbag!"

He struggled back, dragging the bag behind him.

It was sodden, but securely tied and Robshaw and I left it with the sergeant as we scoured the bank for any sign of Cooke having come out of the water further along.

When we got back, Hegarty was standing on the track with his boots on again. The kitbag was leaning against a tree.

"OK," I said, "let's get this bag to Gillman and see what we've got."

THIRTY-TWO

Only Hegarty could have shown such enthusiasm as he tipped everything from the kitbag onto a table in the shared office. He separated out the sodden clothes into civilian and army. The army fatigues had the name William Cooke written in them. Definitely his bag then.

Along with the clothes, there were some personal items but the main interest was a plastic bag. Inside was a wad of documents and a significant amount of money. Some of the money was Chinese but the majority was Sterling.

Hegarty counted it. Fifty British pounds—a considerable sum in those days.

The documents included his British passport, a bundle that appeared legal and a letter. Except for the passport, they all looked to be in Chinese.

"Blimey," Hegarty said. "He really was deserting then."

"What do you think?" Robshaw asked me.

"Maybe," I said. I was distracted by the empty kitbag that now lay on the floor where Hegarty had dumped it. The crumpled canvas didn't look quite natural.

I picked it up. There was a hard edge where there shouldn't have been one. I turned the bag inside out to investigate and found a pouch sewn into the side near the bottom. When I cut the seam a book fell out. A pocket sized ledger. It was sodden, but I managed to open it without destroying the pages. It was a record book with dates and numbers. I also noted Greek letters against each entry.

Hegarty waited for me to look up before he said, "What now, Boss?"

"Do your best to dry these wet pages. I'm taking the rest of the papers and going to lunch." I was thinking about Su Ling's message. "Would you drop me at Goodwood Park?"

Goodwood Park was a classy building close to the botanic gardens. The atmosphere inside was of a bygone era, the nineteen-twenties, perhaps.

The lounge area had elegant furniture, with a lot of wood and shiny brass. The clientele was as classy as the building. I didn't think of myself as a snob, but it was just nice to escape the rowdiness of most of the Singapore bars.

A Malay boy played beautifully on a grand piano, just loud enough to be heard and quiet enough to be background noise while the customers talked about the price of rubber, the next amateur theatre production, where the next dance was to be held or who the latest entertainment for a great garden party should be. I heard no talk of war and I suspected that the same set had been no different as the Japanese prepared to invade a decade earlier.

The only negative was the pall of cigarette smoke which clung to the ceiling like an inverted grey carpet.

I chose a table for two by the doors to the garden so that I could breathe the cleaner air. While I waited for Su Ling, I ordered sparkling water and glanced at the menu.

191

A German gentleman with a thin but friendly smile introduced himself and shook my hand. He knew Pope and had heard about the incident at the market on my first day.

"And how is his daughter?" I asked.

"She's fully recovered," the man said. "May I join you?"

I explained I was waiting for someone and he took that as an invitation to sit and wait with me.

"This used to be known as the German Club," he said as he was poured a glass of wine. "Before the war that is." He laughed and I found him affable.

"If you don't mind me asking, do you come across anything anti-German here?" I was thinking about the Japanese again and whether there was an anti-war issue.

"Not here."

"I mean Singapore generally."

He grinned. "Oh I thought you meant the club, here. No, not really... unless you count the soldiers."

"The soldiers?"

"Nothing specific. You know, they can get a bit rowdy and they still hate us. But I've never had any real trouble."

"And what about the Japanese?"

"It is similar," he said and I thought his smile looked sad. "Of course you had first-hand experience of the soldiers but there is a bit more because of the history. We call it *Hassliebe*—there is a love-hate relationship between the Japanese and Chinese on the island."

We made small talk until I became distracted. Su Ling had entered the club and I couldn't take my eyes off her. The German shook my hand again and gave me his thin, friendly smile. But then between his teeth he said something strange.

"Be careful of that one."

He retreated to the bar and I turned my attention to Su Ling as she approached my table.

She was dressed in a stunning royal blue silk cheongsam with cream trim. The wrist strap also had a matching trim. No longer the party girl from the night before, once more the consummate Chinese business-lady.

I stood and leaned forward to kiss her but she reached out and took my hand in a gesture of formality.

"Just for appearances," she said with a mischievous smile. "Who was your friend?"

I glanced over at the man who was now chatting to someone at another table.

"A barfly, I suspect."

She seemed to study him before focusing her attention back on me.

"Have you eaten?"

I shook my head. "I was waiting for you."

"Eggs Benedict," she said. "Not very Chinese, I know, but I can recommend it highly."

It sounded good to me so we both ordered and she asked for a glass of wine.

We sat in silence for a while and I found myself staring at her.

She took a sip of wine. "Do you know the story of Pavlova?" she asked, breaking the spell and pointing to a photograph behind the bar.

I knew Pavlova was a famous Russian ballerina but that was the limit of my knowledge. I shook my head.

"The photograph is signed because she once danced here at the Goodwood Park!" There was a girlish thrill to her voice as she continued: "The story goes that she was due to dance at the town hall, which is an appropriate and auspicious venue. However when she arrived the hall had been booked by an amateur dramatics society.

Can you imagine? They insisted that Gilbert and Sullivan was more important than any dancing! So as a result Pavlova danced here at the Goodwood on a small stage. It was totally impromptu!"

"You like ballet?"

"Can you tell?"

I smiled. "You look like a ballerina."

"I'm too tall," she said and then added, "Actually I'd rather not talk about it."

For a moment there was an awkward silence.

"That flyer..." she started.

"Yes."

"You said the police thought it might be a date."

"Yes."

She looked at me for a moment and I was again drawn into her eyes that were definitely green.

"What?" I said.

She said, "Forty is nineteen fifty-two. It's the fortieth year since the nationalist democratic revolution—when China became a republic. Forty, February tenth is Lantern's Day, this year."

That made sense. The forty was just part of the date. But that didn't equate to proof of an attack of some kind. Su Ling was clearly thinking along the same lines.

She said, "It could be something to do with the carnival or parade. There will be a lot of lion dancers. So the flyer may just be something innocent.

"You may be right," I said with a smile. "There's something else I want your help with."

"Of course. Anything."

"A soldier went AWOL a couple of nights ago. Today we found his things. They were in the water up near Woodlands Crossing."

"And I can help you how?"

"I'd like you to translate something." I picked up the pack of documents that I had by my feet.

Su Ling stared in fascination as I separated a heavy parchment with Chinese style writing on it and a seal.

"This is a Chinese trading document," she said. "And these..." she took the remaining sheets from his hand and glanced over them, "these are travel documents, rites of passage, for someone called Wan Song Lei."

Wan Song Lei was also the name on the passport. I had a strong suspicion that it was Cooke's new identity.

She continued after studying them closely: "They are all official although I suspect they are forged. I can have them checked if it's of help."

"Not for now, but I'll bear it in mind if I need to."

"And this was in your AWOL soldier's things?"

"In his kitbag."

"What did the soldier say about them?"

"We haven't found him yet."

"Oh, I suppose that doesn't look good then... I mean if you found his things but not the man."

I shook my head and handed Su Ling some more papers.

While she read through, I studied her face. Eventually she looked up and commented: "Various correspondence in Chinese addressed to the same person specified in the travel documents: Wan Song Lei. One of these is about passage to Hong Kong from Singapore. It's for a Filipino cargo boat that is due to leave tomorrow night."

That made me suspect Cooke had planned to leave tomorrow but, for some reason, brought it forward by three days. I wondered why. Did he leave earlier than planned because of my appearance at Tanglin? Why was he going to Hong Kong?

I handed her the letter written on lilac paper.

"This isn't Chinese is it?"

Su Ling took a quick glance to confirm that the language was Japanese. She read through a page then flicked through and read a later one. She smiled. "It's a love letter. Or at least part of one."

"Part?"

"It just seems to start, as though the first page or pages are missing."

"Our soldier is called William or Billy Cooke."

She shook her head then put the paper to her nose before handing it to me to do the same. It smelled faintly of flowers.

"I am certain this is a letter from a young Japanese woman to her lover. She talks of wanting to be with him and the difficulty of their situation. She says she understands how hard it must be for him and that she can only tell her best friend. But they will one day be together and the trade will help."

"What trade?" I said, thinking out loud.

"Wait, I'll read it more thoroughly."

I gave her time and ate my lunch. When she finished, she put the letter down and took a drink.

"It's all quite lovely," she said. "There is no detail about the trade or their jobs or anything personal like that. But there is reference to friends in Hong Kong who can help. I think they planned to travel there and then on to Japan. They were planning to elope. Your AWOL soldier was leaving to be with the love of his life. It's very romantic."

I wondered whether they had been together that night at Woodlands. Had a boat been waiting for them at the jungle's edge. That didn't explain why Cooke's bag was in the water. Unless he'd lost it in the dark. I supposed it could have gone overboard.

"Is there a name? Did she sign it?"

196

"No."

"That's a shame," I said. "I wonder whether they were together the night he was at the causeway."

Su Ling asked how my investigation was going.

"I've found no evidence of the security risk or smuggled guns," I said.

"I meant, about your friend. You said he was forced off the road by another car. Have you found out any more?"

I told her about what Hegarty and I had seen at the crash site; how it looked like the other car had crashed on the opposite side.

"There's a chance it's one of the navy's staff cars."

"Really?" she said. "Can you find out who was driving?"

"I have a list of potential names." Having shared the other documents, it felt natural to show her the list I'd been sent by Colonel Atkinson.

It had names, ranks and Atkinson had helpfully split it by location. Seven of the permanent officers were based at the Keppel HQ. The rest were at the naval base in the north. I reckoned I was down to seven suspects.

She said, "I don't recognize any of these names."

I didn't expect her to. I could see Commander Alldritt at the top of the seven. The name at the bottom seemed familiar. When Su Ling passed the list back to me I read the name the right way up. Lieutenant John Pantelis. I'd seen that name before: on the shipping documentation. Goods In at Keppel Harbour. Signed for and distributed to Tanglin. Signed for as delivered by Sinclair or Cooke.

"What are you thinking?" Su Ling said.

"Just wondering." I hadn't told Su Ling about the pocket ledger we'd found hidden in the bottom of the kitbag. The pages I could open looked like an order book or sales record.

197

"I'm probably just focused on one name because of the AWOL guy, Sergeant Cooke. He worked in the stores and so does this chap on the list. I've seen his initials on everything. It all comes through Keppel."

"You think he's connected in some way to your friend's death?"

"I don't know, but he's just gone to the top of my list of people I'd like to talk to. Only..."

"Yes?"

"I need to find a way to talk to him because I've been banned from Keppel—the navy controlled part anyway."

That gave me an idea. I could try an alternative approach. Dress differently so I didn't look like an MP. Providing the guy at the gate was someone else, maybe I'd get through.

Su Ling said, "I could find out about him, if you like?"

After thanking her for the suggestion I asked if I could see her tonight. "Perhaps we could go dancing at one of the Worlds?"

She smiled and I guessed my suggestion didn't enthral her. "Not this evening," she said. "I have other business tonight. Maybe tomorrow night if you are free."

As we left, I noticed the German watching me out of the corner of his eye.

THIRTY-THREE

Risk is about playing the odds and understanding the consequences. In civilian clothes and with a fedora pulled low over my brow, I walked past the guard at Keppel. I flashed my government ID and hoped he wouldn't look too closely. I was sure my name would be on his exclusion list. Worst case, he would realize who I was and stop me.

He didn't, the gate came up and I was through.

I walked smartly past the Stores Depot and kept going just in case the guard was watching.

Outside the engineers' shed I stopped and looked in. Everyone seemed busy. The gaffer came over and explained they had a problem so couldn't spare any time.

"Not a problem," I said. After all I was just filling in time. "I just wanted to let you know I was still investigating Tom's death."

"Any progress?"

"Maybe," I said. "Just a quick question: did Tom know a sergeant from Tanglin Barracks?"

He shrugged.

"William Cooke," I said. "Probably better known as Billy Cooke."

"Not a name I've heard."

He apologized for the brevity and I watched as he went back to supervising his team.

I delayed a few minutes more and then headed out into the bright sunshine again. I walked back towards the gate, but this time kept close to the buildings, keeping a low profile.

When I came to the Stores Depot, I slipped sideways and entered. The room was a long thin warehouse, crammed with shelves, boxes and crates. Before I could take a step further, a naval officer confronted me.

"Can I help?"

"Lieutenant Pantelis?" I asked.

He considered me with calculating eyes. I guessed him to be in his early thirties, good looking with a thin moustache, and could have probably got a job on the silver screen as a younger version of Errol Flynn. The only thing letting down his appearance was a grubby wedge of a plaster above his right eye.

I reached out and offered my hand.

"Ash Carter," I said.

"How can I help you?"

Rather that shake my hand, he assumed a pose with arms across his chest.

I ignored the rudeness, smiled and said, "Pantelis, that's a Turkish name isn't it?"

I knew about the long-running tension between the Greeks and Turks and thought my deliberate mistake would definitely prompt a response. It did.

He bristled and said, "It's a Greek name. I was born in Brentford but my family is from Piraeus." Then he appraised my appearance and said, "What can I do for you?"

I looked around him. There were four rows of shelves that ran floor to ceiling—about twenty-five feet up. At the far end there seemed to be a filing section and to the left were rooms, possibly offices.

I side stepped him and headed for the offices.

"Hey... you can't just come in here!"

There were three rooms. The doors were half glass, half metal and each room had a large window. No problem seeing out. No problem seeing in.

In the first office I saw a desk, chairs, cabinets and shelves. The cabinets and shelves were crammed with files. The second office also had cabinets, but in the centre of the room was a wide table with maps. There were eight foldable chairs and pinned to the wall was a giant map showing the East Asian Seas.

Pantelis bustled after me, continuing to complain. I ignored him.

The third room had his name on the door. I stepped inside. There was a large desk with an in and out-tray, a blotter and a telephone. Behind the desk were shelves with rows and rows of box files, and against the wall was a metal filing cabinet.

He stepped between me and the desk.

I said, "Where do you keep your most sensitive records?"

His eyes flicked right. An involuntary reflex.

Then his eyes narrowed then he said, "What?"

"Where do you keep the record of your little trades? You know, the black market stuff?"

"Get out!" he barked. He moved around his desk and picked up the telephone. I guessed it was connected directly to the HQ since there was no to and fro with an operator.

Into the phone he said there was a man bothering him. He listened and then said, "He said his name is Carter."

"Ash Carter," I said.

201

He listened again and then replaced the handset. He had a smug smile on his face when he said, "I would leave now if I were you."

"I know."

"You know what?" He sat in his chair and tried to look important, maybe immune.

"I know what you're up to."

Momentarily I saw real fear in his eyes and knew I was right.

"Billy Cooke," I said.

He glared at me and for a second and I thought he was going to say something. Maybe explain or justify himself, but then he looked over my shoulder and grinned.

Two men ran into the stores, their boots echoing in the warehouse like rapid fire. The office door opened.

"Sir?"

It was the Master-at-Arms from the gate with another guard behind him.

He said, "Let's have no trouble, sir. We are going to escort you off the dock."

I leaned on Pantelis's desk and glared at him. The man's chair was on wheels and he pushed back a few inches.

"I'll find out," I said. "Trust me, I will."

At my shoulder, I sensed the guard preparing to grab me and probably try a *come-along* hold. I raised my hands and turned. I nodded to him, one military cop to another.

"Don't worry I'm going," I said and stepped away from the desk. The guard in the office stepped aside as did the one on the other side of the door as I exited.

They followed me to the gate and watched me walk up Anson Road in the direction of the centre.

On the face of it I could have been disappointed that I'd had so little time with the Navy Stores lieutenant. However I now knew what he looked like. And secondly, I'd confirmed a connection with Cooke.

THIRTY-FOUR

Trishaws were everywhere and I hailed one and asked to be taken to Hill Street police station.

Inspector Rahman wasn't immediately available so I stood on Coleman Bridge and enjoyed the afternoon sun watching the boats ferrying goods up and down the river.

A strong smell of rubber wafted up as a row of *tongkangs,* heavily laden with dark grey bales, passed under the bridge heading out to a waiting ship. Today there was also spice in the air: cinnamon, cloves, maybe nutmeg.

I was lost in my thoughts when a voice said, "Wonderful!"

I turned to see the inspector approaching.

He said, "This, for me, is Singapore. Enterprise, enthusiasm, colours and smells to fill your senses to bursting."

"You're a poet, Inspector."

"I really wish you would just call me Anand. And perhaps one day I *will* write poetry," he said wistfully, "but for now there is a job to be done. You have some news perhaps?"

I told him that we had found Cooke's kitbag in the water. But that he was still AWOL.

"Oh dear, I hope that doesn't mean he has drowned. The Straits aren't wide but I for one wouldn't like to swim across."

"There is a possibility he wasn't alone."

"Oh?"

"He may have been with a girl. A Japanese girl."

"You seem to be coming across the Japanese a great deal," he said, "but I am certain it is just a coincidence."

I was less convinced and asked, "Any news of Tai Tai or tracing who hit her yet?"

"I am afraid she has still not woken up and no, we continue to check through the list of members. Of course her assailant may not be a member, but I am hopeful."

"I mentioned the possible date on the flyer to Su Ling."

"And?"

"She said forty means something. It's been forty years since the Chinese revolution so it could be a date. The tenth of February is the end of the Chinese New Year— Lantern's Day."

"Oh goodness, that's the day of the parade! Do you think...?"

I shook my head. I didn't know what it meant. Was it about an attack? Was it something less sinister?

We stood with our hands on the railing looking at the river. I watched a grey inflatable dinghy pull up at the steps and pushed the problem to the back of my brain for processing.

Two policemen tied up the dinghy and headed for the station. The front of my brain was thinking about something else.

"You have a boat?"

"We've got a few. It's not just Customs who need to get out onto the water."

"In that case," I said, "I have a favour to ask."

* * *

It was a long way but I decided to walk back to Gillman so that I could think. On the way, I found a shop selling working men's clothes and bought a black top and trousers.

The clouds swept quickly across the sky until the sun was blanketed out. What had started as a stroll became a brisk walk as I watched the sky darken.

I was almost half way back when it began to rain. My hat did little to keep the rain off me and I was soon soaked. A troop carrier went past and, because of my civvies, I didn't get a second glance. However, minutes later, I was lucky to flag down a trishaw.

The poor cyclist pounded away through the sheeting rain as though it weren't there.

It was still raining when I was dropped at the barracks and gave him a big tip for his efforts. He seemed embarrassed by the money and for a split second I thought he was going to give it back.

I climbed the hill to the officers' quarters and something made me glance back. I don't know why. Maybe it was sixth sense because he was still there. Watching me.

I was still wondering whether I had done something odd to warrant the trishaw driver's attention when I spotted a bedraggled soldier marching around the parade ground. What was the idiot doing, in full kit, square bashing in the rain?

I diverted towards him and, rounding the main accommodation block, found two soldiers sheltering under the arches, watching the man on the parade ground.

"It's not right," one said loud enough so that I could hear.

"What's not right?" I asked.

"Making Franks do that."

I learned that Franks—the young man on the parade ground—had been in the sun this morning and burnt his back. Major Vernon had spotted him and put him on *jankers*. As an example. But not just any punishment. This was deliberate. Franks was supposed to suffer and he was because the heavy straps dug into his burns.

I walked over and told him to stop. He stood to attention and tried to pretend he hadn't been crying.

"At ease," I said and he almost collapsed.

I helped him off with his pack.

"Thank you, sir," he said, "but I've only done sixty-four." He wiped rain water and tears from his eyes before continuing: "I'm supposed to keep going for a hundred and fifty."

I told him he'd done the full distance and to report to M.I. room and get his sunburn checked out. I also said I'd make sure it was all signed off.

The poor man started to cry again. His mates came over. One took the pack whilst the other put his arm around Franks and supported him.

I was fuming and instead of getting into dry clothes, went to the office block intending to confront Vernon. He wasn't there so I ranted at Robshaw instead. I knew I was being unreasonable, it wasn't the lieutenant's fault. Vernon was the CO. It would have to be pretty bad for one of his officers to defy him. It would be one man against another and, in my experience, the senior officer always won such battles.

"Is it common?" I asked once I'd calmed down.

"Pretty much," Robshaw said. "He's quite sadistic... or being generous maybe he's just thoughtless. He thinks it's a stronger message to make someone suffer because of their stupidity. The equivalent of an eye for an eye. Hurt your hand, he'll make you use it. Get ringworm, he'll make you wear wet clothes. And Private Franks is a classic: get sunburn and carry a heavy load so it hurts like hell."

"Heavy load?"

"There will have been a rock in the man's pack."

I shook my head in disgust. "It's going to stop," I said. "Before I leave here, I'm going to make sure of that."

On reflection, I was glad Vernon hadn't been there because I wasn't ready to declare my hand. I would confront him at the right time, on my terms.

Cooke's book was now dry and I picked it up. I flicked through it as I walked back to my room but I was in no mood to do any work for the rest of the day. The sun was out and I hadn't exercised much in the morning so I did my full routine, went for a run along the coast road and then a swim in the pool at the barracks.

I ate dinner alone and went to bed early, setting my alarm for one in the morning.

THIRTY-FIVE

Hoping I looked inconspicuous, I crossed Coleman Bridge. I wore the black clothes I'd bought earlier. The top fitted comfortably although the trousers were too short. My belt didn't really match but I needed it for my torch. However, it was dark except for the well-spaced sodium lamps, and the smattering of people on the street didn't seem interested in my strange attire.

The Singapore River was slick-black with the boats strung across its width for the night. A constant low creak and groan came from below as the boats moved against one another.

On the far side of the bridge I spotted the dinghy at the foot of the steps. I'd asked the inspector for a favour and he'd arranged for the boat to be left for me.

The engine started on my second pull on the cord and I untied from the quay. Within seconds I was under Elgin Bridge and following the channel between tied up boats. The river snaked like a reverse S as it widened and then curved back and narrowed under the Cavenagh footbridge and then immediately under Anderson.

At the promontory, I swung west into the inner roads. The wind was now in my face and water splashed up, stinging my eyes. There were few lights on the water and the little dinghy bounced through inky darkness. I could see the piers, Floating Pier and Clifford Pier, and beyond them the lights of Empire Docks. But I didn't hug the shore. Instead I found a line of anchored ships and followed those.

Even if someone saw me out here, I reckoned they would pay no attention. It was just a police boat on a typical patrol after all.

Initially, the vessels were small and Asian. After a few hundred yards the small ships were replaced by huge cargo boats sailing under flags of many countries.

When I was in line with the end of Keppel Harbour, I turned off the engine.

The Windrush was no longer in dock. In its place was a two funnel American troopship, the USS General William Weigel. It was probably returning from Korea, overladen with maybe four or even five thousand men on board. Many would be wounded and I knew the worst would have been taken to Alexandra Hospital on the island.

The giant American ship dominated the quay and was midway between the cargo docks at the far end and the depots and offices nearest me. A handful of people on the quayside looked like dock workers. I could see the guard at the gate and there was a US MP—we called them *snowdrops* on account of their white helmets—talking to him. I watched as the snowdrop walked to the ship and stood by the gangplank. He seemed relaxed enough and I judged that he wasn't waiting for men returning late from shore leave. The arrival of more MPs with stragglers would have seriously hampered what I had planned.

I decided against the engine and used a paddle to cross the channel. I aimed for the end of the harbour where a double fence ran from the road to the water, separating the public and secure docks.

Just inside the fence, the buildings started, ghostly in the faint sodium lights. My target was halfway between the fence and the troopship. I tied up at the fence and watched the dock. The snowdrop was about eighty yards away and walking towards me. At the end of the troopship, he turned and I decided he was just patrolling to relieve boredom. I'd done it myself many times.

He was now facing the other way and no one else was looking so I pulled myself onto the quay and jogged to the sheds

Once there, I stood still, waiting in the shadows. No one had reacted to my run and I began to move along the edge of the building.

Twenty yards from the Stores Depot, I flattened myself against the woodwork. The building's door opened, shedding a wedge of light onto the quay. A man stepped out and closed the door. He walked to the adjacent building and was gone. A clerk or night watchman maybe? I couldn't tell.

I ran lightly to the door that had just been opened. This was the risky part: I had no idea if there would be someone else inside. Would Pantelis be standing there like last time?

I slipped in and closed the door behind me. I was alone.

This time I could take a proper look around. Six light bulbs hung from the ceiling. They weren't overly bright, but their wide brimmed shades reflected what there was downwards making the most of the illumination.

It was a well organised shed. Pallets with boxes were piled in four rows. Each row had a ladder to reach the highest shelves. As I'd noted last time, the rooms were on the left and I could see metal filing cabinets at the rear. It was a typical quartermaster's store, but bigger and everything was boxed rather than on display and

211

ready for distribution. The one obvious thing that was missing was a secure area. There was no armoury section.

I took a quick look at the labels on nearby boxes to confirm they were the usual paraphernalia then switched my attention to the rooms.

I passed the first office that was more of a storage room, the second which was probably a meeting room, and then stopped at the third door: Pantelis's office.

A quick try of the handle told me the door was locked. Expert lock-pickers made it look so easy but this was navy property and I didn't think it was even worth a try. I took out my torch, reversed it and hit the glass near the door handle. The breaking sound seemed loud in the otherwise silent warehouse, but I didn't pause. If I was caught, I was caught. There was no point being caught half-hearted.

I extracted some shards and eased my hand through the hole I'd made. A flick of the latch and I was in.

To the right of the door were two switches—one for the office, one for the shed lights. I switched off all the lights and used the torch.

Moving fast, I pulled a ledger from the nearest cabinet. It was a record of cargo, goods on ships and cargo transferred to the docks. I pulled another and another. They were the same. I moved onto a row of lever arch folders. Although I had never been involved with shipping cargo, I surmised these were bills of lading—originals that would support the ledger entries.

I pulled out a different style of ledger. This one had financial records relating to customs duty. Another I checked looked like fees for storage at the docks. Big business, I thought, although why companies brought goods to Singapore to be stored and then shipped away later, I didn't know.

As quickly as I could, I flicked through the remaining folders and ledgers. Nothing leapt out at me as interesting. I shone the torch on the desk. It was an ugly grey metal functional thing and immaculately tidy. There was a blotter and a pen holder, containing a number of perfectly sharpened pencils. The desk had two drawers—one small, at the top, and a larger one beneath.

I opened the top drawer to find stationery items. I picked up a metal ruler and closed the drawer.

The second drawer was locked. A small chrome keyhole top left of the bottom drawer. I placed the ruler in the gap between the drawers, just above the lock and tried to work it from side to side. Nothing gave.

I pulled my sleeve down to protect my hand, positioned the ruler against the internal lever and punched the other end with my palm. This time there was a crack, metal snapping from metal, and the drawer opened slightly.

I shone the torch over the contents. It was a neat pile of five identical, hand-sized books with grey covers. I took out the first. It was another ledger with entries entered in the same fashion as the stock movement log at Tanglin Barracks. This was Pantelis's equivalent record.

I removed the other four and for the first time saw a sixth book. This one was half the size and black.

I flicked through the larger ones to confirm that they were identical to the first but with different dates on the covers. The dates ran sequentially. Five ledgers covering two years. I picked up the little black book and turned the pages. It was similar to the other ledgers except it covered less than a year's transactions and it overlapped with the records of three of the others. This was a separate type of record and this one had Greek letters. I visualized Cooke's notebook and recalled the Greek letters I'd seen in that too.

There also seemed to be a cross-reference code that I mapped across to a larger ledger. I found that alpha-theta was a kettle. Eighteen hundred had come in and twenty had gone out via the black book.

Before I could check anything else, there was a click. The building door was opened and the lights came on.

Acting on instinct, I ducked and moved to a position behind the door. I briefly glimpsed someone through the crack in the door. Was it just a clerk or could he be armed? I couldn't see. As I prayed it was the former, my mind processed the options.

The man disappeared down an aisle and I took my chance. Opening the door, I kept low, shoulder-rolling towards the cabinets beside the office. I stood side on and held my breath.

I was part shielded by the office wall and part by the cabinets. That was the upside. The downside was I couldn't see anymore.

I could hear his footsteps: toecaps clacking on the concrete floor.

At first he seemed confident but then he stopped. Was he at the door? Was he looking at the broken glass? Then there were three quick steps and the unmistakable sound of a revolver being cocked.

The man barked, "Out now or I'll shoot!"

THIRTY-SIX

Easing forward, I peeked out from behind the cabinets. If the man with the gun was looking, the game was up.

He wasn't. But he was neither a clerk nor the night watchman. It was Pantelis.

The lieutenant was about six feet away and side on. He knew someone was here but not precisely where.

Should I confront him? I rapidly dismissed the idea. I wasn't ready. So instead, I took a step and did three things. I hit the light switch so that, as Pantelis turned towards the movement, he might be disorientated. In the darkness, I struck out and down with his left arm knocking Pantelis's gun hand as it swung towards me. At the same time, still with forward momentum, I swung an uppercut with the torch in my hand.

Contact.

Pantelis crumpled to the floor, the gun clattering to the ground as he fell. I switched on the lights and checked him. Pantelis was out for the count.

I picked up his gun and stuck it in my belt. A weapon that wasn't signed out by me might come in handy. Then I went back into Pantelis's office and collected his ledgers: the five grey ones and the smaller black one.

With them under my arm, I headed for the shed door and opened it a crack. I looked towards the troopship and saw the snowdrop was still patrolling. He was walking in the opposite direction so I slipped out and retraced my route to the fence.

"Hey, halt!"

I swung around. A snowdrop was standing in the shadows. He flicked away a cigarette and walked towards me. I should have guessed they'd be two snowdrops. This one had just been taking a sneaky break out of sight.

"Evening," I said casually and pointed to the patrol boat. "I'm here on police business."

He glanced at the inflatable and I could see he bought my explanation. POLICE written in large letters on both sides undoubtedly helped.

I continued: "We're looking for an AWOL British warrant officer. I thought I saw someone come ashore just here." I glanced up and down the quay as if looking for places someone could hide.

"Maybe it was just you, having a quick smoke."

"I..." he stammered.

"It's all right, soldier. None of my business."

He nodded and said, "AWOL Brit? No, sir. No activity here tonight."

I climbed into the dinghy. "Right, keep your eyes peeled. He's been on the run for a few of days, must be pretty desperate."

The engine fired on my first pull and I gave the man a friendly wave before engaging the drive. "Don't worry," I called, "I won't mention the cigarette."

I headed back via the shoreline just in case the snowdrop was watching. He might think it strange if I didn't continue my search. With the wind and waves at my back, I was soon at the entrance to Singapore River and then tying up by the bridge.

I'd planned to jog back but I was keen to go through Pantelis's ledgers as soon as I could so I found a trishaw in Fullerton Square and asked to be taken to Alexandra Hospital. If I'd asked for Gillman Barracks, I had no doubt my driver would remember me. The hospital, I thought was a good distraction—and it was only a short walk from the barracks.

My driver tried to make conversation over his shoulder. He asked about my evening, but I didn't reply and he soon gave up.

I'd exited Gillman by climbing the fence behind the MT yard office. Even though I'd been seen by the snowdrop I still wanted to be able to deny I'd been out. The fence was only eight feet tall and easily scalable. In my black clothes, I swiftly rounded the hill back to the Officers' Quarters. No one saw me.

Back in my room I took out Sergeant Cooke's notebook and compared it to Pantelis's. The latter was much bigger and covered a longer period, but I found that every entry in Cooke's book had a matching entry in Pantelis's; the same day with the same Greek letters. Years of ingrained QM training prevented them from deviating from a well-used approach, I guessed. It made me smile at how obvious they had been—providing one could see both books that is.

As far as I could tell, Pantelis recorded the items going out and Cooke recorded their distribution and money paid.

I mapped all the letters and saw that they were trading in everything they could—everything that the army supplied, which was almost anything one could buy anywhere. They traded cutlery to candles, blankets to bully-tins. Each item had a combination of Greek letters and the reference code in the black book took me to the item in the official ledgers.

217

With one exception.

The last trade had happened on the same day Tom Silverman had died. Three hundred omega-deltas had been transferred from Pantelis to Cooke. On the same day, it looked like Cooke had disposed of all of them for three hundred pounds. No wonder they had stopped.

I thought about the fifty pounds found in Cooke's bag and figured that Pantelis took the rest.

So what were they? There was no reference number against the entry in Pantelis's book. There was nothing to tell me what omega-delta related to.

I noticed one other thing. Not one of the trades related to guns or munitions. Not only had I not seen an armoury at Keppel but Pantelis didn't trade in weapons. Or so it seemed.

THIRTY-SEVEN

Corporal Whiteside jerked open his eyes. Had he been asleep? The night patrols had been stood down and from 1am he had been in charge of the downtown MPs' office. He would be the only one there until relieved at eight in the morning.

The desire to close his eyes again confirmed his worst fears. He pushed his face away from the desk, sat upright in the chair and blinked rapidly. *On duty, must stay awake.*

He rubbed his eyes and face and scratched at his short blond hair. His watch said a little after three. *Still five hours of desk duty to do. It's the lack of air in here, that's what's making me so drowsy.*

He stood, walked to the door that opened out onto the street and propped it open. Breathing in the cool night air he glanced up and down the road. All quiet. In fact nothing was expected tonight. It was a dumb job, manning the phone just in case the SIB needed it. The sort of job you give to a rookie National Service guy. He returned to the desk and picked up the stack of papers on the desk—yesterday's reports. He flicked through, found something that looked less dull than the rest and began to read. He jerked open his eyes. *Bugger, dropping off again!*

A check of his watch suggested he'd been out for twenty or so minutes.

Had something woken him? There was a car parked outside. A posh car. Whoever owned it had money. He stood, walked to the door to take a look. A woman in the back seat looked out of an open window at him. Lowering his head to see better inside the vehicle, he realized there was a man in the driver's seat.

The woman beckoned.

Whiteside stepped into the street and to the side of the car. He squatted so that his face was in line with the open window. "Everything all right, Miss?" he asked and thought: not a great light, but she's definitely a pretty one. Chinese, maybe?

The woman placed her finger to her lips and then pointed to the driver.

Whiteside looked in, through the passenger window. The driver had clearly passed out, slumped forward over his wheel. Back at the lady's window, Whiteside said, "Drunk or asleep? Is there a problem?"

The woman spoke in barely a whisper and smiled.

He whispered back, "Sorry, I can't hear you."

She beckoned and he leaned in through the window. Immediately, his senses were assailed by an alluring perfume. He noticed she had long, elegantly crossed legs.

She saw him look and adjusted her cheongsam, so that it revealed less, and then leaned towards him. "He's asleep," she whispered.

"Are you all right?"

She smiled and slid back away from the door. "I'm a little bored." She raised her head. "Won't you come in and entertain me for a while?"

Whiteside took a deep breath. He glanced up and down the street. There was absolutely no one around.

220

What could it hurt? At least I'll stay awake, he decided and opened the door. He slid in, next to the pretty lady.

She adjusted her position and the slit showed more of her leg again. "We'll have to be very quiet," she whispered close to his ear and giggled lightly.

He smiled back, a little awkward.

"So, what's your name, soldier?"

"Peter... Pete. I'm nineteen. What about you?"

"Oh a little older." She laughed quietly. "You can call me Mum if you like. Her hand followed her gaze and she touched his hair. "Nice—" she said, looking him up and down "—all of you."

"You're pretty smashing yourself."

Her hand moved from his hair, lightly down his face and onto his chest.

Her own chest swelled slightly as she touched him. She smiled as his eyes bulged. "You can touch them if you like."

Whiteside placed a hand on a breast and felt its firmness.

She pulled at his shirt and the next moment she was sitting astride him and moved her mouth lightly over his. As Whiteside responded, she kissed him hungrily before probing his ear with her moist, warm tongue.

She whispered, "I have something to relax you."

He blinked, not understanding.

"I have some pills."

But before he could respond, she abruptly pushed on his chest and scrambled off.

"What—?" he started to say but then realized her face was lit up, the interior of the car was lit. A vehicle had pulled up behind them, its headlights bright through the window.

She said something but all he could hear was the jackhammer of his heart and his ragged breaths.

The car behind was a Land Rover. MPs. Maybe even SIB. *Buggeration!*

He squirmed for the door and got out. He didn't register that her driver was now awake and starting the engine.

He glanced in, his mind whirring trying to think of a reason for getting in her car. The men behind must have seen him.

He leaned in. "Glad to be of assistance, Miss."

She smiled. "Friday night," she said. "Meet me at the end of Bugis Street at eleven and I'll show you a good time, my pretty soldier-boy."

His jaw ached from kissing, but the grin on his face stayed with him until morning.

THIRTY-EIGHT

As soon as I saw the Union Flag hanging limply at half-mast, I knew there was bad news. It was the seventh of February.

"Have you heard the news?" the desk clerk said as I entered.

And then Hegarty appeared holding a newspaper and said, "It's the King. King George is dead!"

He handed me a black armband and I noticed he was already wearing one.

"What happened?" I said.

"He died in his sleep on the sixth so we're a day late with the news. Fifty-six and died of a blood clot in the heart. Out shooting at Sandringham the day before. He was still very active. Did you know he had lung cancer? Even though he'd been ill, it was still a shock. And Churchill said—"

I was half listening and half glancing through the overnight incident reports.

"Stop!" I said, holding up both hands.

"But this is—"

"Dreadful news but I'll read the detail later. For now we have something much more immediate."

I spun a report round so that he could read it.

"Get me Corporal Whiteside. It may be a black day but we might have had a near miss with Madam Butterfly."

Peter Whiteside, with boyish charm and as nervous as hell, stood to attention. Robshaw and I sat at the desk in the office. Hegarty stood behind, a serious look on his face.

"So let me get this right, Corporal," Robshaw said. "Last night you were on duty at the Bras Basah HQ. You fell asleep at the desk. When you woke up there was a limo parked at the kerb. You didn't see it arrive, but you could see a driver asleep at the wheel."

"Yes, sir," Whiteside said, his voice betraying his concern.

"Go on."

"There was a woman in the back. She was a looker, if you know what I mean? The window was down and she was leaning out. I think she had been calling to me—that's what woke me up." He swallowed after admitting again that he had been asleep on the job. "I left the desk and went over to the car. As I approached she moved back into the car so that I had to lean in to speak to her. I asked if everything was all right. She asked me to open the door and get in. I did."

Hegarty couldn't contain himself anymore and spluttered, "What were you thinking of, man? Why did you just get in?"

"I don't know. I guess I was a bit mesmerized by her. She was amazing—probably no definitely the best looking woman I've ever seen."

"Was she Eurasian?"

"Maybe. She was tall—well at least I know she had long legs, and Oriental looking, but I'm not an expert on nationalities."

"All right," I said, "what happened next?"

"She patted the seat next to her and I sat. She leaned towards me. It was like I was under a spell. I was mesmerized, I guess. The next thing I was kissing her."

Hegarty asked, "Did she say anything?"

"She wanted to know my name and my age. She said she was older and I could call her Mum."

"Mum?" Robshaw said. "That's new information."

"How old did she look?" I asked.

"I don't know. I suppose she was early twenties, but you know how hard it is to tell with these Chinese-types. She could have been older."

Robshaw said, "But not old enough to be your mum?"

Whiteside laughed uncomfortably. "No, sir."

That didn't surprise me. I suspected the name was to put him at ease. She was probably used to comforting soldiers and could easily have called herself Nan or maybe Nurse.

"Please continue."

Whiteside swallowed, clearly very uncomfortable. "It's in my report, sir."

"I'd like to hear it from you."

Whiteside still didn't speak.

"Soldier, you had better be frank," Hegarty prompted him. "You are in enough trouble already."

I raised a quieting hand to the sergeant and said, "Listen, Whiteside, we all make mistakes. I'd much rather catch a criminal than demote you for a misdemeanour. OK?"

"OK."

"So you were in the car. What happened next?"

Whiteside looked as though he was trying to decide how to explain. Eventually he said, "We fooled around a bit."

"Physical contact?" Hegarty asked.

"Yes, sir. Smooching and caressing, that sort of thing."

"Any penetration?" Hegarty pursued, seemingly undeterred by the young soldier's evident embarrassment.

"No, sir, it didn't go that far."

I asked, "Is there anything else, we should know?"

"She offered me a pill. That's what made me think afterwards."

"What sort of pill?"

"I don't know. Said it would relax me."

"So how did it end?"

"One of our patrols turned up. Interrupted us. I jumped out sharpish."

Hegarty raised his thick eyebrows. "So that's why you reported it. Because if you hadn't someone else would have."

"Yes."

I said, "So what happened to the woman?"

"Her chauffeur drove off."

"I thought you said he was asleep."

Robshaw said, "Must have been faking it."

I nodded. "Did she say anything else?"

Whiteside looked uncomfortable again.

I prompted, "What did she say?"

"That she'd meet me tomorrow night."

That was more new information not included in Whiteside's written report.

"Go on," I said.

"She told me she would be at the end of Bugis Street on Friday at twenty-three hundred hours."

"Jesus!" Hegarty said. "I hope you didn't hold that back because you plan to see her, Whiteside!"

Before the lad could answer, I said, "Did you see a tattoo?"

"No, sir."

"Madam Butterfly is believed to have the tattoo of a butterfly on her hip or groin area. Did you see it?"

"Sorry, sir. I didn't think to look."

"Cast your mind back," I said. "Picture yourself in the car with her. Try and visualize her and look for a tattoo."

After closing his eyes for a moment, he said, "It's no good. She had a mark on her breast. I couldn't quite see it, it might have been a small tattoo or it might have been a mole." He shook his head. "I'm sorry, sir. I was so taken in by her that it wasn't until I was talking with some of the lads that it dawned on me who she might be." He was clearly shaken. "I've had a close shave haven't I, sir?"

Hegarty said, "And yet you were thinking of meeting her tonight."

Whiteside looked on the verge of tears. "I don't know. Maybe she wasn't Madam Butterfly. I don't know. I just... I was thinking I'd be careful. Not take much money, that sort of thing."

I looked at Robshaw and could see we were thinking the same thing. I said, "Whiteside, I want you to make that rendezvous."

"But—" Whiteside began.

"But," I continued, "we'll be there to pick her up. You all right with that?"

"Yes, sir. I guess," he said and looked from me to Robshaw and back. "Will I be put on a charge?"

"Maybe. Maybe it'll depend on how it goes tomorrow night."

Robshaw dismissed him and once the corporal was out of the room, Hegarty asked me, "So do you think it was her?"

"Right MO. I think we just got lucky, very lucky."

Later Hegarty asked if I'd had any more thoughts about Cooke's notebook. I hadn't told him about getting Pantelis's ledgers and I was going to deny it if confronted by Major Vernon. But, as the morning wore on, I reckoned one of two things had happened. Either Pantelis didn't know who'd been in the depot last night or was too afraid I had evidence against him.

I decided to head over to Tanglin and asked Hegarty to drive me.

We found Sergeant Major Sinclair in his office. He still wasn't overly friendly and tiredness pulled at the corner of his eyes.

"A little news of your sergeant," I said.

"I heard you found his kitbag up at Woodlands."

"It looks like he went into the water. Maybe he swam, but more likely he caught a boat."

"And yet you found his bag."

I shrugged, "I agree it doesn't look good."

He nodded and pulled a pile of paperwork in front of himself as if letting me know the meeting was over.

"All the arms come through Tanglin Barracks via Keppel Harbour, right?" I'd checked with the armoury at Gillman and they'd told me their guns came from Tanglin.

"Easier to control that way."

I nodded. "Where at Keppel are they kept? We were there a few days ago and I couldn't see an armoury."

"That's because the secure stuff is over on the island."

"The island?"

228

"Blakang Mati," he said. "It's the large island opposite Keppel. The navy have a secure area there so that's where you'll find the arms."

I nodded. So that's why I'd seen nothing in the Stores Depot. It was also why Pantelis wasn't trading in anything from the armoury. Although I still didn't know what omega-delta meant.

"Would it surprise you to hear that Cooke was trading goods on the black market."

Sinclair bristled but kept it in check. "Yes, it would," he said.

"Well, we have proof."

Sinclair shook his head in disbelief.

I said, "Does omega-delta mean anything to you?"

"No. Should it?"

"You are so sure you run a clean ship here."

"I am."

"How is that? How can you be so sure?"

"Everything is checked in and checked out and reconciled."

"But wouldn't all QMs say that?"

"Maybe but I know it's true. Mainly because it wasn't the case before I got here."

"Eight months ago."

"Yes. Eight months ago. I did a complete stock check. Everything from bolts to biscuits. I made sure everything was counted. I also made sure we identified all the obsolete stock and got rid of it."

"Obsolete stock?"

"There was some pre-war stuff, but also broken items in the stores. One way of gaining control over what you have is to clean up what's there. So, from day one, eight months ago we started afresh."

Hegarty said, "So how come Cooke was trading?"

Sinclair kept his attention on me and shook his head, like he was saying it didn't make sense.

After a moment's thought he said, "Earlier, you mentioned evidence."

I handed Cooke's notebook over.

Sinclair turned the pages slowly and shook his head again. "I don't believe it."

"What don't you believe?" Hegarty said, leaning forward, hands on the quartermaster's desk. "That's a sales ledger. Clear as day."

Sinclair handed the book back to me. "I agree," he said, "but you're overlooking one thing."

"Which is?"

"That's not Sergeant Cooke's handwriting."

THIRTY-NINE

No one spoke for a moment. Did it matter that the evidence of black market trading wasn't in Cooke's handwriting? I wondered whether Sinclair could be mistaken. After all, the records were mostly dates and numbers. The only writing was in Greek—the letter combinations that tallied with Pantelis's own notebook.

We asked Sinclair if he recognized the handwriting at all. Maybe it was one of the other men who worked in the stores?

The QM was emphatic. It didn't belong to one of his men. He also pulled out Cooke's written request for a pass—the one his superior had turned down. I had to agree the writing was different and I should have spotted it straight off.

Left-handed people write awkwardly. And being left-handed, I should know. With practice, it becomes natural, but it's like writing backwards with your hand curled round to compensate. The style in the notebook was obvious. Left-handed. The writing on the pass request was not.

"Telephone message," a voice shouted as we walked back to the jeep. "Captain Carter, there's a telephone message."

Here we go, I thought. It'll be Vernon complaining about last night.

I took the yellow slip off the clerk and read it in trepidation. But it wasn't from the major. It was a personal message from Su Ling.

Important news. Meet me for lunch darling? Haw Par at 1? Kisses SL

Hegarty looked over my shoulder and chuckled. "Getting serious, Boss?"

I checked my watch and swung into the jeep. "Just drive, Hedge."

"Back to Gillman?" he said, "Or early for your date?"

I didn't rise to his bating and just said, "Gillman." There was over an hour before the appointment which would give me time to go through the ledgers again.

We sat in silence until we were going through the centre. When Hegarty spoke, it was serious this time.

He said, "If you don't mind me saying... it's probably best you don't communicate by phone messages."

"Why?"

"Because of Vernon."

I still didn't understand.

He said, "The major doesn't just see all the incident reports, he also sees all the written comms. That slip you just got was carbonated. Vernon gets the white copy and files it in his office. That tall thin metal one with all the drawers. It's his pride and joy. Anyway if there's anything personal you don't want him poking his nose into, I suggest your girl doesn't leave messages that he can see."

"Thanks for the warning," I said. Vernon had all communications in his office. That fact seemed to resonate with something but I couldn't quite grasp its relevance.

232

When we arrived back, I said I was going to my room for a lie down. I suspected he didn't believe me. I couldn't tell him the truth. If I did, he'd know I had Pantelis's ledgers.

I locked my door, got out the books and went through them line by line. I found plenty of transactions of munitions and weapons and realized there was a location code. BM for Blakang Mati, KS for Keppel Stores, I guessed. Items either came into the island or to the harbour and then out to Tanglin or the naval base. The figures reconciled with closing stock. As before, I still couldn't see anything in Pantelis's black book linking his trade to guns. Of course, I didn't have all the paperwork but all the movements in the ledgers looked genuine even when I cross-referenced items in the black book. Either Pantelis was faking the movements or the items weren't going through the official ledgers in the first place.

I opened the ledger showing movements eight months ago and looked for the transfer of the obsolete items from Tanglin to Keppel. Nothing.

I went through a month either side and found a handful of returned items. The most significant were eighty shovels with faulty handles. They came into Keppel from Tanglin but had a BM code. So they'd been taken to the island and were presumably still there. Probably waiting for a supply ship to take them back home. Or maybe to be destroyed. That was how most QM scams worked: mark something to be destroyed but keep it to sell later.

But this was bigger. Sinclair had ordered a clear out when he'd arrived. The items had been sent to Keppel but there was no record of them arriving.

Haw Par Villa was walking distance from Gillman so I declined Hegarty's offer of transport. Instead I asked him to get a complete list of everything Sinclair had disposed of eight months ago. All the alleged obsolete items.

Su Ling was waiting for me at the ornate entrance when I arrived at the villa. I was expecting a restaurant and was surprised to find beautiful gardens with larger-than-life plaster statues posed, frozen in scenes from Chinese mythology.

She kissed my cheek even though there were other people around and it made me smile. Then I noticed a serious expression on her pretty face.

"What's wrong?"

"Not here," she said and led me through the gardens. In the centre was a pagoda—*the* villa. It wasn't a restaurant either but she took me inside to a room adorned with garish murals. There was a single table and chairs set for a meal.

Another door opened and a waiter appeared with food on a trolley. We sat and he served us: noodles with prawns and vegetables.

After the man had retreated she said, "Now we can talk."

She placed her hand on the table and I put mine over it. Finally she smiled and I saw the warmth in her dark eyes.

"I have news about Tai Tai," she said. "You remember the girl from the House of Tokyo?"

"Of course."

She took a breath. "And you remember the girl, Keiji, her best friend."

"The witness. She saw someone run away."

"She has told me that Tai Tai had a boyfriend. A soldier."

I sensed what was coming, but waited.

Su Ling said, "Keiji didn't know for sure but she recognized the name: Billy Cooke. She's sure Tai Tai mentioned him and the letter you showed me was from Tai Tai. It looks like they were lovers and planning to run away together."

I sat back. So, Sergeant Cooke *was* connected to the House of Tokyo in Nee Soon.

"But something went wrong."

"She ended up in a coma at Tan Tock Seng and I suppose he tried to... what do you call it when a soldier runs away?"

"Desertion."

We ate for a few minutes as I tried to make sense of this information. Eventually I said, "I really need to speak to Lieutenant Pantelis."

"That's my other news," she said with a smile.

"Is it as shocking?"

"That depends on your attitude, I suspect. Your lieutenant likes the ladies."

I was hoping for something more than that. I needed to confront him with what I now knew and there was little chance of me getting through the gates at Keppel Harbour.

She was still smiling.

"What?" I said and couldn't help smiling back.

"Not just a few ladies and not for a serious relationship. I have found out where he goes to meet his lady friends. There is a little place in Chinatown called The Red Lion. He goes there most evenings, never in uniform and—I'm told—never picks up the same girl twice. Apparently, he's really dishy."

I wanted to ask her how she'd found out but decided it would be ungrateful and rude. Instead I thanked her and asked what time I could find him there.

"Ten o'clock," she said. "How about you have your meeting with him and then we get together afterwards."

"I'd love to. Dinner? I'll find somewhere special."

"Really?" she said, leaned over the table and kissed my cheek. "All right I'll trust you to surprise me." Then she laughed and added: "No pressure."

She had another meeting at the villa so I left her there. At the gate a trishaw driver asked me if I needed a lift. As I walked back to the barracks I had the feeling that I'd met the man before. He might have been my driver from last night. My sixth sense was up and I suddenly felt like I was being followed, but each time I looked there was no sign of the driver.

FORTY

Sergeant Hegarty stared at me with blank eyes as I walked into the office block.

"What's up?"

"Sergeant Cooke's been found," he said with a shake of his head. "A fishing boat in the Straits picked him up."

"Dead?"

"Very."

I waited for him to say more.

He shook his head again. "Shot in the head."

I said nothing.

"Remember Private Allen at Woodlands Crossing? He mentioned gunshots across the water that night. I reckon Cooke tried to swim across to Malaya and got picked off by a sniper."

"Where's his body?"

"The morgue at Alexandra Hospital."

The cha-boy came in followed closely by Robshaw.

He said, "Have you heard the news about Sergeant Cooke?"

We nodded.

The lieutenant took a gulp of tea. "Ironic. A deserter ending up shot."

The comment reminded me of the story about the man executed at Tanglin after his unit deserted their position at Bukit Timah. True or otherwise. I said, "It's not justice, if that's what you mean."

Hegarty said, "So where does that leave us? We put pressure on the QM at Tanglin. Cooke does a runner and ends up dead."

"Dead-ended," Robshaw muttered.

I didn't think so. But then I hadn't shared my information about Pantelis with them. I couldn't, not yet anyway.

"I learned something at lunch. Remember the girl at the House of Tokyo in Nee Soon?" When Hegarty nodded I continued: "Well it looks like she was the woman writing to our unfortunate Sergeant Cooke. She was his girl."

Robshaw wanted to know the whole story about Tai Tai so I filled him in.

"Crikey," he said when I'd finished. "I wonder whether her attack is linked."

"As a working hypothesis, I'd like to assume so."

"Which means what?" Hegarty asked.

"It means that I'd like to treat her attack as a military issue. I'd like her moved to Alexandra Hospital so we can keep an eye on her."

Robshaw leaned back and put his hands through his blond head of hair. "The police won't be happy."

"I'll persuade Rahman," I said, sounding more confident than I felt. "I'll explain it's in the interest of better relations."

Robshaw said he'd raise the relevant paperwork to request it.

I switched my attention to Hegarty. "Did you get a list from Sinclair?"

"It's in the office—all five pages of it."

"Any guns on it?"

"Oh yes," he said with a grin. "Five hundred M1 Garand rifles. They're pre-war and wrong calibre these days so I see why they cleared out obsolete stock."

Robshaw said, "Are those the guns we're looking for?"

"Maybe," I said.

"No," Hegarty said. "They can't be. I asked Sinclair about them and he said they'd been decommissioned. Unless someone could get the firing parts, the guns would be useless."

After a downpour, I asked Hegarty to take me into the city and drop me at the police station. Inspector Rahman was busy and I said I'd head over to Fullerton Square rather than wait. I told him which route I'd take in case the inspector became free before my return.

At the Fullerton Building I went up the steps to The Singapore Club and asked for Mr Pope. I was shown to the businessman's table by the same window. He seemed delighted to see me and offered his soft hand.

"My apologies for the intrusion," I said.

"Tush tush, my man. It's a pleasure," he said effusively. "How good of you to visit me."

He insisted I sit and ordered me a *stengah*.

I said, "I understand that your daughter, Amelia, is much better."

He looked at me askance and appeared to consider his response. When he spoke he said, "She's still a little shaken I'm afraid. May I ask why you said she was much better?"

Now it was my turn to be confused. The barfly at Goodwood Park had said so. "A German friend of yours told me," I explained.

"German friend?"

"I met him at Goodwood Park."

He smiled like a parent showing sympathy to a child. "You must be mistaken, dear chap. I don't have a German friend and I've never set foot in Goodwood Park."

I wasn't sure what to make of that but I nodded and said, "Yes, my mistake. In that case, I'm sorry to hear that Amelia isn't better."

"She'll get over it. There was no real harm done after all."

There was silence while he drank his whisky. I was hoping he would ask me why I was here. Instead he said, "The Japanese Imperial Army used The Singapore Club as a headquarters, did I tell you that?"

"You did," I said. "I feel uncomfortable asking but... when I met you last time, you asked me if there was anything you could do for me."

He smiled and said, "Of course."

"I wonder if you could arrange for a ride on one of your Japanese junks this evening?"

"Alone or do you wish to entertain a young lady?"

"A young lady."

"Is she pretty?"

"She's stunning."

That's when he told me what he could do.

Su Ling hadn't been impressed by my dance hall suggestion but I was sure she'd like what I'd agreed with Pope.

I must have been smiling when Rahman saw me on North Boat Quay heading towards him.

"Good news, my friend?" he asked.

"Not really," I said, "I was just thinking about something else. My news for you is that our AWOL sergeant has been found dead."

"I'd heard," he said and pointed in the direction of the *Padang*. "Shall we go around this way? The fair is being set up."

As we walked past government buildings, he said, "Do you have any information on what may have happened to your man?"

"He was shot. There are theories but there will be a post-mortem."

"What do you think?"

We stopped for a moment and watched tents being erected. There was a Ferris wheel in the middle of the green and a hive of activity everywhere.

"I don't know," I said. "I think he could have told us a great deal but I've learned something interesting..." I paused and he looked at me expectantly. "There's a connection with the girl in a coma."

"From the House of Tokyo."

"She was Sergeant Cooke's girlfriend. Cooke's desertion and the attack on the girl—they're connected. Not only that, but I think we may have found our trade in guns. It looks like your intelligence about an attack may be right."

He gripped my arm. "It's coming together," he said. "I have news for you too. As you know, we've been visiting all the House of Tokyo's customers. And we are picking up and questioning anyone who is suspicious."

"Good. Let me know if you learn anything." After the inspector nodded, I continued: "About the girl—I appreciate there's a police investigation but I'd like to treat it as a military matter—now that we know she's connected to the death of one of ours."

Rahman said nothing.

"It would be a favour. I'd like her moved to the Alexandra. I think she is key to all of this somehow. If only I could get her story."

241

He inclined his head. "Politics," he said. "But I will do my best to facilitate it."

I thanked him and we resumed our stroll.

He said, "Did you enjoy your boat ride last night?" he was referring to my trip in the dinghy to see Pantelis.

"I'm grateful for the loan."

He stopped and looked at me. "You're being mysterious, Captain. May I ask where you went?"

"It's best that you don't know," I said. "For now at least." A troupe of acrobats started to perform on the green in front of us. We watched for a moment and others gathered round for early entertainment.

Rahman said, "Three days until the final New Year celebration, the parade and pageant. Forty, two, ten."

A street vendor stopped and tried to get us to buy roasted chicken on bamboo skewers. Rahman waved the man away.

The acrobats had built a human tower of five people. A child scrambled up the side and stood on the top. It looked precarious and as the column swayed, the crowd of spectators gasped. But it was all showmanship. The tower became ridged again and the child climbed down. Then one by one the men jumped off to rapturous applause.

When the street vendor was finally out of earshot, I said, "If this threat is real, are you thinking the target is here at the carnival or the parade?"

The inspector ran his hand through his black hair, thinking. Then he said, "Perhaps we could check for empty premises along the route. In case it is the parade."

FORTY-ONE

English through and through, the only clues that said The Red Lion pub was in Asia were the two giant red banners with gold Chinese lettering. They hung either side of the entrance, adding to the vast number of red flags, lanterns and banners that adorned most of the properties in and around Chinatown.

It was early evening and I was dressed in my best suit and ready for my date with Su Ling. I just had to confront Pantelis first.

The streets were packed with party-goers and shoppers and, as I forced my way into The Red Lion, I wasn't surprised to find it equally busy. Inside, red sashes proclaimed the New Year, but apart from that, it now felt like it could have been transplanted from Portsmouth or Plymouth where there would be an equal number of sailors and soldiers with pints in their hands. There were some couples huddled around cheap-looking tables. Others leaned against the wall or a bar at the far end. There were also groups of girls clearly on the lookout for a date. I spotted Pantelis sitting furthest from the door, the plaster above his eyebrow smaller than before and I could see a yellow bruise. There was a half-empty pint glass and an untouched cocktail on the table.

Pantelis leaned in, deep in conversation with what looked like a young Asian woman.

I squeezed through the bodies towards the table.

Pantelis spotted me and stood, a mixture of emotions on his face. Anger, frustration and something else, guilt perhaps.

I briefly wondered if the young woman was a lady-boy but couldn't judge when she looked up at me with alarm.

"You'd better leave," I said and she was up and out without a word or glance back.

"You have a nerve," Pantelis said through clenched teeth.

"Sit down."

"It was you last night, wasn't it? If I reported you…"

"But you won't. Now sit down!"

He complied but continued to glare at me.

I said, "You won't because I have your ledgers and your private record. I know what you've been doing. And I know about your trade with Sergeant Cooke." I sat down and leaned in. "He's dead you know?"

Pantelis's eyes froze for a moment and I figured that he hadn't known. Then he looked down and took a sip of beer.

When he looked back at me he said, "What happened to him?"

"We don't know. He was found earlier today in the Straits of Johor—off Pulau Ubin—with a gunshot wound. I don't know any more—not yet. Not until the post-mortem."

Pantelis looked down and then up again after a beat. "So, what are you going to do?"

"I want to hear it from you."

"What from me?"

"It was you who took the staff car out two weeks ago. It was you who drove my friend off the road."

"Is that what you think?"

"Yes."

He took a breath before quietly saying, "Yes, I took the car but it was for Sergeant Cooke."

"Cooke?"

"He needed to make a delivery in Nee Soon. He couldn't take an army car so he often took one of ours. I just signed it out for him."

I figured he was hiding something, that this wasn't the exact story but I ran with it and said, "So who caused the accident?"

"Cooke. Your friend must have followed him."

"What was he delivering?"

Pantelis looked away. He said, "The usual."

I fixed him with a stare. "But it wasn't, was it? Omega-delta."

He said nothing, just gave me a deadpan look.

"The rifles."

"I don't deal in weapons. That would be irresponsible."

"What was it then?"

"I don't know."

I shook my head in disgust. "I think you're lying. I think you sold rifles to Cooke and you don't care where they ended up."

He said nothing, just looked at me with blank eyes.

I said, "You better hope we find them before it's too late."

I could see him thinking. His left eye narrowed like he was affected by the smoke. He beckoned for me to get closer.

I leaned across the table and said, "What?"

He glanced left and right as though checking no one was listening but it seemed an act.

Again I said, "What?"

"I don't know who the buyer was but what if I were to tell you who the contact was—who Cooke was dealing through?"

"Who?"

"Do I have a deal?"

I fixed him with a glare.

He said, "If I tell you then you don't report me."

"How about you tell me or I punch you in your stupid mouth?"

He shot a glance past me.

"Well?" I said and took hold of his shirt collar with my right hand.

He shook his head.

I held him for a moment and then said, "Fine. I won't report you but you aren't getting away with it."

"We'll see," he said and for the first time I thought I saw cockiness in his eyes. Then he nodded and said, "The big guy at *Dongzing de fangzi*—the House of Tokyo in Nee Soon. Do you know it?"

"The cook?"

"And security. His name is Aiko. He's a really bad guy."

"You traded with him?"

"Me? No, never! But if Cooke was trading with someone there then he'll be your go-between." Pantelis looked past me again and I suspected it was a tactic he'd developed. Perhaps it worked to unnerve junior men, but to me he just seemed distracted. He continued: "We do have a deal, don't we?"

I straightened. "If your information helps."

"Helps?" But before I could respond, he looked past me again and said, "Who's that?"

"Who?"

"Your colleague at the table by the door. Is he part of this?"

I spun around and spotted him immediately: the German guy—the barfly from Goodwood Park.

"What the hell?"

FORTY-TWO

Everyone suddenly seemed to be in my way. When I reached the table by the door, the German was gone. Then I spotted him outside, hurrying away. I squeezed through the door as another young lady came in, and then pushed through the bodies in the direction I'd seen him go. After a few yards I stopped and scanned left and right, looking for someone who stood out, someone running maybe. But I saw nothing. The German had blended into the crowd.

I checked my watch and knew I only had a few minutes. Su Ling would be waiting for me at Floating Pier.

Cutting across town towards Fullerton Square, I struck lucky. A two man MP patrol was checking a bar for drunken soldiers.

"Go to the police station and ask for Inspector Rahman," I instructed them. "Tell him to pick up a guy called Aiko from the House of Tokyo. Tell him it's connected to the security issue."

The two young men hurried off with my message and I continued to the pier.

She had been sitting inside the Bentley and climbed out of the rear as I approached. She was wearing a white cheongsam with gold embroidery. Her matching high heels made her almost as tall as me.

"You look sensational," I said and kissed her cheek.

"And you're in a good suit. My, my, Ash Carter, you do look dashing. Now, I'm intrigued about what you have arranged."

I pointed to the Japanese junk tied up to the pier. "A little boat ride," I said, relieved to see that the water was calm tonight. "And a meal on board if that's meets with your approval."

She clapped her hands and gave me a smile that could have started a Trojan war. We approached the boat along the wooden pier and she linked her arm through mine. When the boards moved beneath our feet, she held on tightly.

"How exciting," she said as we were welcomed aboard by a man in a traditional kimono. He showed us where to sit, amidships and, within a matter of minutes, the giant sails were filled and we cast off, sliding away from shore into the darkness.

The creak and moan of ancient timbers added to the sense of power the *sengoku-bune* exuded. We didn't seem to travel fast and yet it felt like we were riding the back of a huge beast, restrained from taking flight.

We followed the coast east and then looped around and hugged the coast back again until we reached the water opposite the *Padang*. The sails were tied and the anchor dropped.

"This is wonderful," she said as we watched the activity of the fair, the lights reflecting golds, yellows and reds across the still water.

And when a table was set in front of us by a tiny Japanese waiter she laughed with joy again and said, "I see you are romantic after all, Ash."

I had requested a Japanese meal and Pope had happily obliged. The food was cold and alien to my palate, but Su Ling was in paradise. The tiny Japanese waiter poured some more sake in our glasses and slipped discretely back into the shadows.

We watched fireworks and then the activity on the *Padang* rapidly died.

She said, "I'm chilly."

It was pleasantly cool, not chilly, and I got the message. I moved closer and put my arm around her. She responded by pressing up against me. It felt good. Very good. Her hair was close to my face.

"I love your perfume, may I ask...?"

"An essence of ylang ylang," she said, "I have it privately made. I'm glad you like it."

We were looking into each other when she surprised me by saying, "You have lovely grey eyes."

I smiled since I had been thinking something similar. "When we first met, I thought your eyes were green, but they're a rich brown now... which I like," I added quickly.

"Oh," she looked a little embarrassed. "I've been told that my eyes change colour, that they reflect my mood. I'm not sure how it can be true but when I'm happy they appear more brown."

The scientist in me said it was about relative pupil and iris size but I kept my theory to myself.

We sat in comfortable silence for a while, enjoying each other's company and watching the embers of activity on the quay. She had been deep in thought. When she spoke she said, "Tell me a happy story about when you were a child."

"You first. It'll give me chance to think of something."

"Oh, all right. My favourite time was at ballet. I danced from a very early age until I was twelve. I thought I would be a famous ballerina one day. But, as you can see, I grew too tall and, of course, the war happened."

"I should have guessed you trained as a dancer from the way you walk. You have grace and poise."

"And you are a charmer!"

"That may be true, but you haven't told me the story."

"Well it was just generally when I was dancing, but there was a special day that I recall as though it were just a short time ago. We were putting on the Nutcracker Suite at the town hall. I was Clara—my parents were so proud. They sat in the front row and looked so happy for me. Of course it was only an amateur production, but that didn't matter. I remember my father's beaming face and his loud cheer. He was so smart in his uniform."

"Was he British Army? What was his name?"

"Captain Keith. So he was like you. Only he had a big moustache and was much, much older!" The happy expression suddenly vanished and she had a faraway look. "He died in the first few days of the battle."

"I'm sorry," I said.

"It's all right," she said, seemed to shake the melancholy from her head and gave me a warm smile. "It was a long time ago. And my uncle made sure Mother and I were all right."

"I can tell you my first memory. I must have been less than three. It had snowed—that perfect crisp snow that crunches under your feet. I was wrapped up snugly—I remember a hood that was padded with wool. I felt warm and secure. It was very early morning and I was in the garden alone. Although I wasn't really. I remember

251

turning and being surprised that my mother was watching." I stopped for a moment and then said, "For a while I felt like I was the only one in the world."

"What happened?"

"Nothing. Funny it was just a moment in time, a captured memory for some reason. I recall a wooden stool. It was upside down and I pushed it. I think it was a struggle because I used it to lean on and the more I leaned on it, the more it dug into the snow."

"I've never seen snow."

"It can be beautiful, but then it turns brown and mushy and you get wet."

She flicked at my chest with the back of her hands. "Oh you've just ruined a beautiful image."

"We should be getting back." I waved to our Japanese host and pointed to the quay.

As we got underway, she said, "How is the investigation going?"

"To be honest I feel like I'm pushing that stool in the snow. The more I push, the more difficult it seems to get."

FORTY-THREE

On Floating Pier once more, we walked arm in arm across the boards. As we reached the end, her heel stuck and she yelped. I tried to steady her, but in her panic she pushed me off balance and I toppled over the side.

The drop was less than two feet and I was soon back on the pier. The horrified expression on her face evaporated when I started laughing. I shook myself like a dog, working from my head to my feet and then we were both laughing uncontrollably.

As we reached the road, her driver stepped out of the Bentley but she waved him away.

"Come on," she said between gasps, "let's get you sorted." And with that she took my hand and ran.

We didn't stop until we reached the lights and bustle of Chinatown. "You know, we call this *Bu Ye Tian*," she said. "It means: the place of the nightless days. That's because Chinatown never sleeps. Why sleep when there is work to be done and money to be won?"

I'd been in Chinatown a few times, but she led me into an area I hadn't seen before. This wasn't party-lively like Bugis Street and the area around The Red Lion pub. This was different. This was the heart of Chinatown and people were busy about their normal business, like they would during the day. I smelled raw fish and cooking fat. A woman tried to sell us homemade cakes.

"*Kueh! Kueh kara kara!*" she jabbered at me until Su Ling snapped at her and the woman scurried away.

Red lanterns hung everywhere, their glow adding extra warmth to the night. Suddenly she stopped.

"Here."

Without asking, she led me into a clothes shop. It was after one in the morning but the store was busy with customers, shop assistants and other staff working towards the rear.

She pulled a silk suit from a rack and said, "Get out of your wet clothes."

I was shown a cubicle and a curtain was pulled across. Once I had swapped my wet suit for the silks, I pulled back the curtain and Su Ling clapped her hands together with glee.

"I look ridiculous, don't I?"

"Yes." She laughed and held out a pair of black slippers. "Take off your shoes and socks and put these on."

I put on the thin slippers. Normally I would have felt self-conscious and foolish dressed like this but every male around me was dressed in a similar fashion. OK, I was white and taller but I didn't look out of place.

Su Ling picked up my clothes and handed them to the shop keeper. When she gave him an instruction he bowed. She turned back to me.

"He'll dry your clothes and we can pick them up tomorrow."

"We? Tomorrow?" I said, cocking an eyebrow.

"Tomorrow," she said with the flash of an innocent smile.

Then she took me outside and we walked a hundred yards to an ornate building. It had the usual lanterns and banners and a green tiled roof with dancing dragons along the ridge.

"This is where I live," she said.

Inside, the place looked like a restaurant with cloth-covered tables and people sitting around them. It was smoke-filled and had a strange aroma, one that I hadn't smelled before. My face obviously asked a question.

She said, "I obviously don't live down here. I have one of the rooms upstairs."

As we moved forward, I became aware of a *clackerty-clack* and saw that, on each table, the men were playing games.

"Mah-jong," Su Ling explained and we stood over a table watching the frenetic activity. Although many crowded round, there were only four men playing per table. The rest were encouraging and betting loudly. We watched for a few minutes. I could see it was highly strategic with considerable money being passed around and wagered.

We moved on and I saw other tables where men played cards. This was more my game but again I didn't recognize it.

"It's called Fantail," she said and again I could see it involved a great deal of gambling. Both by the players and those watching. Before I could study it for too long, she pulled me away, explaining that the players were very sensitive to outsiders watching them.

With small glasses of rice wine in our hands, she toasted me and knocked it back. I copied her and the rough liquid burned my throat.

Our glasses were immediately refilled and after another shot, I realized I was becoming light-headed.

"What is this smoke?"

Through the mist I could see people at the back, lying on sofas. They had long pipes with a small bowl on the end. Occasionally they leaned over to heat the bowl over a candle. "Is this an opium den?"

"No silly. It's mostly tobacco. And this is definitely not a den."

I knew the majority of the mah-jong players were smoking cigarettes, but the people lounging at the back appeared to be smoking something other than tobacco. I wondered briefly whether this was the sort of club that Madam Butterfly would come to, but then mocked myself for the thought. Of course she wouldn't come here; this was a Chinese club not one where she could pick up a soldier or sailor. I was a rare guest here.

More wine was freely poured and we drank and ate dim sum brought to us on trays. She took me over to a sofa and we sat looking into each other's eyes.

After a while, in an understanding voice, she said "You have some sadness. I saw it briefly when you told me your first memory. Something about your mother?"

"She died." I paused and wondered what else to say. Of course she'd understand because she'd lost her father in the war.

But she didn't say that. Somehow she seemed to read me and said, "You blame your father, is that it?"

"He didn't have time for her—or me. He was part responsible for a bombing raid in the war it caused a firestorm killing countless thousands."

"He dropped the bombs?"

"As good as. He was a strategist. Forget the civilian cost, the end justified the means... and I disagree. My mother's family came from near Dresden—way back. She didn't know anyone there but it didn't change the fact she saw it as a war crime." I found it hard to talk about and it felt like a garrotte round my throat. But I swallowed and continued: "She was horrified and it

256

drove a wedge between them. I sided with her. She died a year later."

Su Ling studied my eyes and I guessed she could read that my mother hadn't simply died. She'd taken her own life. I blamed my father for the murder of thousands. And I blamed him for the effective murder of my mother.

"Were you with her?"

And there it was, the big reason why I felt so bad. The big reason why I blamed my father for her death. It was because I blamed myself. I'd been at university and I could have been with her. I could have given her the support she needed.

Su Ling touched my cheek and I was surprised it was wet.

I said, "I'm sorry." Here I was with the most beautiful woman I'd ever seen, having the best evening of my life. And now I was ruining it.

She stood and took my hand. "Come on, Captain Ash Carter. Let's go upstairs. You've had a long hard day and you need cheering up."

FORTY-FOUR

Finally, the huge Japanese man opened his door. He looked on edge and uncertain and smaller than when he was playing his security role at the House of Tokyo. Perhaps he was dressed for bed.

"Relax," the visitor said in Hokkien, knowing the other man would understand and know who was in control here. "Aiko isn't it?"

The Japanese man bowed his head in acknowledgement.

The visitor said, "Let me in."

Akio looked around the visitor in case there was anyone else outside. When he saw no one, he stepped backwards. The visitor followed him in and shut the door.

"Sit," the visitor said switching to Japanese. Once the big man was sitting, the position of control became stronger and Aiko remained edgy.

Aiko said, "I have seen you at the House. You are a member but I do not know your tile-name."

"I am Jin."

Aiko's narrow eyes bulged for a second, recognizing this wasn't a mah-jong tile but something else entirely. He said, "I have heard of you."

"How?"

"The money... you were very clever," Aiko said. "I heard that you got it from that drugs bust that went wrong—the one with the British soldier. Yes?"

The visitor said nothing.

The Japanese security man said, "They say that's why you are called Jin... because of the money."

The visitor didn't bother explaining the error. He nodded without conviction and changed the subject.

He said, "I am here about the girl."

"Tai Tai?"

"What happened? And I do not want the story you told the police."

"She was trading. I found out and confronted her."

"Because?"

"Because I am the go-between at the House. All deals go through me."

"So you confronted her? You put her in a coma."

Aiko hung his head. "It was an accident. Yes, I hit her but then she banged her head."

"What was she trading?"

"Guns."

"Have you ever traded guns?"

"No."

"You are more of a drugs man, correct?"

"Yes."

"But she had dealt with smaller items in the past."

Aiko shifted uncomfortably in his seat. "Yes, but this was bigger."

"So, you put her in a coma for not sharing a big deal with you."

Aiko didn't respond.

Jin said, "Why did she risk it?"

"For her boyfriend. I think she was planning to leave the House—Singapore."

"It has caused problems."

"I covered it up," Aiko said, with imploring eyes. "I opened the gate and I told her friend to say a Chinese man ran away."

Jin nodded. He said, "But it has made it very difficult. You saw the tall military policeman, yes?"

"Yes."

"He is trying to connect what has happened. First there is a mistake that kills his friend and he has linked it to the girl."

"Are you afraid that the girl will speak when she wakes up?"

"She might."

"I could get rid of her for you."

"I can handle the girl," Jin said. "Now, tell me about the British sergeant."

"Who?"

"William Cooke."

"I don't know him."

"Did you kill him?"

"No. I said—"

"What happened?"

"I don't know anything about him."

The visitor thought that was probably true but let silence fill the air between them as though he doubted it.

Aiko wiped sweat from his chin with the back of his hand. In earnest, he said, "I could get rid of the big MP for you."

"And if you fail, what then? He will have another connection and it will be just a matter of time."

Jin could read the Japanese man's thoughts now. He was trying to work out how to solve the problem. And then his mind must have frozen as he stared into a barrel.

Jin aimed a revolver at Aiko's head.

Click.

"Empty chamber," Jin said. "Just to make you realize I'm serious. Now tell me the name of the man you sell drugs to."

Aiko swallowed. "Six Bamboo. I only know his tile-name."

And then the big guy finally understood that the visitor had everything he needed. He was only two inches off his seat when the bullet blew a hole in his head.

FORTY-FIVE

My watch said it was almost ten in the morning. I'd never slept late in my life before so my first thought was that my watch had stopped last night. Su Ling's scent lingered although she was no longer in the bed beside me. I opened the curtains and blinked in the typical bright sunlight.

I listened and waited a moment, hoping that she was in the bathroom but she wasn't. Then I spotted a note beside the bed. She hoped I had slept well and hadn't wanted to disturb me. She apologized for needing to get to work and hoped I'd meet her for lunch.

Nothing about the note gave a clue to our night of passion and there was no kiss after her initials. But I didn't care. I knew we had something special and words on paper meant far less than action.

My normal clothes were hanging from the bathroom door. They had been cleaned and pressed and I guessed Su Ling had collected them before leaving for work.

I was still grinning as I looked at myself in the bathroom mirror. Images of our lovemaking kept flashing in my head. I thought about her naked body and how funny it was that she kept the silk wrist strap on. "I wear it for luck," she had explained.

I also remembered the quiet, sensitive time, when we talked about my mother again. I told her I felt the guilt and she wouldn't accept it, told me to focus the emotion on my father. And that's when she had told me about her father. It wasn't all wonderful. The memory of him watching her ballet show was all she had because soon after he had left. It turned out that he was already married in England. And like most soldier-fathers, he eventually went home. He hadn't died in the war. That was just her way of dealing with it.

I dressed and, being a neatness freak, I made the bed. On her side, on the floor, was a hand-size book. A diary.

My initial impulse was to take a look but I resisted. It was probably just a work diary but to go through it seemed like a betrayal. I figured she'd need it, so I stuck it in my pocket and decided to drop it off later.

There were people playing mah-jong or Fantail but they didn't pay me any heed, neither did the two members of staff cleaning empty tables as I walked through the lounge and left the building.

I strolled through Chinatown and breathed in the exotic smells. When I reached the main road, I flagged a trishaw and sank back in the seat. I closed my eyes and let the images of Su Ling dance in my mind's eye.

At Gillman Barracks I was heading up to my room when Hegarty flagged me and waved me over to the office block.

"What's up, Hedge?"

His serious face melted into a smirk. "Wow, you obviously had a good night!"

I nodded. "What is it?"

Hegarty led me into the office where Robshaw was sitting at the table and biting his nails.

I said, "Will someone tell me what's going on?"

The lieutenant said, "Cooke was murdered. We've got the pathologist report and his death is suspicious as hell."

I waited for more.

Robshaw handed me a report. As I read for myself, he said, "He wasn't just shot."

I read there was a post-mortem welt around his middle.

Hegarty said, "At first we thought, maybe he'd tied his kit bag round his waist. Maybe he had tried to swim across the Straits but—"

"It was too tight," I finished, studying photographs of the body. "He had a rope round his waist, pulled so tight it left a ring."

Robshaw nodded. "My guess is he was weighed down. The rope was tied to a rock, or something and dumped in the water. We weren't supposed to find the body. Somehow the rope came loose and his body came up."

I said, "And either we weren't supposed to find the kitbag or, whoever did it, didn't find the hidden pocket. They didn't realize Cooke had the notebook."

They listened in rapt silence as I told them that I'd confronted Pantelis who'd told me about Cooke. I didn't mention his ledgers or how I'd found him or implicate the naval lieutenant and they didn't ask.

"It looks like Cooke was trading on the black market with the security man at the House of Tokyo in Nee Soon. His name is Aiko. My friend, Tom Silverman, seems to have been on to Cooke and was driven off the road after a transaction one night. So Cooke killed my friend. He also planned to desert and elope with his girlfriend, Tai Tai. What news of getting her transferred to the Alexandra?"

"Tomorrow," Robshaw said. "Sorry, because of all the paperwork, she won't be released until tomorrow."

"So what's next?" Hegarty asked.

"There's a possibility that this is all about the guns. The M1s that were disposed of eight months ago—I want to know what happened to them. If they are still here they'll be on Blakang Mati—held in the armoury there. Robbo, see if you can find the records. See if you get evidence of what happened to them. And if they're still there, then count them. Three hundred may be missing."

"Will do," Robshaw said. "What about you?"

"Once I've changed, I'm going back into the city. I want to see Inspector Rahman. He should have had Aiko picked up last night. If he has, then maybe we'll have information from him."

I opened the door to my room and froze. The bed had been turned over, sheets on the floor. The drawers were open and my suitcases turned out. My window had been forced open.

I lifted the mattress. Pantelis's ledgers had gone. Cooke's papers and notebook were gone. I picked up my things from the floor and was surprised to find the gun I'd stolen from Pantelis. It had been locked in a suitcase with a wallet containing my ID papers and my cash. They hadn't been taken either. So the thief just wanted Pantelis's and Cooke's stuff. Why not take my valuables? There was only one explanation: they wanted the evidence. They wanted the same information I had.

I knew there was no point in having an investigation. The thief could easily break in—like I had two nights ago. Climbing the fence and getting to my room at night undetected wouldn't have been too difficult. And I was sure the thief would have worn gloves. The only thing

I'd achieve by a formal investigation was having to explain how I'd got hold of Pantelis's ledgers.

After changing into my uniform, I asked Hegarty to drive me to the police station. I didn't mention the break-in.

"Cat got your tongue?" he said as we picked up the coast road.

"What?"

"I've been talking for a few minutes and you've not said a word."

"Sorry, miles away."

"Thinking about your date last night?"

"How did you...? Never mind." I had been thinking about the case and who might have been in my room but I replied, "Yes, I was thinking about my date."

"Details?" he asked.

"None."

He was silent for a while as we drove past Keppel and then around the busy Fullerton Square.

"It comes from the cat-o-nine-tails."

"What does?" I asked.

"Cat got your tongue. The expression comes from punishment on a ship with a whip—a cat."

"Why was it called a cat-o-nine-tails?"

"Ah you have me there. I don't know that."

We arrived outside Hill Street police station and Hegarty asked if he could come in. I said no, which clearly disappointed him, but I felt we were making progress and his inane banter was a distraction. Maybe that was the reason or maybe I was starting to trust people less. Someone had been in my room and taken the ledgers. That could have been anyone. Including an MP. I certainly didn't trust Major Vernon and I had no doubt Hegarty was providing him with updates, probably Robshaw too.

However when I went into the station and asked for Rahman I was told he wasn't available. Sergeant Kee was in the corridor behind and spotted me. He told me the inspector was at Outram Prison interrogating someone.

"A Japanese man called Aiko," I said. Not a question, a statement.

But Kee looked at me askance. "Not Japanese. He is Chinese. The inspector said to let you know we have picked up the man who is the Six Bamboo mah-jong tile."

FORTY-SIX

Aiko hadn't been picked up.

I pressed Sergeant Kee for more information but he just told me to wait. The inspector was expected soon because he had an appointment with Secretary Coates. To kill time and think, I went for a walk around the *Padang* and watched the stall keepers preparing for the evening's custom. After a loop, I walked back into the police station and was told Rahman was now in his office.

He looked up from his desk, his eyes betraying that he'd been up all night. I noticed that the pile of papers in his in-tray was even higher than last time I'd been there. I also noticed that the photograph of his father was no longer on his desk.

He gave me a weary smile.

I said, "Six Bamboo?"

"One of the members from the House of Tokyo. Real name Kim Wan Hoi. We went to question him and he ran. He lives in Yio Chu Kung village. It's notorious for drug dealing and anti-establishment behaviour." He smiled at the expression. "Secretary Coates's phrase not mine."

Of course, I thought, Hegarty updating Vernon and Rahman updating Coates.

I said, "What about Aiko?"

"Ah."

"Ah?"

"I didn't get your message until the early hours. I've bad news I'm afraid. We found him all right, only he was dead. Shot. My working theory is your man, Aiko was a dealer and Six Bamboo—Kim—was his supplier. So Aiko's death could be a drugs deal gone wrong."

"Was there evidence of drugs?"

"No."

I said nothing and Rahman studied me, as if trying to read my mind.

"There's more to this isn't there? What aren't you telling me, Ash?"

"It's connected to my friend's death and Cooke." I paused a beat. "We're pretty sure Cooke was also murdered." I explained the possible train of events and added what I'd been recently thinking through. I said, "Cooke was seen at Woodlands Crossing in a car. I don't think he was alone. I think someone was going to take him across but instead went back and led him through the jungle to the water's edge. Then he shot the sergeant and tried to sink the body."

"Any theories?"

"Nothing I'd like to share just yet," I said. "Unfortunately the person who spotted Cooke in the car didn't recall what the car looked like."

He sat back in his chair. "I'm about to give Secretary Coates an update. Do you think this is connected at all to a potential attack—the security issue—the guns?"

I said, "I don't know."

He studied me again and I wondered if he suspected I was holding something back, wondered if he knew about the obsolete M1s. I wasn't ready to tell him about those. Not yet. Not until there was more evidence.

When he spoke, however, he just said, "As soon as we have anything from Kim, I'll be sure to let you know."

I walked with him as far as the government buildings and then peeled off and headed back towards the Cathay Building and lunch with Su Ling.

She was sitting at an outside table and simply shook my hand when I arrived. Then she laughed.

"Don't be so sensitive, Ash. Underneath this cool exterior, my heart is racing and my body trembling. I just don't want... Not in public anyway."

"That's a relief. I just want you to know I feel the same way."

"Good," she said and then waved over a waiter and ordered for us.

After the man had retreated, she leaned over and said, "I hear a chef at the House of Tokyo is missing."

"He's dead. The police think murdered."

She asked a few questions and I told her what little I knew. Then she nodded. "Keiji is worried and now it seems justified. She has asked for protection."

"Why?"

"It seems she didn't tell the whole truth last time. She saw the incident with Tai Tai and Aiko, the chef. He threatened her. He told her to say she saw a Chinese man running away. But she didn't. The only person she saw was Aiko."

I asked if she knew Kim Song Choi, a customer of the House of Tokyo. She didn't.

I said, "He may have been dealing with Aiko. He may also be connected to Aiko's murder."

After our food arrived, she asked, "What are you going to do about Pantelis?"

"I haven't decided. It depends."

"There's something I've been thinking about. It may be relevant. When Keiji told us about Tai Tai's boyfriend, I may have misunderstood. I translated that her boyfriend was white and a soldier. She said *heitai*. It can mean soldier but it can also apply to a sailor."

"So you're thinking it's Pantelis?"

"It could be."

I shook my head. "But that doesn't fit with the other information: the letters in Cooke's bag and we know Pantelis picks up girls at Red Lion pub."

Su Ling looked thoughtful and shook her head. "You're right. I was thinking that maybe when she said he was her boyfriend it was past tense. Maybe she literally meant he was in the past but no longer."

I thanked her for the idea but I still wasn't convinced. We had a story that fit. Trying to make a different scenario fit...? Well, that was like discarding your hypothesis for another before finding a null result.

I ate a few mouthfuls and then stopped because she was watching me.

"What?"

"Just admiring you," she said, "if that's all right?"

I shook my head at the ridiculousness of it. Su Ling was elegant and exotic. I was in awe of her.

She smiled. "Stop looking at me like that."

"Oh it's all right for you..."

"But I was doing it in a less obvious fashion!" She laughed and briefly touched my leg under the table. "Please, we need to keep this professional—at least looking that way in public."

I accepted her request and focused my attention on noodles instead.

"You were saying," she said. "You said, what you do about Pantelis depends. Depends on what precisely?"

"Precisely what he's guilty of."

She looked at me quizzically, waiting for me to expand on my comment.

I said, "I still don't have concrete evidence although it looks like something will happen on the day of the parade. Maybe there are guns. Maybe there will be an attack of some sort. So I have two days."

"And after that? What will you do then?"

Of course I had thought about it and had a loose plan. But last night had changed things. Now I wasn't so sure. So I just said, "We'll see," and she accepted my answer.

After a brief silence I asked, "Have you found out anything about Madam Butterfly."

She shook her head and for an instant I wondered if she was sad.

"What's the matter?"

She smiled wanly and said, "Oh nothing. I can't help you with that."

I wondered whether she meant *ever* but didn't press for an explanation. Maybe she just meant she hadn't got information yet.

We ate and made small talk until it was time for her to go. As ever it seemed there was no bill to pay. The table was cleared, we stood and she offered me her cheek.

I kissed her and asked, "Will I see you tonight?"

"Not tonight I'm afraid," she said and looked genuinely sad. "Unfortunately I need to work later."

That reminded me of the diary I'd picked up in her room. I patted my breast pocket and realized it wasn't there. I'd left it in my suit jacket, distracted by the break-in.

I said, "My turn to apologize. I found your diary..."

Her eyes seemed to change colour, maybe it was a reflection but I could have sworn they darkened.

"You didn't read it, did you?"

"No. I was going to bring it to you but I seem to have forgotten. I could bring it over later if you need it."

Her eyes shone once more and she smiled. "No that's all right. Tomorrow, my love, save it until tomorrow."

Alone once more I looked around for a trishaw to take me back to the barracks. There were plenty around but it wasn't a trishaw I focused on. There was a skinny Chinese man about forty yards away, watching. And then I realized where I'd seen him before. It was the trishaw man who had taken me in the rain. The same one waiting outside Haw Par Villa.

I started to run towards him. In a flash, he pushed a trishaw driver off his bike and jumped on.

I crossed the road and flagged another trishaw. But instead of getting in the back, I flashed my warrant card. For a heartbeat I thought he was going to resist but he didn't. He just climbed off and a second later I was pumping my legs in pursuit of the other trishaw.

By body mass, I must have been twice the size of the other guy but he was like a greyhound on wheels. Plus he could corner and weave much faster than me. I was standing, pounding the pedals and yet I couldn't close the gap. He headed north and then east and was soon cutting through narrow, residential streets. He twisted and turned and when I rounded the next corner I'd lost him. But I didn't slow and I pressed on to a T-junction. He was nowhere to be seen. Left or right? I gambled. Most right-handed people will instinctively turn left when faced with the choice. But this man wasn't acting on instinct and I'm left-handed. So I turned right.

At the next junction, I stopped. I looked left, right and behind then left again and couldn't believe my luck. He was crossing the street just a stone's throw away. And what's more he didn't look in my direction. I raced after him again and expected to find him about fifty yards ahead when I rounded the next corner. But he wasn't. His bike was right in front of me. Empty. He was walking calmly into a shop-house.

I jumped off and followed.

The windows were too grimy to see inside and I realized this was not a shop in use. In fact the whole street appeared disused and on the verge of demolition. There was only one place the driver could have gone: inside. A partially open door cried out for me to go inside. I swung open the door and entered a gloomy room.

As my eyes adjusted, I saw the trishaw driver standing at the end of the room against the wall.

Only, he wasn't alone.

I knew because there was the unmistakable click of a gun being cocked. I looked left to see the barrel of a revolver aimed at my face. At the other end of the arm was the German.

FORTY-SEVEN

Pointing the gun at me, the German said, "Upstairs please."

I walked forward, towards the trishaw driver. There was a staircase at the back and we went up. The trishaw driver, me and then the German. The stair boards complained beneath our feet and I wondered if they could take our combined weight. But they did.

At the top, the Chinese man opened a door and the three of us filed through.

It was like going from black and white of Kansas into the Technicolor of Oz. Downstairs had been decrepit and dark. The room I was now standing in could have been in a luxury hotel. Heavy velvet crimson and gold curtains blocked the light of the window. There was just one light in the room. It came from a green banker's lamp on a desk which was covered in the same dark velvet. It was the size of a trestle table and I suspected it wasn't a solid desk below that cover.

No longer was I standing on rotten floorboards, but a deep pile rug. It had a gold and green trim, and a cream background but the thing that caught my attention was a sweeping crimson dragon. I was standing on its neck.

The Chinese guy went left and the German stayed behind me and to the right. Behind the desk was another

Chinese man. He wore a dark grey suit and looked like a thousand other businessmen except for one thing. He had a milky-white right eye, that I guessed was a severe case of cataracts.

On the desk in front of the white-eyed man were seven ledgers. Five large and two small. Pantelis's and Cooke's private books.

"Welcome," the man said. He didn't stand nor did he offer me a handshake.

"Who are you? What's going on?"

White-eye shook his head. "Captain Carter, you are in no position to ask questions." He nodded slightly towards the gun I knew was still in the German's hand behind me. And then he smiled, "But I have not brought you here to threaten you. I have brought you here for a little quid pro quo."

I glanced at the trishaw driver and realized I'd been played. He had wanted me to see him. He had wanted me to follow him here.

White-eye continued: "I would like a little information and I want to help you in return."

"How can you help me?" I asked.

"First," he said, "I want to know what these books mean. Why do you have them?"

"They might help me solve a case. They might be related to why a friend of mine died."

The other man looked at me, unblinking through his one good eye like a mortician might study a corpse. I figured he was judging whether I was lying or not. Or maybe he was just waiting to see if I'd say more.

I didn't.

He said, "What are you investigating, Captain?"

I thought, *what the hell, maybe this man can actually help me* and said, "A security issue. Secretary Coates—

276

the police—have intelligence of an attack. And it looks like it will happen this Sunday—on Lantern's Day."

He said nothing nor did he blink.

I said, "Do you know anything about it?"

Behind me the German spoke first. "We've heard nothing about an attack on Sunday or any day for that matter."

"Where does Andrew Yipp fit in?" White-eye said, still studying me. "Why are you working for him?"

"I'm not."

"You are spending a lot of time with the girl for someone who is not working with him." He paused and then shook his head a fraction. "Either you are working for him or you are a fool. You do know who he is?"

"But who are you?" I said.

"You honestly don't know?" the German asked. He had moved so that he was now off my right shoulder. I guessed he wanted to see my face.

"I don't know."

"And you are concerned about some sort of attack."

White-eye said, "Tell me about the ledgers."

"You said quid pro quo," I said. "Tell me something I don't know first."

The German started to speak but White-eye raised his hand to quieten him. He would tell me.

"Who is Su Ling?" he asked.

"She's Andrew Yipp's niece and works for him as a translator."

"Is that all she told you?"

"Yes."

"Did she also tell you he raised her? Did she tell you that she is his mistress?"

Bile burned my throat and I knew White-eye could read my reaction.

"You cannot trust her," he said. "She is not genuine. She is his lover not yours. Whatever she has done she has done for him."

Which meant that by default anything I told her, she was passing on to him. Of course she was. Deep down, I always knew it. I just wanted to believe there was something else. As his employee and niece I could accept it. As his mistress? I was being delusional.

"Quid pro quo," White-eye said.

"The ledgers might be evidence of a trade in guns."

The German said, "For the attack you mentioned?"

"Yes."

The man behind the table studied me before asking, "Who?"

"Who is trading in guns? Who is going to attack? I don't know. That's what I need to find out. The ledgers point to a British Army warrant officer but he's now dead, most likely murdered."

"And he was trading?"

"It looks like he sold them to a Japanese man in Nee Soon. A place called the House of Tokyo."

"Dongzing de fangzi," the German explained.

"Of course," the other man said. "One of Yipp's businesses. You know he owns most of Nee Soon village?"

I didn't but I wasn't surprised. From my pocket I pulled the flyer with the red circle and lion's paw. I showed it to the man at the table.

"Do you recognize this symbol?"

He smiled and I thought for a split second that he did but then he shook his head. "If it had been a dragon instead of a lion's paw then I might have recognized it." He glanced at the German who let out a laugh. "But no, I can not help you with this picture."

"It may be linked to the attack," I expanded hoping he'd say more but he didn't. He simply passed the flyer back to me. Then he looked down and I knew the meeting was over.

He said, "We did not meet and if you ever come here you will not find me. Understand?"

I did. Everything here was temporary. It could be folded and rolled up and moved in an instant.

"I'd like the books back, please," I said.

White-eye looked up and held my gaze. "No."

"I may need them to prove my case against the men involved."

"In that case we will see. But not yet. Maybe after we have found that you are telling the truth." Then he raised a finger and indicated for us to leave.

The German led the way downstairs, no longer concerned about holding a gun on me. They had what they wanted and they knew I was no threat. I may not know the Chinese man's name but I figured I could find out. He was Yipp's biggest rival and, although there were no secret societies, I had no doubt that White-eye was the head of the second one that didn't exist.

From the decrepit shop we emerged into bright sunlight and the German held out his hand.

"I apologize for the gun and the subterfuge," he said. "But you should be aware that spies are everywhere. You are being watched all the time. The only reason—"

I nodded. There was no need to explain. The only reason I had picked up on the trishaw driver was because they had wanted me to.

Then he surprised me by delving into a pocket and extracting a sheaf of documents. They were the other papers found in Cooke's bag.

He said, "We are keeping the ledgers but there's no more need of these. I assume you'd like them."

I took the pile and shook his proffered hand.

"If you need me... for whatever reason," he said with a knowing smile, "then you'll find me at the Goodwood Park club. And if I'm not there—"

"You soon will be," I finished for him.

FORTY-EIGHT

I used the Cathay Building as a landmark and cycled the requisitioned trishaw back to where I'd eaten with Su Ling.

My mind was in a thousand places and my stomach churned. I had been such a fool. A damned fool.

I eventually found the spot where I'd taken the bike and a skinny young Malayan staggered up to me. He was in tears and I soon realized they were tears of joy at seeing his prize possession returned.

"How much do I owe you?" I asked him.

He looked confused and then patted the air with both hands. He could have meant calm down or slow down but I judged he was telling me it was all right, that I owed him nothing.

"No," I said. "I took your bike. How much business have you lost?"

He reluctantly gave me a figure and I gave him double. At which point I think I made a friend for life but I patted him on the shoulder and headed back to Hill Street Station.

I breathed deeply and slowly but the sick feeling was still there when I arrived so I kept walking. I walked along the river and turned at the Government building. I began to amble and soak up the atmosphere around the

Padang again. Although the sun was relentless, there was a cool breeze off the sea and I imagined the saline air, filling my lungs and purifying my body.

I had played cards for years. I liked their mathematics, their dynamics, especially in the game of Bridge and also Poker—although I confess to playing this less well. I liked the feel of cards in my hands and their distraction. So I headed for where I was certain to find some: a NAFFI and I knew there was one just before the Raffles Hotel.

I bought a pack of Waddington's Number One and sat on a bench outside Saint Andrew's Cathedral, overlooking the *Padang*. I tore off the plastic and shuffled them, they were stiff at first but soon became pliable and so comfortable I could cut them with one hand. I tried not to think about anything but the cards brought back memories of the fortune teller. I wanted to think about anyone but Su Ling and here I was almost encouraging the memory.

I put the cards down for a moment and watched an odd-looking chap on the green practising fire-eating. I looked back at the cards and wondered if they could help me. I pulled out three kings and placed them on the bench to form a triangle. Spades was traditionally Swords and the King of Spades was the head of the knights. The head of the army: Gaskill. Diamonds represented wealth but more specifically merchants. The king was clearly Yipp. I remember someone once telling me that Hearts were originally Cups and represented the Clergy. I was outside the bastion of western religion right now but it wasn't religion I was thinking of. It was politics. A bit of a stretch maybe but the King of Hearts was the Governor. Or maybe Secretary Coates. I had three kings. I covered each king with his queen, jack and ten. The queen's didn't work so I removed all bar the

Queen of Diamonds. That was Su Ling. The jacks however made more sense. Diamonds was Yipp's henchman Wang. Gaskill's was Atkinson and Coates was—who, me? Rahman? I decided the latter because I thought of the tens as the pawns: the employees and members, the soldiers and the police. I wasn't the Jack of Hearts, I was more like the Joker. I was in the middle and I'd been acting like a fool.

I pulled out a Joker and shuffled it one-handed with the court cards. I stopped as I realized a little girl was watching me intently. She must have been about six or seven, blonde hair in ringlets, a puffed out white dress with a bright pink ribbon.

"Are you doing tricks?" she asked with such enthusiasm that I found myself smiling.

"I can read your mind," I said fanning the cards for her to select one. "Take one, remember it, and put it back. I will read your mind and tell you what it was."

She took the middle card, studied it and placed it back where I wanted it. I then proceeded to shuffle the cards very obviously with both hands and watch her excited face as I did so. Eventually I frowned. "Oh dear I don't seem to be able to do it."

I turned them over, fanned them out in my right hand and said, "I can't find it."

She looked at the cards and a frown started to form on her own face. "It's not there," she said and as she did I reached up and pulled her card from behind her ear.

"The Ten of Diamonds," I said to accompany her squeal of pleasure.

She clapped and asked me to do it again but her mother must have heard the squeal and grabbed the little girl's hand to lead her away.

I leaned back on the bench, put my hands behind my head and closed my eyes. All I had needed was the innocence of a six-year old to snap me back to my senses.

"Captain Carter?" a voice said and I opened my eyes.

Colonel Atkinson stood over me with a wide grin and his broad moustache. "Taking a well-earned break?" he asked.

"It seems that way."

The colonel sat beside me and copied my pose, hands behind his head, his feet outstretched. After a minute he dropped his arms. "I'm just about to go inside." I realized he was referring to the cathedral. "Care to join me?"

I declined the offer. "It may be wrong of me, but I'm finding this moment of peace and tranquillity far more spiritual than I could gain from being inside, I'm afraid."

"I know what you mean."

We sat in silence for a while and I sensed him relax.

"It's guilt," he said.

"Sir?"

"Why I feel I need to seek God's forgiveness."

I gave a nod as though I understood. "About the war?"

"It was a mistake," he said. "Do you know the story?"

"I know you were here during the invasion."

"Yes, the general made it sound like we both transferred before the invasion but I was still here. We had seventy-thousand front line soldiers, we had a vast superiority of numbers but strategically it was a disaster. I can admit that now. Not that I had any say in it, I was just a captain back in forty-two." He shook his head. "Ten years ago and sometimes it feels like last week."

"It must have been awful."

"The Japs attacked on the eighth of February. As I'm sure you know, we weren't ready. By the second day they were coming from every which way. They had their

284

heavy artillery on the island and they were slicing us apart. Percival decided we'd defend the Jarong Line—"

I knew this from the history Private Evans had recounted but I let him talk.

He pulled at his moustache before continuing. "There was an order to set a second defensive line west of the Reformatory Road. Everyone was called there, men from half destroyed regiments and reserve. But the message wasn't clear. The Jarong Line started to break because brigades were wrongly ordered to fall back. I was trying to muster a rag tag group of Australians and reservists—an ill-armed local brigade—and in the confusion some of my men thought they had the same order. I lost control and the Jarong Line broke up."

He swallowed hard and I waited for what was to come next.

"It was just a misunderstanding. By the time I found out it was too late." He swallowed again and looked away. When he put his hand to his eyes I was pretty sure it was to wipe away a tear. "I thought some of my men were cowards. I thought there was a risk of mutiny. So… I had three men executed… as an example you realize."

"It must have been awful," I said for a second time.

"You have no idea."

He was right. I had never been in a war. I had never experienced the chaos, the panic, the desperate need for clear orders and strategy.

He said, "The Japs came on the eighth. I executed the men on the tenth—God they were just reservists—and the war was all over by the fifteenth." He looked at me then and smiled wanly. "I pray that you are never in that situation, Ash. I pray to God that none of us is in that situation ever again."

FORTY-NINE

Should Atkinson have felt so bad? If I had been convinced of their guilt, maybe I'd have done the same although I suspected he had overreacted on limited information. Whatever, it was a nightmare he would probably never escape.

He shook my hand warmly and I watched him enter the cathedral.

I picked up my cards, tore up the Joker, and handed the pack to a passer-by. I thought about going back to Gillman but decided to call by to see Rahman in case Coates had said anything of worth.

When I arrived at the station I was surprised to see the inspector outside talking animatedly with Robshaw and Hegarty.

"There you are!" Rahman cried as he saw me approach. Then he started speaking so rapidly that I had to ask him to slow down and cover one thing at a time.

I said, "How did the meeting with the secretary go?"

Rahman tried to calm himself by first exhaling. "I did not see him. That's what I was saying. There has been a most urgent development."

"This Kim chap that you've picked up—he's talked?"

"No. Well nothing of use yet. No, we have found something in his home. Under the floorboards he had a box of the flyers about the attack."

Robshaw said, "So we have confirmation he is involved."

I held up a hand and focused on Rahman.

The inspector continued, "We also found a lion or dragon dancer's uniform, so again it seems to confirm that this is about the celebration but more than that." He sucked in air to compose himself again. "We found newspaper clippings. Pictures. The photographs are of the general."

"It's an attack aimed at General Gaskill," Robshaw added, stating the obvious.

Rahman held up his hands apologetically, "But I must have my meeting with Secretary Coates. I asked Lieutenant Robshaw here because no one knew where you were. So, my plan was that he could inform the general."

"The parade isn't until tomorrow. There's no rush. Let's all see the secretary and then let's all inform General Gaskill."

Rahman smiled and I could see he was grateful for the inclusivity. However, when we arrived at Coates's door, the secretary asked to see me and the inspector, but not Robshaw. A petty political game, I figured, but the lieutenant accepted the exclusion with grace. A few minutes later the inspector and I were in front of the secretary giving him an update.

At the end, he unnecessarily told us to meet with the general and determine what action we'd take. He also asked to be updated once we had a plan. Then he focused on me.

"You haven't mentioned Andrew Yipp," he said.

"No, I haven't."

"You have just told me that the police have a suspect in gaol but you haven't located the guns. What you haven't explained is how you have confirmed there are guns."

"It's complicated and to be honest it's not a hundred per cent. It is more important that we find and stop the attackers rather than worry about how they obtained the weapons."

If I had overstepped the mark with my abruptness, Coates didn't let it show. Instead he placed his hands together in a thoughtful manner.

"Andrew Yipp," he said, after a pause.

"What about him?"

"He will be behind this. Directly or indirectly, it will be him."

"We have no—"

"Then find the bloody evidence." He paused and smiled beatifically and I figured he had unintentionally let his feelings show.

"If there's anything against him, you can be sure we will act."

Coates nodded. "Just find something."

Hegarty drove the four of us up to Fort Canning but stayed outside with the jeep.

"I've not been inside before," Robshaw said as we waited for the clerk to let General Gaskill know we were here. "What about you, Inspector?"

Rahman seemed a little distracted perhaps lost in his own thoughts. "Pardon?"

"Have you been here before?"

"Oh no. Sorry. Never."

I said, "There's nothing to worry about. The general may be a little blunt but he's a nice guy."

Rahman smiled nervously. "That's very good to hear."

I glanced at Robshaw's straw-coloured hair that looked a little wild after the drive here. "However, Robbo, he may tell you to get your hair cut."

The lieutenant rapidly smoothed down his hair and a moment later the clerk returned. We were asked to wait in the library and told the general would see us as soon as possible.

I sat in a chair and looked out of the window, Robshaw hovered at the bookcase, reading titles and Rahman paced anxiously. I watched the light change and then Hegarty jump out of the Land Rover and start attaching the canvas roof.

Huge drops splattered on the library window before Hegarty had finished but he just managed to get back inside before the torrential downpour began.

It had stopped before the clerk knocked on the library door to tell us the general was now free.

He led us along the corridors that rang out with our shoe fall and took us to the room where I'd met with the general and Colonel Atkinson previously.

I patted Rahman on the shoulder and whispered, "Really, he doesn't bite."

"Let's hope you're right, my friend," he whispered back. And then we were through the door and standing in front of the general's desk. He stood up and his big frame seemed to fill the bay window behind him.

We saluted and I introduced each of us.

"We'll stand, if you don't mind, gentlemen. I've been sitting down, hunched over this desk all day so far and at my age..." He arched his back to emphasize discomfort. "Now what news do you have for me?"

I said, "In brief, sir, we are now convinced there will be an attack of some kind in two days' time. During the parade to be precise."

Gaskill nodded. He didn't need further explanation.

He said, "I'll inform Colonel Atkinson to work with you on tightening security."

"We believe that you, personally, are the target of the attack," I said.

"Me personally?"

"We found your picture with other things associated with the crime," Rahman said. "We are most concerned—"

Gaskill raised a hand quieting the inspector and gave me his avuncular smile. "I will be all right."

"Sir, this is a serious threat and I urge you to take the necessary precautions," I said.

The smile vanished and he held my gaze.

He said, "I don't run away."

"I'm not asking you to run away, sir. I'm asking that you implement the standard procedure for an attack on this position." I had discussed it with the others and we were of one mind. The general should be in the bunker. To deliberately place himself in harm's way would be reckless.

The general glanced away and the light briefly highlighted his beak-like nose. He looked like an eagle considering his position, and remained silent as he turned back to me.

I took the opportunity to continue: "Your bravery is not in question, sir. But just imagine the propaganda coup an enemy would achieve should you be assassinated."

"And who is the enemy?"

"We don't know... yet. The most obvious would be the communists."

"You don't know," the general said, nodding as though it explained everything. I suspected it explained our weak position. After seven days I knew the target and I knew when—although not precisely. I didn't know the location and, even worse, I was still unable to confirm the weapons. I sensed the case getting weaker as we stood and waited for the general to say anything more.

I was sure he was about to deny the request. And once denied, it would be nigh impossible to reverse.

So I gambled.

"Sir, can we speak alone?" I didn't have a plan yet, I didn't know how I would convince him. It was just a delaying tactic.

He dismissed the inspector and Robshaw and then gave me five minutes.

My arguments were weak. I just didn't want him to commit either way in front of anyone. And by the time he said my time was up, I'd at least got him to accept that the bunker was a possibility, that if I could find my concrete evidence, he would use it. And I would have right up until the start of the parade to present my case.

A mark of my semi-success was the key he handed to me. It was a key to the bunker. I knew the contingency was for the general and his staff to lock themselves in and only a trusted few held a key to release them once it was safe. Of course they had a key to lock themselves in, but once inside they could hear nothing. The only contact was by phone. The heavy iron key, I now held in my hand, was more symbolic than anything and dated back to a practice before telephones had been installed.

All I had to do now, was find my evidence.

On the drive back to the barracks, Robshaw and Hegarty wanted to talk. I sat in the rear, arms either side of the seat, my eyes shut. The roof was down again and I let the wind buffet my face as though it could drive away any negative thoughts. But it didn't work. I was thinking about Su Ling again. Thinking about the irony that a one-eyed man had tried to make me see the obvious.

"We need to find the guns," I said when we pulled up outside the office block. "Get the men on the streets and go over the parade route. We need to check every building that could possibly—"

"But aren't the police doing that?" Robshaw asked.

"By all means coordinate with them, but if there are guns out there, intended for an attack on the parade, we need to find them."

I didn't wait for another response. I was already walking up the steps to the officers' quarters. There was a diary I needed to check.

FIFTY

Bugis Street was humming with activity. It was ten in the evening and things were just starting to get more lively. I noted that the people were mostly locals, all colourfully dressed and in party mood. Bright awnings hung down from all the buildings that lined the street, sheltering much of it from the drizzle that had begun half an hour earlier. The sky was exceptionally black due to the cloud cover, but the lights along the street gave a daylight effect.

Corporal Whiteside tried to look casual as he leaned against a wall at the junction with Victoria Street, a main thoroughfare across the city. He held a bottle of beer and pretended to drink from it as he waited. Hegarty and I stood on the opposite side of the road, hidden from view by the street sellers. Twenty yards either side were plain-clothed MPs ready to rush into the road and prevent any car from leaving.

This was our trap to catch Madam Butterfly.

I had spent the rest of the afternoon in my room. The first thing I'd done was open Su Ling's pocket book and read her appointments. Unfortunately it was written in some kind of short hand Chinese that I couldn't read. However there were the occasional English words and times.

I couldn't help check all the known days when Madam Butterfly had struck. Each day had multiple entries but I couldn't be sure what they related to.

"Two minutes," Hegarty whispered.

I ordered some roasted chestnuts from the street vendor in front of us and handed the hot bag to Hegarty.

He shook his head. "Too on edge."

"Take one and pretend to eat it then."

I shrank further back so that I wouldn't be spotted—in case there was someone who might recognize me. Did I expect Su Ling? Based on Whiteside's description it could have been her. I didn't see a tattoo last night, but then again it had been dark and I wasn't looking for one.

There had been one entry in the diary that had sparked my interest. Three hours before we staked-out Bugis Street, I asked Hegarty to take me for a drive. First we went to Keppel Harbour and I sent him in to speak to the carpool guy.

He wasn't gone long and I was concerned our man had gone home for the night. But he was still there and he confirmed to Hegarty something I suspected. When he'd said the car had been a mess, he was referring to blood. There had been blood on the dashboard, front seat and inside the door.

"What does it mean?" Hegarty asked me.

"It means I'd like you to take me to see Tom Silverman's girlfriend." He drove us back to where we'd dropped her off five days ago and within ten minutes I was knocking on the door to her accommodation. A diminutive old Chinese lady answered the door, but I was soon welcomed in to meet Mei Fen.

The little lady fussed and offered me tea but I explained I wouldn't be long.

I then asked Mei Fen to sit and I told her that I was making progress.

294

"You know who killed him?" she prompted.

"I do," I said. "I haven't worked it all out yet but you can be sure he isn't getting away with it."

"Can you tell me who?"

"I think it's better you don't know." I nodded and hoped she understood. "Like I say, we will get justice— and soon."

She accepted that and shook my hand, her tiny cold fingers dwarfed by mine.

Before I left I had a quick favour to ask. I pulled out Su Ling's pocket book and asked her to translate tonight's meeting.

It was an address in Kallang, an industrial area on the far side of the river. And the entry was for two in the morning. I was briefly relieved that it wasn't for now, in Bugis Street, but then I later figured Madam Butterfly might not put these dates in her work diary, if she recorded them at all.

Just after quarter past ten, a woman approached Whiteside. They spoke for a moment and she melted back into the crowd. If it was the right woman, the pre-arranged signal was for Whiteside to place his bottle on the table. He didn't. It stayed clutched in his nervous hand.

"Too short, anyway," I whispered. "The woman we're after is almost as tall as Whiteside over there." I was picturing Su Ling in high heels. "Taller in fact."

I realized my mistake as soon as I said it. How would I know how tall she is? Whiteside had only seen long legs. He'd not seen her stand. And other reports were inconsistent. However, Hegarty didn't seem to spot my disclosure.

295

He glanced up the road, busy with cars and rickshaws. Except for the people drinking, everyone was on the move.

"We need to move," I said. "Standing around, even in the shadows, makes us stand out."

"Can we move under an awning? This drizzle is almost as bad as back home."

His comment made me smile. We started to stroll and I signalled the other plainclothes to copy.

I said, "You've been in the Tropics too long, Hedge. You've forgotten what cold and damp means. This is refreshing."

Then the sergeant grabbed my arm. "Bloody hell!"

"Not too obvious," I said, glancing Whiteside's way, "Stay relaxed."

Another woman was talking animatedly to our bait. It wasn't Su Ling, at least I didn't think so from a distance of thirty yards, but she was the right height.

I looked for a limousine, but couldn't see one. In fact there was no vehicle waiting anywhere. Maybe she came on foot this time. Maybe the plan was to walk to a car parked on another street.

Suddenly we couldn't see our man. The ebb and flow of people had resulted in a melee at the end of the street.

Hegarty did a small circle, walking into the road and back, trying to see through the bodies.

By my side again, he said, "I can't be certain but I don't think the bottle is on the table."

We were heading back. We reached the roasted chestnut seller opposite Whiteside. The woman had hold of his sleeve and was pulling at it. Whiteside was resisting.

We closed in but my eyes locked with Whiteside's. He mouthed something desperate and it took a few repeats for me to get it.

He was saying: "It's not her! Help me!"

I signalled one of the plainclothes who pushed through the crowd to Whiteside's table. In a swift move, he broke the woman's grip on Whiteside's arm and, ignoring her protestations, pulled her away and into the crowd.

Nothing happened for another five minutes. The crowd thinned and occasionally, Whiteside glanced our way for reassurance, I guessed.

The MP who had intervened walked past, heading back to his original position. "Bloody Ruby!" he whispered and Hegarty groaned.

He looked at his watch. "It's not looking good. One chat up and a lady-boy. Shall we call it a night?"

I said, "Let's give it until eleven."

Eleven o'clock came and went. The rain stopped and the clouds began to separate. There was still considerable activity on the streets although it had gradually thinned as couples had met and restaurant goers departed. The chestnut vendor began to pack away his stove and an odd shop light went out.

"She's not coming," I said more to myself than the sergeant. "Let's go home."

Thirty minutes later I was back in my room. I put on the black clothes I'd bought two nights ago. I took Pantelis's gun from my kit bag, checked the rounds and stuck it in my belt. Then I changed my mind. I didn't need it. This wasn't about confrontation; it was about observation. I needed to know what was going on.

Two minutes later I slipped out over the fence behind the MT yard and jogged down the road.

I had an appointment in Kallang.

FIFTY-ONE

Uncomfortable in my hiding place, it took me a good thirty minutes before I was used to the smell of sewage, gas and diesel. This was the industrial region in a wedge between the Rochor and Kallang rivers. I'd jogged as far as Commercial Square and decided to risk taking a taxi. I knew my destination was somewhere near the little civilian airport at Kallang but wasn't sure of the exact location.

The driver showed no interest when I asked for Kampong Bugis and I asked to be let out at the end of the road just after a gas works.

I'd found the building—a warehouse beside the smaller of the two rivers and hunkered down behind oil drums. From here I was hidden but had a clear line of sight of the entrance.

The moon was at its zenith and only a few days off full. However I had a route to the warehouse that was mostly in the shadows.

This part of the industrial area was deserted. Once I'd left Kallang Road and the taxi behind me, I'd seen no one.

I had located the warehouse and noted it had two doors, large enough for a truck. One of them had a smaller pedestrian entrance. There were no windows but there appeared to be a long skylight in the roof. I found a wooden box and a barrel and moved them to the rear of the warehouse.

I found my hiding place behind the drums, the river stink in my nostrils, and waited.

There were noises from boats on the river and out at sea. I also heard cars and the occasional metallic noise from somewhere on the site. These gradually diminished and nothing happened until one-thirty when a lorry drove up. I couldn't see the make but it looked like a Bedford fifteen-hundred. The vehicles the army used. With half panel sides and a frame that could be covered in canvas, I judged it to be empty.

The driver got out and opened the twin doors to the warehouse. He drove the vehicle inside and closed the doors. Then the skylight told me interior lights had come on.

After another five minutes, a smaller van and a car appeared. A passenger from the van jumped out, opened the doors and both vehicles followed the first. This time the doors weren't closed until two men were standing guard outside. They leaned on the front wall and lit cigarettes.

Another few minutes passed and another Bedford-type lorry arrived. Only this one was covered, and by the way it was driven I guessed it had cargo of some kind.

Hugging the shadows, I crept to the warehouse wall. I could hear voices inside making no attempt to be hushed, unconcerned about being overheard.

At the rear, I climbed onto the box and then the barrel and took hold of the top of the wall. I pulled myself up and over the edge and lay flat for a moment drenched in moonlight, exposed. If someone came around the back and looked up, they would see me for sure. No one did.

The roof was corrugated, probably asbestos, and not easy to cross. I squirmed over to the skylight and looked down into the warehouse.

On the ground, about fifteen below, I could see two rows of benches. Between them a long trestle table ran along the middle of the room. Around the outside were empty wooden crates. People sat on the benches and others either appeared to be ferrying items or clearing up.

I counted twelve people, all men, all Chinese. I figured that the second lorry to arrive had transported the workers. The first truck was close to the far end of the tables. I could see things being unpacked from sacks and repacked into boxes. The boxes were being loaded into to the truck.

The boxes had writing on the top.

I strained to see as much as possible, by pressing my face to the edge of the window. A box lid was raised and I saw the writing clearly: US Army Medical Supplies.

My surprise was met with a cracking sound.

I had just enough time to register the noise when the roof gave way beneath me.

A huge section of asbestos collapsed into the warehouse and I fell with it. Flat onto my stomach.

Dust billowed and I quickly stood.

Six men were already encircling me. They didn't have weapons, but they looked like they meant business. Not one of them was over about five and a half feet and yet they all looked fearless.

The other men started to close up behind. Six against one, twelve against one. The odds weren't great.

I tried to look relaxed and raised an apologetic hand. I was about to say sorry for dropping in, but before I opened my mouth, the first man stepped and kicked.

I blocked it and punched him in the head. I swivelled, expecting the next attack to come from behind but it didn't. These guys weren't a one-at-a-time bunch, they were all-at-once. Every single one of them attacked.

I ignored the blows and focused. Hit, move, hit. I floored three before my vision started to blur. The attacks were too intense, too rapid.

It was like being on the ropes, your opponent in control. All you can do is take the blows and hope he wears himself out or the bell saves you.

But this was no boxing ring and there was no bell.

And then the attack just stopped.

I heard a bark: "Stop!"

Somewhere in the back of my mussed-up brain I recognized the voice.

A woman. Strong. Commanding.

I was on one knee and pushed myself up to stand. My vision cleared and there, before me, was Su Ling.

She said, "You were lucky the armed men were outside."

Behind her I could now see the two smoking guards. They both had revolvers aimed at me.

I looked back at her. This wasn't the woman I'd spent lunch with. This was a different Su Ling. Her eyes were dark and cold like she didn't know me. Or I was dirt on her shoes.

I said, "I'm sorry."

"What are you doing here?"

"I thought..."

"What? That you would find your missing guns here? Tonight?"

I said nothing but she was right.

She shook her head. "Why have you betrayed me?"

I scrabbled around in my head for an explanation that would make sense. The German. The white-eyed rival.

The information they had told me about Su Ling. She was more than Yipp's translator. Niece was a euphemism for lover. She was using me and maybe she was Madam Butterfly.

"Were you on Bugis Street tonight?"

She looked at me quizzically and then almost spat her next words with disgust: "Questions with questions, Captain Carter."

"Did you not go to meet Corporal Whiteside because I warned you?"

"You are talking nonsense."

"Did your father really watch you dance?"

For a fraction of a second I saw her features freeze with the truth behind my question.

She didn't respond but after a few beats signalled to someone I guessed was out of sight behind the truck. Then she said, "What do you think is going on here?"

"Something you don't want the authorities to know about."

She laughed mirthlessly. "Is that the best you can do?"

I stepped over to the nearest bench. The table was covered in dust. More than had been caused by the falling roof.

"Drugs?"

Su Ling pointed to a box and one of the labourers opened the lid. Inside were bandages.

She nodded and the man lifted a section away to reveal something under the bandages: bags of almond-coloured powder.

She seemed to wait for me to understand.

I said, "Opium?"

"No. This is ground poppy seeds."

From my limited knowledge of opium, I believed the drug was made from the lactose from the poppies. Not the seeds themselves. I looked at the sacks that were yet to be opened and wondered if I wasn't being shown the whole thing here.

I said, "Why the cloak and dagger routine for poppy seeds?"

She smiled without any warmth. "This isn't a question and answer session, Captain. I am merely showing you that this has nothing to do with guns. This has nothing to do with any security threat real or imagined." She paused for effect and then said, "This is none of your business."

With the slightest movement of her head, she instructed the men to move.

The two guns came close to my face and strong hands ripped my arms. They quickly lashed my hands behind my back and then bound my arms at the elbows, squeezing my shoulder blades together until I bit my tongue against the discomfort. Finally they jerked me to the ground and bound my ankles.

I looked up at her. "What are you going to do with me?"

"I could throw you into the sea, Captain. I doubt you would ever be found and no one would ever know."

"Is that what you did with Sergeant Cooke?"

"Really, your fantasies are beginning to become tiresome." She sighed and for the first time I sensed real disappointment with me. "I did not arrange for Cooke to be killed. I had nothing to do with him. None of Mr Yipp's men had anything to do with him."

I was picked up by four men and carried beyond the truck. There were offices set against the wall and I was dropped onto the floor inside one.

Su Ling waited for the men to leave us before she said, "I will come back in a short while." And then she closed the door.

I was trussed up, and after a little squirming decided that there was nothing I could use to cut the bindings. So I got myself as comfortable as possible and watched the door, waiting for her to return. I heard the sound of boxes being opened and closed and loaded. Later I heard the warehouse doors open and two vehicles start up and leave.

Then the door opened and Su Ling was framed by the warehouse lights. She dropped something on the floor close by.

Her voice remained cold as she said, "It's a pen knife. I'm also going to leave the key in the door. I am sure you can get out but we'll be long gone by the time you do. Do not try to find out where we went. And I would like my diary back."

I nodded.

"And one last thing. If it had been Wang here tonight, you would have been feeding the fishes by now."

I nodded again and said, "I'm sorry." I meant it but I could no longer see her face. And she closed the door and locked it.

I wriggled over to the knife, lay on my back over it and slowly tried to saw through the bindings on my wrists. I heard the last vehicle leave. The lights went out and the doors clunked shut.

I was alone.

FIFTY-TWO

The man who called himself Jin walked into Tan Tock Seng Hospital.

There was just a smattering of night staff and no one gave him a second glance as he walked past the reception and along the corridor. Anyone he saw either had their head down, half asleep or were busy with some emergency.

Jin climbed the stairs to the second floor and walked towards the ward where he knew Tai Tai was being treated. A secure room had been arranged and there would be a policeman standing guard—even though no one knew why. He stopped at the corner and took a quick look around.

The policeman was sitting in a chair, head on his chin. So much for *standing* guard.

Jin's plan had been to send the man a drink and then wait for him to need the toilet. There was just one policeman so when he needed a break, the room was no longer guarded. But if he was asleep... well it could all be so much quicker and easier.

Jin was considering the risk when an orderly came out of the girl's room. The man opened and closed the door and walked away. There was no attempt to keep quiet but the policeman didn't stir. Perfect.

When he was sure the corridor was clear, Jin rounded the corner and walked straight to the room. Without a pause, he took hold of the door knob and was inside. He'd planned an excuse in case there was someone waiting inside but there was no one. Just the girl.

She looked peaceful and if hadn't been for the drip running into her veins, Jin would have guessed she was sleeping rather than in a coma.

She was pretty, for a Japanese girl, he decided. She had an unusually delicate bone structure, almost Indian but with alabaster skin. And she looked much younger than nineteen. She could probably pass as a school girl, which he figured was part of the attraction.

He took a long breath. He had to do this and quickly. He couldn't risk her coming out of the coma before the New Year's parade. If the MP Captain realized her involvement he might connect the dots... might see the truth of it all. It was too great a risk.

There was a chair beside the bed with a spare pillow on it. Jin picked it up and stood over the bed.

Her little chest moved almost imperceptibly under the sheet.

He swallowed hard. This wasn't him. OK he'd killed the Japanese security man from Dongzing de fangzi but he was scum. He deserved to die. But this little girl... All right she was involved but she was no drug dealer.

He placed the pillow over her delicate face. She didn't stir.

Tai Tai just got mixed up with the wrong man. That was all.

He leaned on the pillow and tried to block out the mental image of a pretty girl beneath it. She began to move and he pressed down harder. And then it was over. She had hardly reacted. Maybe she never knew.

Jin lifted the pillow and looked at her face. She still looked like she was sleeping. Yes, he told himself, she's just asleep.

He returned the pillow to the same spot on the chair and stepped towards the door. Through the narrow window he could see no one outside except the sleeping guard. He turned and took one last look at Tai Tai.

"I'm sorry," he said.

He slipped out of the room and down the corridor. Again no one confronted him or even paid notice. Perhaps they thought he belonged there.

Once outside he walked two hundred yards to where he'd parked his car, well beyond the hospital. He sat in the darkness and breathed deeply. This had to be done. When he got home he would look at the photograph and remind himself. There was no room for sentiment.

It was an eye for an eye.

FIFTY-THREE

Yesterday I had spent the evening and night with the most alluring, beautiful woman I had ever known. Now, the darkness brought with it dark thoughts. What had I been thinking? I had believed the white-eyed gangster, the rival of Andrew Yipp, and betrayed the trust of the girl I was head-over-heels about. And the reason I did it was because I somehow thought she could be Madam Butterfly. But she hadn't been playing me in the same way as that woman had conned the other men. Otherwise we would have just had one date and I'd have ended up with a lump on my head and a hole in my wallet.

And from my misapprehension I'd projected the other issue: the possible attack in two days' time and the guns.

I cut through the final bonds and tried the door. But of course it was locked.

My eyes had become accustomed to the milky-grey darkness caused by the moonlight through the roof. Outside the room was lighter than inside and through the keyhole I could see the key still there.

I found a piece of paper and pushed it under the door. Using the penknife, I jiggled the key in the hole and within seconds had it out—on the other side of the door. It fell onto the paper and I pulled it through to my side.

The warehouse was empty. All the tables had gone and the asbestos had been cleared away but there was still a hole where I'd fallen through the roof.

I walked out of the building and down the road. I kept on walking the two miles back to the city centre. My dark thoughts still swirling in my head, the river stink thick on my clothes.

I took my mind off my failure tonight by thinking about what I knew and what I didn't know. Secretary Coates had information from the police about a security issue—a potential attack that looked like it would be on the day of the parade. In fact Su Ling herself had realized the meaning of the date. Forty was nineteen-fifty-two.

The police had found Aiko dead but found the guy he was dealing with—Kim aka Six Bamboo. The police had found the flyers and a lion or dragon dancer's costume at Kim's home and he was now being interrogated.

We had no sign of guns although we had discovered obsolete M1s had been shipped to Keppel eight months ago. I had compared Pantelis's ledger with the one found on Cooke and identified a trade that look remarkably like they may be the guns we were looking for. But Pantelis denied it and Cooke was dead.

Aiko and Tai Tai. What was her role, if any, in all this? Her friend had lied or been confused. There had been no one else involved. Tai Tai's coma had been caused by Aiko. And then there was the boyfriend. Su Ling translated *heitai* as soldier but it could refer to a sailor.

If only Cooke wasn't dead or Tai Tai able to talk. They were the important pieces in this that would make sense of it. Maybe.

I had crossed Fullerton Bridge without noticing it and was now standing in the square. It was after three in the morning and the lights inside The Singapore Club blazed. I wondered if Pope was up there drinking his watered-down whisky. I should thank him for the boat trip and dinner. Of course that looped my thoughts back to Su Ling and my betrayal. She couldn't be Madam Butterfly. White-eye had been lying. Su Ling hadn't been brought up by Andrew Yipp. Her father had watched her dance when she'd been twelve.

At dinner on the junk I'd learned she was twenty-four which meant she was probably twelve in nineteen thirty-nine or maybe nineteen forty if she'd just had a birthday. She said her father was Captain Keith. I didn't think Keith was a common surname and he must have overlapped with Atkinson's tour of duty. I decided to ask the colonel in the morning.

It was probably irrelevant but the positive action lifted my spirits enough to say yes, when a trishaw driver asked if I wanted a lift.

As I sat back in the seat I realized how much my body hurt. I'd fallen fifteen feet, flat on my chest and taken a beating from a gang of crazed Chinese men. I was lucky nothing was broken, though at that moment I didn't feel the slightest bit lucky. I was tired and I had a headache. Had I taken a blow to the head? Probably. A quick examination said I had. There were a couple of lumps on the back of my head, my right eye socket felt sore and my jaw was tender.

I asked my driver to drop me a mile from Gillman so that I could walk for a while.

Before I paid the man I said, "Tell the German I will be at Goodwood Park tomorrow. Tell him I want the Japanese letter back. Tell him I can trade."

The man looked at me blankly for a second and I thought I'd misjudged. These men have a thousand spies and I just happened to pick someone who wasn't.

But as I turned away he said, "You trade what?"

I swung back around and the man still looked at me with his unreadable expression.

"I have information about Andrew Yipp," I said. "Tell him to be there at lunchtime."

FIFTY-FOUR

On my back, eyes on the ceiling, I stared at the lizard. There was no point in trying to sleep. Daybreak was more than three hours away but I couldn't rest so I showered and dressed. I put on my suit and looked at myself in the mirror. It felt peculiar to be setting out for the day wearing anything other than the usual shorts and short-sleeved shirt but I no longer felt like an MP. Dressed like this was somehow liberating.

I packed everything into my suitcases and said farewell to the room and lizard.

At the bottom of the steps, I went into the office.

The night-duty clerk was Corporal Franks. He gave me a double take. Maybe it was the suit or suitcase or maybe it was the marks on my face.

"Quiet?" I asked, dropping my cases by the door.

"Quiet," he said.

"I need a favour."

"Sir?"

I took his tone to mean yes. I said, "Take a smoke break."

"But..."

Of course he wasn't allowed to smoke on duty but I knew he'd take little persuasion. "Five minutes," I said. "And Franks..."

"Sir?"

"Leave the keys."

As soon as he was outside, I took the large bunch of keys from the duty desk and found the ones for the offices. The second one I tried opened Major Vernon's door.

There was the tall metal cabinet with a huge number of drawers. I tried a few but they were locked. However I doubted this was where he'd file what I was looking for. I turned my attention to the credenza beside his desk. There was a key hole but the two doors weren't locked. Inside were hanging files with dates on the tabs. I delved into one and pulled out a list: Staff movement. Names and ranks of people arriving at the barracks and leaving. Bingo!

I located a sheet from a year ago with ten names and was scanning it when there was a knock on the door.

Franks looked in, awkwardness etched on his face.

"Sir, the major has just driven up through the barrier. I saw his face in the spotlight. You have about a minute. God knows what he's doing back here at this hour."

I stuffed the papers in my pocket, closed the drawer and tossed the letter opener on the desk.

Outside the office I handed Franks the keys and thanked him. I was through the entrance door just as Vernon started up the path.

It was still dark and I was up close before he realized it was me and how I was dressed. He stopped, looked me up and down and then more deliberately at the suitcases in my hands. "Going somewhere Carter?"

I guessed he'd been drinking, his tone slightly off due to too much alcohol.

I didn't break my stride.

"You need me, I'll be at The Queens Hotel," I said and headed for the gate.

"I hope you aren't giving up on the Madam Butterfly case!" he yelled after me. But I didn't respond and I didn't turn round. I was starting afresh and Gillman was not in my plans.

It was almost half past five and still dark. A car stopped on the coast road and I thought it was a taxi. But it was just a guy who'd been out all night. He said he was in textiles whatever that meant. The car smelled of booze but he seemed sober enough. He was heading home to somewhere in the north of the city and I expected him to drop me in the centre. But he kindly took me all the way to The Queens Hotel.

The night manager looked at me dubiously when I asked for a room until tomorrow.

"You'll have to pay for the night," he said.

Of course. If the attack was going to happen tomorrow then I wouldn't need the room another night but then it became clear what he meant: If I wanted the room now, I'd have to pay for last night.

He was probably playing me. What the hell? I showed him my government ID and told him to charge it to Secretary Coates.

I checked my watch and asked to use the phone. Just before six in Singapore which would be ten in the evening in London.

The night manager showed me to the manager's office I'd used last time. After asking the operator for Whitehall in London, I waited a good three minutes before I was put through to my father's office. He often worked late so I hoped he'd still be there. He wasn't but his clerk was. The same lady I'd spoken to before. She sounded tired and I guessed she was about to pack up for the night.

I said, "I need a favour, Sam."

"From me or your father?"

"My father if he'll do it. Otherwise..."

I thought I heard her sigh then she said: "What is it?"

I asked her to write down the list of names that I'd taken from Vernon's office, the men who had left a year ago.

She said, "And what do you want him to do with those?"

So I told her about Vernon's fencing club. "I want to know how much they've received back," I finished.

"And when do you need this by?"

"I'll call same time tomorrow."

Again the sigh.

"Please, Sam, this is really important. Do what you can but I need it for tomorrow morning here." And I did because, based on my current thinking, I wasn't going to be around after tomorrow.

"I can't promise," she said in a voice that said she'd do her best.

I thanked her, ended the call and went to find my room.

It was on the second floor and I flopped onto the bed suddenly dead tired. I didn't recall falling asleep but woke up with bright sunlight in my eyes because of a gap in the curtains. I'd slept for three hours and still felt groggy even after splashing my face with icy cold water.

I needed a clear head. The parade was just a day away and I still didn't have all the pieces straight in my mind. Being away from Gillman Barracks would hopefully give me a different perspective. I felt the need to break from the confines of military thinking and see the bigger picture.

I also wanted to park the Madam Butterfly case. It was a distraction and yet my mind kept returning to it.

315

Not because of Vernon, more likely the betrayal of Su Ling.

Today there were things I needed to do and resolve. Then I could properly focus on the likely attack.

First things first. I needed to make three more phone calls.

FIFTY-FIVE

Undeterred when Su Ling refused to take my call, I left a message.

"Please tell her that I will return her pocketbook," I said. "I'll be at the Cathay Building at two today. I would be very grateful if she would see me briefly." I added the last line in the hope that she didn't just send an assistant to pick up the diary.

My second call was to Fort Canning and was put through to Colonel Atkinson.

"Have you found the guns?" were Atkinson's opening words.

"Not yet, sir. That's not why I called. I wondered if you could check the records for me. I'm interested to know where a Captain Keith served up to and during the invasion."

"Here in Singapore?"

"Yes. I also wondered what happened—whether he was killed, sent to Changi or escaped."

"It's not a familiar name, but I'll check for you."

He said he'd let me know and I told him where I was staying. He didn't question why I had moved out of Gillman and for that I was grateful.

My final call was to Gillman. I asked for Hegarty but was put through to Robshaw. Again the other man spoke first.

He said, "Where the heck are you?"

"The Queens Hotel."

I could hear him processing that but he didn't question my reasoning either. Instead he said, "That girl in a coma..."

"Yes?"

"She died last night. Since the paperwork was in motion, she's now been moved to the Alexandria but she's in the morgue."

"Natural causes?"

"Looks that way."

I thought for half a second. I'd decided Tai Tai was pivotal to the case. There was something just out of reach that I wasn't getting and now she could never tell me herself. Too frustrating. Too convenient.

"Ask the coroner to make absolutely sure. Double check. No – tell him to triple check."

"Will do. Was there anything else?"

"Is Hedge there and available?"

A moment of muffled talking and Hegarty came on the line.

I said, "Can you chauffeur me around for a few hours?"

"Yes. Where shall I pick you up?"

"The Queens Hotel."

"Why—?"

I cut him off. "Bring Corporal Whiteside with you. How long before you can be here?"

"I'll pick you up in half an hour."

While I was waiting I went back to my room and lay on the bed. There was a crack in the ceiling and may as well have been the lizard from the barracks, since neither moved.

I stared at it and thought about guns going from Tanglin to Keppel and then Pantelis selling them back to Cooke. Tai Tai was his girlfriend. Or was she? Was this all the wrong way round? And if it were then what did that mean for the guns? What did it tell me about Cooke's murder? I played a few scenarios through my mind and decided that I would know for sure if someone needed Tai Tai dead. So that she couldn't talk. So that she wouldn't point her finger at the guilty party.

A knock on the door broke my train of thought and I followed a porter downstairs where Hegarty and Whiteside were waiting.

The sergeant grinned to mask his surprise. "Out of uniform now?"

I smoothed my jacket and nodded.

"But you're still on the case?" he asked.

"At least until the end of tomorrow," I said. "But for now I'd like you to take me to Goodwood Park on Scotts Road."

"I've never been inside before," Hegarty said as we got into the jeep, me in the passenger seat, the junior man in the rear.

"Sorry, Hedge," I said, "you aren't going in this time either. I'd like you to wait outside... unless there's any trouble. In which case you can come in and rescue me."

He laughed. "What about Whiteside? Mind telling me what you need him for?"

I swivelled so that I could see the young man behind.

"I just want you to keep your eyes peeled. I want to know if you see the woman you snogged in the back of the car."

He nodded meekly.

"You think we'll meet Madam Butterfly," Hegarty asked as he turned up Orchard Road and put his foot on the accelerator.

I shrugged. "She's in this city somewhere, Hedge. We just need to know where."

We arrived twenty minutes before my appointment with the German—assuming he'd received the message that is. Since I hadn't eaten since yesterday lunchtime my stomach complained as I walked across the lounge and smelled fresh baked bread.

The waiter showed no surprise when I ordered a full English breakfast as an early lunch. I also asked for some of the bread with butter while I waited.

It didn't disappoint. The bread was still warm with a hint of yeast and the butter oozed over it like nectar.

I had barely begun when a side door opened and the German appeared. He surveyed the room first before deciding I was alone and it was safe to join me.

He hung back a second as my breakfast was served. Then he sat down opposite me.

"Hungry?" he asked.

"Like I haven't eaten in a week."

He smiled and nodded. "I should leave you in peace then and let you eat."

"Have you brought the letter?"

The smile faded momentarily. "You said you have information for me."

"Who is your boss?" I asked. "The man I met—the one with the cataracts?"

"A business man."

Now it was my turn to smile. I recalled how Su Ling had introduced Yipp and said, "A business man, a merchant and philanthropist."

"And not forgetting a politician."

320

"He's on the Elected Assembly?"

"Not yet. But one day. One day things will be different. At least we hope so for Singapore's sake."

"Is he sympathetic to the Communist cause?"

"I don't think you should be asking me that."

"But I am."

"In which case I am not answering."

"Why all the secrecy? Can you at least tell me that?"

"Because he is a ghost."

I shook my head, not comprehending.

The German explained: "Chen Guan Xi travelled to China a few months ago and was refused the right of re-entry. According to your Secretary Coates, he was a threat and so invoked the Internal Security Act. And therefore you never met him because he is not in the country." He paused and took a sip of water before fixing me with gimlet eyes. "You said you have information to trade for the letter but I am already saying too much." He patted his breast pocket suggesting that he did indeed have the letter on him. "What do you have for me?"

So I told him about Yipp's warehouse beside the Rochor River. His expression told me that he didn't know about it. He also didn't know what they had been doing.

"Bottles of opium being crated up?" he asked.

"That's what they said and that's what it looked like."

"Interesting. Although I too have no idea why." He watched me eat and seemed to be thinking. Then he asked, "Will you tell me what you were expecting to find, Captain? You went to a great deal of subterfuge to watch them packing medical supplies."

"Guns maybe."

"Because of the rumoured attack?"

I watched his face as I ate for a moment.

321

He reached into an inside pocket and handed me the Japanese letter found in Cooke's bag.

I thanked him and said, "Could you also assure me of something? As far as you know, is your boss or any of his men planning anything tomorrow night?"

"Oh I'm sure they are." He laughed and continued: "There's the parade and people are bound to party. Oh and the Ho Ho Biscuit Company—one of his businesses—has a float." When he saw I was serious he added: "There will be no trouble from us. Not even the rivalry with Yipp will be a problem. That is all under the water."

I figured he meant like a duck's feet paddling. An observer couldn't see what was going on beneath the surface.

He said, "You want assurance? I can give you assurance. The guns have nothing whatsoever to do with us. I can also reaffirm that we have heard no rumours about an attack or the acquisition of guns. It looks to me, Captain Carter, as if someone wants you to think there are guns."

"And why would they do that?"

"That, Captain, may be the pertinent question."

FIFTY-SIX

Did the German's final comment bother me? Not really. I had also been thinking that the whole thing could be Secretary Coates's mechanism for getting me to find leverage against Yipp. Or maybe it was leverage against Gaskill.

Hegarty drove back down Orchard Road and stopped outside the Cathay Building. I positioned Whiteside outside and asked him to look as casual as he could.

Su Ling kept me waiting ten minutes before the elevator doors opened and she stepped out. For a moment I thought that she would change her mind and go back up. She stood still and regarded me as the doors clunked shut behind her. Perhaps she was composing herself or deciding what to say. Whichever, she eventually started to walk towards me, her eyes straight ahead, unfocused as though I were invisible.

When she stopped a few feet away, her eyes met mine and I registered how green they looked. The cool air-conditioned atmosphere of the foyer seemed to drop a notch as we faced one another, neither speaking.

I opened with, "Hello."

"You have my pocket book?"

"It's here," I said digging it from my pocket and holding it out.

She took it but said nothing.

I said, "I'm sorry."

"So you said last night. Thank you for returning this." She tapped the book in her hand. "I hope—"

"I have a small favour to ask," I interrupted. Her expression said *you're joking!* but I held out the letter from Tai Tai to Billy. I said, "Something's been bothering me. The relationship and the trades between Sergeant Cooke and Pantelis. Please could you look at this and tell me whether you think it could be left-handed."

She smiled then although it was mirthless.

As she took the letter, I moved slightly to one side. I wanted Whiteside to get a good view, just in case he hadn't moved already.

Su Ling studied the paper and I could imagine her thinking about the pen strokes; how would she have written the letters. Then she handed the letter back to me and gave me a quizzical look.

I said, "The ledger entries were by someone left-handed but Sergeant Cooke was right-handed."

She nodded. "I can't be sure but I would bet that these Japanese characters were drawn by a left-handed person."

"I know it's an imposition, but—"

"What? You are asking me to find out whether Tai Tai was left-handed? The answer is no, Captain Carter." She started to turn, hesitated and continued: "I'd rather I never had to see you again."

And then she was back at the elevator and I was alone in the foyer.

My motives had been two-fold. Yes I'd wanted to find out if Tai Tai was left-handed but I'd also wanted

Whiteside to get a good look at the woman I'd spent the night with. Could Su Ling be Madam Butterfly?

"Better looking," Whiteside said when I asked him.

"So you're sure it's not the same woman?"

"Both looked Eurasian but like I said, the woman you just met was a knock out, Captain. The woman I was in the car with was sexy, but... well, just not as good looking."

I pumped the young man's hand and then felt awkward for showing how relieved I was to hear his judgement.

"Where to now, Boss?" Hegarty wanted to know.

"Hill Street Station. Let's find out how the search for the guns is going."

We scooted around the fort to reach the station and, when we got there, I suggested the other men come inside with me.

Rahman met us at the reception, his eyes bulging with excitement. And when he spoke, his words came out like rapid fire.

"Where have you been? I've been trying to get hold of you for over an hour. I asked at the barracks and they couldn't tell me."

"What's happened?"

The inspector looked from me to the other MPs at my shoulder and said, "Can we speak in private?"

I followed him into the corridor where he turned and gripped my arms. "We have some news of the guns. Kim has talked." He glanced about, checking no one could overhear. "I've been delaying things because I wanted you to be with us when we go there. But..."

"Yes?"

"It's awkward. I appreciate you are an MP..."

"Not really, Anand. You know the situation."

325

He smiled. "Well it's good to hear that! It's just that... This is a big deal for me... for the police. You understand?"

"You don't want to share the glory with the army. Is that what you're telling me?"

Now he looked contrite. "It's..."

"It's fine."

I walked back into the reception area and spoke to Hegarty, asking him to find out the latest from the coroner at Alexandria Hospital. And if he hadn't performed the autopsy to make sure he did it soon.

The sergeant was disappointed but accepted my instruction without complaint.

When they had left, I asked Rahman, "So where are the guns?"

"Geylang Village. According to Kim, they're stored in a shop-house there."

We jumped in a waiting black Austin 5 and were followed by two more, crammed with policemen. Our car just had a driver and the two of us in the rear.

"Tai Tai is dead," I said.

"Yes. It is a great pity. You said you thought she could help us if only she came out of the coma."

"What happened?"

"I do not know the detail but I understand they did not know she had died in the night until the orderlies came to prepare her for transportation in the morning."

As we weaved through the streets I recognized them from when I'd chased the trishaw driver and met the white-eyed man.

I said, "There was a sentry outside her room?"

"Yes, of course."

"So no one could have got in?"

"Her room was permanently guarded. Surely you don't think she was murdered?" He sounded shocked at the suggestion but I couldn't shake the idea.

I looked out of the window. We were now beyond the ghetto and in an area I didn't know.

"Even if she was murdered—" Rahman said thoughtfully, "although I can't see why—even if she was, hopefully it won't matter now if we find the guns." Then he pointed. "Here. This is the street. We'll stop at the end and walk."

Our driver pulled to the kerb and one of the following cars parked behind us. The second car continued up the road and stopped about eighty yards away.

As we stood on the pavement, surveying the row of shop-houses, I became acutely aware of how heavily armed the police squad was. Rahman had a holstered pistol but the other five men had rifles, two handed, at the ready.

Four policemen from the second car mirrored us until Rahman gave a signal. As his men responded by putting up a cordon at each end of the street, civilians rapidly melted away until we were the only ones outside.

The shops looked clean and well-presented but that belied the state of the buildings. Tiles were missing and most upper floors looked in need of paint, if not new window frames.

I suspected our target was equidistant between our two groups. It was correct. Rahman left one man by each cordon, sent two men to the rear, and posted another two outside the shop. That left me and the inspector and four policemen.

We entered a hardware store and immediately an elderly Japanese man—who I guessed was the shopkeeper—came at us with a stick. Rahman barked something at the man which made him hesitate. Then two of the officers grabbed him, forcing the old man to the floor.

At the rear I could see three Japanese women cowering. Rahman marched forwards and spoke to them, his tone commanding but placatory. The women bowed and the eldest, possibly the old man's wife, but more likely his daughter, spoke. Rahman replied and then called over his shoulder.

"Let the old man up. He's harmless."

Once the man had been released, Rahman spoke to the woman again. She pointed at the ceiling and he explained, "The upstairs rooms are not safe but Chinese men have been there recently."

I said, "Nothing to do with these people down here?"

"According to the woman."

We went through the back of the shop and into a yard behind. The two policemen who Rahman had sent back here dropped their aim once they realized it was us coming through the door.

The inspector repositioned them and pointed to a staircase. There were the two of us and five of his men.

Rahman looked at me. "You don't have a gun," he said quietly. "For your safety, I'd like you to hang back. We'll both wait until it's clear."

He kept one man at the foot of the stairs and sent the remaining group up the flight. What happened next shocked me.

The men charged to the top. The first man there front-kicked the door, ducked to one side and the other three opened fire.

"Stop!" I yelled. This was crazy and I remembered what Robshaw had told me about the raid in Chinatown, a couple of weeks before I arrived. The police went in shooting and ruined the MP's operation to catch a guy called Webster.

The gunfire was over almost as soon as it started. One of the men shouted, "All clear!" and we raced up the stairs.

In the gloom, I could see the room was empty. There were no Chinese gangsters, just five policemen and me.

A stench of old cigarettes, piss and something rotten rose up and filled my nostrils.

One of the men pulled a makeshift curtain from a dirty window and I could see the room itself was virtually empty. The floor had dusty, bare wooden boards. A square table had four chairs and four beer bottles. More bottles were scattered around the room along with cigarette butts and newspaper detritus.

A bucket in the corner by the window explained the toilet smell. There was also a box with scraps of food. Maybe the remnants of many meals.

"What's this?" One of the men held up a piece of paper.

It was something I'd seen before.

FIFTY-SEVEN

"Exactly the same," Rahman said as he turned the flyer of a red paw print in a circle in his hands.

"Not exactly." I pointed to the Chinese lettering. "This looks different."

The inspector asked one of his men to translate.

"Attack the parade," the man said.

Rahman looked at me but didn't say anything. He didn't need to. We may not have found any guns but we had more evidence of what would happen tomorrow.

I took the flyer and walked back to the stairs and the sunlight. Something bothered me. As I suspected, the image and writing were hand painted. Surely a flyer like this would be mass produced. If they weren't then that would explain why Yipp and white-eyed Chen said they hadn't seen it before. Because there were so few around.

Which raised the question: why make them?

"Captain!" Rahman called me back into the room.

He was looking up at a square outline in the ceiling. A hatch, most likely. He pointed to the floor and I could see scrape marks in the dust. The table and at least one chair had once been under the hatch.

The inspector signalled to the men and they dragged the table over. One man stepped onto a chair and then the table. He pushed the square area and it lifted. There

330

was no hinge so he pushed up on one side to reveal a hole about two feet square.

The man gripped the edge and jumped so that he could see over the edge. When he shook his head, someone passed him a torch. He removed his jacket and jumped again, this time with so much spring that the table toppled over.

With a jerk and a wriggle he levered himself up and into the space above.

After the crash of the table, it fell silent except for our breathing and the scuffles over our heads.

Then the man cried out. "Sir!"

He reappeared in the hole, panting with excitement. "Sir, they are here!"

"Guns?" Rahman asked.

"Crates at least. Looks like they could be, sir."

"Can you get one down?"

"Difficult. Easier with two."

The table was repositioned and Rahman looked at me. "What do you think? Want to take a look?"

I didn't waste a second. I was up on the table and handing the inspector my jacket.

This time, the men below held the table and I imitated the move of the policeman already up there. At least, I did my best, because I was bigger and broader and had to lever one arm at a time before pushing up and through.

The roof was only a few feet above us so I needed to crouch. Combined with dodgy looking rafters it made progress awkward. I followed the policeman's torch and was soon looking at a pile of wooden boxes. They had His Majesty's crest and Property of The British Army stamped on the lid and were padlocked. I knew these crates. I'd seen hundreds of them. Inside would be up to twenty rifles.

The policeman shone his torch around and we counted six boxes. Maybe one hundred and twenty rifles.

I could have waited but the wood looked old so I lay on my back and stamped my heel down on the nearest crate.

The wood splintered and we tore the lid away. The first thing we saw was oil cloth. Long items were wrapped in it. It's how rifles used to be stored. So there was no surprise when I pulled one out and removed the cloth. In the torch light I read *M1 Garand* on the stock.

"It's them by God!" I shouted. "It's them."

I passed the rifle down for Rahman to see and then we manoeuvred the box to the hatch and fed it down to waiting hands. Within minutes, we had all six boxes down and open.

As I expected, there were one hundred and twenty rifles.

Rahman shook his head. "So, if three hundred were traded by Cooke, then we have less than half and all of them are missing the firing pins. I suppose that could be easily rectified?"

I was holding one of the rifles and took it outside for a better view. I looked down the barrel and then handed the gun to Rahman.

"That's not what bothers me," I said as the inspector also looked at the barrel. "It might not be by much, but each of these has been damaged. Deliberately so, in my estimation. These guns have been rendered useless."

We turned and looked back at the boxes and rifles we had laid out on the shop-house floor.

"Why would somebody buy damaged rifles?" I pondered.

FIFTY-EIGHT

Although Rahman didn't have an answer to that, he said, "Perhaps the other one hundred and eighty weren't damaged."

We were back in the Austin 5 and, under Rahman's instructions, heading for the fort.

"We should inform the general," he said.

"We've found guns but they can't be used in an attack."

"Does that matter?"

"What do you mean?"

He placed his hands as though in prayer. "What do you want the general to do?"

"Follow the security plan," I said. "I want him in the Battle Box."

"And he said that if you found the guns then that's what he would do." He looked at me shrewdly. "Does it matter that you know the guns we found were useless?"

I sat in silence for a while, watching the streets and thinking about all the questions I still had. Did it matter? Probably not.

"But we have another whole day," I said eventually. "Another day gives us time to find the rest of the guns."

"And if we don't?"

"Then I'll tell the general we've found them."

That made Rahman laugh and I guess he was right. In effect the outcome was the same.

"In that case, back to the station," he said leaning forward so our driver could hear.

When he sat back, I said, "I didn't know you could speak Japanese."

He studied me for a second and then the realization must have hit him. "Ah, in the shop."

"Yes. You spoke to the old lady."

He nodded. "I know a few words."

To my inexperienced ear I thought he sounded more proficient than that, but I said nothing. I was thinking. I replayed things in my head.

"Penny for them?" he said snapping my attention back into the car. It reminded me of Hegarty and his need to tell me the etymology of phrases.

"Just thinking," I said but didn't expand on it. Instead I said, "Do you know The Red Lion pub?"

"It's not a place I would patronize, but yes I know it."

"It's just a little ironic. The Red Lion is so British, and one of the most common names for pubs. I was once told the reason is that the army used pubs to recruit soldiers back in the seventeen hundreds, and chose pubs as recruitment centres. So that people knew, they were called The Red Lion."

"Is that true?"

"I have no idea but the irony is we are chasing a red lion," I said referring to the image on the flyer. "Only this one represents the enemy."

We agreed that Rahman would hold onto the guns, just in case we didn't find the others. If the general knew they were useless, he'd never agree to my plan.

I suspected it was too early for what I wanted but I went for a walk around Chinatown. I found Happy

Palace, the bar where the lady-boy called Angel had tried to pick up a soldier. She wasn't there and I didn't find her in any of the other drinking haunts.

However the walk cleared my head and I decided I would visit Fort Canning after all although I wanted to speak to Colonel Atkinson rather than the general. I also wanted to avoid telling him about the guns we'd found, if at all possible.

Atkinson was in the garden looking out to sea when I walked across the courtyard.

"Good to see you," he called, and waved.

When I joined him, he said, "I hear you came mob handed to see the general yesterday."

"Yes, it was a mistake. I should have come alone but there's so much division here, I thought—"

"You thought to involve others." He smiled reassuringly and I suspect he had sympathy for my role and what I was supposed to do. However, when he continued he said, "Politics is a funny old game. One may try to do the right thing but it isn't always the prudent course."

"Will the army and police ever find a balance?"

"Oh it's not that, Ash. It's the government not the police. One day, and maybe not far off, this will not be a Crown Colony. This will not be a British controlled government."

"And where does that leave the army?"

"Not here, I'm afraid. That's the best I can do with my crystal ball. But you didn't come here to talk about sand running through the hour glass."

"No, I wanted to ask you a question, if you don't mind. I also wanted to think about the security here."

He began to walk and as I stayed in step, he asked, "What would you like to know?"

335

"You remember the names of the people involved and the battalions?"

"Of course. They are burned in my memory. Percival was the commander and we had thirty-eight infantry battalions and three machine-gun battalions."

I said, "What happened to the Indian 4th on day one?"

"Day one? You mean the 44th. There wasn't a 4th. It was the 44th Indian and Taylor's Australian battalions that met the first wave of attacks. On the second day Percival formed the defensive line, when it was already too late. That's when I got involved. And you know the rest." He went quiet and I let him walk in silence lost in his own thoughts.

After we'd done a loop around the garden, I asked, "Did you ever come across a Captain Keith?"

"That's not a name I know. From the time of the war?"

"That's what I thought."

He shook his head, "If you gave me a couple of days I could probably list all the officers here at the time. But I can tell you now that no one was called Keith."

He said he needed to get back to work and invited me inside. But I declined. Instead I headed for the Battle Box. Somewhere in the recesses of my mind a plan was forming. It wasn't complete yet but I needed to make sure I knew the layout of the bunker. I also needed to be sure my key worked.

I stood in front of the solid iron door and pulled the four inch key from my jacket pocket. It looked dusty so I gave it a clean. There was something between the teeth and I rubbed the sticky substance away before trying it in the lock. It worked just fine, clicking the tumbler like it had just been oiled. Which, knowing the army, it probably had.

I flicked on a light switch that was one of those sticks with a bobble on the end: never updated from when it had been constructed I guessed.

The room was unchanged from the first day I'd been here, the large table with a relief map of South East Asia, dominating the centre. The rest cold and sparse, not helped by the grey-orange lighting.

If this were as sumptuous as the main building—and I imagined the library—I suspected the general wouldn't have needed so much persuasion to come here. As it was, even I would have objected.

I turned off the light, clunked the metal door closed and removed the key.

My watch said it was an hour to nightfall. So I strolled back to the area around Happy Palace, found something to eat and waited.

I didn't have to wait long. When Angel spotted me, she thought about running but then she looked down at her high heels and shrugged.

"I've not done anything," she said as soon as I gripped her forearm and steered her over to a table.

"I didn't say you had," I said.

"Then what?"

"I have a proposition for you."

She looked at me long and hard possibly wondering if I meant a sexual proposition and then realizing it was something else.

"How would you like to make some money?" I said, needing no answer. "I have something I want you to do for me."

After I'd explained it, she negotiated on the price, which I'd expected. Then she asked "When?"

"Soon. I want you to go to The Red Lion at this time each evening. When you see a black ribbon hanging from a lantern outside, then that's your signal."

"I can't keep—"

I doubled the price, as I'd expected to. For me this was still good value. For her, it cost virtually nothing. Then I added: "It's just for a maximum of two days."

"And the taxi?"

"Of course I'll pay for the taxi—both ways."

There was a telephone message waiting for me at the hotel. It was from Hegarty.

It said: **Tai Tai was murdered**.

FIFTY-NINE

Dead was one thing. Murdered meant something altogether different. Relevant. I rang the Gillman office.

"Suffocated," Hegarty said when I was put through. "The coroner had natural causes originally but I asked him to triple check. And, like you suspected, he found something. There were little spots around the eyes. He hadn't been suspicious at first because suffocation would normally result in much more obvious damage."

I said, "But she'd been in a coma."

"Right. She will have hardly struggled, hardly known about it."

"Small mercies," I said and ended the call.

I lay on my bed thinking, looking at the crack and imagined it was the lizard.

Something was troubling me. Rahman had said we should focus on the attack and that the trade in guns was secondary. We could worry about who did what afterwards. However to my mind Tai Tai's murder changed everything. It told me that she was important.

I was already pretty certain that the ledger found in Cooke's bag was Tai Tai's, that she was the intermediary selling Pantelis's goods—at least some of them. And most importantly the three hundred omega-delta items, I was pretty sure were the guns.

So where did the security man, Aiko fit in? He'd led the police to Kim who had the dancer's costume and leaflets. Then under interrogation, Kim led us to the place in Geylang.

We'd found some of the guns but they had been decommissioned, damaged beyond repair.

There were so many elements that didn't make sense to me and I played them over and over in my head.

Then I stopped myself. The main thing that didn't make sense was motive.

Yipp didn't know about the flyer or guns, I was sure of that. Secretary Coates would have loved to pin the security issue on Yipp but he couldn't. Maybe Yipp was head of an illegal secret society but he was part of the establishment, not someone about to cause an uprising.

And what about his rival? Chen was undoubtedly secretive but his low profile was necessary. He desired political influence over Yipp's commercial control. The flyer suggested the threat was from a gang and yet neither man knew anything. A thousand spies might be hyperbole, but surely they would have known.

Flyer, guns, dance costume, motive.

Eventually I managed to break the cycle and think about why I had come to Singapore in the first place. Tom Silverman must have seen something suspicious and probably believed Pantelis was up to no good. He had followed him to Nee Soon, but not for the first time because he'd told Mei Fen what he was doing. I wondered if the first time was the deal making and the second, the transaction.

Tom had sent me the telegram.

He must have known that I couldn't come immediately. Did he think the transaction would come much later? It didn't seem reasonable. If he suspected Pantelis was trading arms, he would have needed an immediate response. And yet he'd sent the message to me in Palestine. That logic bothered me. I thought about the sequence of events again. Then I tried to imagine I was Tom.

If it had been me, I would have confronted Pantelis. If I'd had time I might have gained some evidence. But Tom Silverman wasn't me. He would have gone to someone else with his suspicion. Not his gaffer. It would need to be someone in a position of authority—in the military. Commander Alldritt then? But Alldritt was a protectionist. He had stonewalled me about the car. I had no doubt he would have stonewalled Tom.

So what next? If I were him, would I have gone to the police? No, I was used to the culture by now. There was an us-and-them mentality. The white British and the natives. The police, policed the latter. The government then? No. Tom Silverman had gone to the military police. He'd either been stonewalled again or filed away as a minor issue. At best, they hadn't appreciated the magnitude of the issue. At worst they were complicit. That's why he'd contacted me. He needed someone he could trust and someone who would act.

Only I'd come too late. I should have telephoned. Perhaps if I'd not been wrapped up with my own issue in Palestine I would have called the Singapore Provost Marshall's office and made things happen.

341

Perhaps. Life was full of what could have been. If only I'd protected my informant in Palestine. If only we'd moved his family in time. But I hadn't.

And I was getting nowhere.

I thought about the flyers again, how they looked homemade but definitely pointed to an attack on the parade tomorrow.

I let the events play over and over in my head. I thought about Commander Alldritt and his obstruction. I thought about Major Vernon and Sinclair and Atkinson. And thinking about Atkinson's story reminded me of the journey to Woodlands Crossing with Evans, the war history buff, talking about which battalions had met the first wave of Japanese invaders. The car journey made me think of Hegarty and his phrases like "brass-necked" and his favourite one, "red herring".

Round and round in my head. I had nothing.

The card trick I'd shown the little girl was about sleight of hand and misdirection. Hegarty's phrase: red herring.

What if I had everything? I swung my legs out of the bed, delved into my pocket and pulled out the key to the Battle Box. I rolled the sticky substance between my finger and thumb, thinking. It felt like clay.

The flyer was a misdirection. The dance costume and clipping about Gaskill could be misdirections because they came from Kim. And I no longer believed he was the buyer of the guns. Because he was Aiko's contact not Tai Tai's.

And then there was Japanese. Not the people, but the language.

There was no point in trying to sleep, the adrenaline was pumping through my veins and my mind was hyper active.

If I had everything then what did that mean about the motive?

I paced the room and within an hour I had a firm plan.

My uniform had been laundered by the hotel and my shoes, which I'd left outside the bedroom door, had already been polished. I dressed and looked at myself in the mirror. This would be the last time I'd wear this. There was no sentiment, just an acknowledgement that it would soon be over.

I went down to the lobby to use the phone, asked for London and gave the Whitehall number to the operator. When Whitehall accepted my call, I asked to be put through to my father but as before, his secretary answered.

"Sorry Ash, he's not available," Sam said.

"It seems he never is."

"Well..." I wondered if she was going to make an excuse for him or even tell me something I suspected: that the Department of Energy was a cover for something else entirely. But she didn't. After a hesitation, she said, "I checked those names for you."

I waited expectantly.

She said, "I tried to trace all of them but I haven't had much time. So far I've only managed to reach three."

Was that a good statistical sample? No. But then this wasn't a science project. I would probably accept two providing the answers were identical.

She said, "None of them has received a thing. And from the way they talked I don't think any of them expected to."

A hotel porter flagged a taxi for me and I asked for Gillman Barracks. I was acknowledged at the barrier and walked up to the office. The same clerk was on night-duty: Corporal Franks.

"Captain Carter!" he said and looked flustered. "Sir, shall I take a cigarette break?"

"Not this time, Corporal," I said. No subterfuge this time. I was well beyond subterfuge. I held out my hand. "Just the keys to his office please."

I opened Vernon's office door and turned on the light. If Vernon found out, I wouldn't deny it. I knew now that I wouldn't need to.

His tall filing cabinet seemingly with a hundred drawers had a key hole at the top. I riffled through the bunch and realized not one of them would fit.

Oh well. On Vernon's desk was a silver letter opener. It had his initials on it. I put the tip in the keyhole and punched the handle with the heel of my hand. The knife bent at the tip but the drum shifted. Another punch and a jiggle of the knife and the lock disappeared inside the cabinet. I was in.

I imagined it could take all day to go through all the documents in the drawers so I pulled some out randomly and quickly established the filing protocol. Reports were split into incident reports—which were the majority—other reports and telephone records. The three types were kept separately. Everything was otherwise in date order.

I guessed I was looking for some time around the 22nd of January, the date of Tom Silverman's telegram to me.

I doubted this would be an incident report and I started with telephone messages. I looked at the date and then went back a few days. I found two calls from Tom Silverman for Major Vernon. No messages were left.

I put the papers back and started on the other reports. Dated the twenty-first, I found a short statement taken from Tom.

I pushed the drawers back so that the room looked undisturbed. I didn't want Franks to get in trouble for this. However I tossed the bent letter opener on Vernon's desk. I liked the idea that he'd guess I'd been in here and would worry about it.

I had been in and out within twenty minutes. I'd paid my taxi driver well and he was still waiting at the barrier for me. He drove me to a café near the *Padang* where they served breakfast all night and I watched the dark sky gradually lighten.

Before the first rays of sunlight broke across the South China Sea, I had paid for my meal and walked up to Fort Canning.

Atkinson and Gaskill were already at their desks when I arrived. We sat in the general's office and I told them about the guns we had found, the expected attack on the parade tonight and confirmed the target appeared to be the general.

I told them my plan.

Gaskill said he would have extra guards at the fort.

"It's the last thing you want," I said. "I need you to act as though nothing has changed and then last minute we execute the emergency security plan. I want everyone thinking you'll lead the parade. Then you go into the bunker."

With their reluctant acceptance, I asked to use the telephone and called Gillman Barracks.

Franks answered.

"The major has not arrived yet," he said.

"I'd like to speak to the lieutenant, please."

It took ten minutes for Robshaw to pick up the phone. "Sorry, sir," he said, "I was out having breakfast."

"I need a favour."

"Anything."

345

"You might not say that when you hear what it is," I said and when I told him he paused for a second and I imagined him running a hand through his blond hair.

Finally, he said, "What time?"

"Nine o'clock. Do whatever you have to but clear the HQ of everyone except the major."

"I can do that," he said and I started to suspect he was enjoying the prospect. "I'll get everyone to Gillman to talk through the parade plans."

After ending the call, I headed for the police station.

Inspector Rahman wasn't expected for another half an hour so I stood on the bridge and watched as the wharves came alive. The water ran thick and slow. Boats that had been strung across the river overnight were untied and the *godown* doors cranked open. Wares appeared on trollies and were run down to the water's edge where they were loaded onto the boats. Minutes after the first labourers started hauling bales and boxes, the first customs men appeared.

From the moment I arrived to the time I headed back to the station, the river went from quiet to frenetic. Another work day was well underway.

"You look tired, my friend," Rahman said as I entered his office.

"I've been up all night."

"Worrying about the attack tonight?"

"Something like that," I said. "I've had things to do and decided to tell the general about the guns."

"I think that was wise."

The clock on his wall showed eight thirty-three. He offered me tea and I accepted.

Once it had been served and we were alone once more, I said, "So the general's agreed to follow the contingency plan. He and the colonel will sit out the parade in the bunker. I will release them—" I held up the key "—when the coast is clear."

"Excellent."

"But one thing," I added. "I don't want anyone else to know. As far as the men are concerned, right until the last minute, I want them to expect the general. Anand, I'm only trusting you and Major Vernon with the information. So tell no one else for now."

"Of course. But why Vernon?" Bemused, he shook his head. "I thought you didn't like him."

I laughed. "Is it that obvious?" The minute hand moved.

"Yes."

I watched the long clock hand click another minute. "I trust him as far as I can throw him. Unfortunately Vernon needs to know."

I could see Rahman wanted me to say more, but it would have to wait. I asked him to join me at Gillman early afternoon so we could go over joint plans for the evening.

And then I left to confront Major Vernon.

347

SIXTY

I strolled up Bras Basah Road and stopped on the steps of the HQ. Robshaw had done a good job. The place was silent except for a sergeant at the desk.

He looked up sharply as my shoes clacked on the marble floor.

"Sir?" he said. His eyes were full of concern.

"Is Major Vernon in his office?"

"Yes, sir."

"Then I need you to leave."

"I can't do that, sir. Major Vernon gave a specific order. This desk needs to manned at all times."

I handed the man a pack of cigarettes. "Take a break. I'll cover for you."

The sergeant still looked uncertain.

I said, "It's an order—from me."

That did it or maybe it was my tone. Whichever, he scooted outside as if his life depended on it. And maybe it did.

I walked past the desk, turned left to Vernon' door and knocked.

After a count of ten, Vernon called for me to enter. I waited. A minute later I knocked again, a little more urgently. Vernon immediately called out this time. I continued to wait.

When I knocked for a third time he barked at whoever was knocking on his door. I waited and knocked again. This time I heard him scrape back his chair and stomp towards me.

The door swung open. He glared at me, his face and neck flushed with anger.

"What the hell—?"

I punched him in the stomach.

He doubled over, winded.

When he straightened he spat his words. "What the hell do you think you're doing? I'll have you hanged for that!"

"That one was for me. This one's for Tom."

I punched him in the gut again. This time he sunk to the floor, coughing and glared up at me.

"You're a fool!" he said through clenched teeth.

"Maybe," I said. "My friend Tom Silverman was a fool too. He came to you for help and you ignored him."

Vernon didn't deny it.

I said, "He needed you to investigate but you just passed it over to Commander Alldritt, didn't you?"

Vernon said nothing but his eyes told me the truth of it.

"You may as well have killed him."

"You're an idiot. You won't get away with this."

"What, hitting you? I think I will. You have no witnesses and quite frankly you aren't in any position to complain but I'll come to that in a minute."

His eyes narrowed.

I said, "It all ends tonight, Major. You will lead the New Year's parade."

He looked surprised, not following me.

I continued: "If I'm right about the attack tonight then I'm done. If I'm wrong then it won't matter."

"You've lost your mind. You aren't making any sense."

"Far from it. I've spoken to the general and he's agreed that you can lead the parade. There's something that I didn't tell him though. I didn't tell him about your fencing club scam."

He shook his head as though I was talking nonsense again. This is what my father's secretary had confirmed. Sam had checked whether ex-MPs from the 200 Provost Company had received any money. They hadn't.

I said, "You will do two things."

"It's a proper savings scheme."

I clapped my hands on his ears and his head jerked back with the shock percussion. He slumped against the wall and looked up at me with unfocussed eyes.

"Shut up and pay attention," I said. "You will pay back all the money you've taken to men who have left—like you promised. Except there will be no deductions for fencing equipment—I know how this works, you see."

He looked at me with defeated eyes.

"Agreed?" I said.

"Agreed."

"You'd better," I hissed, "and you'll do something else."

He just looked at me.

"You'll stop with the sadistic punishments. No more full kit drills for men with sunburn or ringworm for example. From now on, I'll be watching you. No matter what happens tonight if you don't change your ways then you'd better keep looking over your shoulder. Because one day I will be there and next time it won't be a warning."

He nodded weakly and I was happy that he'd got the message.

"Now stand up," I said, pulling him to his feet, "and be the Provost Marshall that the men need you to be."

I spent the afternoon at Gillman with the sergeants reviewing the parade route. Lieutenant Robshaw had arranged for a map to be pinned to a table tennis table in the common room. He'd also had his haircut, reducing his pride and joy to a neat stubble.

Inspector Rahman joined us with six other senior officers just as we were discussing high risk buildings and sections. He thought the exposed pinch point of Anderson Bridge could be an issue and we'd already identified Fullerton Square as high risk.

"A sniper on the Fullerton Building would have a good view and wide range," Robshaw said.

We discussed resources. The RMP had eighty-five men available and the police could provide almost two hundred. We agreed that the police would cover the highest risk locations we marked on the map except for the bridge and Fullerton Square. The RMP would have two men on top of the Fullerton Building and men either end of the bridge.

The police would generally patrol the outside of the parade route and the RMP would cover the inside. The lion or dragon costume the police had found pointed to acrobats or dancers as a potential threat. We therefore agreed that units would walk alongside any acrobatic displays. One of the sergeants had the schedule and list of entrants so we allocated police and RMP teams to these.

"What about the general?" Rahman asked.

I hadn't planned to tell the men yet but they knew the police had found the clippings about General Gaskill that implied he was the target.

I said, "I don't want it to leave this room but as a precautionary measure, the general and Lieutenant Colonel Atkinson won't be joining the march."

There were a few expectant nods in the room.

Robshaw said, "We should allocate a unit to the fort."

"No," I said. "The Battle Box is secure enough and the general wants as little fuss as possible. He'll just sit out the parade just in case."

"So, who's leading the march, Boss?"

"Major Vernon," I said.

After the mutterings of surprise and dismay had died down, Hegarty grinned.

"Well lads," he said rubbing his hands, "change of plans. We all stay at home and hope there is an attack tonight!"

Everyone laughed and I dismissed them to get prepared.

Rahman was about to leave when I said, "I'd like us to work together on this."

He nodded and said, "How do you want to play it?"

"You take your best man and I'll take Sergeant Hegarty. We don't track anyone in particular. We move up and down the line and keep an eye out for trouble."

"One team," he said. "I like that."

We shook hands.

I checked the time. We had two hours.

"Ironically," I said, "I actually need something to happen tonight."

"An attack you mean?"

"Yes."

He shook his head, not understanding.

I said, "If it happens then I'm free. My deal with Coates is over."

"Ah," he nodded and shook my hand again. "Then good luck I suppose, my friend. Let us hope for a happy ending."

SIXTY-ONE

Closing my eyes, I could hear the distant mumble of voices, men preparing, falling into ranks. The near-full moon was high in a clear sky and lit Fort Canning above us. Hegarty and I stood on Stamford Road at the foot of the hill and greeted Inspector Rahman and Sergeant Kee as they joined us.

We heard the marching band strike up and knew the soldiers had begun their descent from the fort. Waiting at the *Padang* on St Andrews Road was the pageant. They would tag onto the rear once the parade reached them.

The lead motor cyclist appeared, rolling at walking pace, and a second later we saw the band: Royal Marines wearing red jackets, black trousers, white helmets, brass trimmings, and playing brass instruments.

Behind them was Major Vernon, resplendent in full whites with the addition of a black armband. All the men had armbands in mourning for our king.

After Vernon, a sergeant major twirled his baton, leading four blocks of soldiers from Tanglin Barracks.

As the sergeant major passed I said, "Ready?"

"Ready," Rahman confirmed.

We tucked in behind and to one side of the sergeant major and walked across Hill Street heading south.

We could hear the carnival now. People cheered and drums clashed as we reached the *Padang*. We turned right and I saw the floats start to move to join us. Firecrackers banged and whistled and I was happy to see Vernon looking nervous. There was a despatch rider waiting with the front of the pageant section and I waved him over. We'd spoken in advance and he knew to stay close in case I needed him.

We moved back and forth, staying together as a unit but checking all directions and suspicions. Now and again I spotted the motorcycle rider and was happy he stayed within shouting distance.

The head of the parade crossed Anderson Bridge and went on into Fullerton Square. Suddenly the crowds were ten, fifteen people deep, jostling and shouting. But it was good humoured and I sensed no trouble.

Red, white and blue bunting festooned the square and was strung in waves across the front of the Fullerton Building. The upper windows of the building were closed, faces pressed against the glass, but The Singapore Club had its first floor windows open. Club members leaned out, some with Union flags unfurled, all waving and cheering. I think I saw Robshaw on the roof but it was too dark to be sure.

After Fullerton, the parade headed up Battery Road. We turned and started back against the flow.

"Boss?" Hegarty said beside me.

"Just thinking. I'm sorry that the general wasn't here to receive the applause back there."

After the soldiers came three acrobats with giant red flags. *Health, Prosperity* and *Happiness* they said in both English and gold Chinese characters. The men twirled the flags and moved in a dance routine, weaving in and out of one another's path, their flags swirling first high then low. Then came the first dancing dragon, gold and white with twelve men in a costume. It jumped, snapped giant jaws and snaked, the men inside working incredibly as one living organism.

As the carnival moved, men with flaming torches walked beside and around the entertainers, providing illumination that, in its flickering, added to the excitement and mystique of the dancing.

A series of floats followed, advertising Chinese companies including Ho Ho Biscuits but there was no sign of white-eyed Chen or his German henchman. Then came acrobats performing somersaults and building human towers, like the one I had watched at the fair.

The first of the lion dancers were next. Three lions: golden, red and green each with two people inside followed by three musicians with a drum, cymbals and a gong.

Hegarty had been quiet for a while. Rahman and his sergeant were over to our right.

"What's going to happen?" Hegarty asked me.

"What do you mean?"

"You know something."

"Do I?"

He stopped and looked into my eyes.

"Yes, you do."

I started walking again. "We should keep checking."

"Tell me."

"Tell you what?"

"What's going on?"

I said nothing.

More floats passed us at a snail's pace followed by dancers and then three scantily clad young women leading chained tigers. Then more lion dancers and dragon dancers. I discovered there were two types of dragon dancer, ones inside a costume, like the lion dancers, and ones where the body was long and thin, controlled by men using bamboo poles outside the body and incredibly long tails. Red and gold were the predominant colours for the dancers but no one looked like they could be carrying a rifle.

I reckoned the top of the parade would have been turning right to cross the river again about now.

I waved the inspector over and said, "Let's make our way to the front again."

He didn't disagree and we fell into a routine of checking and switching sides, looking ahead and looking back, looking at the crowd and the buildings. I saw no sign of real trouble, just drunken revellers here and there.

I couldn't see where they came from, but a series of explosions made a few people around me jump. Gunpowder thrown into flames, I decided. I'd seen and heard it before, and it didn't have the same report as gunfire.

Hegarty was alongside me again as we left Fullerton Square behind us.

"I'm not going to tell anyone," he said, "if that's what you're worried about."

"There's nothing to tell."

"Then why are you so relaxed? My heart misses a beat every time I hear a bang but you don't even flinch."

"I have a theory."

"Yes...?"

"That I'm not going to tell you."

Hegarty stopped again. "Why?"

I kept walking and said, "I might be wrong."

We turned right, crossed Coleman Bridge and then left along River Valley Road, past Hill Street Station. From here we would continue to loop around the hill below the fort and then turn up Orchard Road. Midway it would turn up Grange and from there the army would continue their march on to Tanglin. The pageant would loop around along Patterson, rejoin Orchard and then head back to the *Padang* via Stamford Road.

We kept walking and looking and checking that each unit was in place. By the time we reached the bottom of Orchard I had the sense that the conclusion was approaching fast. I signalled to Rahman to turn around and we worked our way back again.

"At least tell me something," Hegarty said.

"Red herring. It was your explanation that made me work it out."

"But you might be wrong?"

"I might be wrong," I said.

We passed the tigers and the second batch of floats. We were midway through the first group of lion dancers on Tank Road when a loud explosion occurred close by. Suddenly there was chaos. People were screaming and running. A lion was on fire. Then I saw gouts of flame shoot from a shop-house across the way. The crowd stampeded. I stood my ground as bodies pressed past me in panic.

"Hedge!" I shouted, but got no response.

Then I saw him looking desperately around. He had his pistol out, aimed at the burning building. Other MPs and police started to appear, also waving their guns.

Hegarty ran to my side. "What shall we do?" he shouted over the clamour.

"Where's the inspector?" I shouted back, but just then I saw Sergeant Kee on the floor. Another policeman was damping out his flaming clothes.

We ran over.

His face was blackened and there was blood on his nose and neck.

"The inspector?" I asked him.

"Went inside."

"When? Just now or before."

Kee swallowed and tried to compose himself. He was shaking and Hegarty wrapped his coat around the man.

"Before," Kee whispered and coughed. "He was... suspicious. Told me... told me to wait."

The police were now thick around us and a medic took Kee from us.

I stood up and scanned the crowd.

"Rider!" I yelled. I cupped my hands to my mouth and yelled again and again.

Eventually I saw the man waving to me. He was off his motorcycle and pointed to where it lay on the ground, only yards away.

"Boss?" Hegarty said running at my side towards the bike.

"I'm going to the fort," I told him.

I jerked the bike up and threw a leg over.

Hegarty said, "What shall I do?"

"Ignore this," I said and gunned the engine. "Get to the head of the parade and check on Vernon... just in case."

I left him then, weaved in and out for a short distance and then had some space to accelerate.

I raced through the pageant, sounding the pitiful horn and screaming for people to get out of the way. At the end of Tank Road, I cut away from the parade and opened up the throttle. I sped around the hill back to the fort back to General Gaskill.

And I prayed I'd not miscalculated.

Two MPs blocked the road with guns raised, alarmed at the motorbike tearing up the drive. I slammed on the brakes, let the bike slide and leapt off.

"Sir?" one of them said, realizing who I was but still a bit jumpy.

"Any trouble?" I shouted.

"All quiet here, sir."

I ran past them, round the barrier and under the gateway. The courtyard was in darkness except for lamps outside the main house and the Battle Box. I could hear firecrackers from the carnival and a low hum of voices and music. Apart from that, the fort was silent and my running feet crunched loudly on the courtyard stones.

When I reached the Battle Box, the door was shut and locked. As expected.

I took out my key and opened the door.

The room was empty.

I entered and relocked the door, took a seat by the table and waited.

Within a couple of minutes I heard a key in the lock.

The door opened.

SIXTY-TWO

On the edge of the *Padang*, the man who called himself Jin ducked below the sea wall and climbed over the rocks. He levered aside two medicine-ball sized stones and located the hole just wide enough for a slim person to crawl through. He was one of very few who knew there were old plans of Fort Canning; security plans that marked the sally ports. This exit had been covered by a metal grid, maybe a hundred and fifty years old. Jin had removed it easily a few days ago and replaced the stones.

He squirmed into the hole. There was no dignity in his progress, but he was beyond caring about dignity. After crawling a few yards, the space opened up and he was able to crouch. This was where he'd previously stowed his suitcase though he didn't expect to need it. Everything had been well planned and the suitcase was merely a contingency.

He began to shuffle forwards awkwardly, but with a practised rhythm. He knew that speed was essential and had timed himself to take twelve minutes to make the tunnel and climb.

Initially the passage sloped gently downwards, but then started to rise, until the height increased and he could stand with a stoop. He trudged through the ancient tunnel for a long time until the stone stairs began. They were wet with water that dripped from the two-hundred-year-old walls.

Forbidden Hill, that was the old Malay name for the mount. It was sacred. Before the British, the islanders believed the spirits of the dead lived here. But the British had not respected the locals' beliefs. They never did. Cannons had been fired to clear the hill of the ghosts and the fort had been built. But the ghosts were here now. He was here, Jin the spirit.

He reached the top of the steps where a modern metal gate blocked the entrance. Hidden in the tunnel by the gate, Jin located the rifle he'd stowed here and slung it over his back. He placed his hand on the latch and looked out into the courtyard.

Darkness. No staff. No guards.

SIXTY-THREE

Night gave way to the figure of Inspector Rahman as he stepped into the light of the Battle Box.

"Quick!" I said, "Lock the door and take a seat."

Rahman came over. He was breathless, "Where's the general? Is everything all right?"

He picked up the chair and moved it to the side, back to the wall. He looked at my revolver out on the table and leaned his rifle against the wall beside him.

"Everything is fine," I said. "How did you know—?"

"Your sergeant told me where you were headed," he said and started to rise. "But if there's no trouble, what are you doing here?"

"Waiting for someone to come through that door."

He sat back down, his eyebrows cocked like he didn't know what was going on.

I said, "Do you know the origin of the phrase red herring?"

"No."

"Sergeant Hegarty told me. It comes from saboteurs who used kippers to distract the hunt. It made me think. Sometimes things are a distraction from the real issue. Sometimes those things are deliberate."

The dim grey-orange light flickered and I figured it would be on a separate generator to the main house.

The slight movement of the light made Rahman's face seem animated but it wasn't. His eyes were frozen for a moment.

I said, "I was trying to find out what happened to my friend. It looked like it dead-ended at Pantelis: the guy who drove Tom's car off the road. It could have ended there but it got messy didn't it?"

Rahman said nothing.

"But let's forget that for a minute," I said. "We had information about a secret society and a date that we worked out coincided with the parade. We had intelligence about guns and your team found them. Your team also found the dragon dancer costume and the newspaper clippings with Gaskill's picture."

Rahman nodded. "And there was an incident on Tank Road. We could have been killed."

"Good intel or misdirection," I said. "Coates wanted so much to believe there was a secret society behind this—to get Yipp—that he bought it, totally."

"Me too."

"But that wasn't the red herring."

"It wasn't?"

"No, the misdirection was General Gaskill."

Rahman frowned.

I said, "The real target was Colonel Atkinson. Where Gaskill went, Atkinson would follow. Get the general into this bunker and Atkinson would be here too."

Rahman looked down and I wondered if he was studying my revolver.

"It was to shoot the person who came through that door."

"But it was me," he said.

"I knew it would be you," I said.

"How?"

"Well firstly, you opened the door with a key."

"But before that?"

"I put two and two together. I should have realized straight away when I saw the photograph on your desk. I thought you were emotional about your father and uncle's deaths but it was worry I saw. You had to cover yourself. You told me they died on the first day and then you had to work out how many days to the anniversary."

Rahman said nothing.

"Because it was the third day."

Rahman shook his head but I knew I was right.

"You told me they were in the 4th Indian Infantry. But there wasn't a 4th and the only Indian's involved on the first day were in the 44th Infantry. But even that didn't matter because you are Singaporean. Your family is from Singapore. Your father wasn't in any Indian regiment. He was a Singaporean reservist under Atkinson."

Rahman said, "They weren't cowards. They weren't deserting. There was a misunderstanding. Cooke was a deserter. My father, uncle and the other man were loyal soldiers."

"So you wanted revenge."

"Atkinson had them shot outside Tanglin Barracks as an example. I was there, you know. I saw those three men murdered. Atkinson ordered his men to do it but they wouldn't so he did it himself."

His voice quavered. After a pause he continued: "Atkinson was just a captain in those days, but I recognized him. I'll never forget the face of the man who executed my father and uncle."

"Weren't you worried the colonel would recognize your name?"

He laughed a hollow laugh then. "I was more concerned you had seen the names on the photograph on my desk. But my father and uncle spelled their name Rahamaan..."

"Is that the rifle he used?" I said, nodding towards the one leaning against the wall.

"The same make with bullets designed for big game. The men took a long time to die; blood loss through the many holes. An arm and a leg blown clean off. It was a barbaric way to kill someone. And they leave the wall there like..." the inspector choked with the emotion and his voice trailed off with, "...like it's a proud memorial."

I waited for him to compose himself. He sat up a bit straighter and gave a flicker of a smile.

"The key..." I said. "You copied it. I noticed a tiny bit of clay."

He nodded slightly.

I asked, "When? How?"

"At the shop-house when you went into the attic."

"Why take that risk? I thought the police had a copy."

"Historically the chief has had one and my original plan was to take that. But it was safer to copy yours rather than ask for our copy."

Now that I had him talking, there was something else I wanted confirmed.

I said, "Tai Tai was the contact, not the Japanese security man. She had a buyer, a customer at the House of Tokyo."

Rahman said nothing.

"That was you. You were a member. When I met you there you were talking to the madam."

"Before I got promoted I had been there undercover."

"At the time you said you didn't speak the language but you do. You told her to keep quiet and to only give the mah-jong tile list to you—so I wouldn't see your name."

"Yes."

"It was five wheels, wasn't it? That's why the madam said it. She wasn't giving us an example of a tile, she was getting back at you. You led us to a drug dealer and made it look like he was the buyer of the guns. Kim never confessed to anything, did he? Because he was never involved."

Rahman said nothing.

"The madam knew you were a member but Aiko and Tai Tai knew you had the guns. So, you had to get rid of them, didn't you?"

He swallowed and, after a pause, said, "I didn't know how much Aiko knew and I never intended anyone else to get hurt."

"Like I said, things got messy. Even the best plans get messy."

"How did you realize?"

"I thought Tai Tai was the key to this, if only she would talk. You were the only one who knew. You couldn't risk her waking up and talking to me."

Rahman's eyes narrowed. He said, "Are you going to shoot me?"

"I haven't decided yet," I said, and it was the truth.

"So I want to kill Atkinson. It's revenge, plain and simple. Like I suspect you took in Palestine. Are we really that different, Ash?"

"Yes."

He glanced at the rifle and I wondered whether he considered trying to use it before I shot him. I doubted it.

He looked back at me.

I said, "You killed innocent people to cover your tracks."

He laughed then and said, "I bet you—"

But he didn't finish the sentence. There was a clatter. The light went out and the table overturned, knocking

367

me backwards. My chair tipped me over and I sprawled in the darkness.

When I looked up, Rahman had the door open. He hadn't locked it and now he was getting away.

I pulled out my revolver and fired three rapid shots, but too late.

The door shut again plunging me into darkness.

SIXTY-FOUR

Shining my torch around, I saw the rifle on the floor. I also saw how Rahman had killed the lights. There was a handle, low down on the wall: a switch between mains and backup generator electricity. He must have tested it. That's when the lights had flickered.

I opened the door and scanned the courtyard.

Had he gone for Atkinson in the house? Rahman didn't know where he was hiding and the building was still in darkness.

He wouldn't head for the gate. So where?

Then I heard it: a metallic squeak that took me a second to figure what it was: the sally port. That's how he'd got in. That's where he'd gone.

I sprinted to the gate. It was shut but unlocked.

I pulled it open and crouched through the aperture. The air was dank and musty. Far off I heard the sound of feet on stone. I shone my torch and found a flight of steps descending into the blackness beyond my light's reach.

I went down as fast as I could, my free hand over my head to feel the ceiling.

Twice I almost fell but jammed my elbow against a side wall to stop myself.

At the bottom I had to crouch. It was probably five and a half feet high and difficult. But I tried to run. I used the torch handle on my head like a miner's lamp to make sure I didn't hit my head.

I lost track of time. Maybe I'd been running for five minutes. Maybe longer. I stopped and listened. The tunnel wasn't straight so I couldn't see more than thirty yards ahead but I thought I could hear the scuff of Rahman's feet. The air was also fresher. As I ran again I noticed a sound like bones scraping and rolling over one another.

And then I heard other sounds: the creaking of metal and a clang.

I pressed on and saw the faintest of lights ahead. The sound of rattling bones echoed around me and I realized it must be the sea, crashing on the rocks, echoing through the passage.

The end of the tunnel. Then I found a discarded jacket. It appeared to be a police uniform so I figured Rahman probably had a change of clothes waiting for him.

I could taste the salt air as I crouched lower and was then on all fours until I reached an exit gate. A padlock held it tight shut. Rahman had shut and locked it. That's what I'd heard in the tunnel.

Although I figured the lock was new, the gate looked ancient with rust.

I squirmed around, lay on my back and kicked as hard as I could. The gate creaked and came away from its frame. With a heave, I managed to create a space wide enough to squirm through.

When I stepped onto rocks I realized I was on the coast, close to the Stamford Canal. The passage had come under the cathedral and the *Padang*. The fair was right in front of me. There were so many torches it was like daylight. And Rahman was walking casually, less than fifty yards away, between stalls towards the Ferris wheel. Maybe he thought he had more time. Maybe he thought I'd be less likely to spot him walking in a different jacket and carrying a suitcase.

Glancing over his shoulder, he could see I was rapidly closing the gap and began to run. He appeared to be heading for the densest section of crowds. But they soon impeded his progress and then I lost him for a moment. When I spotted him again he'd switched directions, keeping to the less crowded routes between stalls.

As we raced east across the *Padang* I lost ground when the crowds got in the way. When they thinned, I closed the gap again.

I was less than twenty paces from him when he tore through a tent selling fabrics. The poles collapsed and rolls of bright material fell like flags in the wind. Customers spilled left and right, blocking my way.

I could no longer see him. I climbed onto a table and scanned the crowd.

He'd put on a fedora and was walking again, but I recognized his shape and brown jacket. He was going in the direction of the river.

I leapt from the table and started running again. At first he seemed to be heading for the head of the river, maybe one of the bridges there. Then, as he saw me chasing him again, he switched right along North Boat Quay.

People were thick along the quay. The official fireworks would be by the monument at Empress Place. We were heading in the opposite direction, against the flow. There were also food stalls and dancers along here. I kept losing him, slowed by the throng of bodies.

"Military Police!" I yelled hoping people would get out of my way and ploughed through the gaps.

We passed Elgin Bridge and then he did the same trick with a stall, grabbing hold of a tent pole and pulling the whole thing over. The crowd reacted. There was a moment of chaos and my route was blocked. By the time I could move again he was nowhere to be seen. I ran on and got to Coleman Bridge.

There I stopped, breathing hard, and scanned ahead for anyone running. And then I caught sight of someone walking in the shadow of a *godown* on the opposite side.

I crossed and ran to where I'd seen him. There were few people and no stalls here but neither were there any lights. I checked each alleyway as well as wharf ahead. Not a sign. I didn't think Rahman could have made it to the next bridge without me seeing him again.

I went to the edge of the quay and looked up and down. There were stone steps leading down into the water. *Tongkangs* and *bumboats* were strung across the river for the night. Hundreds of them.

And then I spotted him below, crouched in a boat.

I pulled out my gun, aimed it at him and shouted, "Stop there or I'll shoot!"

Rahman looked at me for a second then scrambled into the next boat, rolling to get away from any shot.

I rushed down the steps and leapt into the nearest *tongkang*. I almost fell as the craft jolted beneath me. I grabbed the side and almost dropped my gun. But I didn't stop. I ran and leapt to the next boat.

Rahman was also moving. He stepped lightly across from his boat onto the next. He seemed an expert in balancing on the flat bottomed boats. I tried to copy his style but he moved swiftly and much faster than my clumsy efforts. If he got to the other side too far ahead of me, he could disappear into the warehouses beyond.

I made a decision. Rather than cross carefully, I threw myself from boat to boat, lurching and jumping, jumping and lurching.

I was getting closer.

Rahman turned at the sound I made as boats crashed side by side. The ripples caused by my approach rocked Rahman's boat. He missed his footing and fell partially into the water.

By the time he recovered, I was just one boat behind.

Rahman reached the steps on the far side.

I stepped on the prow of the last boat and launched myself at him. Just as he reached the top, I caught Rahman's heel knocking it sideways. He stumbled.

I landed heavily on the steps. Winded, I launched myself again and swiped Rahman's legs as he tried to stand.

I scrambled over him. We were both breathing heavily.

Sprawled on the floor, Rahman pushed himself up with his left arm and I guessed unnatural angle of his other meant it was broken.

As Rahman struggled up I saw that he a revolver in his good hand.

I aimed my gun at him in return.

"Give up, Anand."

"You could let me get away. I have tickets for the cruise ship at Clifford Pier."

"You aren't going anywhere."

"But Atkinson is a murderer. If you were me—"

"I wouldn't have killed the girl."

There was a percussion of explosions and the sky was lit with multiple colours.

"The finale," he said.

Above the noise of the celebration I heard police whistles. I saw lights bobbing towards us as men ran with torches.

"I could shoot you," he said.

I held out my other hand for his gun and said, "Put the gun down and come quietly."

"This isn't justice." Tears ran freely and his aim dropped a few inches. "Atkinson murdered those loyal men. It was brutal."

I thought he would release his weapon so I went to take the gun. I sensed other men around me now. I could see police with their guns pointed at the inspector but there was also a gang of Chinese who I thought seemed familiar. Yipp's or White-eye's men probably.

"Happy New Year," Rahman said with no feeling.

When I realized what was happening it was already too late. The inspector swiftly raised the gun to his own head and pulled the trigger.

The gunshot echoed off the warehouses but was lost in the sound from across the city.

The firework show reached a crescendo of flashes and bangs. And then for a moment there was silence before the clamour began again as the people returned to focus on enjoying the celebration, to eating and drinking, to gambling and fortune-telling, to dreaming of a bright and prosperous future.

SIXTY-FIVE

I promised a full report in the morning and just walked away. No one tried to stop me.

I collected my suitcases from Queens and walked to Raffles Hotel. Although the bar and street outside were alive with revellers, I felt a strange emptiness. I was free from Secretary Coates but it had not been a satisfying conclusion. Not yet anyway. I would spend one more night here—enjoy the luxury of Raffles and then leave. Where to? I still hadn't decided. Maybe I'd go to Changi Airfield and hitch a ride on a military plane. Go to wherever it was headed.

My new room wasn't a disappointment but cost almost double what The Queens was charging. The mattress was so comfortable that I don't remember falling asleep and it was midmorning by the time I woke up. Clearly, I'd had some sleep to catch up on.

I went out for a run and took the road east, past Yipp's warehouse, past Kallang and along the coast road until my lungs burned. Then I turned around and pushed myself harder.

Back at the hotel I showered, put on my suit and then strolled to the police station.

It was the first time of my many visits that I hadn't asked for Inspector Rahman, which felt odd. The foyer was as busy and hot as ever, as though nothing had changed. It was just another day. However I could tell from the desk sergeant's eyes that it wasn't. And then the senior officer who took my statement looked the same. Neither voiced their feelings but there was a sense of loss and confusion. What had happened? Why had the inspector shot himself?

During my run, I'd thought long and hard about what I was going to say. I decided to keep it simple. I said Rahman had seen his father executed by Colonel Atkinson ten years ago and had wanted to confront the colonel. I didn't say that he had caused the explosion on Tank Road. Instead, I explained that he had taken advantage of the attack to visit the colonel at the fort. I didn't mention why I was waiting for him and my deductions. I said nothing about buying the guns as a distraction to get Atkinson where he wanted him. Nor did I mention Aiko or Tai Tai. It was superfluous information I decided.

I just said that I'd explained the colonel's remorse and that Rahman had had a change of heart. He couldn't go through with the plan and I supposed he took his life because the hatred had kept him going for so many years.

My rationale for doing this? The best I can do is to say I had found myself liking the guy. Yes, he'd been manipulative but he had been right. We weren't that different. And I very much doubt I would have shot him.

So, in my version, he hadn't done anything wrong except consider confronting his father's executioner. This way, I figured, at least his family would get his pension.

Whether or not the police officer believed me, he didn't say. He just wrote my statement down and asked me to sign it.

He told me they were holding my service revolver as evidence and would return it to 200 Provost Company in a few days. The fact that I didn't have a weapon any more suited my plans fine.

I should have gone to see Vernon and given him a report as well but I decided against it. As far as I was concerned, it was over. I was out of the army—for a second time in three weeks. I thought about going to see Hedge and Robbo to say goodbye but I didn't. Instead I decided to walk the streets of Singapore for one last time, to soak up the atmosphere partially, but mostly to prepare myself for what was to come.

SIXTY-SIX

There were just two things I needed to do. I went to The
Red Lion and tied a strip of my black armband to both
of the lanterns outside, just in case one fell off or was
removed. My second thing was to find the club where
Su Ling had taken me, the place where we'd spent the
night in each other's arms.

I found a Chinese boy cleaning tables and gave him a
note I'd written for her. He understood that it was
important she got the message and I gave him ten
shillings to seal the bargain.

It had gone ten o'clock and I had been waiting in Yipp's
Rochor warehouse for over an hour when I heard
someone at the doors. The pedestrian section creaked
open and the lights came on.

"Are you sure?" Pantelis said and I slunk back into
the shadows.

Angel laughed and pulled on his hand. "Come on.
You said you wanted a bit of excitement."

She led him towards the office where I'd been bound
and left by Su Ling. I could see from his face that he was
half unsure, half aroused.

"In this room," she said.

"The stuff's in there?"

She laughed again. "That and more, sexy!"

The lure of sex was so great, so easy. I knew I'd fallen for it myself and here was Pantelis, in a remote place he didn't know with a lady-boy who'd been paid by me.

As instructed, she encouraged him into the office ahead of her and then shut the door. But she was on the outside and she turned the key I'd left in the lock.

"Well done!" I said, emerging from my hiding place.

"The rest of the money," she said without preamble, holding out her delicate hand.

Once she had the cash she ran for the warehouse exit, her heels clicking on the concrete floor. At the same moment, Pantelis started to hammer on the door. His shouts turning from anger to panic in a matter of seconds.

I stepped over, let him yell for a few more minutes and then turned the key.

"Jesus!" he said laughing nervously. "Is that part of your—"

He did a double take as he realized it was me in the doorway rather than his date.

"Captain Carter?"

I said nothing.

He said, "Thank goodness you came. Did you hear me calling? I was trapped."

A punch to the solar plexus shut him up and he crumpled to the floor, gasping.

I said, "I should have realized I was missing the obvious."

Pantelis just looked at me.

"You were driving the car that night," I said, "not Sergeant Cooke."

He said nothing.

"Your MT guy said he'd had to clean up the car. Then he told me about the bodywork but he'd been talking about the interior. There had been blood hadn't there?"

Pantelis looked away.

"The gash on your head," I said. "You did that in the crash. Head wounds bleed a lot and you made a mess inside the car. That's what the MT guy was telling me."

"Yes, I was driving. It was an accident. I knew he'd been following me. I wanted to scare him."

"By forcing him off the road at speed?"

"It was just a nudge. I didn't mean—"

I said, "You killed him whether it was deliberate or not. Though I think the court will say it was deliberate. Tom knew or suspected what you were up to. You didn't just want to scare him. You wanted to shut him up."

A smile flickered at the corner of Pantelis's mouth.

"What?"

"Commander Alldritt already knows about the accident."

"He knows you killed Tom Silverman?"

Pantelis said nothing.

I took out his gun, the one I'd knocked from his hand five nights ago. I pressed it against his forehead, hard. His eyes went wild with fear. Then he took a shuddering breath and tried to sound calm.

"You're not going to shoot me."

"Let's find out," I said. "Start talking. Tell me everything you know about what was going on."

"Cooke and I had been trading for months. We used his girlfriend at House of Tokyo."

I crouched in front of him and looked him in the eye. "So you sold the M1s to Cooke and he traded through his girlfriend Tai Tai." I emphasized girlfriend to watch for a reaction. He was good because he stared back at me with dead-eyes.

"Yes."

I punched him on the nose; just a light tap but enough to cause blood to trickle.

"Stop lying," I said. "You first lied about Cooke taking the navy car and running my friend off the road. Now you're lying about him dealing with Tai Tai. You were in contact with her—you were her boyfriend or had been." I knew he hadn't killed her because Rahman had, but Pantelis didn't know that so I asked, "Did you kill her to stop her talking?"

"No, no, I swear I didn't."

"OK so who did you trade with? Tai Tai or Cooke?"

"Cooke. He was trading with Tai Tai." I knew that was another lie but saved it for later. I stayed quiet and let Pantelis fill the space like a liar often will. *Embellish your story and make it more convincing.*

He said, "I'd traded with Will for almost two years. All sorts of stuff but I think he panicked over the guns… even though they were decommissioned."

I said nothing

"He had second thoughts about the guns but it was too late by then. He came to me for more money. He wanted to run away."

"We'll come back to that," I said pretending for the moment that I bought his story. "So how did the big Japanese security guy fit in?"

"Aiko. I don't know."

"Guess."

"He was also a trader though mostly drugs she said. He had underworld connections so we didn't want to deal with him. Anyway, I think he wanted a cut."

"Did you know who the buyer of your rifles was?"

"Not the end one, no."

"Did you care?"

381

He wiped away the blood and seemed to be regaining his confidence. "They were duds."

"But the buyer paid three hundred pounds. It doesn't sound like he knew they were duds. Or maybe he thought he could recommission them?"

"Maybe."

"You were selling guns and didn't care who was buying?"

He said nothing.

"Let's go back to Cooke. What happened to him?"

He looked up at me as though he wanted to speak but his mouth wasn't working.

"Tell me," I said. "What do you think happened?"

"Will wanted out. I gave him some money from the deal. He had travel documents. I think he was going to Shanghai or Hong Kong or somewhere."

"His kitbag was found near Woodland's Crossing. Do you think he was going to Malaya first?"

"Yes," he said like he was thinking, and I reckoned he was pretending to work it out, pretending we were a team solving this.

"So who shot him?"

"I don't know."

That was a lie. I said, "I think he came to you for help."

Pantelis said nothing.

"I think he was afraid and you were the only one he could turn to."

"I was afraid too."

"You drove him up to Woodlands Crossing. Maybe you planned to take him across to Malaya, help him escape."

His eyes said he was smarter than that and I knew then that I was right. Pantelis had tricked the sergeant.

He'd wanted the guards at the crossing to see Cooke and never had any intention of taking him to Malaya.

I said, "You took Cooke into the jungle and shot him. You snagged his bag in the water so we'd find it. You hoped a stone would weigh him down so he'd never resurface but in case he did you hoped the guards would think bandits shot him across the Straits. That hasn't happened before and it would have been a remarkable and lucky shot."

Pantelis said nothing.

"But you made a mistake."

I saw surprise, perhaps disbelief in his eyes then. I said, "You should have checked his bag more thoroughly. You found his papers and you added the travel documents. You probably put in the money too, to convince us that he was the dealer. It must have been hard to throw away fifty pounds like that but the gun deal alone netted three hundred pounds. That didn't make sense to me. He would have all his money with him and yet it was only fifty pounds."

Pantelis said nothing although I could see I was right.

"And there was Tai Tai's letter. You removed the first page because that letter was to you. You'd been her lover at some time not him."

He shook his head unconvincingly. "And that was allegedly my mistake?"

"No. You didn't find the notebook. The one he'd obtained that proved the trade. My theory is that you had been trading with Cooke and Cooke dealt with Aiko. I think Aiko got the evidence and one or both of them was trying to blackmail you or maybe Cooke was just protecting himself, I don't care. But what I do know is that the notebook wasn't his. It was Tai Tai's. She was left-handed, he was not. She was your partner in the gun trade, not him."

Pantelis swallowed but didn't comment.

I said, "You killed him and dumped his body in the water."

Pantelis looked at me with cold eyes. "You can't prove any of this."

"I can prove you were the driver the night Tom Silverman was killed."

His little smile flickered again.

"You killed Sergeant Cooke."

"Like I say, where's your proof?"

"I can prove you've been trading on the black market."

"Really?" he said practically smirking now. "All you have are codes in a book. Link those to the guns? That's circumstantial. I'll deny it."

"But I know the truth."

"And who are you?" he said and started to stand. Suddenly he was full of self-confidence. "You'll report me to Commander Alldritt. He'll thank you and file it away."

"Why?"

Pantelis was standing now. He looked up and his eyes were shining. He knew he'd get away with this.

"Because Alldritt doesn't want any trouble."

"But he's got plenty of trouble," I said.

Pantelis looked confused.

"Working out why you disappeared," I said.

"What?"

I had talked enough. I shot him between the eyes, walked out of the warehouse and let the Rochor River swallow Pantelis's revolver.

SIXTY-SEVEN

An hour later, a taxi dropped me at the foot of Mount Faber, the place where Su Ling and I had had our first date and talked about the stars. As I climbed the path through the trees, I recalled her stories of romance and mystery. An overcast sky seemed fitting tonight.

The path opened up and I continued to the crest where we had lain in the grass, where I had fallen asleep with my head in her lap.

The lights of Singapore city were just as bright, just as energetic, as if they were declaring their indifference: life-goes-on. Get over it.

A movement of shadows told me someone was coming up the far side of the hill. And then I saw her outline distinctly, her elegant walk. Su Ling.

She came within four feet and stopped. There was no kiss or handshake but I didn't expect one. When she spoke her tone was less harsh than the day before but there was still no warmth.

"You wanted to see me," she said.

"Can you ever forgive me?"

"For wanting to meet me here?"

"For not trusting you."

She didn't respond immediately and I wished I could have seen the colour of her eyes although my heart knew they were green for me now.

"You have already apologized," she said then paused. "Maybe you have no need to apologize. I am Eurasian, but my family is Chinese. My loyalty is, and will always be, to my family. Do you understand what I'm saying, Captain?"

I think I did. She was telling me that she worked for Yipp and would have betrayed me for him.

She said, "But I did have feelings for you. I just..."

I wanted to reach out to her then, to hold her, but I sensed it wasn't what she wanted. I had something I needed Yipp to do but in that moment, I realized that she had something she needed to tell me.

"It's all right," I said. And then because I couldn't think of anything appropriate I continued: "Tell your uncle that Secretary Coates means to entrap him."

"He knows this."

"Tell him that there is a mess in his warehouse near Kallang and he needs to clean it up before the police arrive tomorrow morning."

She looked at me long and hard and I felt a frisson of guilt for using her to cover what I'd done to Pantelis.

When she spoke, it wasn't about the warehouse, it was about what had been on her mind; why I think she had stopped mid-sentence before.

"Madam Butterfly is not a single woman," she began quietly. "It is an informal group that you would probably call self-support. They... they have all been betrayed by men. By army men."

I said nothing as she paused again. There suddenly seemed to be an unusual chill wind blowing off the sea. I stuck my hands in my pockets and waited.

"These women grew up without their fathers because those men did not take responsibility for what they had done."

"You aren't talking about me."

"No," she said and her voice was stronger. "This is not about you. This is about girls abandoned by their soldier lovers and their children who had to grow up mixed race without their white father."

And then I understood this was about her. Her father hadn't been around. Maybe Captain Keith was a made up name just like her story of dancing for him was imagined.

I said, "Captain Keith..."

"My mother never knew his last name." She paused and her stance seemed to soften. "So you see, I could not tell you who it was because of my sympathies with them."

I nodded but said nothing.

"Are you going to do anything with this information."

"No."

She started to pull off the wrist band. "I want you to have this."

"As a reminder of you?"

"Something like that."

She handed it to me and for a second our fingers touched. There was no spark or energy like I'd felt the first time. I resisted an urge to raise the material to my nose and breathe in her scent. Instead I just stuck it in my pocket.

"Goodbye, my brave captain," she said and this time offered her hand.

The shake was formal and deliberate, rotating her wrist more than an up and down motion. She wanted me to see something and watched my eyes for the realization. Then she turned and walked swiftly away, down the hill, in the direction of the city.

I stood for a moment and thought about the implication of what I had seen. On her right wrist was a tattoo. It had been covered by the wristband and then it was exposed: a tiny delicate butterfly.

I stood still, looking at the spot where she had been. The urge to run after her was strong, but I waited until it had passed.

Then I turned and walked slowly down the path and kept walking. I followed the coast road past Keppel, through Fullerton Square, over the bridge past the Government buildings, past the *Padang*, back to Raffles Hotel.

I'd planned to have one more night in Singapore. But as I walked, as I breathed in the ever-changing air, I decided to stay. For a while anyway.

Acknowledgements

I was brought up on stories from my father's time as an MP in Singapore and so, when I first decided to write crime-thrillers, this was naturally the first one to try. Unfortunately my early efforts weren't good enough and I'm grateful to everyone from the Authonomy writers' community who helped me learn my trade, especially if you recall critiquing chapters of *The Jin Deception*. Also thank you for voting it to the top of the charts and to Harper Collins for the subsequent professional critique. Of course the biggest thanks must go to my father, who not only inspired me with his stories but has also been a thorough editor. He accompanied me on one of the research trips to Singapore—and had to put up with staying at the sumptuous Goodwood Park Hotel. On that trip we fortuitously met Ian Johnson (Capt) and he has been exceptionally helpful in filling in gaps about the military and political situation of the period. I would also like to give a shout out for the men who served at Gillman Barracks and the team at RedCap70. You'll know I've taken some liberties, but hopefully you'll forgive me.

Thank you to my official editor Debz Hobbs-Wyatt and my unofficial one, Pete Tonkin. As always your insights were invaluable. Finally, to my wife, Kerry: Thank you for your support, enthusiasm for 52, and looking forward to *Singapore Girl*.

Read the next exciting instalment…

SINGAPORE GIRL

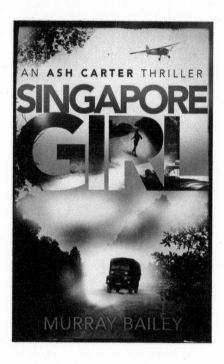

When a headless body is found on the causeway between Singapore and Malaya, Ash Carter is asked to investigate.

This second adventure takes him through Malaya visiting Johor Bahru, Kuala Lumpur and Penang. Is the murder a warning by the Chinese Communists or a drug lord? Or is this something else entirely?

The third adventure:

SINGAPORE BOXER

Ash Carter goes undercover with a private protection force
in central Malaya looking for a missing man. He soon
discovers there's much more to the investigation.

Someone is happy to kill Carter so that he doesn't find out
what's going on. Intrigue, deceit and deception – will Ash
be able to uncover the truth, before it's too late?

The first Alex MacLure thriller:

MAP OF THE DEAD

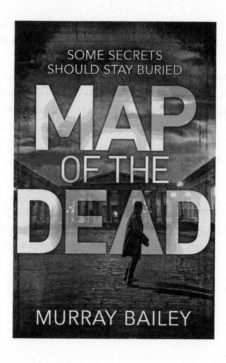

Within days of solving a 3,000 year old puzzle, a researcher
dies in suspicious circumstances.

With only a few clues and a mysterious object Alex
MacLure follows a trail from London to Cairo. He must
crack the code and expose a shocking, inconceivable truth
before the secret is buried for ever.

IF YOU ENJOYED THIS BOOK

Feedback helps me understand what works, what doesn't and what readers want more of. It also brings a book to life.

Online reviews are also very important in encouraging others to try my books. I don't have the financial clout of a big publisher. I can't take out newspaper ads or run poster campaigns.

But what I do have is an enthusiastic and committed bunch of readers.

Honest reviews are a powerful tool. I'd be very grateful if you could spend a couple of minutes leaving a review, however short, on sites like Amazon and Goodreads.

Thank you
Murray